MW01139050

TEARS OF A HEART

(Book 0: Kan Savasci Cycle)
Revised and Expanded Edition 2016

Kan Savasci Cycle of Books

Book 0: Tears of a Heart

Book 1: Tower of the Arkein

Book 2: Into the Fold (*in the works*)

ACKNOWLEDGMENTS

There were many who helped with the crafting of this book. I'd like to thank all those who took the time out of their busy schedule to help me flush out the book, improving upon the characters, world building, grammatical issues, and depth of story. My Beta/Alpha readers, you're invaluable. To those who read and reviewed the first version/edition, thank you for taking the time to write a review and allowing me to be understand what works and what doesn't.

FOREWARD

The Kan Savasci Cycle is a work of passion I created, whilst working two jobs. I have spent a significant amount of time building first the world, knowing that in history environment often shapes culture, followed by the peoples, characters, religion, politics and economic systems. I have used my life experiences (everything from working in the sciences, to traveling the world, to martial arts training, federal law enforcement and military experiences, as well as loves come and gone) to make the world as vivid and beautifully real as I can, while still retaining the ephemeral feel of an epic fantasy.

I wanted to mention to new readers, Tower of the Arkein was originally intended to be Book 1, and as such can stand alone (Think of Batman Begins and the Dark Knight, or to a certain extent Star Wars a New Hope and the Empire Strikes Back). Yet, I wanted to really flush out the world, and therefore, wrote Tears of a Heart first. This allows for a greater character arch, as well as more depth for the discerning reader. Think of Tears of a Heart as a prequel, introducing origin of characters and world.

In short, you can start with Tower of the

Arkein and still very much enjoy the story, the characters, and the immersive world. For those who love greater depth, the history, and world building, as well as hidden Easter eggs for later books which, both Tears of a Heart and Tower of the Arkein contain, I suggest starting with Tears of a Heart. For those who value action above all else, start with Tower of the Arkein.

PRAISE FOR THE KAN SAVASCI CYCLE

"TEARS OF A HEART is lyrical literal fantasy, excellently-written by an accomplished author." *Mallory Heart Reviews*

"This is the first in a series that will be a great epic fantasy." *Author Jodi Woody*

"The language is expressive and at times achingly beautiful and almost bardic." *Read Bookworm Read*

"Overall, a deeply enjoyable story and a fantasy world I'd love to see more of in future books." *Author Emily de Courcy*

"I really enjoyed Chase Blackwood's writing style. It was flowing, moving and beautiful in a way that seems to be rare these days." *Katelyn Hensel for Reader's Favorite*

"Chase Blackwood has created a world and a story that will have readers enthralled, just like the way they are enthralled with the world of Lord of the Rings by J.R.R. Tolkien." - *Divine Zape, Reader's Favorite*

"Every bit of this book is action packed, it's an amazing plot, and Blackwood has a way of drawing you in to where you just keep turning pages..." - *Instagram Reviewer: @meggsba_booknerdigan*

"It is fast paced, well-developed and very well-constructed." *Rabia Tanveer, Reader's Favorite*

"I heard that this book was good and I agree! I loved the story line and characters, especially Aeden! The plot was refreshing in the sense that the adventures were exciting and unique compared to some other fantasy novels that tend to get predictable after awhile" - *Book n Basics*

"Fantasy fiction doesn't get much better than this and I tip my hat to Chase Blackwood." *Ray Simmons, Reader's Favorite*

"Ultimately, this was an amazing read. It is a book that was hard to put down. I constantly wanted to know what was going to happen next." *Bridgett Brown, Goodreads*

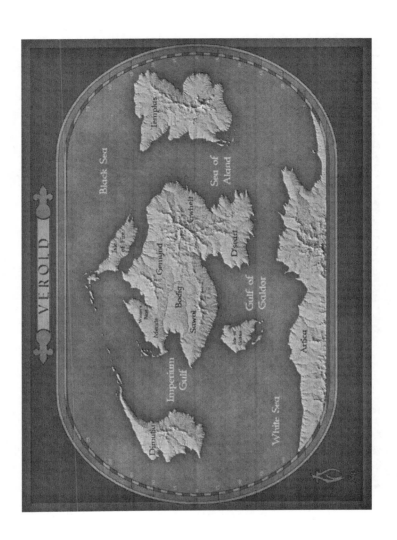

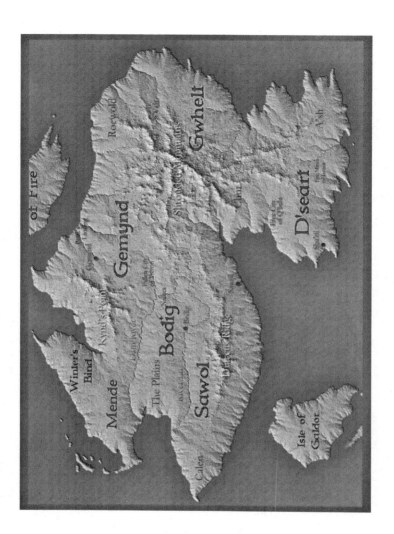

PART ONE
Thane Sagan

Prologue

"A hero isn't defined by his actions but by the deeds that others think he accomplished under the light of unscrupulous men."

Anonymous - Tower of the Arkein

An azure sky slashed at the mounting gray clouds in a vain attempt to paint the scene in the colors of Lenton. It failed as a tepid wind blew in from the north. It carried the sounds of leaves torn from branches, sleet slicing cruelly through the air, and a hidden mystery blanketed by time, waiting to be uncovered.

The frigid wind attacked a lone man's hungry body as the thin mountain air grasped for his very breath. The man glanced up at the gray sky and shivered. Cold stinging nettles of snow bit at his face. He tugged on the Bodigan scarf that clung to his head like a well-worn glove. His cheeks were red and burned and his lips were cracked. They were the idle discomforts that would have discouraged less ambitious men.

Sheets of frozen water gusted over the tattered remains of a stronghold lost to the years. They were the broken stone fortifications that shyly revealed fragments of their former self in the light of hazy distance. The sight gave the man strength.

Blood struggled to pump to his shaky legs as he unconsciously clenched and unclenched his hands. You see this man's hands were his trade, his livelihood. He was an annalist, a chronicler of history. It wouldn't serve him well to have travelled hundreds of miles through some of the most unforgiving terrain to find that he couldn't write of his discoveries.

Another gust of wind snapped over a stone and slapped the annalist in the face. It felt as if the very weather were struggling against him. Fear crept into his heart like a dull shadow at the first hints of afternoon. The annalist couldn't help but worry it was the arkein work of the very man he was writing about.

An old Q'Bala expression leapt to his mind, *"Fear is but the crucifixion of man upon the planks of past and future."*

Was it possible that his writings had summoned the attention of the most powerful man of his time? It was rumored that merely uttering his name would unleash the torrents of seventh hell.

The annalist stumbled on an icy slip of terrain. His mind shook loose his growing anxiety and he pressed forward. He knew the consequences if he failed. They were too grave to fathom. If a thousand Bodig soldiers had died to bring him thus far, he could muster the strength to climb a little farther.

The annalist crested another small rise and came upon the tattered ruins. The secret whisperings of the *Syrinx* were true. A once impenetrable town of warriors had been reduced to molten ash and twisted stone.

Buildings lay broken and crumbling along the mountainside. A light peppering of snow rested serenely upon everything. The scene was reminiscent of shattered teeth. White and black scorch marks scoured the surface of gray stones. Wooden beams the length of draccus weasels were scattered and torn asunder.

It appeared as though war had descended upon the town from the sky, but the annalist knew better. The unthinkable had occurred. A draccus fiend had visited these parts. It was something that hadn't happened in an age, at least according to recorded history.

The annalist knew otherwise.

He tripped as he stepped over a cracked wooden beam. His eagerness to uncover what he had glimpsed made him hasty and clumsy.

Mumbling a silent curse under his breath he weaved around some large foundational stones. At that moment, the clouds parted and a shaft of light fell through the broken sky. The light fell upon a floor of carefully carved stone.

Half-collapsed walls of crumbling gray formed a semicircle about the center of the shaft of light. It was as though the hand of Ghut swept down through the heavens to guide him. There, in the center of the shaft resting in a bed of fractured earth, lay a massive chest. Gold and silver leaf once adorned most of its surface but presently only covered parts. Two heavy iron clasps were held fast by a strong lock.

It felt almost too easy after everything he had endured. His dark eyes searched about for any sign of subterfuge. The annalist carefully observed every detail until he was fully satisfied that what he saw was what rested before him.

The annalist dusted off some snow and examined the lock for a moment before circling the chest. The clouds overhead moved and the light faded. Once again, the world was cast in shades of ashy granite.

He leaned forward rubbing his fingers along the back of the chest. It was as he suspected, the hinges were made of copper. The annalist scraped gently at the patina, flecks of corroded metal flaking off in a shower of green.

He pulled a small flask out of his pack and

uncorked the lid. He held the flask away from his face, knowing the contents were poisonous when inhaled and the vapors could cause blindness. In a deliberate, practiced motion, he poured the contents onto the hinges and stepped away.

The reagent reacted with the copper, hissing slightly as a light brown gas lifted lazily from the hinges, vaguely reminiscent of a startled snake. The annalist watched from a safe distance as a tight grin made its way onto his face. Anticipation gripped his heart and squeezed it in a vice-like grip.

When the reaction was complete and the gas dissipated, he moved toward the chest. Using a blunt tool, he struck the hinges. With a muted thump, they broke and fell into the copper stained snow.

The annalist wedged open the lid with a few deft movements. Ever cautious, he glanced behind him before eyeing the contents within. To a king a chest of gold and gems would be a welcome gift. To an annalist, books, scrolls, and words were of immeasurable value, for in them lie the truth.

Parchment laden with a simple rudimentary script lay entombed in the heavy chest. A thin layer of wax covered each sheet, protecting the contents from the elements. He leafed through the sheets reading through each quickly; a list of sacred items, the history of a dozen weapons, and the lineage of two schools of philosophy. His excitement grew with each sheaf of parchment. He was closer than he had ever been to uncovering the true beginnings of the Scourge of Bodig.

He paused as he read through a genealogy. His hand trembled slightly as he came upon the name he had been searching for. *Kirin D'Velt, son of the Kovor*. His bowels iced over, it was the subtle feeling of cold spreading through one's stomach after drinking from a mountain spring. Then he felt his hand go cold. His fingers lost their dexterity and a wave of fear swept over him.

A cold sweat burdened his brow. His heart thumped oddly in his chest like a trapped bird. The annalist clenched his shaking hand into a fist and struggled to clear his mind.

Fearful breaths settled into a steady rhythm. Blood once more flowed unrestricted into his fingers. He opened his eyes not realizing they had been closed. The fallen parchment lay upon the snow, the names glaring at him defiantly.

The rumors were true; the most feared man in the Middle Kingdom was once a prince of the fabled Thane Sagan. A man with more stories attributed to his greatness, his villainy, and his power than Magis himself.

Burdened by fear, driven by duty, and devoted to the point of pain, the annalist continued. He knew he had to start at the beginning. No complete truth could be gleaned from some distant assessment. Anyone could do that. The annalist, however, had been tasked with the far more intimate and far more dangerous task of uncovering the layers of history that shaped *Kan Savasci*.

He took in a shaky breath. The air felt cool in his lungs. The annalist shuddered to think he was peeling back the layers of *Tui Faaroa* as he was known to the Amevi Tribes of Dimutia, and *Touja Keventaminen* to those tattered souls in Templas. It seemed that no part of Verold had been left untouched by the arkeinist's reaching hand.

Hungry for more, the annalist pulled out more sheaths of parchment. His heart pounded away in his chest with the intensity of an angry dog. Finally, the pieces of a greater puzzle and the early history of the legend he was tasked to truly understand were beginning to come into focus.

Chapter 1

"The heart of a warrior is something shaped over time, molded in the forge of fire." Proverb of the Thane Sagan

Kirin D'Velt was not quite what his father had hoped for. Although he had wished for a son, he hadn't wished for that son to rob him of the one woman he had truly loved. Instead of the tall, strong, and independent leader he had prayed for, the gods had decided to test him with a weak, pink little boy, a mockery of the kovor lineage.

This child was sickly and starved for attention. His pale skin would wrinkle into contorted lines of discomfort as he cried at all hours of night, burdening the widow who had been chosen to care for him. His screams of discomfort could be heard through thick stone walls and caused the kovor, Kirin's father, to lay awake at night wishing the boy had died and his wife had survived.

As the boy grew he became less sickly. A steady diet of motherly affections, hearty foods, avoidance of bad smells, and an old herbal elixir of Templas origins all lent to improved health. A thick head of white hair, marking him as different, grew wildly. His awkward features slowly became handsome and his gray eyes were often described as bewitching. The trouble was he was too smart for his own good. He questioned authority when he should have followed. He daydreamed when he should have trained, and he argued when he should have listened.

Therefore, on Kirin's thirteenth birthday the kovor was worried. It was a year that was considered sacred. The number thirteen demarcated the number of gods in the Thane Sagan pantheon. It represented the number of hidden mysteries within the gevecht and it also represented the yearlong trial that awaited Kirin to prove his manhood. Kirin wasn't in the least excited.

An older man with a thinning head of hair stepped into Kirin's field of vision. The movement was deliberate, graceful even. He wore simple leather armor with a fearsome cat emblazoned in the center. The cat stood for the solidarity of his people. It adorned the armor and shields of all who passed their coming of age tests. If all went well, Kirin would join them and too wear the insignia of his family lineage.

It was the beginning of Lenton and the snow had recently melted, leaving the ground muddy. A cool wind swept down the mountainside and played with the fine wisps of hair on the old man's pate. Kirin was reminded of a particular children's fable, *A Night's Cool Shadow*, in which nymphs used dance to steal the king's treasure.

He had an inexplicable affinity for women at a very young age.

"Kovor's son, holder of the gevecht, and future memory of our people, it is time," the old man said.

The images of the dancing nymphs were yanked from his head. Kirin eyed the man's leathery face for a moment, his heart heavy. These were the dreaded words he had feared for years. Every boy and girl of the Thane Sagan had to prove themselves. It was simply part of life. For the son of a kovor, the testing was more grueling and rigorous than for most.

S'Vothe, as their foothold of land up in the mountains was called, had been attacked numerous times over the ages. Kings, emperors, and caliphs all attempted to wrest control of these tepid lands from the Thane Sagan. Only once had they been conquered. These constant raids and attempts at uniting foreign lands to appease the masses at some faraway home, left the Thane Sagan ever watchful and ever prepared. It was one of the reasons for the rituals of becoming a true member of their society and of becoming a warrior.

"Time for what?" He asked innocently enough.

This earned Kirin a stern look. It was an almost perfect imitation of his father.

"You can play your games. Your wit may

have served you well among children, but there will be little use for it in your upcoming trials."

"We're all children under the eyes of the gods," Kirin said.

"As I said, I will not be roped into your attempts at humor or argument." The venerable master looked about the village for a moment then leaned down to whisper to Kirin. "Do you know what wisdom is?"

Kirin paused, sensing a trap, but his clever mind and quick tongue couldn't be held down by something as feeble as the fear of faltering.

"Wisdom is the accumulation of knowledge over time."

The master smacked Kirin quickly on the back of the head. Kirin was shocked at the speed of it.

"I didn't ask for a definition young man."

Kirin was about to speak up when the master smacked him on the back of the head once again.

"Wisdom," the master resumed as if nothing had happened, "is learning to keep your mouth shut when you have nothing of value to say."

"And learning to dodge quick-handed old men," Kirin whispered to himself.

The master chose to ignore his last comment.

"You're still the kovor's son and have a part to play, so play it," the older man said as he nodded a greeting to the village blacksmith.

Kirin took a subtle step backward waiting for a hand to smack him again. None did. He glanced about and took in a breath.

"With patience in my heart, dedication in my mind, and steel within my soul, I stand prepared." Kirin responded with the words he'd been taught over the years, although they sounded hollow even to his own ears.

If it were up to him he'd forgo the tests altogether and spend more time hearing about the greater world, chasing Dannon, and enjoying the company of his best friend.

The old man's face remained passive but his eyes grimaced slightly as if an insect had landed on his face. It reminded Kirin of the expression his father too often wore, like a well-worn mask.

A few months ago, he had been training all day in the biting cold of Vintas. The snow fell in swirling mists as if angered by the wind. His fingers had grown numb on the hilt of the spathe sword he held in his hand. His teacher admonished him again for maintaining an overly tight grip, yet every time he loosened his grasp the sword would feel weak in his hand and shudder uncomfortably when he parried a blow. And there in the shadow of a building overhang stood his father. His features were stern, proud, and unflinching.

As the hours froze upon the frigid ground the

other students were allowed to seek warmth
indoors and fill their bellies with a hot meal.
Kirin, however, was forced to practice the ancient
movements of fighting and defense cleverly
disguised within the gevecht. Ever watchful, ever
judgmental, his father stood like a pillar,
galvanizing the teacher to push Kirin toward
greater levels of discomfort.

Finally, as the sun began to set and the true
chill of Vintas tore down the harsh rocks of the
Barre Mountains, Kirin performed the
movements with precision and skill. His body
ached, his bones shivered, but he denied his
father the pleasure of seeing weakness upon his
face. His mind clung desperately to fanciful
images of another land, of a time away from
home.

The teacher finally nodded to him, releasing
him from training for the day. Kirin passed his
father, glancing hopefully at his face, wishing for
a smile, a nod of approval, a hint that he had
done well. Instead his father's eyes looked at him
critically. The kovor grimaced ever so slightly as
he saw the white-knuckled grip return to the hilt
of the spathe sword.

"Very well, follow me," the old man turned
on his heel and without waiting for a response
stalked off.

Kirin only hesitated for a moment before

following the man. As an ever-curious boy he already knew the shape of what was to come. The Thane Sagan were a small and tight knit community with few secrets, save for the coming of age rituals. Somehow the details remained locked inside the hearts of each who had undergone them.

It was rumored that no two rituals were alike; the master shaped the rituals to fit the personality of the warrior being tested. In Kirin's case, there was a lot to be tested and the hope that he could still be molded.

The old master kept a quick pace as he moved down a worn stone path. His leather armor shifted with his gait as he passed several buildings. The buildings were of gray stone with thick timber roofs. They formed defensive postures alongside the steep mountain face. Small windows punctuated the stone. The wooden roofs were lacquered in sage oil and merriwood fungus, a combination that granted a degree of protection from fire.

Along the mountainside, wooden enclosures fenced in areas dotted with goats and sheep. Small plots of land were sectioned off within these larger tracts for simple farming. Not that much grew in the soils of the Barre Mountains.

Older men could be seen in the gardens, but being that it was Lenton, they were simply removing the straw covering the soil, while others worked on fixing or sharpening the tools they'd need once the soil was ready for planting.

Kirin knew that come Sumor many of the younger children, he included, would train in the evenings after a day of plowing the soil and planting the seeds for their annual crop. He remembered as a boy the year a heavy and unexpected Sumor rain devastated their crop. The mighty Thane were forced to practically beg the Guelder, a village to the east, for their surplus crop.

Despite his youth, he understood the grumbling protests of Gosselin, his adopted grandmother, "it isn't right to beg for help, the previous kovor would have used our hunger as a tool for greater discipline."

Kirin noted the biggest complainers were often the older women, grandmothers they were called by everyone once they had reached a certain age. At that time, he was still young enough to be watched over by them as they spun yarn, weaved clothing, and mended leather straps from broken or worn armor.

Those were the days when he spent most of his time exclusively in the buildings huddled by the mountainside. The stone buildings of the village formed family-clusters of buildings. Each had an area used for cooking, cleaning, weaving, tool making, playing, training, and stories by the night fire. He had been forced to learn each to better understand every aspect of Thane life to one day become a better leader. Although forced may not have been the best word, for in truth Kirin enjoyed learning. He soaked in everything he could and often attempted to improve upon the old ways, vexing those entrenched by tradition.

As they continued down the path they passed a small training arena. Only yesterday had Kirin been swinging a wooden sword, moving through the forms of the gevecht. Today a dozen youth were sparing. Devon, a thickly built boy only months younger than Kirin, smiled and waved while he pinned down another boy.

Devon's face was splattered in mud. His blond hair was plastered to his head. From his lopsided grin one would never have expected that he was sparring the third best the Thane had to offer. Kirin had been the best, only occasionally beat by Devon. It was the foundation of their, at times, tumultuous relationship.

"Time spent alone will do you well," the master said, startling Kirin from his thoughts, "perhaps you'll learn how to clear your mind of the unnecessary clutter" he continued as one weathered finger poked Kirin roughly in the head.

Kirin had almost run into the master and felt his face flush in shame. It took a moment for the words to register and another moment for him to realize where the old man had taken him.

Before Kirin stood the Shrine of Patience, or as he and his friends knew it, The Gates of Boredom.

"Well?" the old man said with just a hint of a frown.

Part of Kirin wanted to refuse the rituals altogether. He hated being coerced almost as much as he hated stupidity and hypocrisy. To refuse would invite physical punishment and excommunication and that'd take him away from Devon and Dannon. Instead, Kirin cleared his throat and looked longingly back toward the heart of the village before returning his gaze to the grizzled warrior before him.

"I'm ready," he said.

A stern look from the older man reminded Kirin he had a part to play.

"With the moon as company and the air as food, I shall practice my silent coventry," a reluctant Kirin stated from memory.

He caught the first glimmer of positive emotion on the old man's weathered face, watching a smile pass like a wisp of a cloud on a hot day. Kirin smiled back before stepping through the open door. Without word or further ceremony, a heavy wooden door was closed and Kirin was cast in darkness.

Chapter 2

"Strength flowers from the well of eternal struggle." Principles of the Gevecht

There is little to write about Kirin D'Velt's time in solitude. It is thought by some that during this time he figured out the hidden powers of the mind. Others believe he perfected his body through hidden exercises. Some have rumored that when he grew bored of solitude he called down lighting to distract the town so he could walk and feel the fresh air. Other versions claim that he simply fell into a meditative trance and stepped out as if only a day had passed. As with any good story, embellishments come with time, subtly shaping it until the narrative becomes fiction, myth, and then legend.

According to Thane Sagan records, Kirin spent sixty days in solitude. Sixty days of darkness. Close enough to the village to hear the playing, training, and voices of his people. Far enough away that he could not distinguish individual words. The last seven days were without food to test his mental resolve while physically exhausted. The records were short, efficient, and dry, as with most things Thane Sagan.

On good authority word had it that Kirin D'Velt was bored out of his mind. The days passed slowly. He practiced and rehearsed lineage histories to keep his mind sharp. He ran through the gevecht to keep his body strong and limber for the upcoming trials following his solitude. Supposedly he had learned the art of atori, clearing the mind of unwanted thought. Most of all he slept.

Chapter 3

"Intensity is a matter of the mind willing the body to overcome fear." Proverb of the Thane Sagan

It was on the sixty first day that the heavy wooden door to the Shrine of Patience was opened. Light spilled in, casting the lone figure in a bath of warm luminescence. Kirin stood and stretched briefly before stepping out, his hand shielding his eyes.

"Today begins your first day of recovery, do as you wish."

Kirin struggled to peel his eyes open, but the light was still blindingly bright. It didn't matter. He'd recognize that deep voice from anywhere. It was the voice of the kovor, the voice of his father. There was no warm embrace, no pat on the back. Instead there was the discerning look of a father who was ascertaining the resolve of his son. With a placid expression, Kirin emerged, hiding any hint of hunger, weakness, or lethargy from his step.

Kirin nodded a brief acknowledgement as he stumbled down the path away from the sun's reaching grasp. The sunlight felt good. It was the warmth of a blanket after a long night of shivering. A gentle breeze rustled the leaves of the eschew trees and lightly caressed his face. A smile graced his lips. There was nowhere else he'd rather be.

Kirin side-stepped a larger man ambling toward him. His eyes were still struggling to adjust when the man spoke.

"I see you're out, I'll be keeping an eye on you," the broad-shouldered man said, holding an intimidating axe over one shoulder.

The man's name was Borin. Borin was the father of Dannon, a young girl Kirin once had the pleasure of kissing late at night behind the main dining hall. Her father had caught them just as Kirin was sliding his hands toward her well defined rear end. Kirin received an angry warning filled with a detailed account of what unpleasantries he would be subjected too if it were to occur again. Dannon had been instructed to stay away from that irascible kovor's son.

Kirin nodded his head and headed away from Borin. He didn't want to give that man any more reason to keep Dannon from him.

Kirin took a lone path, circumventing the main fortifications of their small town and walked to a small glade along the mountain. At the glade were the Sacred Pools of the gods, statues of Enlil and Balder resided within the embrace of Ansuz, carved into the mountainside. A good cleansing was what he needed anyway, especially if he were to accidently run into Dannon again.

After a bath in the geothermal spring and a

change of clothes, Kirin felt like he had emerged from a cocoon only to realize he hadn't transformed into a butterfly. Presently he needed to satiate the rumblings of an empty stomach.

The familiar sight of heavy stone buildings, squatting by the mountainside, felt comforting. The jagged peaks protecting them to the north slashed at the blue sky with a quiet strength. The puffy white clouds of Lenton hung fat and lazy in the air.

It was his favorite season.

The sounds of clanging steel filled the air as Kirin approached his extended family compound. As he rounded the perimeter one of his friends caught his eye. It was Devon. Devon glanced toward the lead instructor. With a small nod, he was released early from training and jogged to Kirin.

"Hey stumpy! How was the Gates of Boredom?" He asked as he approached slightly out of breath.

Devon often began their conversations with some mild insult. At first it had annoyed Kirin. It wasn't until he spoke of it to Ayleth that he gained a new perspective. She had explained that Devon was merely jealous. He was jealous that Kirin was the son of the kovor. It made sense. After that Kirin never let it bother him again and actually grew to enjoy the subtle rebukes.

"You know I'm not supposed to talk about

it," Kirin said.

"Come on, I'm sure you had plenty of time to daydream in there!"

"More than enough time, but don't let my father know that," Kirin said with a smirk, although part of him wanted to tell his father that his first test hadn't worked and nor would any of the others. Maybe that would elicit a response other than the quiet reticence the kovor seemed to wear like a second skin.

"No of course not," Devon said wiping some sweat onto his pants, "you were meditating or practicing the gevecht the entire time to be sure."

"That sounds about right," Kirin said as he skirted a building and approached the entrance to one of the dining halls.

Devon laughed. It would have been disconcerting had Kirin not known him for most of his life. It was the laugh of a man rather than that of a boy, full of resonance and confidence.

Kirin ducked into the dining hall, followed by Devon's bulkier frame.

Sturdy wooden tables and chairs rested heavily in the center of the building. A few simple tapestries of another time hung along the walls, offering another shade of gray to accent the earth tones within. Thick candles burned along the perimeter. Black fingers of soot reached up the walls as shadowy extensions of the small flickering flames. The smell of fresh bread and roasting meat along with hints of rosemary clung to the walls with desperate abandon.

Kirin glanced about, realizing he had come a touch early. The familiar sights and smells were tantalizing to his rumbling stomach. He glanced back toward Devon who merely shrugged. They worked their way toward the kitchen to check on the progress of dinner.

"Young D'Velt, a pleasure to see you out," a tall man with overly thick hands said. "And the gifted Devon I see."

"Master Cook, it's great to finally breathe something other than the scent of a thousand desperate Thane," Kirin replied with a smile, he liked the cook.

The cook smiled as he gripped a hot iron handle with his bare hands. He moved the pan with a flick of his wrist tossing the contents within. A sizzle and fresh waft of savory steam permeated the air.

"What's for dinner?" Kirin asked eagerly.

"Of course, you must be starving!"

He grabbed a cloth, wiping his hands and dabbing at the sweat accumulating as slick beads on his forehead. The Master Cook then looked about conspiratorially before tossing a warm mini-loaf to Kirin and another to Devon.

"Thank you!"

"Our secret. Now get out of here you two," the cook made a shooing motion with his massive hands.

Devon darted out the door with Kirin quickly in tow, each clutching a fresh loaf in their hands. They slipped past the compound toward the mountain. A narrow path weaved toward a lookout position enshrouded by some trees. It was under the shade of these trees that the pair dug into their bread and simply sat in silence looking out upon the distant valley. Comfortable silence, Kirin felt, was the mark of a solid relationship.

"You ever wonder what's out there." Devon said breaking the lull.

Kirin laughed, "Did you forget who you were asking?"

"Yeah I guess. It's been nearly two months."

"Two months and a day," Kirin corrected him.

"That bad huh."

"Yeah, I wouldn't want to repeat that anytime soon."

They lapsed momentarily into silence as they chewed on their small meal.

"Anything exciting happen while I was away?" Kirin asked.

Devon glanced up toward the sky. His brow furrowed a bit as he thought on the last couple of months. He ran a thick hand through his blonde hair before he finally replied.

"The snow finally melted and it's warmed up enough so that we can train longer into the evening now."

"I know it's warmed up. I wasn't dead, I was simply locked up," Kirin cut in.

Devon chuckled and almost choked on a small piece of bread.

"Well then, let's see," Devon paused a moment in recollection, "Instructor Fulk broke Warin's arm, he cried like a little girl," Devon grunted to himself as a half-smile lingered on his lips.

"That must've been entertaining," Kirin said.

"It was, even Dannon laughed. Warin was acting more of an ass than usual that day. We think Master Fulk did it on purpose," Devon mimicked the breaking of Warin's arm as he related the story.

At the mention of Dannon, Kirin's throat went dry. He swallowed the bread he was chewing and suddenly wished for some water. Devon carried on oblivious.

"Gosselin challenged your father not two span ago over the food rations, Ayleth tried to calm her down, but couldn't," Devon continued, his expression changing.

Kirin knew what Devon thought of women's opinions. He was also torn in that Gosselin had raised him as a grandmother. Ayleth had shown him more warmth than his father ever had, yet his father was the kovor. He was to be respected, not challenged publicly.

"She shouldn't have done that," Kirin replied.

"By the thirteen I don't know what she was thinking!" Devon spat. "Women are always complaining, bickering or gossiping."

Kirin didn't respond. He knew how Devon got around certain subjects. This was one of them. He always wondered why his friend was so passionately distrustful of women. It was still a mystery; one Kirin was unwilling to probe further. Only once had he tried and it ended with them wrestling halfway down the hill and caught by the Master.

"I'd move south if I could, I hear they treat women the way they're supposed to be treated there," Devon mumbled.

Kirin looked over at him. He shook his head as he thought of a response.

"If I could go somewhere it would be over the Shrouded Mountains to the land of the Three Kingdoms," Kirin said.

"If you can make it past the witches of the mountain!" Devon snorted.

Here it began, Kirin thought. At least he had diverted Devon away from a sensitive subject.

"They're probably just a myth. You know how the stories get built up with each telling. In one version, they're beheading children in another they're flying from the sky breathing fire," Kirin said waving his hand dramatically.

His father had told him about the witches. Kirin remembered it clearly for it was one of the few one-on-one interactions they'd had. The kovor had simply stated, *"Remember with many stories there is only a kernel of truth. Not all witches are bad."*

"I think you're confusing the draccus fiend with witches," Devon retorted.

"Maybe, but you know what I mean. Anyway, draccus fiends are a perfect example, they no longer exist, yet they're still talked about as if they were seen flying around yesterday."

At this Devon seemed shocked as if Kirin had stated the moon would no longer appear in the night sky. A wicked grin struggled to remain hidden on Kirin's face as he glanced briefly at the clouds.

"Of course, draccus fiends exist; for the kovor's son sometimes you say the stupidest things!"

Kirin suddenly became serious.

"I wish I weren't the kovor's son," he said at last.

"What?" Devon said, exasperated as he looked upon Kirin. He noted the solemn look and immediately changed his tone, "Why not? The kovor is the most honorable position in the village!"

"There are other ways to maintain one's

honor than bossing people about and making their son's life miserable." Kirin responded.

"The honor doesn't come from the position, but is demanded by it," Devon said.

"I knew what you meant, but there's more to life than what people perceive you to be. Most are so caught up by their own problems that they couldn't give two shits if it didn't involve themselves."

"You think your father's like that? That he doesn't care?"

"Oh, I know he cares about the village, and the crops, and the defenses of our people..."

"Just not about his own son," Devon filled in.

"Exactly," Kirin whispered.

"You really don't like him, your father I mean," Devon said, slightly in shock.

"You wouldn't either if you were his son. He didn't even raise me. He wants nothing to do with me. Ayleth is more a parent to me than the kovor ever has been."

At this Devon spat, "women shouldn't raise men. They're too emotional and too weak. They lack the logic and strength required to raise a true warrior."

For some reason this struck a nerve. Kirin was already feeling heated and dove into their newest argument with relish.

"If logic and strength were the only attributes

that defined a warrior we'd live in a society without compassion, compromise, and loyalty."

"Bullshit, loyalty is part of strength," Devon said.

"I'll admit it's a strength," Kirin replied.

"You see, I'm right," Devon said proudly, inflating his muscular chest.

"I'm not finished; although it's a strength it is rarely logical. Logic is self-serving. It is cold-hearted and cannot exist in the same realm as emotion. Loyalty is an emotional bond not a logical thought."

"Whatever, I'm not trying to philosophize with you, plus you just had two months to think on these things."

"Two months and a day," Kirin corrected feeling a smug smile creep onto his face.

"You know what I'm saying! Anyway, a boy needs a father, that's all."

This silenced Kirin and the smile that graced his features faded like the warmth of a dying fire. Devon had a point, a boy needs a father. Silence enveloped them once more in its quiet grasp. Their minds worked as the sun began its slow descent through the heavens.

Chapter 4

"Words are but spoken memories waiting to be remembered." The First Kovor

A week passed by entirely too quickly.

Kirin had spent the evening after supper along the hillside alone. Simple tombs containing the ashes of the fallen were enshrined within stone, resting peacefully on the earth. A gentle wind stirred the tufts of green grass sprouting from the sun-kissed ground. Lenton's feminine energy was both warm and soothing and Kirin basked in its tender glory.

Kirin wiped a tear from his face and glanced once more at the statue before him. It was a stone carving of his mother. His father had spent months carving it himself. Although this was normally a job for a stone mason. The kovor felt that it wasn't right for another man's hands to create the final resting place of his beloved's remains. So, after several failed attempts, he finally finished the monument to his deceased wife.

The statue was crude but elegant. Its simple lines showed a beautiful woman with a broad smile. Upon her shoulder was an angel of sorts. It spoke of the countless hours the kovor had spent lovingly crafting it, a shrine to a lost love.

Kirin leaned forward to look more carefully

at the angel. It was in the shape of a baby girl. It was strange his father would choose to add an angel to his mother's statue. The Thane knew of angels from the stories of other lands, but they didn't believe in them.

They believed in the power of the thirteen gods. They believed that all life was part of a greater cycle of balance. When one died, another was born. If the death was caused unjustly a revenge killing was necessitated to restore the proper balance. Once properly avenged the lingering soul would be allowed to pass through the gates of the thirteen and be admitted into the afterlife. Kirin knew that his mother had passed through the gates and was watching down upon them with love in her heart and a smile on her lips.

Kirin had often wondered what she was like, but his father never spoke of her. He heard a few stories from Gosselin about her, but only after she'd drunk too much ale. One interaction in particular clung to him with an unusual tenacity. He remembered coming home from apprenticing with the village's main armorer, Jarin the Fist. He was a tough man who had earned his nickname from once knocking out Merek, a rather large man, with a single strike.

That night Ayleth was already asleep. She often began her days early, rising with the sun. Gosselin on the other hand would often stay up late, drinking spiced ale and slowly mending clothing while staring at the fire. He remembered her old wrinkled hands working diligently with the mending needles as if they had a mind of their own. She worked them as she talked. Her eyes were far away. And she spoke of his mother.

"… so strange your father would choose a foreign woman to marry. Everywhere she went her snow-white hair garnered attention, we all knew when he brought her back that there was love between them, but there was something more, something unspoken, something that danced and hummed in the air about her like a second skin…"

Gosselin had at that moment made eye contact with Kirin. Her old, tired eyes narrowed and she seemed to catch herself.

"I've said too much my boy, off to bed and not a word you hear, not a word."

He knew better than to repeat her words. The Thane rarely spoke of the dead, it was better to leave them in peace.

In regard to his widowed father, people whispered. It wasn't natural for a kovor to be without a wife, but he never took another. Kirin simply believed it was because he was stubborn, but when Kirin let his anger subside, he knew that his father still held his wife close to his heart.

He wasn't sure why he still came to the Thane cemetery. Maybe he felt if he spent enough time at her resting place he would learn more about her, feel her, know her. Perhaps it was one of the few places he could be left alone with his thoughts.

Most of the Thane Sagan believed it wasn't right to visit the dead except for on their name day. This, however, allowed Kirin time alone to ponder on the wider world, the reasons for why things were, and to daydream. He would find himself asking his mother questions. Often, they were simply the idle wanderings of a growing mind, but at times they were dilemmas he felt were too big for him to handle. Today, however, he asked for her guidance and her strength for the upcoming trials.

With a final prayer, he stood and walked back to the cluster of buildings. They were cast in the mountain's shadow as the sun had set, illuminated by the wash of light that fell upon the sky before night truly descended.

Large fires burned in central pits to keep the shroud cats, bears, wolves and other animals away. He passed a group of adolescents who had already completed their coming of age trials. They were drinking watered down ale and joking by the fire. Their easy countenance and nonchalant attitude bespoke a quiet confidence. They ignored him as if he were nothing more than a feral cat. Amongst the Thane even a prince had to earn his name before gaining respect.

Kirin slipped into the building where Ayleth,

Gosselin, and Dimia lived. They occupied one end of the building, while Kirin had been given a small room on the other end. He was soon to take a new name and become a man.

It wouldn't do for the son of the kovor to be sharing a room with others.

He removed his boots and lay atop the furs of his bed. He closed his eyes and attempted to wrestle sleep into submission. He failed miserably.

There was a light knocking on the door. Kirin rustled out of bed. He opened the door half expecting a raiding party to take him bound hand and foot to his next challenge. It was only Devon.

"You awake?" He asked.

"Can't sleep," Kirin responded.

"I probably wouldn't either," Devon said entering his room, "I just wanted to let you know, Dannon saw the Medicine Man preparing something yesterday, it might be for your ritual."

Dannon had captured Kirin's eye some time back, much to the chagrin of her father. She was young, lively, and spirited. She was just becoming a woman and her gentle curves bespoke a hidden beauty that yearned to be embraced, touched.

When Dannon had been younger she struggled to make sure all games were fair, sharing the same uncommon desire for universal rectitude as Kirin. Devon on the other hand would often try to circumvent those rules in an effort to win. The challenge with Dannon was, she was unpredictable, and Kirin had the hardest time figuring out what she wanted or what she was thinking.

"Dannon?" Kirin said trying to mask his buried desire. "Did she ask about me?"

"Yes, she asked. For some unknown reason and despite her father's wishes, she seems to be quite smitten." Devon said as if relaying some annoying bit of news. "Although who knows with her, she's always changing her mind."

Kirin blushed and looked away trying to hide his discomfort before responding, "Did she tell you what she saw the Medicine Man preparing?"

"No, that was it," Devon said offhandedly.

"Well, next time you see her, tell her," Kirin paused to think of something good.

"I don't want to be some messenger boy between two love-struck, smooches," Devon said with exasperation.

Kirin smiled and continued as if Devon hadn't laid bare his discomfort, "Tell her that she filled my thoughts and dreams, distracting me from properly finding peace in the Shrine of Patience."

"Lame," Devon uttered under his breath.

Kirin fixed Devon with a stare of pleading desperation.

"Fine, but if Borin follows through with his promise and beats you silly I'll stand there laughing."

"Really!" Kirin said, attempting to sound hurt.

"I'd take you to the Medicine Man afterward of course," he said as if to make amends.

"Deal," Kirin said almost too quickly.

"Alright, I better let you get some rest."

"If I can," Kirin said as he watched his friend leave the room.

The morning came sooner than he had hoped. It was the incessant chirping of the birds that had jostled him out of a rather disturbing dream. He was able to get some sleep, just enough to make him feel groggy. Kirin stumbled as he dressed, splashed some water onto his face and stepped out.

He almost ran headlong into the looming figure of the kovor. He needed to stop daydreaming and pay more attention. He was liable to walk off a cliff one day.

"Let's get some breakfast," his father said formally.

This took Kirin by surprise. Despite the cloud looming in his mind, he stood up a little straighter and did his best to hide the surprise from his face. The prospect of sharing breakfast with his father on the day he was to begin a new trial caused his stomach to turn. Although he had shared many a meal with him, rarely was it just the two of them, and never at his personal request.

The two walked in silence to the dining hall. The morning was cool and crisp. Birds sang their birdsong as the sun struggled to rise over the distant mountains. Long shadows stretched across the stone hewn path lending a surreal air to the scene.

Kirin fidgeted as he watched the tall, strong figure of his father walk ahead. He always felt nervous around him. He feared him almost as much as he was angered by him.

Too quickly they arrived at the dining hall. Once inside Kirin positioned himself behind a wooden chair opposite his father. He took a moment to study his stern features. There was now a touch of gray to his otherwise blonde hair. His graying hair was tied back with a simple leather strip as was the custom of all warriors who had passed their trials. The white fur of a shroud cat graced his broad shoulders, marking him as the leader of their people.

"Sit, you needn't stand on formality with me today," he said with a hint of emotion in his voice.

Kirin sat without hesitation glancing across the hall toward the adjacent kitchen hoping to catch sight of the Master Cook. Instead he glimpsed the Medicine Man. His father's voice stole his attention.

"How was the Shrine of Patience?" he asked.

Kirin glanced about, unsure if this was yet another test. He didn't like being alone with his father, although part of him had craved it since he was a boy. He reflected momentarily on how odd and conflicting emotions could be.

"There is no one else here, you may speak freely," the kovor's voice split through Kirin's head like a hammer upon ice.

At first Kirin thought of refusing to answer just to stir an emotional response from his father, but he knew that'd only make his next trials more grueling. He needed to think of an answer to placate him all the while showing that he didn't really care.

"It was challenging, but a good lesson," Kirin finally responded.

His father raised his eyebrows at this, "and what lesson was that?"

Kirin's hadn't anticipated that question, but he hadn't thought through his response either. On a better day, he wouldn't have fumbled so carelessly with his words, but today he was tired and nervous. Anger bubbled quietly beneath the surface as Kirin's hands unwittingly balled into fists. How was it that simple words from his father could cut through him like a Sagan blade through fresh wool?

"Patience," was all he managed to spit out.

His father regarded him with an austere look, "patience, how would you define this newfound knowledge?"

"Awareness of the passage of time without attachment to each moment," Kirin blurted out.

His father leaned back bringing a hand to his jaw, rubbing it for a moment.

Kirin wasn't sure what this meant as he eyed him with a nervous stomach and a vacuous expression.

"Do you know why I've invited you to breakfast?" the kovor asked.

Kirin looked at him then about the room, his eyes once more wandering to the kitchen looking for the Master Cook. It was strange not to see him there.

"Honestly?" Kirin asked.

"Of course, I expect nothing less."

"You lacked good dialogue and wanted to start the day with a thoroughly good conversation," Kirin said flatly.

"You are the kovor's son! You make light of the situation in some failed attempt at humor yet no one is amused," he said heavily.

"I am," Kirin whispered.

The kovor decided to ignore the last statement and instead fixed him with an angry glare. Kirin's anger boiled over and he spoke.

"You have lured me here to begin the second phase of my trials. We are awaiting the Medicine Man for it to begin."

It was at this moment the Medicine Man stepped into the dining hall with two plates of food. Kirin watched him enter, surprised at the uncanny timing of his words. The kovor's look of surprise lasted a moment longer and gave Kirin a moment of satisfaction, albeit fleeting.

Without a word, the Medicine Man placed the dishes before them and stepped back, but didn't leave the room. The kovor nodded to him in greeting then looked back to his son.

"Anything else you wish to say?" the kovor said with genuine interest.

"Good morning Medicine Man," Kirin said, turning to the older man, purposefully sidelining the kovor's question.

The kovor narrowed his eyes momentarily before also turning to the Medicine Man.

"Should we eat this while still hot?"

"Please do," he replied.

Kirin didn't say anything. He was still angry at being talked down to. The sooner the breakfast was over the better.

The kovor had already dug a fork into his food and began eating. Kirin decided to do the same. His first bite was aromatic, tasty, and quite different than anything he had eaten before. It was quite easy to shovel the food into his mouth.

Before he knew it, he had finished his meal. His stomach was pleasantly full and a mild sense of euphoria settled over his mind. Strangely his anger had dissipated like a late morning fog.

As his emotions softened he glanced about. His father and the Medicine Man were watching him closely. A slow smile crept onto his face as amusement sought to befriend him. For some reason, he found the whole situation ironically comical.

"It's time," the Medicine Man said.

The kovor nodded and stood. Not knowing what to do, Kirin stood as well. He felt slightly dizzy, maybe he had overeaten. He burped aloud and giggled.

"Let's go," his father said, gesturing to the door.

Kirin stepped past him and through the doorway into the early morning. Three tall men in ceremonial leathers stood waiting for him. Their faces were painted with white stripes. The lines resembled the pattern found on the shroud cat. Their leather armor was segmented, covering most of their bodies, giving them an insect-like appearance. Kirin's demeanor changed as his mind struggled to comprehend the significance of their presence.

Without warning they moved forward

placing heavy hands on his body. He could feel the years of training in the strength of their grip. Had he struggled he would have only managed to injure himself, despite years of body hardening exercises. Kirin managed one quick glimpse of his father stepping out behind him. The kovor gave the briefest nod before a black hood was placed over Kirin's head.

Chapter 5

"The mind is a fragile thing, waiting for a single event to crack its shell." A common saying of the Gwhelt

Kirin's mind began to spin. Being carried with a black hood over his head wasn't his favorite way to travel. His body began to break out in a cold sweat despite the warmth of the rising sun. It was a bad start to an unpleasant day.

He struggled to guess where they were traveling. The sunlight was filtering through the black linen on his left, letting him know they were traveling south. It felt as if they were traveling down a hill. His mind churned over possibilities, trying to figure out where they were taking him. The harder he thought, the more his growing headache intensified. He didn't want to think about what they would do once he got there. His muscles tightened in fearful anticipation. The image of his father's angry, stern face flashed through his mind. Was this a trial or a punishment?

The group began to slow their hellish cadence. It seemed Kirin was going to get his answer before he desired. His heart was already beating quicker and he was feeling simultaneously a surge of energy and an intense desire to get some sleep. Nausea was beginning to settle deep within his stomach.

The cloth covering his head was suddenly ripped free and the light of day temporarily blinded him. A startling display of colors danced in his vision as his eyes fought to focus. The world came together in a collage of blurry images.

"How are you feeling?" one of the men asked.

Kirin opened his mouth to speak and instead vomited onto the tough mountain grass. The three men were no longer holding him, but instead formed a circle about him. Kirin was on all four, heaving for a moment, before struggling to regain his bearings. It had now become abundantly clear that he had been drugged. His mind was ablaze and unable to resolve thoughts into the focus needed for clarity.

He pushed himself to his feet and staggered. The men's faces looked fierce with their white war paint. He took a couple of steps and steadied himself, suddenly feeling an incredible urge to defecate.

One of the men stepped forward and placed the skin of a shroud cat onto his back. It must have been a juvenile, for the fur of a full-sized cat would have completely engulfed him. A strange thought to have while men held him down. Two armored men quickly strapped the fur onto his limbs as he howled in frustration and confusion.

"You are a shroud cat, proud and strong," the tallest of the three said, his face appearing to change shapes as he spoke. "You have the strength and stamina of the powerful animal, but beware, for you are hunted!"

Kirin glanced down at his arm to see it was covered in fur. His hands had claws. His head pounded in confusion as thoughts slipped away like pollen in the wind. He growled fiercely and ran into the woods, the trees twisting in his vision, smelling much like mother's milk.

Chapter 6

"Reality is the thin veil that shades the world in a thousand hues of gray." Testament of Khein 3:22

For twenty days Kirin was kept in a drug induced state. His days and nights bled together in a hyper-aware amalgam of emotion, color, and sensory overload. The normal distinction between the senses simply did not exist. Colors held scent, shapes were in constant flux, sounds held color, and all sense of self was lost in the agitate froth that had become his reality.

Kirin at times was the wind, whispering through the trees, feeling and seeing everything. At times, he became the earth, still, slow, and cold, yet humming with a quiet unseen rhythm. He ran and he hid. He jumped and he played. He sat and he stared. The hours were nothing more than a distant thought created by an elusive mind. Time held no sway in his state. There were moments that lasted an eternity. At one point a butterfly held his unwavering interest. The next moment he watched as the clouds took on an infinite number of hues transforming into ever moving geometric patterns.

It was on the twentieth day that the three men watching him began to reduce his dosage as per the instructions of the Medicine Man. For an entire week, they continued to feed him lessening amounts of the potent plant that forged a new reality in his mind. It was during this week that the Medicine Man stood nearby, watching Kirin as he convulsed, vomited, and struggled with the shape of reality.

Each passing day brought greater moments of lucidity. The world as he knew it and the world as he had come to know it were colliding, and his mind was struggling to cope. Flittering images of a fragmented past invaded his long moments of wonder and awe. Crisp thoughts of a tangible nature tugged at him with greater intensity. Despite this flurry of mental activity, who he was had been lost to the wind.

Eventually Kirin was brought back to the village escorted by three tall warriors and the Medicine Man. He was unable to form words for it seemed he had forgotten how to speak. His eyes were alert, bordering on paranoia. He could walk on his own and was able to distinguish between sights, sounds, and tastes to varying degree.

His father visited him briefly but no record of that visit exists. He mostly recovered under the watchful eye of the Medicine Man for the next thirty days. It was on the cycle of the new moon that Kirin finally spoke.

Chapter 7

"Experience defines the man." Proverb of the
Thane Sagan

"Tell me of your experience," the Kovor
asked, facing the young white-haired Kirin.

"There are few words to describe it and I
have gaps in what I can recall," he replied, his
voice sounded strange to his own ears, his mind,
however, was strangely calm and devoid of
emotion.

"Nevertheless, I want to know what you
learned."

Kirin glanced about the room. Candles were
lit and cast pools of yellow light on heavy stones.
Carpets from the faraway D'seart Kingdom
graced the floor, providing a vivid splash of
color. Furs lined the chairs, lending a sense of
warmth and comfort. It was the private quarters
of the kovor; few others were afforded such
luxuries.

Kirin's eyes focused off into the distance. For
a moment, he debated refusing, but he was tired
and not in the mood for a beating. A lie would be
transparent and stupid, which left the truth. The
truth was often heavier, more outlandish, and
more layered than any lie could conceive of
being.

With a small inhalation and feeling older than his thirteen years of age he began, "The Shrine of Patience made me acutely aware of the passage of time despite being unaware of the passing of the sun and moon. I had time for idle speculation, excessive thought and self-reflection. This last trial was different." He paused as he attempted to assemble the fragmented memories of the last couple of months. "It tore me apart and spread me across the expanse of heaven and earth. I felt there was no separation between things. I couldn't remember the names of common objects; yet could somehow recall the names of things I have never seen nor understood."

The kovor was leaning forward, listening intently. Kirin looked toward the wooden beams bracing the ceiling. "Time had no meaning, only the moment held me."

Kirin then stopped, watching his father nod in approval. It was a rare sight. Normally he would have flushed with pride or been filled with an anxious excitement, but not today. Today he noted the emotion and remained silent.

"You have shaken loose the ancestor that clung to your mind and plagued you with incessant thoughts. You have shown that patience and time can be used for introspection and awareness. You have assumed the form and taken the strength of the shroud cat."

Kirin reflected on his father's words. He

gazed upon his face for a moment and searched for any emotion. To his surprise, he found pride upon his father's features and sadness lurking in his eyes. It was not the usual mask of displeasure the kovor normally wore.

"What ancestor did I shake loose?" Kirin asked.

His father's face paled slightly but otherwise remained unchanged.

"That is for another time. Perhaps you should ask the Thirteen," he said gravely.

Kirin was not placated by his response. He knew there was something more the kovor was withholding.

"You blame me for mother's death and think she lingers," Kirin stated flatly, still looking intently upon his father.

The kovor's expression changed into one of surprise followed by anger.

"How dare you disrespect me? I'm your father, I'm the kovor. Never in a thousand thousand years would I have thought to do such a thing to my own father."

"Did your father ignore you, give you away? Did he poison you and make you nearly lose your mind?" Kirin responded, emotion starting to well up from a hidden pit in his heart.

The kovor faltered for a moment some of the anger leaving his eyes. Eyes that now looked heavy and tired. Silence hung thickly between them for a span of heartbeats, as heavy as a sodden blanket. He then spoke quietly and calmly.

"You were a twin, the only surviving twin. Your mother had passed through the gates long ago, although, you possess many of her strengths and some of her weaknesses."

He fell silent for a moment. It was the most the kovor had revealed about Kirin's mother in his young life. His father's eyes were momentarily filled with emotion. The moment passed and a hardened resolve fixed itself onto his chiseled features.

"It was your sister that lingered," he said finally. "She was the ancestor clinging to you, forcing her child-like qualities upon your mind."

The news shocked Kirin into silence. He was born with a twin sister. She too had died upon birth. It was believed that twins were the mark of a god's interference. One baby had been graced by divine intervention, leaving the parents with a miracle and with disruption. Two mouths to feed were always harder than one when food was carefully rationed and calculated for. Yet, he was the one who had survived, that would mark him as the child of a god, not the kovor's true son. That would explain the kovor giving him away at a young age, the additional training, and the trials.

"I've tried to be a father to you Kirin," was all

he said after a lull, his voice barely a whisper.

Kirin remained silent and motionless as if any movement would startle the moment to flight. His father cared. He could see it in the set of his shoulders, the unshed tears in his eyes, and the stern look upon his face. The trials were his hopes of helping Kirin see the world for what it was. Perhaps he had succeeded.

"I know," Kirin responded.

He thought of saying more, of telling him he loved him, he forgave him, he understood the pain he felt, but he didn't. Instead, he looked to the ground and gave his father a moment to compose himself.

In a deep and clear voice, and after a moment of silence, the kovor spoke. His words were careful, yet warm.

"You will one day have a son, lead our people, and bury my ashes beside your mother. It is my hope you'll be a better father and a better kovor than I've been. That is why you must finish your trials. Only one final trial remains, and this last is specifically for you, Kirin, as the son of the kovor."

Kirin remained silent but sat forward in his chair. The last trial was the only one he had been aware of as a necessity. The previous two trials now made greater sense. Despite this knowledge, he sat and waited for his father to continue.

His father glanced at the flickering candles;

their yellow flames cast his features in shadow and light.

"There is little else to say. You know what must be done. I suggest you pack only what you need, lighter is better. Several seasons may pass before you find what you're looking for. I guarantee Sumor will be done and the cool of Hearvest will roll in, but more than likely Hearvest will pass and Vintas will fall before you accomplish your task."

Kirin looked at his father and could see a hint of pride, a touch of nostalgia, and the merest sign of concern upon the corners of his eyes. His father caught his eye for a moment before speaking again.

"There is a strongbox in the back where we chronicle the events of our people. When you come back it will be your duty to improve your reading and writing so you can carry on the tradition of maintaining the record of our lineage."

The kovor leaned back in his chair. He placed his steepled fingers near his chin as if in thought. Silence filled the air as Kirin glanced back toward the trunk in the corner. A heavy weight began to settle upon his chest as he realized the burden his father carried, a burden that would one day fall upon his young shoulders. He didn't want it.

"Behind the strongbox is a small room, the armory of the kovor lineage. I want you to pick out a bladed weapon and a long-range weapon. Listen to your heart, for those weapons will become an extension of you."

Kirin nodded as he listened to his father. He waited a moment longer, waiting to see if he had anything else to say. He did not. Kirin pushed back his chair and stood. He crossed the room passing the heavy gold and silver leaf covered chest and paused at the threshold of the Kovor Lineage Armory. He glanced back, his father nodded to him. That was all the approval Kirin needed.

He entered the small room. His skin prickled as he felt the weight of history and death upon the stagnant air. It was the subtle feel of the smell of turning leaves in Hearvest.

A wooden rack stood to his left, holding a series of long swords. They looked heavy, strong, and too big for him to easily handle. Above them mounted to the wall were knives of all shapes and sizes. On the adjacent wall were longbows leaning against the cool stone side, their wood was the sandy color of the yew tree. Above them hung two medium-sized bodark bows distinguished by their yellow-orange hue. He reached for one and took it down. The well-oiled wood felt light and strong. He tested the bow and placed it to the side.

Strangely the other bodark was strung. It seemed highly unlikely his father would have forgotten to unstring a bow. A strung bow would warp the wood and weaken the bow string. He tested it and was surprised to see it felt as supple as the first, despite clearly being older. Faded runes were carved lightly into its frame. Kirin liked the runes and set the bow aside.

On the right wall were traps, spears, and blades of various sorts. It was a bladed weapon he was after. From his training, he knew he wanted something with enough reach to hurt someone without it being a burden to carry. It needed to be sharp and well balanced.

He reached for a medium-length straight sword and paused. Above it was the Sword of Sagas. It was his father's sword, before that it was his father's father's weapon, dating all the way back to the First Kovor. Was this a test? Did his father leave his sword in the armory to see if Kirin was bold enough to claim it? Somehow Kirin doubted that. He admired its lines. It was a large sword, too big for him to properly wield anyhow and certainly not conducive to carrying around for days on end.

He let his eyes slip from the magnificent blade and looked once more upon the simple spathe. It looked almost ugly in comparison, drab and gray. Most training was done with a straight-blade sword. They trained with a wooden version of the spathe; it was what he was familiar with. He swung the weapon a few times. It felt strong and solid. He set it aside as a possibility.

His eyes wandered over a few other similar scythes, towards axes he had trained with but was less familiar with, until they paused on a type of sword he had never seen before. It was simple yet elegant. The blade had a gentle curve to it as was evidenced by the curved scabbard. The scabbard and the handle were of the darkest black, likely why he hadn't seen it at first, as if it were trying to remain hidden in the shadows.

He had to move a small stool in order to reach it. Kirin stood atop the stool and ran a finger along the scabbard. It was as smooth as fire-hardened glass. His fingers tingled at the touch and a deep-seated curiosity tugged at his innards.

Kirin grabbed the sword. It was lighter than he had expected. Perhaps it wasn't of good quality or the metal wouldn't hold against a standard spathe. He unsheathed it; the gentle note of steel rang lightly in the air. The leather grip felt solid. The balance was excellent as though they had folded the blade into the tang for that very purpose. The steel had the deep undulating pattern of metal that had been heated, folded, and forged to remove all imperfections, with the most perfect hamon he'd ever seen. A subtle pattern of blue lent an aura of beauty.

Kirin knew the blue was from the process of heating and rapidly cooling the blade by quenching it in a bath of special salts and water. He'd apprenticed briefly with the blacksmith and asked enough questions to understand hot bluing, but he was too small at the time to weld the heavy forging hammer to be of much use.

With a few quick swings, he fell in love. He ran a finger gently across the oiled edge and drew a drop of bright crimson from his finger. It was far sharper than he would have thought. He sheathed the sword, grabbed the bodark bow and stepped out.

His father was still seated where he had left him. He was leaning back in his chair with his eyes partially closed. Without opening them he spoke.

"So, you made your choices?"

"Yes," Kirin responded.

The kovor opened his eyes and leaned forward, his eyes bright and interested. All hints of sadness were gone. He reached forward for the bow. Kirin handed it to him. The kovor traced a finger over the fine-grain wood, lightly pausing on the runes.

"You have chosen a fine bow, but I'm curious. This bow is nearly twice as old as the other bodark, why chose this over the other?"

Kirin shrugged, "I liked the runes."

His father grunted, "Either you've a good eye or you're lazy. This bow never needs to be unstrung; it was touched by the hands of the divine."

The kovor handed the bow back to him. His

eyes then froze on the black sword Kirin had chosen. They narrowed as his brow furrowed.

"Where did you find that?" He asked.

"It was above the other weapons, hidden in shadow."

His father's eyes widened briefly before a mask of composure settled over his features. He reached out as if to touch the sword then paused and retracted his hand.

"This is a very old sword indeed. I had almost forgotten it was ever there."

Kirin waited for him to say more, but he didn't.

"Where's it from?" Kirin asked.

"Templas."

Kirin looked at the sword more carefully, eyeing the detail and craftsmanship.

"Do you think I should choose another?" He asked.

"No." The kovor's voice was firm. "The sword chooses the owner, not the other way around. There is a reason you picked that sword, let's only hope it's an honorable one," he paused and then whispered so quietly that Kirin could barely make out the words, "Let's hope you've not been touched by Kurat's devious hand."

His father paused long enough to look at Kirin carefully and placed a strong hand onto his shoulder. It was the most affection he had received from the man in a dozen years, and it felt good.

"Go now and pack, for tomorrow you will leave."

With those final words, Kirin gathered the bodark bow and Templas sword and left to pack. His shoulder still felt warm from where his father had touched him. With a faint smile and a loose grip on his sword he crossed the room.

"Kirin," his father's voice reached out to him as he stood at the doorway. "There is a secret tied to that blade, one I cannot tell you until you've passed your final trial and become a man. Perhaps, upon your return we shall share a drink together as father and son and discuss its true name."

Kirin's eyes searched the kovor's for a moment, probing for any hint of amusement or jest. There was none. His father, as usual, was gravely pensive.

Kirin nodded his understanding and walked out into the cool night. He wasn't sure if he was more startled by the revelation that he had chosen a sword with a secret or that his father had treated him more like a son than he ever had.

Kirin only took a few steps before stopping, thoughts stirring up a mental storm. Kirin had uncovered the mystery of his final trial. He learned he'd become the keeper of records and upon his return would be groomed to take over as the kovor. He learned that he once had a twin sister that died during birth, marking him as touched by a god, and not just any god, but possibly Kurat, the god of the arkein. Despite all of these revelations, it was the kind words, gentle touch, and temporary pride he saw in his father's eyes that affected him most.

Maybe his father actually had cared for him all along and Kirin had been too young and too immature to see beyond the peddling challenges of youth.

Chapter 8

"At the heart of ceremony lies tradition, the backbone of any healthy civilization." A Common Sawol Saying

Kirin woke early that morning. The night prior he had oiled his sword, applied wax to the scabbard and leather grip, and packed his bag. He had followed his father's advice, doing his best to keep it light while still packing warm clothing in case he was away through Vintas. He even spent some time figuring out how to most comfortably wear everything. At first it was a daunting task. How did he position his sword, bow, arrows and pack so that they wouldn't interfere with each other?

He had tried by placing his sword at his hip so that the arrows could sling across his back. The problem was the quiver would dig uncomfortable into his spine. The sword at his hip swung awkwardly. He'd trained with the spathe both at his hip and upon his back and over time grew to prefer a sword strapped tightly to his back. Although it had initially been quite awkward drawing a sword from his shoulder, he had practiced until he could draw and slice through a straw-man in the time it took to blink an eye. The first time Devon had seen him do it, he simply stood there silently in awe, a rare treat from a boy who had an opinion on most everything.

Kirin slung his curved blade across his back so that he could draw it with his right hand. He attached the quiver to the pack so that the arrows rested slightly lower than the grip of his sword. His bow fit perfectly across his back. He moved about, imagining various hero-like scenes. Most scenes involved Dannon watching from a safe distance as Kirin saved her.

Once he'd worked up a small sweat, he placed everything neatly in a corner. Beside his pack, bow, quiver and sword was his leather armor. The pieces were simple and functional, just enough armor to protect certain parts of his body while allowing for unhindered and rapid movement. With one final glance at his stuff, he slipped out in search of food and his best friend.

Kirin slipped through the household with the silence of a thrush mouse. He cut through the night as he avoided the large fires. The stars shone brightly, blanketing the heavens like a thousand phosphorous candles.

He skirted a nearby building and nearly stumbled upon Dannon. She stood mostly in shadow, only a sliver of firelight outlined her features. Her young, lithe form and long auburn hair were as beautiful as a kalon flower in full bloom. His heartbeat quickened at the sight of her. She hadn't noticed him yet. Her slender back was to him as she glanced about.

He struggled to think of something clever or interesting to say. As the seconds scraped by he worried she'd turn around and catch him simply standing there, staring at her like an oaf.

"Dannon," Kirin whispered as loud as he dared in case her father was nearby.

Great, that should sweep her off her feet, he thought.

She turned to look at him. Her gray eyes bordered on purple and were as lovely as a Sumor sunset. They lit up when she saw him and she skipped over to him. Her young body moved distractingly under a lace tunic tied tantalizingly at her narrow waist.

Her smile slipped from her face as she looked at him.

"What're you doing here?" She asked.

Had she caught him looking at her body? He couldn't help himself. In so many ways he was disciplined. He could train for hours under the most miserable conditions, yet melted before the judgment of a teenage girl.

"I came looking for you," he lied.

Her face blushed lightly as she gave him a gentle shove and a mock stern look. She was so beautiful when her brows knitted together.

"You found me," she replied. "You know my father doesn't want me to see you."

"He made that abundantly clear," Kirin said as he recalled their last interaction.

Dannon laughed, her eyes sparkled in the moonlight.

"Not so loud," Kirin whispered.

"So, the future kovor is scared of getting caught with a girl at night, interesting," she said teasingly.

"I'm not scared," Kirin replied a little too quickly.

"No of course not, and the mouse doesn't run from the cat."

Her smile caused his heart to thump oddly in his chest. She wasn't the most beautiful girl in the village, but there was a beauty that she held that shone through her eyes that had so enamored the young Kirin. He longed to kiss her again and for some reason became so fixated on trying to make that happen that he failed to listen to her.

"Am I boring you?" She asked more seriously, crossing her arms across her developing chest.

"No, of course not."

"Then you're simply daydreaming again. Perhaps I should leave you to it," she said turning and looking away.

This wasn't going as he had planned. Somehow, he had seen everything playing out differently in his head.

"Wait, that's not fair," he said softly.

Dannon regarded him for a moment, her eyes hardening into two fierce pools of defiance.

"What is it future kovor? Do you command me to stay?"

"I can't command you," he replied sheepishly.

"That's right you can't."

Kirin now struggled to think of a way to change the tone of the conversation. How had it gone so wrong? He felt if Devon were here, it would be different. Probably because he didn't give two shits what women said. That tactic, however, didn't seem appropriate at the moment.

"Devon said he saw you," Kirin said trying to change the subject, desperate to see her smile or laugh at least once more.

"He did," was all she said. She stood there for a moment staring at him. "Devon told me you thought of me while in the Shrine of Patience," her brow momentarily knitting together again.

"I did," was all Kirin managed to say.

There was a moment of awkward silence. Kirin ached to look upon her lips, but instead looked away as if he were afraid they would blind him like the sun. The courage he had demonstrated so blindly with his friends was nothing more than the hint of a shadow on a full moon. His only recourse was to fill the void with words.

"I hoped I would see you again," he said, the truth now spilling forward.

"Why?" Dannon asked.

"Isn't it obvious?" Kirin replied, this time courage filling his words as confidence inflated his lungs. "You fill my thoughts and dreams. You're dangerous! I cannot spend a waking moment without thinking of how you smell, imagining your smile, and remembering our kiss."

Dannon dropped her arms and looked about ready to speak, but then stopped herself.

Kirin felt naked before her. Why had he said all that? Devon was right, he was crazy.

"I have to go, my father's waiting for me," she finally replied.

"I leave tomorrow for my final trial," he blurted out; hurt she hadn't returned his affection.

Dannon regarded him for a moment. She glanced to his mouth before she leaned forward. Kirin didn't move as if he were afraid of startling a butterfly. Her warm lips graced his for a heartbeat, yet the feeling of her touch remained. It was gentle, leaving his lips tingling and his mind foggy.

"So you don't forget me," she whispered before she turned and walked off.

Kirin stood there for a moment, dumbfounded and smiling stupidly. Dannon still liked him! He was so excited, he almost forgot why he had ventured out in the first place.

He watched her disappear around a corner before remembering he was making his way to the kitchen. Kirin walked past a stone building. His lips still inflamed with the purity of her touch.

"Hey stupid," Devon said, startling Kirin from his revere.

"What in the gods are you doing sitting in the dark?" Kirin asked as he tried to mask his surprise.

"Why are you smiling like the village idiot?" Devon replied.

"I saw Dannon," he said.

"Why am I not surprised! You're damn reckless is what you are, on the night before you leave no less."

"I'm reckless?" Kirin said his mind felt sluggish and a further retort was still forming when Devon spoke.

"Yes, you're reckless! Great come back, by the way. Did she rob you of your wit too?"

"No," Kirin said.

"No," Devon said mockingly, "Anyway halfwit, I've been waiting for you."

"And I came looking for you," Kirin lied again.

What was it about lies that flowed so readily

from the tongue, when truth felt so heavy and burdensome? Dannon was one of the few people he felt he could open up to, even if she sometimes made it frustratingly hard.

"Whatever," Devon continued, running a hand through his blonde hair, "So you find out what your next trial is yet?"

"I did." Kirin paused, glancing around the corner, "Wait for me. I'm going to sneak in to get some food."

"Sneaking out at night, consorting with Borin's daughter, and now stealing. You're setting quite the example as the future kovor."

"How about you either shut it or help the future kovor steal some food so he doesn't starve to death during his damned trial."

Devon tossed a heavy sack at him. Kirin grunted as he caught it. He peeked inside, dried meats, D'seart bread, and dried fruits were packed tightly within.

"This'll do," Kirin said with a grunt of approval.

"I knew there was no way you'd leave without getting something to eat," Devon said with a smile.

Kirin laughed, it was true. Part of his test was surviving alone with nothing but what he brought. Water would be easy to secure, but food he would have to find, trap, or hunt. It would be far easier to start off with a little something extra.

"So, what's the final test?" Devon asked as if he had been waiting to know for days.

"I'm the kovor's son, I think you know."

"No! You're supposed to hunt a shroud cat?" He said incredulously.

Kirin nodded, suddenly feeling a hint of pride stab at his insides. The two of them had been competitive since a young age. Despite Devon's greater strength, Kirin had a height and skill advantage, allowing him to win most of their competitions.

"My father let me choose from the armory as well," he said.

"What did you get?" Devon asked, struggling to hide his curiosity.

"A bodark bow with something written on the upper limb and sitting groove. Also, a Templas sword."

"A Templas sword? You don't mean from the Templas Empire, do you?"

"Yup, sharpest damned blade I've ever held."

"Of course it is!" Devon paused for a moment before he whispered, "Can I see it?"

"Tomorrow, I want to try and catch some sleep before the ceremony."

Kirin looked up at the night sky trying to discern the hour. He had a rough idea from the constellations' positions in the heavens. There were constellations for each of the thirteen gods.

By his estimate there were only a couple hours of darkness left.

"You're lucky," Devon said, starting to walk off.

"Why's that?"

"I don't start my trials until the end of Sumor," Devon stopped, half turning to Kirin.

"End of Sumor," Kirin repeated as if reliving a memory. "If they stick you in the Temple of Boredom I carved something into the wall, perhaps you can keep yourself entertained trying to figure out what it says."

"I can't wait," Devon replied sarcastically as he too looked to the sky.

Dawn stretched slowly across the heavens like an awakening feline as slim fingers of light proclaimed the early morning hour. For Kirin it was the start of his final trial. In a few hours, he would leave S'Vothe and venture into the wild.

Once settled upon the fur covers of his straw filled mattress, he fell into a fitful sleep, dreaming of Devon, Dannon, and his father. The first hints of fear crept in like a shadow tugging quietly at his intestines. It was a short sleep, infused with subtle hints of lavender.

The sun watched sanguinely as crowds gathered. Younger boys scrambled to get a better vantage point as older women complained of the weather. A cool wind blew in from the north whispering a sorrowful song of repose.

Oblivious to it all was Kirin. He stood proudly at the center of a small dais. Behind him stood the Medicine Man and the Kovor. To his right were five senior warriors clad in ceremonial armor. To his left were five leather-clad women nearly as fierce looking as the men.

"Kirin D'Velt of the kovor lineage, step forward," the kovor shouted.

There was a shuffling in the crowd as people jostled for a better view. Those who had passed their own tests stood in silent remembrance. It was the youth who wore expressions of impatience and curiosity.

Kirin saw Devon standing next to his father. A goofy grin was plastered upon his face as he watched the ceremony. The stern gaze of Borin was farther back as he stood next to his wife and their daughter Dannon. Her eyes were bright and attentive, but she didn't catch his gaze.

Kirin took a step forward. The Medicine Man then stepped forth to stand beside him. The kovor then continued.

"The shroud cat has long been the standing symbol of our lineage, dating back to the First Kovor and the Time of the Reckoning."

Those who were familiar with their history remembered the stories of the great battle nearly two centuries ago. It was the time when the Caliphate of A'sh under Rajah had last attempted to wrest control of their lands. The time when the First Kovor and a group of warriors had captured three fierce shroud cats and released them at night upon the camp of the enemy. The wild cats had torn through the camp in a bloody rampage reminiscent of a Vintas gale. The story had grown to become legend among not only the Thane Sagan, but a warning taught to all D'seart royalty thereafter.

Kirin's father continued, as the crowd listened. It wasn't every day the son of a kovor underwent their final trial.

"The stripes we paint upon your face symbolize the patience, strength, and the mental toughness you have learned and displayed these last months."

The Medicine Man carefully painted white stripes onto his young face. Kirin could feel himself transforming into the powerful animal before his people.

"Upon your return a new name will be granted to you as the rightful heir to the kovor lineage," his father continued, "a name that you'll ponder, learn, and make your own. Let it smolder in your heart and give you strength so that you can give strength to our people and one day lead with the conviction and power of the First Kovor."

Kirin's father paused, letting the tension build in the crowd. The taking of a new name was done with great reverence. It was said that a proper name chose the person.

"You shall become *Aeden* of the Thane Sagan. Now go forth and prove your worth."

With that, Kirin soon to become Aeden, walked forth through the crowds past the squat structures of their village and into the untamed wilderness of the Gwhelt.

Chapter 9

"There is no other thrill than that of the hunt."
Saying of the Thane Sagan

It was Kirin's second month away from home. Sumor was in full effect. It was hot and humid. The day before it had rained intensely for nearly an hour, passing as quickly as it had come. He spent half the day drying his clothing. He found some tracks that were likely that of the shroud cat, but the rain only worked to wash them into oblivion.

Hunger and fatigue defined his Sumor. It seemed to last an eternity as he tried to sign cut under the unrelenting sun. Evening showers drenched the lands, soaked his clothing and dampened his spirits. Buzzing mosquitoes and incessant flies kept him awake at night and pestered him during the day. The traps he would set were half as often tripped by the rain as they were empty. In fact, at times it felt as though nature were testing his very resolve. The lessons he had learned about patience were the only thing driving him forward. Most days were simply spent looking for water or trying to catch food. He spent more time identifying edible herbs and plants than he did trying to find the elusive shroud cat.

And so his days passed. When Hearvest

finally came with its gradual cooling and shorter days he hardly noticed. It wasn't until the chilly winds forced him to dig for warmer clothing and the leaves began to turn that he truly realized how long he had been away. Despite all that time, he felt no closer to finding a shroud cat.

When Kirin first set out, he had grandiose ideas about setting traps with larger game to lure the shroud cat in. He imagined capturing it alive and riding it into the village. He knew the last part was pure fantasy, but part of him wanted to make his father proud and to prove he could pass his trial faster than those before him. He'd prove that he had the blood of a god coursing through his veins.

There were days where he spent half the time daydreaming. Kirin sat theatrically upon the back of the fearsome beast, somehow having learned to tame it. Devon gasped in shock as he sauntered by. His father smiled proudly. Borin looked on with respect and fear as Dannon swooned. He'd slip off the back of the terrible beast and sweep Dannon up into his arms and ask her to marry him. With each passing day that fantasy faded further into obscurity and then into absurdity.

It was therefore a shock, that on his fifth month from home he acquired clear sign of the animal. Distinct tracks and fresh scat indicated he wasn't far. The day passed quickly as he followed the animal's sign. It left distinct prints in the dirt.

A tuft of hair was caught on a branch. A few steps away a broken twig indicated a large animal's passing. The final indicator was scratch marks on a tree. He was close. His excitement grew and it ironically became harder for him to concentrate as he daydreamed of catching the beast.

Of course, as fate would have it, he wasn't yet meant to catch the creature. Days of tracking lead him nowhere closer. He knew that shroud cats could travel over twenty miles in a day and claimed massive tracts of land as their own. In order to secure their claim, they sprayed an incredibly musky odor onto large trees often shredded by their vicious claws. It was then, that he stumbled upon an idea he couldn't believe he hadn't thought of before.

Kirin finally figured out how he was going to capture the much-feared shroud cat.

Vintas came early that year. The air was still, quiet, and cold. A fine blanket of snow cast a delicate beauty upon the land. For Kirin, it was ideal. The snow made it all the easier to follow the tracks of anything that passed before him.

As luck would have it, the tracks of a shroud cat cut a distinct path ahead. The footprints were headed south. Kirin had been south only a few days earlier, for he had been tracking a group of elk. He figured the shroud cat was doing the same. As his instructor used to say, "*If you want to catch a predator, first you must find its prey.*"

Kirin continued to follow the shroud cat's footprints, splitting his attention between its tracks, large trees with claw marks, and any elk sign. Large piles of elk droppings were ahead. He spent a moment examining the dark pile. The round droppings were not quite firm enough to be frozen, despite resting on fresh snow. He stuck his finger into the dank mass. It was cold but still moist, less than a day old. Kirin hastily wiped his fingers on his pants and forged ahead.

He continued following the tracks across a small stream. It was at that moment when he saw what he had been searching for. A large juniper tree still oozing sap from jagged claw marks. Clearly the large cat had been here recently. As he approached, the repugnant smell of the shroud cat's territorial markings filled the air. He looked about for another juniper of equal size. He found one. Its green nestles were covered in a fine layer of white powder, glinting in the sparse light like a thousand diamonds.

Kirin took out his sword and made some swift cuts into the tree, doing his best to mimic the claw marks of the great cat. He then laboriously removed his equipment to get at his pack. Within was a container holding the sap and residue of a shroud cat's territorial spray. He uncorked the lid and was hit with the sour odor.

Kirin took his time using a stick to apply the contents of the jar onto the freshly slashed tree trunk. Despite his caution, a piece of sticky residue found its way onto his pants. When he was done, he stood back and admired his work. Good enough, he thought.

He glanced about the clearing, scouting for a suitable vantage point. A large tree sat anchored opposite the juniper he had just defaced. Kirin began the arduous task of climbing. The branches were cold and his hands were becoming numb. He ignored the discomfort, knowing he could huddle up and rest once he found a suitable position. His plan was perfect, sit and wait for the cat to investigate the "intruder cat's scent" and then pick it off with arrows shot from his bodark bow.

Plans and reality, however, are often like oil and water. Kirin was only partway up the tree when the distinctive crack of a branch caught his attention. He glanced up in time to see a massive shroud cat hurtling down toward him. Shock wasn't quite the word he would have used to describe it. Sheer and utter terror combined with temporary paralysis was a better description.

Fortunately, in his mind-numbing state, he had fumbled his grip and slipped. To Kirin it felt as if the world had slowed to a crawl. Individual snowflakes hung suspended in the air. The air was still and bone cold. His stomach traveled into his throat, where it throbbed uncomfortably. The gray stripes highlighting the aggressive features of the massive predator's face, burned an image into young Kirin's mind.

Thunk!

Kirin hit the ground and immediately rolled to the side. A second later the sharp claws of the shroud cat tore at the earth. Kirin leapt to his feet only to stumble backward over a large root. His bow fell off his shoulder and lay to the side. A couple of arrows had fallen out of his quiver and something may have broken in his bag.

The deep throated roar of the large cat filled the air. The deep pulsing sound tore at his insides like a rat trapped in a jar. Kirin pushed himself to his feet pulling his Templas sword free. He positioned himself as if he were squared off from a much larger man. A small part of him hoped the intense training he had received would work against a beast this size. Another loud roar startled him loose of any preconceived notion of bravery.

Still the cat did not approach.

Several long moments stretched off into silence and forever burned themselves into Kirin's memory. The thick white coat, of Vintas fur, bristled behind the heavy head and above its brawny shoulders.

Kirin briefly contemplated climbing the tree, only to recall the cat had come from high up the conifer. Running was clearly not an option. He glanced at the fallen bow and discarded arrows. They seemed small and feeble. His options were narrowing. He needed a plan.

Kirin simply stood there, stupefied, with his sword held resolutely in front of him. His fingers were firm upon the grip but loose enough to maintain blood flow. His stance was strong, slightly wide and stable. His shoulders were in line with his hips and his head was straight. Despite his fear, the thousands of hours of training became his pedestal.

The large cat roared again and lunged.

Kirin merely had time to stiffen and observe. He remarked upon its sheer speed, despite its great size. He marveled at the large teeth exposed in its open mouth. He could even recall the spittle clinging to the back of its black lips.

What he hadn't anticipated, was his sword sinking into the roof of the beast's mouth. The hot flow of sticky blood that spurted forth as the beast slumped forward, spraying internal fluids onto his clothing and face.

Kirin, still maintaining a grip on his sword, fell back. He wiped at his face, attempting to get the blood out of his eyes. He kicked himself backward, desperately creating space.

He braced himself for the cat's second lunge. It didn't come. Kirin opened his eyes not having realized they were squeezed shut. His heart continued to pound away within his chest like an angry drummer.

There, before him, lay the shroud cat, wheezing its final breath. Sitting on the snowy dirt, dumbfounded, he watched as it twitched and finally lay still.

He had done it. He had killed a shroud cat.

A cold sweat broke out and he shivered. It was the closest to death he'd ever been and it was simultaneously terrifying and invigorating. His heart continued to race. His mind buzzed with adrenaline. Kirin felt more alive than he could ever remember.

He continued to sit there struggling to deal with the conflicting emotions that twisted through his mind like a festnia vine, twitching and convulsing under the light of a partial moon.

Finally, Kirin gathered himself and stood upon shaky legs. He inspected his kill. It wasn't until he walked the length of it that he realized the magnitude of his feat. Although feat wouldn't be how he'd describe it. More like sheer, stupid luck.

Kirin patted himself down, checking absentmindedly for wounds as he had been taught. He was still fully intact.

He gazed at the animal stupidly for a few moments before feeling inclined to pray.

"Kegal, accept this soul as a gift to my mother, so that she may remain safe and guarded while she watches over us, in your name and in the name of the sacred thirteen I pray."

A weight was lifted off his chest. His mind cleared and he realized he had work to do. With this realization, he fumbled within his pack for a proper cutting knife and set about removing the animal's organs.

The fur was soft and thick. The cat's skin was still warm. He slipped in the knife, wincing despite knowing the animal to be dead. Kirin struggled to cut through skin and muscle, exposing its organs to the Vintas chill.

Steam rose in small clouds from the internal cavity of the great beast. Kirin reached deep within and gripped hold of its insides and in a few quick movements pulled out its organs. He tossed the offal to the side. His hands felt slick with blood and internal bodily fluids. The smell was overwhelming.

Wiping his forehead on his sleeve, he then began the task of carefully skinning it. If it was anything like a rabbit, the skin and fur should come off like a jacket. He knew it would serve as his proof. He also knew that once measured, it would serve to distinguish him amongst the few who had killed the much-feared monster.

Kirin, soon to become Aeden, dragged the skinned fur to a nearby stream and rinsed it free of blood and dirt. He nearly slipped into the slow-moving water as he attempted to drag the water-logged fur out. Kirin fell back into the soft-packed snow panting; his hands numb from the effort. After a moment's rest, he laid it out to dry, stretching the mighty length of fur over a virgin patch of snow.

The next three weeks dragged by slowly as he found some mineral salt from a geothermal hot spring. He covered the shroud cat skin with the salt and allowed it to dry. Once dry he followed the time-old Thane tradition of using the hot spring water to soak and tan the fur.

He was exhausted, hungry, and ready to go home by the time the skin was conditioned enough to last the journey home.

Chapter 10

"Single moments are suspended from celestial strings waiting for memory to retrieve them." Canton of Sawol

It had snowed lightly the night before, leaving everything covered in a fresh blanket of powdery silk. Glancing up, Kirin could see the sun's feeble light struggling to reach through the partially obscured sky. Light flakes of the purest white began to fall.

He reached out, trying to grab individual snowflakes, only to watch them melt upon contact with his skin. Kirin paused and took in a deep breath. The air smelled faintly of pine needles and tilled earth. Finally, permeating everything was a tranquil silence that hung in the air like the final inaudible note of a masterful bard.

He daydreamed as he walked, imagining his homecoming. Kirin's excitement was growing with each passing day. Each lumbering step took him closer to home. He missed his friends, the food, his bed, even his father.

In his waking dreams, he could see his father standing proud announcing his return. The Medicine Man proclaimed the shroud cat skin was the largest ever caught. Dannon was standing there impressed by his skill. He would then run up into the hills and talk to Devon of how it had transpired. He'd ask him about his own trials and if Devon had found his carvings in the Shrine of Patience. The look in his best friend's eyes; admiration, pleasure, and a tinge of jealousy, would make the whole ordeal worth it.

Kirin slipped on a smooth stone and used a tree to regain his balance. Excessive daydreaming could be a dangerous business. Complicating his movement was the skin of the shroud cat, rolled and strapped to his pack. It was a symbol of strength and pride.

Kirin felt content. Soon he would become Aeden of the Thane Sagan, son of the kovor, warrior and leader. With a smile, he looked into the distance, recognizing the jagged peaks of the Barre Mountains. It was the range that had protected his people from those to the north for over a thousand years.

He paused and took in a deep breath. Kirin thought he could smell rosemary and sage spiced meat in the wind. He imagined the smile of the Master Cook welcoming him as a massive hand patted him heavily on the back.

A distant rumbling tore him free of his mind's wanderings. He looked to the sky expecting the clouds to be dark and the flash of lightning to greet him. Instead, they were much the same as before. Blue sky peppered with drifting gray clouds. The flittering snowfall had ceased. A light breeze from the north swept southward.

Shrugging as much to himself as to the unchanged weather, Kirin trudged along. He had thought of stopping to rest but that slipped his mind. Instead he was determined to make it to his village by nightfall if possible. He quickened his pace and adjusted his rhythm, settling into a march.

As the hours passed underfoot, the subtle odor of burnt wood drifted through the air. A feeling of discomfort grew deep within his belly. Kirin couldn't place it, but a feeling of fear swept over him like a cold wet sheet placed over his naked body. He increased his pace, slipping occasionally over the snow-covered surface.

Again, the sound of a distant rumbling filled the air. The tone and pitch were different than that of thunder, deeper and more ominous. Kirin crested a small rise and could see black trails of smoke rising in the distance. His fear had been a hidden warning that now took on a new hue. Abandoning any sense of normalcy, he broke into a run. Branches slapped him in the face and snagged on his bag. His sword chafed at his back and a cold sweat glistened on his skin.

Kirin maintained his hellish pace for two solid hours. His heart thumped heavily in his chest. The wind howled at his ears, bringing the sounds of fire and death. Smoke clouded the air and stung at his eyes. His breath came in wheezing gasps, but an unseen hand was guiding him ever closer to home.

A monstrous shriek filled the air and tore at his insides. Kirin's bones rattled and his teeth chattered within his skull. Fear danced in his vision as he peeled his eyes open. There, suspended in the sky, was a draccus fiend. It was a beast that by all accounts should no longer exist. Its massive body swept through the air with angry purpose. Its gaping mouth spit streaking flames of draccus fire over the landscape.

It was impossibly big. Black scales seemed to soak in the sunlight. Its sinewy body spoke of power beyond Kirin's fragile comprehension. The thick neck supported a monstrous head with teeth large enough to be seen from his vantage point. Yellow and blue were the hues of flame that streaked from its gaping maw, followed by the horrendous shrieking thunderclap of air rushing to fill a void.

It was fear wrapped in terror, reining death upon his home.

Kirin wasn't far from his village now. He paused at the edge of the tree line, frozen. Before him was the steep slope leading home. A home that was now engulfed in flame. There were no shouts, no cries of fear or pain. Instead, the steady rhythm of buildings ablaze filled his ears.

Slowly the vice-grip of fear squeezed tighter. His legs were rooted to the ground. Thoughts of running came and fled his mind. He brought his hands to his ears in an effort to ward off the terrible sounds of destruction. Kirin's mind shut down as desperate hands pleaded inaction. All thoughts of courage escaped in a wisp of smoke as the mother of a shattered reality gave birth to stillness.

The rumbling sounds of shrieking fury stopped. Kirin peered into the sky only to see it blackened by smoke. He stood slowly and looked about, his ears ringing and his mind numb. Ash and smoke hardened the air into a congealed, unbreathable mass.

With fear in his heart, he worked his way up the hill toward his village. Desperate thoughts struggled with the flavor of hope as he stumbled over loose rocks and blinked away the stagnant air.

A sudden gust of wind spat thick curling fingers of smoke into his face and sucked the air from his lungs. Kirin coughed as he crawled over molten stone. He was too dazed to notice the distorted shape of rock. Its edges were blackened and held the appearance of melted wax.

He dropped his pack with trembling hands and a wild look in his eye. Feeling dizzy from emotion and sick to his stomach, he stumbled forward. He searched about desperately. The earth was discolored as if death had graced the soil with pouches of burnt ink.

Kirin's bowels turned to liquid as he saw the crisp remains of a villager. The body was too blackened to recognize. Clothes were fused with skin and bone and the smell of overcooked meat hung thickly in the pungent air. The smell ripped through the fabric of his being and snapped his fragmented reality into the present.

Kirin tripped on a piece of chest armor, emblazoned with a single powerful cat. It was the armor of the old master. It was partially melted, resting upon a bed of ebony ash. The master was dead; reduced to charcoal waste, smeared upon the lifeless terrain.

Kirin glanced about, seeing more scorched bodies litter the ground. Too many had died. Scattered remains flaked off, carried by the fitful wind, fanning the final flames of death. The quiet crackling of burning embers sputtered and popped in the distance.

A hefty axe lay next to the charred remains of a man. Next to him was a smaller body, burnt and twisted. Part of the head had been protected by a low stone overhang. He knelt beside the smaller one and saw the auburn strands of hair that had escaped the draccus fire. Dannon. She had died beside her father.

The world spun as Kirin struggled to

maintain his grip on reality. He wanted to shout but his voice was stuck in his throat. He wanted to run but his legs felt like rubber. Instead, he fell to the ground and cradled Dannon's disfigured head in his unsteady hands.

His mind fell blank. With eyes squeezed shut, Kirin whispered a prayer to each of the thirteen Thane gods. He begged them to let her pass through the gates so that she could live peacefully in the afterlife. He implored them to take him instead, but his words fell upon deaf ears.

He didn't know how long he sat there. His back began to ache and his body felt cold. The smoke had dissipated enough to see the remains of the village. Broken buildings lay shattered upon the earth beside the blackened remains of all that burned.

Kirin slowly lowered Dannon's head to the ground. He drew his Templas blade and carefully cut off a lock of her untouched hair. He tied it into a simple knot and placed the lock into a pocket.

He stood on shaky legs and began looking about for wood to create a pyre. He needed to properly care for the bodies to appease the gods. He needed to do something, anything.

The wind picked up again fanning the flames of death and scattering the ashes of the fallen. Kirin coughed as ash lodged in his throat and created a gritty film on his teeth. He wiped his eyes on the back of his sleeve. There was no wood, no kindling, no straw. Everything had burned.

As he looked about, he stopped before the broken remains of his father's house. All thoughts were stripped from his mind. Once again, his legs turned to jelly. Kirin tried to be strong, but all strength failed him. His knees eventually buckled underneath him, as though felled by an axe. He collapsed before a blackened body that lay twisted on the ground. It was still gripping the Sword of Sagas, the sword of his people.

It was Kirin's father, there could be no doubt.

Kirin had always felt his father to be invincible. He had never seen him cry or complain. The kovor had been a strong and fair leader, looked up to by his people. Kirin remembered seeing his father break stone with his bare hands. Yet now he lay there, burnt, befouled by death. His face scorched beyond recognition.

Suddenly the weight of it all, fell heavily upon him, like a waterfall unleashed by unseen hands. All sense of self lay broken upon the smoldering remains of his home. Tears soon flowed in racking sobs of harrowing despair. Ragged gasps of air filled his lungs in acrid spurts of smoky sadness.

Kirin finally succumbed to his fate, wishing he too were dead. He wailed loudly, damning the beast who did this and taunting it to finish the job. He held his sword high over his head and screamed until his voice was hoarse. Then with a throbbing head and an emptiness beyond words, he sank back to the ground and curled into a ball as the voices of his people faded into memory.

PART TWO
Heorte

Chapter 11

"Witchcraft is nothing more than the deviant use of the arkein." Book of Galdor a Brief History of Verold

The annalist stood deep in the Shroud Mountains. It was morning and a thick layer of mist clung to everything it touched. The air was still and cool, yet whispered of something greater. Silence. There was the notable absence of birdsong, tree branches swaying, or insect calls. It was a profound silence of great depth, an artificial silence, a warning for those who knew to listen for it.

With deliberate and quiet movements, the annalist strode forward. In his hand rested an ambit in which sat a bloodstone. It was a curious artifact from another realm imbued with a unique quality, an attraction to the arkein.

The annalist glanced again at the cracked surface of the crimson stone. It rested idly in its cradle. Days had passed and his hunt for the witches was as successful as putting out a bonfire with a cup of water. His anger simmered slowly to a boil. His hatred for this task, for the man he sought, threatened to rob him of clarity of thought. Yet, he had still felt a hint of emotion uncovering the destruction of the Bane of Verold's village.

It was a justified emotion in the annalist's eyes; a feeling necessary to uncover the hidden depths of truth. It in no way changed how the annalist felt toward *him*. Instead, it was the beginning of a story. The first broad brush strokes of a painting. A painting with angry, red brushwork; leading the annalist to the answer he sought.

How to end an impossible war?

His head started to pound slightly, the lingering effects of a days-old headache. He rubbed absentmindedly at his temples and distracted himself with thoughts of his undertaking.

Pieces of knowledge coalesced into solid shapes as he recalled what he knew of the witches. History wove a deceptive web of mistruths. Partial accounts, folklore, and vivid imaginations sprouted the legend of the witches of the Shroud Mountains. They were known as the Witches of Agathon.

Stories of disfigured women cast from an

ancient school of magic were whispered in the discreet corners of the civilized world. Most knew the witches were nothing more than children's stories. The tales were meant to frighten and to educate.

"If you don't obey your parents you'll end up like the Witches of Agathon," or some used them in a derogatory sense, "there goes that Agathon girl," referring to a woman of less than stellar appearance.

Yet, as with many stories they originated from somewhere. The annalist had spent years peeling back the layers of fiction, the witches being one of his favorite. He parsed truth from legend and stitched together the most likely fabric of reality. What he uncovered was a story that would frighten any child and disgust any adult.

The bloodstone swiveled in its bronze cradle, a scarlet arrow pointing to his right. The annalist paused and listened. Straining past the terrible silence, he could discern the whispering voice of an impending storm.

He was getting close. The skin on the back of his neck tightened.

Fear wasn't a foreign concept to him, for he had seen more atrocities than any single person should ever have to endure. One of which was too recent and too fresh to recall. Yet, the lingering feeling grew in his heart.

He knew that Aeden had fled his village and passed through these very mountains on his way to Heorte. He knew that he had stumbled upon the Witches of Agathon.

What he didn't know, was what elements of the stories he'd heard were fiction and which were fact. Unlike Heorte, where everything was catalogued and recorded, the Gwhelt lay untamed and unchronicled.

There were stories that stated Aeden pretended to be lured in, only to cut the witches down with his Templas blade. Others said Aeden stumped them with a mental puzzle that drove them mad. It was also possible that he never met the feared witches of Agathon and had safely stumbled past their domain.

For an annalist, details and facts were of incredible importance. They held the power of truth, a once valuable commodity that had since dwindled in importance. The annalist was nothing if he wasn't thorough. The annalist knew that for him to succeed against one of the greatest arkeinists Verold had ever seen, he had to be meticulous in his craft, nothing less would do. And so, there he was, deep in the Shroud Mountains, trespassing on the lands of the Witches of Agathon. It wasn't a place he had hoped to ever visit, yet one he had imagined many times.

The bloodstone swiveled slowly in its cradle.

It was time.

"I've come searching for the lost arkeinists," the annalist shouted.

His voice seemed to echo against the very mists. Shadows slithered through the gray morning as if in reaction to the broken obmutescence. A chill ran up his spine and the bloodstone began to spin more rapidly in its cradle.

"Who dares break the silence!" a voice screeched from multiple directions.

"I, the annalist dare, for I seek the truth of one who passed."

There was nothing for a moment. A lull filled with depth, permeated the air, giving it weight and texture. The annalist struggled to stifle a shiver that threatened to rack his body in a spasm of uncontrolled contractions.

"There's no such thing as truth," a loud and shrill voice replied. "Especially for one whose heart is so filled with anger and hatred."

"Leave this place," another voice chimed in.

"You cannot hide the truth from me no more than I can hide the moon or the sun from you," the annalist responded. He continued, "I know what you are."

The annalist's skin prickled as the blanketing mist seemed to grow denser. His head throbbed with the intermittent silence, so penetrating as to numb his mind.

"And we're aware of your kind, annalist. The world had abandoned you long ago," the witch's voice pined.

"As they did your kind," he responded.

"Tell us of what you seek annalist, for we grow bored of these sounds."

"Tell me of the boy Aeden who passed through here," he said.

The silence grew thicker and the bloodstone spun more rapidly. The annalist searched about, but the mists were too thick for sight. His ears strained, but rang with stillness. His mind struggled, but resisted thought as languor fought to gain hold.

"We will not speak of him."

"Why not?" the annalist pleaded.

"Fear of the Sight," was the echoing response.

The annalist had anticipated as much. He placed the bloodstone into his satchel and began to remove his special tools. He sat gracefully upon the moist ground and leaned against the wide trunk of a tree. He placed a black leather-bound book in his lap and turned the pages. Beautiful flowing script of the deepest crimson graced the pages. The annalist paused on a blank sheet and dug once again into his satchel.

"Wait!" the witch shouted. "We have remembered the white-haired boy."

Chapter 12

"Providence is a state of intense destiny."
Testament of Khein 6:19

Kirin/Aeden had left the massacre of his people and traveled west. The images of death plagued his days and haunted his nights. Sadness clung to him with a sticky tenacity. A pit had formed in his stomach that couldn't be satiated by food or water. At times, tears would flow unbidden from his eyes. Each drop tickling and itching at his irritated skin. His future now loomed uncertainly before him, smothering his childhood in a dark embrace.

It wasn't until his second week of mindless wandering that a new emotion fought to gain hold. This emotion was more powerful than the last. The darkness that had grown about him receded, giving way to a bitter red cloud.

Anger seethed deep within his chest.

The anger that grew, started as a seed, comforting him during his bouts of sadness. It blanketed him during his periods of hysteria. Yet, it could do nothing for his sense of isolation. He had no one. No home, no family, no friends. It was a pervasive feeling of loneliness that could only be described as the aching pit of a starving heart.

With eyes open, his heart bleeding emotion,

and his mind numb to the pain, he stumbled through the misty Shroud Mountains and vowed his revenge.

It was in this heavy time of internal conflict that he accidently blundered upon the Witches of Agathon. Few dared seek them purposefully and those that did, rarely lived to tell the tale.

One day, as he hiked through the dense, snow-covered woods of the Shroud Mountains, it occurred. The cold of a thousand Vintas nights descended upon Kirin like a bucket of icy water. An unnatural chill permeated his skin and sank to his bones. His mind struggled as though the weight of a bank of snow had settled upon it in a deliberate act of quiescence. All the while a wall of gray crept ever forward.

Slowly the mist parted, revealing a small clearing. The shape of a figure dissolved before his very eyes. It seemed to flicker like a candle before resolving into clarity. To his surprise, it was a beautiful young woman, oblivious to the cold.

Her hair was unlike any he had ever seen, golden and radiant. Her eyes were large and unwavering, of the deepest blue. It was the fair skin of her naked body that caught Kirin's attention. Her hair barely covered the swell of her rounded breasts. She was seated with her long legs folded together, casting the gentle curve of her sex in shadow.

Desire battled the anger in Kirin's heart as his mind struggled to stitch reality together. He felt warmth radiating from her and was drawn closer to quench the terrible chill that rattled his bones. With each step, he watched her blue eyes gaze upon him with the promise of passion, warmth, and an endless embrace.

The young woman shifted positions, displaying her gender for the briefest flash of temptation. Kirin remained fixed to his position. A hidden string seemed to lure him ever closer as arousal threatened to rob him of proper thought. He took a step forward without realization. Anger simmered quietly in the background, stirring him to action.

"Who are you?" He asked.

She tilted her head quizzically, her shifting hair playing with the curve of her breast.

"You don't understand me?" Kirin tried again.

She continued to look at him but didn't say a word. Perhaps she was a mute. It seemed to him that if she could speak, even if it were a different language, that she would have said something.

He glanced about, realizing the woman had stolen his attention for far too long.

The scene remained unchanged. The steel curtain of fog lingered, suspended thickly in the air. Green tree needles were cast in shades of gray and half obscured by the morning weather. Towering trunks were lost above him in the soup that cast him in perpetual gloom.

Nothing felt right.

The forest was too quiet. He strained to hear anything beyond his rhythmic breathing and beating heart. Silence echoed back in response. His gaze settled once more on the naked girl before him. The warm tones of her skin belied the cold air and hinted at an inner radiance that transcended the drab that hung around them.

Suddenly, the clarity he had learned from his trials and training, set in. He rid himself of the throbbing silence as he tore his gaze from the beautiful nude before him. It was a trap and she was the bait. The soft note of ringing steel graced the misty forest, as Kirin drew the Templas sword. Anger now burned brightly within.

"Stop!" shouted a voice from seemingly nowhere and everywhere.

He glanced toward the naked woman, but she remained seated. The voice couldn't have come from her. He advanced toward her with his sword held steady before him. The single word still ringing in his ears, it had been in Sagaru, the language of his people.

"Leave my imp alone!" the voice shouted again.

This time Kirin was sure it hadn't been the girl. "Show yourself then," Kirin shouted to the surrounding forest.

The imp girl stood, her hair shifted, exposing her magnificent breasts for a beat. She turned and blew Kirin a kiss before trotting off into the surrounding mist. A sudden longing to follow her nimble legs into the gray, swelled within him. The feeling quickly faded and left him feeling all the more alone.

"What have we here," the voice came back, this time closer and distinctly behind him.

Kirin spun about, his sword cutting an arc through the air.

"Careful boy, that looks to be a sharp blade you carry." There was a hint of mockery and a trace of fear in her words. "Why didn't you follow my imp into the woods?"

"You set her as bait to lure me," he responded.

"Clever boy, or perhaps I read the bones incorrectly, and I should have sent a young man instead." Laughter followed, hollow and short.

Again, Kirin circled about, seeking the person he spoke with. The reaching grasp of twisted trees and the watery shroud of condensation, were all he could see.

"What have you brought us beside yourself?" she asked, this time the voice took on the characteristics of a woman, softer, warmer, and curious.

"Nothing," he said hastily.

"Come now, you cannot pass without sacrificing something. Surely you have heard of us?" The voice inquired more menacingly than before.

"You're the witches of the mountain."

"Yes," she hissed.

"You seek my blood then?"

"Come now, do we seem so cruel?" Another voice sounded off from beyond the haze.

"I'm of the Thane, it'd be wise of you to leave me be." He said with greater bravery than he felt.

"Of course, your gray eyes gave you away boy," said the first voice, her patience seemingly wearing thin.

Were they so close as to see his eyes? He looked about in desperation. Only after a moment, did his breathing fall under the control of years of training.

"Why lure me in with the girl?"

"She needs your help young warrior, only the strength of your burning passion will keep her alive," the second voice chimed.

"I was once told that the viler the intention, the greater the lies used to entrap their prey. You wield your lies like I do my sword."

"Come now, no need for insults. Our lies are far defter than your childish swordplay."

Silence followed for a short span. A span that seemed to stretch for an age. Kirin glanced about, waiting for an arrow to come hurtling out of the mist.

Nothing came.

He struggled to discern the direction of the voices. It should have been easy in the silence, but it wasn't.

"What's your name boy?" the first witch asked.

"Aeden," Kirin said without hesitation, uttering the name he now earned.

Another silence followed, but unlike the first, Aeden could hear the muted whisperings of an argument. He quietly sheathed his sword and unslung his bodark bow, nocking an arrow. With short, controlled steps he moved toward the source of the discussion.

He paused behind a tree and struggled to make out their voices. It sounded as if a third had joined the row.

"Who named you boy?" a new voice echoed from the gloom.

"My father," he stated, looking about.

"Lies," another witch shouted.

Silence followed. Aeden knew he couldn't get a clear shot without something more than the vague direction of a voice. He replaced the arrow in his quiver and slung his bow. Slowly he backed away from where he had last heard the voices. Spinning on a heel he turned and fled.

The morning mist swirled before him and solidified. Aeden stopped just before an invisible barrier. He withdrew his sword and attempted to hack at the barrier. It was no longer there and he simply slashed ineffectually at empty air.

"He has the gift of Sight!" the second witch blurted out.

"It's not time for you to leave boy," the first witch intoned.

Still holding his sword steadily before him he asked, "When then can I leave?"

"Perhaps never," another witch answered with delight.

"Do you know what your name means?" the second witch asked.

"Fire," he replied.

"It means more than just fire, it is the name of rebirth, strength, and in the old tongue has another meaning altogether. You've been marked for greater things."

"Then let me go and accomplish them," Aeden said.

Hushed whispers permeated the chilled air. Aeden stood, listening, straining to make out the words. It was another language and too quiet even if he were to understand. The whispers grew more heated, rising to a crescendo before falling quiet, the last words echoing into silence.

"Ridere af tannin."

The first witch then spoke, "You cannot leave without first answering three questions. If answered properly, then we will talk of letting you go, not before."

"And if I don't answer properly?" he asked.

"Then you will know of your fate soon enough. Will you answer our questions?"

"I've been answering everything so far," he responded.

"So it has been," she said, her voice slipping through the fog like a snake, quick and sharp.

Before Aeden had a chance to ask any questions, hesitate, or stall for time, the first witch spoke.

"Who is your mother?"

How could that be the first question? Aeden knew so little of her. His father had only mentioned her once. None dared speak of her, save for an inebriated Gosselin. What could he say to satiate their curiosity? What could he say to save himself from their wrath?

"I never knew her, she passed into the arms of the Thirteen upon my birth," Aeden said, having decided the truth was better than any lie he could fabricate.

The air grew still and cold.

"Is your father the kovor?"

He hesitated in answering because in truth he no longer was, for he had died. Was this a trick

question and they already knew the answer?
Were they taunting him with the death of his
father? He was suddenly unsure of himself. They
hadn't stipulated any rules. Was he allowed to
answer with more than one word? Now he
wished he had clarified their meaning before
beginning.

"Not anymore," he replied as honestly as he
could.

"Do not play games with us Aeden of the
Thane," the second witch spat.

"I don't play games," he said.

Aeden stood, waiting for death's hand to
grab him. It never came. Instead he waited for
time's slow step to march forward. Only one
more question, and he'd either be free or killed.

One of the witches startled him with their
next question.

"Is it your intent to seek the Isle of Galdor?"
the second witch asked.

"I don't know of this place; how can I seek
what I don't know."

This seemed to startle the witches and stirred
them into debate. Aeden listened for the tone of
their voices, his grip tightening on his Templas
sword. Had he answered incorrectly? He had
never heard of the Isle of Galdor, for all he knew
it was a city in Templas, or an island mountain in
D'seart, or was once the Emperor of Heorte.

"We have two more questions for you

Aeden," the first witch continued as if there had been no pause.

"You've already asked your three questions," he said.

"There are no rules but those we make, unless you wish to answer no more." The last words sounded more like a threat; one Aeden didn't intend to see through.

"I'll answer."

"Of course you will," it was the second witch. "Do you seek greater power?"

Aeden was caught off guard and had to pause to think.

He had never been excited about the prospect of taking over as the kovor. As a child, he preferred to follow than lead. But now that his people were dead at the hands of a draccus fiend, he supposed he would have to become more powerful. He would need to be strong enough to kill a draccus fiend, to avenge his people and assure their ascension to the afterlife. The prospect was daunting but also gave his anger a sense of purpose.

The image of charred bodies flashed through his mind and made him sick to his stomach. He took in a shaky breath and fought to stifle his emotions. Aeden took another calming breath before responding.

"Yes, I seek greater power."

"Then we have one final question of you," the

third witch now spoke.

Aeden turned, as though he knew where the voice was coming from. It was a pointless gesture.

"Will you retain your sense of honor once you become powerful, and spare us witches of Agathon, as we will spare you?"

"Yes," was his response.

"Then, before you leave, we will need two things," the first witch said. "Put away your sword, for our imp will come to collect."

Aeden did as he was told. Once the Templas blade was sheathed, the beautiful naked girl from earlier, approached out of the shroud of fog.

He let her get near. The smell of her, wild flowers and honey, overwhelmed him. He fought the urge to reach out and touch her, yet somehow, he knew if he did, the contract he had just made with the witches would be broken.

She leaned forward, pressing ever so gently against him, and with the flick of a wrist produced a knife that sliced cleanly through a lock of his hair. He was startled but didn't let it show.

The imp regarded him for a moment before gently taking one of his hands in hers. Her hand felt small, delicate, and soft. In that moment, he knew that if she wanted to reach forward and cut his throat, he'd let her, if he could just get a chance to grace those sweet lips with his own.

She worked carefully and quickly at removing part of his fingernail. Her movements were precise and painless. The small rise and fall of her breathing had him transfixed. She could have cut off his finger and he would have been none the wiser.

When she was done, she stepped away wordlessly. He admired her small form before glancing about the small clearing.

"You are free to go Aeden of the Thane. Remember your promise."

Chapter 13

"The taste of something new is not always the most pleasing the first time around." Canticle of Bodig 12:6

On Aeden's fourteenth birthday, he arrived in Heorte. The passage of time had been nothing but a burden upon his young shoulders. Time had whittled away at his heart, casting memory to shadow. The anger that had fueled his steps finally simmered to a low, rolling boil, bubbling silently away, deep within his tattered soul.

Therefore, it was of little surprise that the expansive valley was lost to his thoughts.

If he were to look upon the greater map of Verold he would see the rolling hills far to the north, gently giving way to the sea. If he were to travel far enough to the west, he would see the famous white-sand beaches of Heorte, resting amidst the delta of the middle kingdoms. But he had not traveled that far, and he was not looking upon a map.

Instead, Aeden saw nothing but the repeated pattern of self-doubt, fear, and guilt.

It was on a warm Sumor day that he found himself on one of the many roads leading to the great city on the shores of the River Lif.

Irrigation streams carved channels through the valley, sectioning off parcels of land for farming. Aeden had never seen farming on such a scale. The thoroughfares were made of crushed stone and were plied upon by thousands of groups. Travelers, troupers, farmers, merchants, and the nobility all made their way over the vast network of roads.

The route he took led to the heart of Bodig. By the third day he could make out the great Red City. Massive walls of maroon-hued sunstone enshrouded the city. The early morning light graced the sunstone and cast it in luminescence, giving it the appearance of a giant gemstone.

To his left, the River Lif carved a wide, slow-moving channel. Its waters shimmered in the morning light, feeding the great vine of the central kingdom.

There was almost too much for Aeden to process. He had grown accustomed to the quiet of the forest. The sights and sounds sparked lucid fragments of crumbling memory. A brief flash of him sitting about a campfire settled in his mind.

He was back in his village, sitting next to Devon after a long day of training. Their bellies were full and stories of faraway lands were told to amuse and to educate. He would purposefully position himself to watch the firelight play with Dannon's delicate features. That night was the story of the Great Empire to the West. How one man set about uniting three massive kingdoms.

Aeden blinked back tears and attempted to clear his throat of the constant lump of sadness that now resided there. He glanced down; surprised to see he was clutching the lock of Dannon's hair. He tucked it back into his pocket and followed the movements of the boats plying the River Lif in an effort to distract himself.

Brightly colored sails flapped in the subtle wind. Flags demarcating noble houses of trade snapped and fluttered. Dark-skinned men appeared as insects in the distance moving about the wooden decks. Aeden couldn't help but wonder what Devon would think of it all.

Thoughts consumed Aeden, swallowing the hours as the sun rose into the afternoon sky. He had followed a trouper's caravan to the walls of the Red City. A series of piers stretched out to his left. Boats of various make and shape were docked. Men were busy casting lines, offloading cargo, or shouting orders. Smaller skiffs lay anchored, awaiting their turn, sails folded and tucked away.

Soldiers stood alert along the road leading to the huge gates. They had the solid look of pillars, sweating under the Sumor sun. The symbol of an oak tree with a single sword underneath emblazoned their red chest armor. Aeden quickly wrapped his bodark bow, quiver, and Templas sword within the folds of the great shroud cat's skin that he carried upon his back.

He huddled ever closer to the multi-colored wagon in front of him, its wheels creaking over the gravel and stone. Aeden was temporarily cast in shade as they squeezed through the massive archway of one of the main entrances to the city. Huge metal gates stood open, the black bars stood in stark contrast to the differing shades of red brick that comprised the walls. The bricks themselves were partially transparent, as if they struggled to retain the color within. A shove from behind snapped him out of his fascination and forced him into the city. He was surprised at how many people were making their way into Bodig. It reminded him of the mass elk migrations he had seen back home.

Once within the city walls he left the relative safety of the lumbering trouper caravan. The smells of spices, humanity, and rotting foods flooded his senses. A dizzying array of colorful stalls lined the great artery leading deeper into the capital. People shoved, shouted, and bargained as they clogged the streets. Small alleyways twisted off the main road like branches of some great tree. Smaller shops lined the alleys cast in shade by red canvas strung overhead. Bins of spice stretched into the twisting depths of each alley he saw. He never knew there were so many spices in all of Verold.

Foreign words were uttered all about him. People pushed past him as he watched a small group of children beg for food. All the while the swelling tide of humanity pushed him ever deeper into the heart of the Red City. Hopefully toward a place of greater quiet, he thought.

Aeden passed another wall and another open gate. He paused, briefly running a hand along the strangely translucent, red stone. This second section was nearly as busy as the first. People continued to push their way through the crowds like rain upon an open mountain.

Almost immediately the stench of feces, blood, and death hit him like a fist to the stomach. A cacophony of squeaks, squeals, barks, and hollers trumped the haggling shouts of the populace. Live animals of every shape and size imaginable were chained, caged, or otherwise enclosed and for sale. The ground was a slippery mixture of dung, urine, and water, all running in thin runnels over faded stone.

Flies buzzed about in angry clusters. They droned around incessantly. They were attracted by the ever-present metallic tinge of blood. Small rivulets of red ran from the stands where animals were killed. Impatient customers watched in agitated boredom, swatting at flies as butchers worked their craft. The scene was fascinating, gruesome, and mundane.

Aeden pushed his way past the throngs of people, moving as quickly as he could toward the next section of the city. His nostrils burned and his stomach was twisting into knots of nausea. People pushed into him as he passed others, funneling through one of the numerous choke points within the Red City. Again, he found himself in a glowing red tunnel and a moment later he was in another section of Bodig.

The main roadway was still full of people but surprisingly less than there had been in the previous two districts. The alleys here were nothing more than smaller streets lined with housing.

In an attempt to leave behind the drum of humanity, Aeden ducked down the next alley he saw. It weaved past tight doorways of multistory buildings. He had never seen buildings this tall. There were windows above windows above windows. It seemed strange to him to have so many people crowded into so little land. Where did they all work? How did they farm the lands? Was each building a massive family unit? Suddenly he yearned for some open sky and some fresh air.

A fork in the alley presented itself. Aeden took the branch to the right. It crossed another street that was nearly as wide but less busy than the main artery he had used to enter the city. He crossed the street deciding to stick to the alley. It was quieter.

Unobtrusive buildings sat huddled together in stony silence. He passed an open doorway and peered inside. An old woman was busy weaving as two children paused to look up at him quizzically. He must have struck quite a chord, for they walked to the door and continued to watch him as he walked down the alley, disappearing around a mild bend.

It was beyond the bend that a small square rested. A few trees were planted and provided shade from the sweltering sun. The cobbled plaza showed signs of cracking and wear from the searching roots of the trees. There were a few benches situated in the shade, beckoning him to rest. There were a scant few people in the plaza. Most were older folk, sitting in quiet contemplation under the shade of the wide leaves. Aeden saw that one of the benches was free and decided to claim it.

He removed the heavy burden from his back. His shirt stuck to him in sweaty discomfort. Aeden wiped at his brow and looked at the others nearby. They were staring at him as if he had just climbed out of the fiery pits of hell to enjoy the day. He stared right back. After a few moments, they looked elsewhere, as if the mere act of staring was too much work in the heat of Sumor.

Aeden took a swig from his dwindling pouch. His lips were cracked and the water stung at them painfully. His stomach rumbled in response, reminding him of his hunger. He dug through his bag, remembering he had a couple strips of dried meat.

As he tore into the meat, he watched a man set a small cushion down in the center of the plaza. The man then carefully placed a jug next to him and sat.

Aeden's attention was enraptured by the subtle grace of each movement. He sat stupidly, chewing slowly like some grazing animal as he watched the gray-robed man settle himself. Each action was taken with the care a mother would place on a newborn.

The man's shaved pate reflected dully in the afternoon sun. His face was calm and unlined as if age had yet to touch his features. It was his eyes that most captivated Aeden. There was something familiar, inviting, and peaceful about them. They spoke of an older soul peering out wisely upon the simple world, casting a light of compassion to those in need.

A longing in his heart threatened to tear at the fragile fabric Aeden had stitched about himself in an effort to evade thought and feeling. He blinked back swelling emotion and looked about. Aeden realized he wasn't the only one whose attention was fixed on the newcomer. The man seated in the center gazed slowly at everyone present. He brought his hands together and nodded his head to each in turn.

More people filtered into the plaza as if an unseen energy beckoned them closer. Aeden was briefly reminded of the lure he felt toward the imp in the Shroud Mountains. This was different however. He didn't feel desire well up inside him; rather the feeling was more akin to the gentle peace of a still body of water.

The man then reached into his robes and withdrew what appeared to be a dried and stretched animal skin. On the skin were carefully painted words. It wasn't Sagaru, the language of the S'Velt, leaving Aeden ignorant of its meaning. The man then placed the skin before him so that the words faced those who wished to read them. Aeden glanced about, noting the reactions of the people, trying to gauge the meaning of the words.

A few people stood and left, their faces a mask of resigned frustration. A few of the newcomers nodded their heads as if in approval.

Another group of robed men stood toward the back. Aeden noticed a bald-headed man with intense eyes and kind features. Beside him was a younger man with shortly cropped hair. The third man was taller than the other two, with darker hair and paler skin, and stood with fidgeting hands.

Aeden was unsure what to make of the situation. He returned his attention to the man seated in the center of the plaza. His eyes were now closed. The figure appeared to be mumbling quiet words intended for unknown ears. The words were echoed by others in the crowd.

It was a prayer.

Aeden was so transfixed, that he failed to notice as more people began to fill the plaza. Soon a small group of Bodigan Guards arrived. Aeden caught their menacing glare. He glanced down at the swords swinging by their hips and the simple chain mail armor covered by red shirts. He decided it was time to leave.

Aeden looked back at the robed man as he gathered his pack. The man met his eye and smiled briefly and warmly. He extended a hand as if asking Aeden to sit. He sat without thought.

The seated man nodded his head as if in respect. He then calmly poured the contents of the jar over his head and onto his robes. It would have seemed bizarre if the man hadn't moved with such practiced ease.

Glancing across the plaza, Aeden saw the guards begin to cross the square. A small group of bystanders attempted to slow them as the robed man struck two stones together. Each strike caused a shower of sparks to fall about him and a distinct crack to fill the still air. The sounds felt thick and heavy in the humidity of Sumor.

On the third strike the guards were able to shove past the discontent crowd. Aeden watched them approach. They had drawn their swords and were rapidly moving toward the robed man. One final strike of the flint caused sparks to ignite the liquid on his robes. Within seconds his entire body was engulfed in flame. Aeden couldn't have been more shocked if the sun had decided not to rise.

A gentle breeze swept the hot burnt air across the plaza. The guards stopped their advance and simply stood, transfixed, with their swords hanging limply by their sides. The group of young, robed men, fell to their knees and began praying in the direction of the man aflame. Everyone else stood in silence and shock.

Sacredness cast its weight upon the plaza and etched a place into each and every heart. All the while the flames licked at the sky as the man remained motionless. It was his silence that most astonished Aeden. His discipline in the face of incredible pain. His stillness in the final moments of his life.

The flames seemed to leap ever higher as everyone stood quietly, reverently. A few people were now bowing their heads and a young girl wept soundlessly. The smell of the fire carried the scents of burnt skin, fabric, and the gentle note of geranium oil.

The sounds of crackling as skin blistered and burst permeated the humidity. Thin wisps of smoke clung to the air and stung the eyes. Each second slower than the last.

Finally, the robed man fell forward as the fire claimed him and extinguished the spark of life he once held.

Imperial soldiers pushed their way into the plaza. The spell that bound the group together was broken. The guards seemed to remember themselves and raised their swords as they turned to face the crowd. The crowd sensed the impending danger and began to disperse. Aeden knew he too should leave, but felt an aching desire to support the burning man with his presence.

A hand grabbed his, startling him. Two words were uttered in broken Sagaru, "We go."

With that, Aeden was led away from the immolation, his mind reeling with thought.

Chapter 14

*"The Holy Order of Sancire predates the first age
and has lent a heavy hand in shaping the course of
history." Book of Galdor a Brief History of Verold*

Questions began to burn an aching hole
through his mind as he was led away from the
chaos. The sounds of shouting slowly faded like
the last embers of daylight. Aeden followed a
bald man down a serpentine alley. He recognized
the man; he had been part of the robed group of
three. Where were the others?

Aeden watched him struggle slightly with a
limp as they crossed larger streets and passed all
manner of buildings. It was a blur to Aeden for
he couldn't remove the image of the burning man
from his mind.

"Wait," Aeden said, planting his feet.

The man stopped and turned to face him. His
intense eyes bore through him as if reading his
very thoughts and examining his soul. Aeden felt
naked before his gaze and hardly noticed the
light wrinkles about his eyes, the scar running
down one cheek, and the faint smile that touched
his lips.

"Who are you?" Aeden asked, the question
suddenly sounding stupid to his own ears.

The man hesitated as if he didn't quite
understand the question before responding. "I

am me, who else could I be?" he said in his thick accent, the barest hint of a smile creasing his eyes.

"Why did you take me from the plaza?"

"Plaza?" the man asked in confusion.

"Why did you take my hand," Aeden said, pointing to his hand in exasperation.

"You are not safe there," the robed man replied, pointing to where they had come from.

"Where am I safe?"

"With me safe."

Aeden shrugged. It was like communicating with a child.

He looked about, hoping a more enticing alternative would present itself. It didn't. He felt the illusion of control slip through his fingers like melted snow. Aeden sensed he had been swept up by the current of some mysterious hand, flowing uncontrollably toward some unknown catastrophe.

"We must continue before they come," the man said.

Aeden glanced at him, watching him nod gently. The man nodded again and smiled as he grabbed Aeden's hand. They continued through the maze of a city.

It felt strange to have another man hold his hand, perhaps it was their custom. He didn't resist as they cut down a larger street, the milling masses pausing to stare. A tall, white-haired adolescent in leather armor with a large shroud cat skin on his back being led by a smaller, limping man in gray robes must have cut a curious sight.

They passed the stupefied throngs and came to a quieter part of the Red City. In this section the buildings were taller and the street was a touch wider. The red-tinged cobblestones carved a path up a hill toward a building with a single ivory tower reaching for the hot sky. The tower was capped with a steeple copper roof. A single copper circle caught the sunlight, glimmering above the roofline.

There was a series of steps leading up to the white stone building. Its neighbors appeared to shy away, their red faces revealing their shame before the salient construction. The building's bleached skin was vaguely reminiscent of fresh milk. It was pleasant to see something not the color of crimson, Aeden thought.

He struggled to control his expression as the bald man led him up the steps to the massive copper doors. On each door hung a large circle nailed to the center. He hardly had time to appreciate the exterior as he passed through the doors and into the cool interior.

Tall graceful columns were punctuated by copper plated archways. Gray cushions adorned the floor in carefully placed rows. The floor itself was a simple light-gray stone, illuminated by two circular openings in the ceiling. The central nave was flanked by two corridors. Thick candles rested silently before smoke stained walls.

A tug on his hand broke his gaze. Aeden continued to follow the man through the massive building toward a small wooden door in the back. The door was open and they entered a smaller and shorter corridor. The ceiling was a half circle of vaulted stone. There were a few open rooms that punctuated the otherwise austere hallway.

They passed the rooms and emerged into an open courtyard. A stone pathway cut a square about a garden of fruit trees, flowering plants, and what appeared to be vegetables. The air was heavy with the scents of wild flower and sweetened by an unknown citrus. Aeden breathed in the perfume-like smell as he passed arched supporting columns.

Before they could get much farther a fat robed figure stopped them.

Aeden's attention was inexplicably drawn to the larger monk. A simple rope sash was tied about his waist. It was mostly hidden under a rotund belly that pressed heavily upon his worn robes. His eyes were set too close together, exacerbated by a stern expression expertly painted upon his portly features. His closely cropped hair did little to hide the fact that he was balding. His eyes were small and beady. In all, the man reminded Aeden of an oversized mole.

Aeden was so mesmerized that he hardly noticed the fat monk begin to speak. He spoke in hushed whispers to the one who had led him thus far. Aeden couldn't understand a word that was said, but the facial expressions and hand gestures were enough to garner understanding. He wasn't welcome and the scarred monk shouldn't have brought him here.

The man who had taken him into the building pointed to Aeden and murmured something unintelligible. The discussion ensued. Finally, the larger man waved a chubby hand dismissively and stalked off. The one accompanying Aeden turned toward him and took in a breath, recomposing himself. After a moment, he smiled and spoke.

"I am sorry for him; he is not of good temper. You are now with us, a brother. I take you to room and then food."

Aeden nodded as if he had spoken with the clarity of a nightingale. The robed man then led him toward the cloisters adjacent to the courtyard. The entire complex was larger than Aeden would have imagined.

They entered a room with several wooden chests spaced evenly along the wall. The room was otherwise barren. The robed man paused by one of the trunks and pointed.

"You," was all he said, pointing a finger

toward a wooden chest under a window.

Aeden opened the storage box and found a single blanket inside its otherwise empty interior.

"You put now," the man said, gesturing for emphasis.

Aeden glanced up to see him indicating his pack and animal skin. Aeden, however, was reluctant to part with his items for they were his only reminders of home and all that he owned.

"No light hands here," the man stated as if those words should bring comfort, his intense eyes gazing through him, laying bare all insecurities.

With a final nod of encouragement, Aeden placed his pack into the chest. He closed it, hoping to find a lock of some sort. There was none. It would have to do for now, what other options did he have?

The man then rubbed his stomach and pointed to Aeden.

"Do you mean to ask if I'm hungry?" Aeden asked.

"Yes. Let us eat food together," he said.

Aeden nodded his affirmation. All he had eaten was a strip of dried meat. His stomach grumbled as if it too wished to voice its hunger. The man turned toward the opposite side of the courtyard.

It was there that a small kitchen sat adjacent

to a rather large dining hall. The dining hall itself was stark, simple, and to the point. Wooden benches graced the tables. A few candles provided light and a sense of warmth.

"Do not speak," the man whispered to Aeden as he indicated a seat at the table.

Aeden and the man weren't the only people within. Approximately two dozen men with short cropped hair in gray robes sat on the benches. They had watched him enter with curious eyes, but none said a word. Two of them smiled, while the others remained expressionless. A few made quick gestures with their hands.

Aeden nodded to them and mimicked the gesture he had seen the man at the plaza perform before lighting himself on fire, two hands placed together at chest level. This garnered a few raised eyebrows in response.

His escort disappeared into the neighboring kitchen and soon returned with two cold bowls of stew. They both sat and ate in silence. It reminded Aeden of home. It felt good being amidst a group, even if they were strangers.

It was strange what one misses when memory stirs.

Chapter 15

"The Church stifles curiosity with fear and prejudice to maintain the parochial." Library of Galdor

The following day Aeden woke early. Odilo, the bald, limping monk who had recruited him was by his side. He covered his mouth as if to indicate they weren't to speak. Aeden complied, looking about groggy eyed. It had taken him a good, long moment to realize he wasn't on a forest floor, but instead in the heart of a large building within a massive city.

The night of tossing and turning returned to him in a flash. He had only just truly fallen asleep. Most of the evening the ceiling overhead seemed threatening, like a boulder resting precariously on a ledge, waiting to fall. The air felt stuffy and was filled with the smells and noises of over a dozen men.

He did his best to blink away the tired feeling in his eyes. His mouth felt sour and his back was sore. The perfect time to begin chores he thought. The sun hadn't even made its way to the horizon beyond the windows.

He looked about in the candle light, his eyes adjusting to the gray shapes moving about in a languid stupor. They performed simple chores; folding blankets, sweeping floors, and emptying chamber pots. Aeden joined them. The movement felt good.

Once the chores were completed, he was led to the main hall. Aeden recognized it as the one he had entered the day earlier.

The vast space looked different in the darkness of morning. The great circular windows above were cast in shadow. The pillars appeared as dark trees amidst a stone clearing. Yellow candle light cast the stones in warm hues.

The monks shuffled through the open space to the cushions laid out upon the floor. They took seats and began to pray aloud. Their voices were the deep sounds of rumbling thunder upon a grassy plain.

Aeden closed his eyes and felt himself transported. What would Devon think if he were here? Aeden couldn't imagine a more different life than the one he'd been leading back home. His hand slipped into a pocket and gently caressed the lock of hair he had taken from Dannon. Tears began to swell in his eyes and he opened them, his hand falling back to his lap.

Aeden looked upon the audience that had gathered for Morning Prayer. It was a feeble effort to distract himself. There was a scattering of older patrons of middling wealth who graced the open areas and mumbled the appropriate responses to the prayers. Many of them were looking at him intently. His long white hair and leather armor must have looked like a wolf among sheep.

He hastily wiped any remnants of tears from his eyes. His face flushed red and he dropped his gaze to the floor, casting shame to the pits of hidden sorrow.

Aeden's legs grew numb before they were finally finished. He noticed that one of the younger monks had been looking at him on and off with a look of curiosity and compassion. As soon as he caught his eye however, the monk averted his gaze. He looked familiar. Was he also at the plaza the day before? Images of the crowd standing in quiet reverence as a man burned before them flashed through Aeden's mind.

The monks formed a solemn line. Aeden shuffled behind a tall and awkward looking monk. He followed them as they worked their way to the refectory for the morning meal. He recognized the dining area from the day prior. It was a stone vaulted room, with an entrance to the kitchens on one end and a smaller subsection with a stout wooden door on the other end.

Once seated about the table, the monks began to fidget with their hands; pointing, communicating, gesturing. Aeden took it all in with the wide-eyed curiosity that only youth can maintain.

He didn't eat much despite being hungry. His stomach was unsettled and his mind was anxious. The environment was so new. Everything had changed in an instant. Aeden felt like it wasn't long ago that he was sitting in the Shrine of Patience, counting each passing hour. Now he sat in a dining hall half a world away. Every sudden gesture or movement caught his attention and caused his muscles to tense. He felt like a fish plucked from water, gasping for breath.

He nibbled on some barley bread as he watched monks slowly finish their meals and stand. They filed into the kitchen with their plates. He watched a pale young monk leave as Odilo tapped Aeden on the shoulder and gestured for him to follow into the corridor.

"We are busy today, you and me," he said.

Aeden nodded, slightly startled at hearing someone speak.

"Follow and we begin," Odilo said, gesturing for Aeden to fall in behind him.

Odilo led him away from the dining area past the courtyard, down a corridor to a closed room. A thick wooden door rested heavily at the end of the stone walkway. Odilo worked the metal latch as Aeden waited, looking about.

With a small shove, Odilo pushed the door open. A wisp of humidity and the smell of lavender immediately accosted him. Aeden paused at the threshold looking inward.

Behind the wooden door were two large

baths of water lined by stone. The waters were calm and still, small clouds of steam dancing at the edges. An old man sat in a chair, struggling to get up as they came through. He had the look of a man startled from the dream world.

Aeden couldn't help but wonder how they kept the baths warm. His mind raced through a few possibilities before he realized Odilo had continued past. He watched Odilo approach the old man and decided it was safe to follow. He stepped into the room, pulling the wooden door closed behind him. He glanced at the large stone baths before looking over at the two monks.

Odilo and the old man engaged in a verbal exchange. Aeden watched the old man as he spoke. He had a sore under one of his eyes that was most distracting. It seemed to have a life of its own, jumping up and down as the man spoke. After a moment, the old man fell quiet and Odilo turned to Aeden to translate.

"Your hairs must be cut," Odilo said.

Aeden's hand moved reflexively to his hair. Perhaps he had misunderstood.

"What do you mean?" Aeden asked, hoping he had misheard.

"We cuts your hairs," Odilo said slowly, miming the action of scissors cutting hair.

There could be no mistaking the words. Aeden glanced back at the door. He thought about leaving. He had no ties to this place, to this man.

They wouldn't understand the shame of cutting one's hair short, of admitting defeat. For the Thane, long hair was a sign of respect and strength. What would his father think? Would Devon let his hair be cut without a word, without a fight?

Odilo placed a reassuring hand on his shoulder, his piercing eyes gazing intently upon him.

"I understand you do not want. You are here now, here is different than old home. Old home is not good here, people will want to damage you," Odilo said struggling with Sagaru.

"I don't understand," Aeden said.

Odilo paused as if contemplating how to explain his meaning.

"Like this," he said, pointing to the scar running along one side of his face.

Aeden looked at the scar for a moment, his imagination quickly taking the reins. He was tempted to ask how Odilo had gotten it, but somehow felt that now wasn't the time.

He glanced at the old man, his gaze inadvertently fixed on the puss filled boil under the old man's eye. Odilo nodded to Aeden encouragingly, as if he were a young boy about to attempt a daring feat. It was foolish he realized. He was still of the Thane, long hair or not. Nothing could take that from him. Not a draccus fiend and not some old man with scissors.

The old man struggled to move toward Aeden and indicated that he sit in the wooden chair he had been occupying. Aeden sat. His back was rigid. The old man seemed unconcerned as he began to cut Aeden's hair. White wisps fell to the ground in a cloud. The grimacing image of his father appeared in Aeden's head.

"I will avenge you father," Aeden whispered quietly, knowing his father's immortal soul still clung to this earth, waiting to be released.

The old man wheezed something unintelligible in the Heortian language. Aeden attempted a smile. The old man merely nodded and snipped one final piece before standing back.

With little fanfare, the torture was complete. The old man issued a satisfied grunt as he patted Aeden on the back. Odilo smiled and nodded his approval.

"Very good," he said. "Now you get clean." Odilo pointed to the bath water. "Give me cloth. I take to room with your stuffs."

Aeden glanced at the old man and Odilo before stripping down and handing his clothes over to Odilo. As he was about to slip in the water, he shouted a quick word at Odilo's retreating back, "Wait!"

Odilo turned with a quizzical expression upon his face. Aeden walked to Odilo and fumbled through the pockets of his rumpled clothing before his fingers graced the lock of Dannon's hair. He held it tightly in his fist and thanked Odilo.

The bald monk limped out of the damp room leaving Aeden alone with the old man. The old man had collapsed back into his chair and fell asleep. With a shrug Aeden lowered himself into the water and bathed.

His skin began to prune and wrinkle by the time Odilo returned for him. Odilo brandished a gray robe, much like the one he was wearing, along with a simple rope sash. Aeden got out and slicked the water off his body with his hands before taking the robe. He slipped it over his head and found a simple pocket tucked into a fold. He placed Dannon's lock of hair into the pocket before tying the sash about his waist

"Yes, very good," Odilo said before gesturing for Aeden to follow him. "I show you place now."

Aeden's eyes lit up. He was curious about the monastery and had almost woken up to explore as the others slept. Yet, the thought of Odilo getting into trouble caused him to remain in the stuffy cloisters, lying awake listening to the others fart and snore.

Odilo led him back down the corridor toward the large open cloisters. Sunlight now cut a path diagonally across half the courtyard, casting some of the plants and grass in light.

"Here is plant foods," Odilo said pointing to rows of plants in the large courtyard. "We make many foods here and eat them."

Aeden nodded as though Odilo had just explained the phases of the moon. They didn't linger long as Odilo led them down a corridor to a set of stairs. They worked their way to the second floor, where Odilo pointed out the rooms for the sacrist, the cellarer, the tithe counter, the abbot, and the almoner.

"Monahan," Odilo made the impression of narrow eyes and a fat build, obviously indicating the angry mole-like man they encountered yesterday, "he stays here, you and him better not together."

"What did he tell you yesterday?" Aeden asked.

"He no want you here, tell me not allow more new people," Odilo stated matter-of-factly.

"What's his position? Does he have authority?"

Odilo regarded him oddly for a moment as if trying to understand his words before finally replying.

"He counts money. I find new people. We have same *power*," the last word was a struggle upon his ungainly tongue.

"It seems there are a few unhappy monks

here," Aeden said, thinking on the faces he saw at prayer and around the dining table.

"Happiness lives in here first," Odilo pointed to his head, "then here," he pointed to his heart, "too many forget what it is."

Aeden nodded but said nothing. Odilo reminded him of one of his gevecht teachers. His teacher often used parables to relate a tale. It was within the story that the greater nugget of wisdom resided, like a gem within a stone.

Aeden thought on his words as they walked down an open-air corridor, lined by columns, looking down upon the cloisters. They rounded a corner and came upon the library.

"Here live books," Odilo said.

Aeden was curious. He had heard of books in stories and once seen his father working on parchment, but he had never seen a real book before.

"Can I see?" he asked as he made his way inside.

"Yes, but no talk."

Aeden stepped into a relatively large bifurcated room. On the far end were small desks with two scribes busily writing upon virgin sheaths of paper. On his end of the room were two, tall glass windows. They cast the morning light upon the rugs on the floor and the chairs lining the walls. It felt inviting. Two large wooden shelves were filled with books. Aeden marveled at them and reached for one before Odilo placed a hand on his arm.

"No read now," was all he said.

Aeden was led back downstairs and shown the kitchens, the storage area by the refectory, the area behind the cloisters, the central nave and adjacent prayer areas before being taken down into the crypt.

The stairway down was tight and confining. Another stairway led to a different area below the monastery. Odilo said it was for bad monks and hadn't been used in years. The smell from that corridor was stale and unpleasant. Aeden was thankful they didn't visit there.

The stairway ended at an opening to a low, stone vaulted ceiling. It was mostly dark, save for a flickering candle by a small desk. An old monk, who appeared to have been startled awake, sat there. He hardly glanced up as they passed. He remained hunched over a wide book and grumbled something unintelligible to himself.

Odilo had grabbed a small candle from a stack and lit it before moving deeper into the large space.

The crypt was accessed through the kitchen on one end and the grand nave on the other, spanning the length of those areas. It was a large basement filled with grains, simple spices, religious symbols, and supplies. It was an organized mess where everything appeared to compete for space.

It was, therefore, odd that Aeden caught sight of a solid, red door at one end. There were no storage bins, no bags of grain blocking it. In fact, the area around the door was devoid of anything, as if it preferred to be free of clutter.

It was out of place the way a lone flower in a field of grass was. A thrumming energy seemed to radiate ever so lightly from the door, beckoning him. Whispering voices echoed ever so faintly in the shadowy recesses of his sleeping mind.

Once again, he found himself drawn toward something. Without asking for permission, Aeden strode toward the door. It took a moment before Odilo noticed Aeden wander off.

Aeden glanced at the door and noticed faint script upon the frame. It wasn't in a language he recognized. It had a feeling of permanence the way the carved statues of the gods at the Sacred Pools did back in the S'Velt.

Aeden reflected on the door for but a moment before placing a hand upon the red wood. That's when Odilo shouted.

"No!"

Aeden froze with his hand on the door, much like a child caught with his hand in the apple barrel.

"You no go there. No one go there," he said sternly. Any hint of a smile that had once graced his eyes was replaced with two hard, cold pools, devoid of laughter.

Aeden's hand slipped away as his faced reddened. He felt ashamed. Already he had insulted the only person here who had spoken with him, the one man who had shown him kindness in nearly a year.

He was desperate to ask what lay beyond the door, but he knew the rules were different here. Aeden stifled his curiosity in an effort to appease Odilo's displeasure.

"I'm sorry," Aeden finally managed as he stepped away from the door.

"How do you feel?" Odilo asked with concern, grabbing Aeden's hand and examining it.

Aeden was surprised by the question. He felt bad for going where he wasn't supposed to on his first day there. He felt bad because it seemed this man was trying to help him. His mind tingled with curiosity. He was tired and lonely. Sadness clung to his heart and threatened to overwhelm him. But he said nothing.

Odilo dropped his hand and watched him intently before speaking, "You no need sorry. This place is not for you," he said, a touch of warmth returning to his voice.

Chapter 16

"The inquisition came about to unify methods of interrogation through questioning, torture, and tribulation." A Brief History of Verold, Library of Galdor

The following morning Aeden awoke with a startling headache. He had been dreaming. More specifically he had been dreaming of the final moments of his village. The screams and thundering echo of destruction were trumped by the pleas of the villagers. Each villager had visited him, begging for release, for vengeance, for a clear path to the afterlife.

Aeden rubbed at his eyes a moment and sat in stupefied silence as the monks moved about in relative darkness. They had begun their morning routine. He had already garnered stares for not having begun. He didn't care. It was the look from the fat, mole-like monk, Monahan, that most galled him. There was something about the man that he didn't like, and it was already apparent the feeling was mutual.

Aeden stared back at Monahan for a moment in defiance. Monahan pointed a finger at him, but said nothing. Speaking before sunrise was forbidden. Monahan stalked off and Aeden smiled at his small victory. He pushed himself up and with effort moved through the morning rituals. He made it to the afternoon relatively unscathed.

It was an odd day in which the normally blue sky and buttery brilliance of sunlight was cast in grey shadows as storm clouds settled their bulk over the Red City. The air was stuffy with the tepid weight of humidity.

A shadow had descended upon the monastery of the Holy Order of Sancire, Bodig. Thick clouds watched the monks toiling within the courtyard gardens below.

Sweat clung to Aeden's back as he worked alongside Odilo and another monk named Adel. Adel had been at the plaza with Odilo for the immolation. It was an event that had befuddled and shocked the young Aeden. He could still see the bald monk burning when he closed his eyes. He sometimes wondered if that's what it had been like for those in the S'Velt. The day his village had been destroyed.

He was amidst another one of his mental wanderings when he caught Adel's eye. The young monk smiled and nodded. Aeden smiled back and nodded his own subtle greeting before resuming his work. Putting his hands into the soil felt good. The earth was cool and comforting.

It was strange how different the monks were. Adel's friendliness was quite in contrast to a tall skinny monk named Bosco and a shorter fat monk named Jerome. They had taken a dislike to

Aeden from the moment they had locked eyes. How was it they already disliked him? It would have bothered him more if he wasn't already consumed with other thoughts.

Aeden spent the day listening to the idle jabber of the monks in the guttural tones of Heortian. It was a much rougher sounding language than Sagaru. At times, he almost felt like he could understand them. Maybe it was the context of movement, tone, and facial expression. It didn't matter, he was among people, and he felt a semblance of peace. The aching loneliness that haunted his trek through the Shrouded Mountains was slowly being washed away by the presence of humanity.

Thoughts slipped away like silken shadows as thunder echoed against the monastery walls. Aeden glanced to the sky looking for the black sinewy shape of a draccus fiend. Instead of fire, he was rewarded with thick drops of water. It had started to rain. Relief settled into his gut.

He held up his thick hands and let the water slowly cleanse them. His eyes were now closed, and he could hear the monks shuffling into the surrounding corridors, and out of the inclement weather.

"We move in now," Odilo stated simply, pulling Aeden from his moment of blissful silence.

The monks stood under the shelter of the stone-vaulted ceiling, staring out at the garden courtyard. The rain fell and splashed upon the dirt and stone. The falling drops seemed to remain suspended within the air for a moment before deciding where to fall. It was peaceful.

Distant shouts yanked at his insides. They held the distinct tone of fear.

Aeden tore his gaze from the gentle scene of rain. He glanced about to ascertain the source of commotion. The monks all seemed to be doing the same. They were sheep bleating their pleas of ignorance.

Odilo spoke loudly and calmly directed the monks to the grand nave. Aeden's stomach tightened, wasn't that the source of the sound? He didn't question; however, he was a guest within the monastery and Odilo his host.

The monks began to shuffle to the main prayer hall. Aeden was part of the crowd behind Adel, wishing he were in body armor with his sword strapped to his back instead of the useless grey robes of Salvare.

The distinct sound of boots on stone and the tune of armor alerted Aeden to danger before he saw it. The monks entering the nave were shoved to the ground by soldiers. The grand nave was ringed by men in chainmail with polished helmets and long swords upon their hips. What were they doing here? Were they allowed in the house of Salvare?

Rough hands fell onto Aeden. He ducked and turned away from the force. The knight was momentarily off balance. Aeden shifted his weight and brought up a hand. He purposefully stumbled and grasped the knight's wrist. As Aeden regained his footing he used that sudden change in momentum to fold the soldier's wrist and pull him to the ground. The clatter of armor on stone was louder than he expected. Aeden quickly slipped back with his hands in the air, palms forward.

A couple of soldiers looked over, but only saw their comrade on the ground and monks backing away. There was a moment of silence and confusion, broken only by the fallen man's cursing. A few more monks entered the nave and moved toward the center as the standing soldiers helped their fallen brother to his feet.

The fallen knight continued cursing and looked about, but appeared confused. Aeden smiled. The victory was small and temporary. It faded rapidly like the light before an oncoming storm.

Aeden took a moment to look around the grand nave. His stomach slowly turned uncomfortably within his gut. It seemed that moments of silence often preluded inexplicable acts of violence.

Fear tugged at his sleeve. He did his best to

ignore it.

A few of the older monks looked angry. Most, however, looked frightened. None were fighting back. This surprised Aeden. The Thane would never let such a thing occur. His insides boiled as he looked at each soldier. Each knight wore a tunic over their chainmail, emblazoned with the image of a single, golden draccus fiend.

There was no way this could end well. Aeden's insides churned as he looked about for Odilo and Adel. He found Odilo. He was with two other men. They were speaking to the knights. If they had been seeking a response, they failed to get one.

Where was Adel?

Aeden saw heads turn to look toward the entrance of the nave. His skin tingled with anticipation. Aeden reluctantly tracked their gaze. The knights toward the great doors shrank away from an impossibly large figure.

All eyes seemed to track the massive man's movement. The air about him seemed to shimmer with an oppressive, unseen energy. It was as though a nightmare had stepped into the realm of the living to reveal itself before them.

This nightmare wore a helmet of the darkest iron. A single line of red metal formed a menacing stripe across his eyes. Perforated holes covered the lower portion of his mask. Black chainmail was evident under a black tunic, with a single red sash tied about his waist. Light shrank back and wrapped the figure in shadow.

He took several steps into the grand nave. Candles flickered and monks scooted away. There, before the great beast of a man, was Adel, looking like a frightened child attempting to be brave.

The man spoke, his voice echoed deeply, yet he did not shout.

Aeden moved subtly toward Odilo. He wanted to know what was happening.

"What's he saying?" Aeden whispered as he slid next to Odilo.

"He seeks people from yesterday," Odilo translated in a muted whisper.

Aeden nodded his head. He must have been referring to the crowd present for the burning monk in the plaza. Fear and fascination gripped him. Thunder rumbled somewhere in the distance. The echoing rumble warned of danger. Aeden was too distracted to listen.

The man paused in the center of the room and slowly looked around. His movements were almost mechanical. His demeanor was menacing. The dark folds of his tunic and black chainmail obscured his movements and repelled the light. Even the guards ringing the room avoided direct eye contact.

He spoke again and once more Odilo translated.

"Those at place with burning monk have done illegal by the emperor," he paused for only a moment struggling for words as he translated, "stand and come for question."

The man's voice grated against Aeden's head and made his skin crawl. The last word compelled him to move. A restraining hand tore his attention from the dark armored figure.

"Don't look at face or you do his bidding," Odilo warned.

Aeden felt his heart beating heavily in his chest. His breathing became shallower. The world about him seemed to slow and shrink as his hands grew cold. Anger seethed within. It was a silent call to battle.

"Patience, one goes to fetch the city guard," Odilo whispered, keeping a hand on Aeden's shoulder.

The dark features of the tall man suddenly turned toward Aeden and Odilo. The big man seemed to be scanning the area, as if searching for the source of anger.

Odilo began a chant to Salvare, seeking peace and wisdom. The chant spread like a fire, soon taken up by all the monks. The grey-robed men seemed to relax as they found purpose through prayer.

The low tones of the chant permeated the space and seemed to still the guards. The tall black-clad man, however, was unimpressed. He moved through the monks like a ship through water, oblivious to the sounds of prayer and repulsed by the words of the chant.

"You," the man said, now looking at Aeden, the word was in Sagaru.

Aeden remained silent. How did the man know Sagaru? How did he know it was Aeden's mother tongue?

"Yes," Odilo responded in broken Sagaru.

"Why do men of the Gwhelt reside here?" the man said in his grating voice.

Aeden took in a breath thinking of an answer. Odilo spoke before him.

"Salvare judges not men of origin, but of purity of heart," Odilo said, placing a hand upon his own chest.

The tall man was silent. Dark eyes behind an inky black helmet, regarded them. Those eyes were shrouded in obscurity. Somehow the air about him seemed thicker, heavier. Aeden's mind buzzed with the burden of his presence.

"Perhaps an examination of that heart would reveal the truth."

Aeden's blood went cold. Fear swept over him as the words settled upon him with the weight of an anvil.

"Peace, Inquisitor, we are men of peace," Odilo replied calmly, yet Aeden noticed his hands were shaking ever so slightly.

The chanting had stopped.

Every eye in the room was focused on the two men. The small, bald head and scarred face of Odilo was cast in shadow by the hulking figure of the Inquisitor.

"There is no peace in this world, it is one of shadow and fear," the Inquisitor stated coldly, "words you will come to understand."

The words were bleak, threatening, and full of intent. Fear threatened to squeeze Aeden's heart until it stopped. His eyes grew wide as he watched the Inquisitor reach forward. Time seemed to slow. Thunder rumbled a distant warning. Fear turned to anger.

Without thought Aeden exploded forward and shoved the Inquisitor. It was a rapid and powerful movement that would've sent his friend Devon stumbling backward off of his feet. It was a move he had practiced hundreds of times. The power, timing, and strength had even up-ended his master once. The Inquisitor, however, only took a step back, slightly angling his body as he drew a dark blade.

An angry veil seemed to mask his features. Aeden stood before him, feeling naked without a weapon. His hands were up and his feet were set to fight. It seemed he would meet his ancestors sooner rather than later. Aeden braced himself for the inevitable when a commanding shout echoed from the entrance of the monastery.

Aeden looked to the doorway. Lightning flashed somewhere in the distance. Dozens of men were stepping in from the rain, dressed in the red tunics of the city guard. Following them were ordinary citizens of the Red City.

The imperial guard seemed uncertain, almost fearful. Many looked to the Inquisitor for guidance.

More citizens filed into the nave. Once again, the monks began their prayer. The chant soon reverberated off the walls. The sounds danced off wet armor and burrowed into the nooks and crannies of the stone structure.

"He will be punished," the Inquisitor said to Odilo in a menacing whisper.

The Inquisitor looked slowly around the nave as if daring any to approach, before signaling the Imperial Soldiers to leave.

Aeden stood in silence, watching the procession of armored men file out of the monastery. His shoulders slumped. His fingers tingled as blood began to circulate normally. His heart thumped audibly as he realized he would live another day.

Chapter 17

"Metering punishment is far easier than receiving it." Canton of Sawol

That evening Aeden found himself in a room with the abbot, a balding man with a nasally voice, Monahan, an older bear-like monk named Blaise, and Odilo.

"You be punished," Odilo translated as the abbot spoke, "the emperor is no friend of Salvare, but your actions have brought light onto monastery and danger to us all."

Abbot Filbert consulted briefly with Blaise. Monahan stood nearby, clearly trying to impose the strictest punishment the book of Khein would allow.

Odilo took a step closer to Aeden and whispered, "Friends in Bodig work to protect us and you."

A hint of a smile touched Odilo's eyes. The abbot looked to Blaise then back to the ground, shaking his head. His narrow eyes and stooped shoulders spoke of a man tired and burdened to the point of breaking.

The posture of the monastery's leader didn't invite comfort. In S'Vothe the kovor had to show strength. His father once told him, *"strength fills one with the power to do right by others, without it we fail."*

Odilo seemed to sense Aeden's faltering courage. He took a step closer and whispered.

"Faith in Salvare, you can then see beauty in the darkness."

Although there was no need to whisper, for no one else spoke Sagaru, the quiet words were oddly reassuring.

Aeden nodded his head then looked over to the fat, mole-like monk. Monahan was smiling. Aeden's discomfort seemed to fuel that man's happiness. Aeden straightened his back and took in a calming breath. He wasn't going to give Monahan the satisfaction.

Aeden then looked to Blaise. The large monk stood quietly; there was a hint of sadness in his eyes. He liked the man despite not knowing him. He reminded Aeden of the Master Cook for some reason.

The abbot seemed to remember what else he needed to say and continued. Odilo struggled to translate from the guttural tones of Heortian to the lilting tones of Sagaru.

"You live alone, below," Odilo began as he pointed toward the ground, "until High Priest gets back to city and talk to King Benbow."

The abbot rubbed at his brow as if it were all too much for him to handle. Monahan seemed a little upset, as if he had hoped for a more severe punishment.

"Question?" Odilo asked.

"Yes," Aeden said, finally able to voice all the frustration, confusion, and anger he felt. "Why am I being punished? What if I just leave? I don't belong here anyway. Maybe I can talk to the king..."

Odilo's eyes were heavy. He was nodding his head slowly as he listened to Aeden's rant. When Aeden was finally done, he placed a gentle hand on his shoulder, as seemed to be the custom in Bodig.

"Trust Odilo. Now is safer here. You no want Inquisitor trouble. I keep you safe, Salvare watch after you now."

Aeden blinked back the rising tide of emotion that threatened to spill out. He swallowed the heavy lump in his throat and nodded. He could spend time alone. If he survived the Shrine of Patience, he could certainly survive in the monastery cells.

Chapter 18

"Solitary confinement bleeds the soul and starves the mind." Canton of Sawol

The solitary cell within the Monastery of Bodig was cold, dark, and moist. It carried the vague smell of remembered pain and the subtle hues of forgotten fear. They were the whispered reminders of all those who had once been abandoned and punished.

It wasn't the faint smell of human waste, or the subtle taste of sorrow that most bothered Aeden. It was the powerlessness he felt, coupled with the loneliness, that most attacked his wayward heart.

He had endured the Shrine of Patience through long bouts of sleep, interspersed with dreams of Dannon. Now she was gone and so was Aeden's family, his home. The foundation he once took for granted no longer existed. It lay broken, twisted in ruin. Thoughts preyed on his mind and the subtle fingers of insecurity played upon Aeden's emotions with the grace of a master bard.

Why had he decided to trust Odilo? The monk seemed like an honest man, but what if he wasn't? Aeden didn't owe anybody anything, yet here he stood, waiting. Anger blanketed him as he paced the cell. It was his only comfort to combat his rising sense of fear.

Again, Aeden found himself staring at the sliver of light under the doorway. The faint light played with the layered shadows and helped to form an elusive picture of insinuated lines and broken forms. The light was his link to a greater world. And somehow that world had decided to swallow him whole as he had become ensnared by the political winds of the Heorte Empire.

His mind struggled to cope with the scope of his predicament and failed. He yearned for guidance, for answers, for the stability of his old life. But no, that life had been ripped from him. He could never go back, not until he was ready and able to avenge his people. Not until he was powerful enough to free them from the bounds of purgatory.

There was the sound of footsteps walking the corridor.

Aeden stopped his pacing and strained to listen. They were approaching. The light under his door was obscured. A sound at the door indicated keys being inserted into the lock. He could easily overpower any of these monks. He could escape. But where to?

The door opened and light spilled in. Aeden shielded his eyes.

"I bring you food and apology," Odilo spoke. "I also have candle, and old book in Heortian and Sagaru."

Thoughts of escape slipped away like a mountain breeze. He realized he couldn't hurt this man. He wouldn't.

"Thank you," Aeden said.

Aeden placed the food onto a stone bench that also functioned as his bed. The thick candle he placed next to it, thankful for the warmth of the yellow light. The book he held delicately in his hands as if it could break at any moment. He had never touched a book before. In the S'Velt they worked on sheets of parchment and coated them in a waxy substance to protect against the elements. There were few parchments, for it was the sole role of the kovor to keep the records of the people. Most couldn't read or write. There was no need. He had been one of the few, groomed to take the role of kovor after his father.

His father was gone.

The image of the Sword of Sagas laying upon the ground flashed through his mind. He needed distraction. Anything to take his mind from the haunting sorrow of complete loneliness.

"Why is this book in Heortian and Sagaru?" Aeden asked.

Odilo smiled before responding, "The Holy Church of Salvare go to many place to teach, including Gwhelt."

Aeden nodded his head and placed the book down.

"What will happen to me?"

Odilo took a step farther into the room, looking briefly about, before finding his eye. There was a hint of sadness in his eyes rimmed by an underlying determination.

"The High Priest has important friends. Archduchess Cynesige is one, and she will speak to king for us," Odilo paused, "For you. Abbott and sacrist working now for this."

Aeden thought about this for a moment. He didn't know who or what the archduchess was, but he was happy they were working to fix the problem. Otherwise he could simply overpower the next visitor and escape. It was an odd sense of comfort in an otherwise cold world.

"Read, relax mind, and focus," Odilo said, "Running won't fix your heart."

Aeden looked up startled. Had he read his mind? Was he looking at the exit too long and Odilo guessed his intentions? If so, Odilo showed no fear, only compassion.

"I will be back for you," Odilo said as he stepped out and closed the door.

Chapter 19

"Boredom can become an incredible tool for learning." Learning and Mental Humors, Library of Galdor

Aeden spent the next couple of weeks learning Heortian. He had nothing else to do but study. If he allowed his mind to wander, he would happen upon images of his home, of all that he had lost. Distraction was crucial to his emotional well-being.

Odilo had visited on several occasions, but he had sent another monk to see him more frequently. That monk was named Adel.

Adel was an interesting, young monk, only a couple years older than Aeden. He enjoyed Church doctrine; he liked games, and had a strange sense of humor.

Aeden quickly grew fond of Adel. It might have been partially due to his circumstances. He had so little human contact that he clung to whatever was available. But he knew that Adel was honest. Adel spoke from his heart, a rare trait that Aeden very much appreciated.

It was Adel who helped him learn Heortian faster, helped him pronounce the strange words, and helped him learn the alphabet. Adel had him reading aloud, albeit slowly, within a week.

Therefore, on his third week in confinement he had been expecting Adel to visit. Instead it was the abbot, Blaise the sacrist, Monahan and Odilo.

The cell felt even more confining with all of his visitors. His heart was beating quickly. Monahan was holding his robes to his nose to ward off the smell. Odilo was smiling as was Blaise. The abbot looked tired, yet relieved.

Before Odilo spoke, Aeden already knew the answer. He smiled as he turned to the monk who had taken him in.

"We make you free," Odilo said with a grin on his face.

The abbot spoke in Heortian. Aeden understood some of the words, enough to know that he wouldn't sleep another night in the monastery prison.

The sacrist gave him a hug and smiled, but otherwise remained silent. Monahan launched into a long speech. His eyes darted about, but held disapproval, anger, and a hint of what appeared to be disgust. Aeden was so awash with excitement and relief that he didn't pay much attention to the ill-tempered monk.

He was free. Aeden gripped Odilo firmly on the shoulder and thanked him before stepping out of the cell and back into the realm of the greater monastery, after a much-needed bath of course.

Chapter 20

"Games are what adults play to remember how to be children." Saying of Sawol

Another week passed and Aeden was becoming more comfortable with his new routine. Memories of his time in confinement had faded to be replaced with the familiar tasks of the monastery.

The first few days had been challenging. He had to acclimate once again to social interactions and human contact. The sounds of others talking, burping, farting, were at first repulsive. But the repulsion soon faded to be replaced with a need for greater depth of human interaction.

Some of the monks went out of their way to congratulate him. In a way, he had become a bit of a celebrity. Having laid hands on an Inquisitor and lived, was all some talked about. The action was polarizing. A handful of monks went out of their way to avoid him. An even smaller group went out of their way to taunt him, namely those associated more closely with Monahan.

Aeden did his best to fit into the monastery. Each routine was a form of escape from his mental prison of thought and allowed him to slowly feel more normal. It was the simplicity of life within the walls that most appealed to his still fragile mind.

Life at the monastery was easy. It was filled with prayer, chores, plenty of eating, and as Aeden had come to find out, games.

The days themselves passed slowly at first. Every day was very much like the day before. He would wake to the sound of ringing bells just before the crack of dawn. He had grown accustomed to waking at odd hours from sleeping in the forest. He had a semblance of the routine simply from hearing the faint tones of the monastery's ringing bells as their song reached into the bowels of the monastery's solitary cells.

After the morning bell the monks would start by rolling their thin sleeping mats and they would place them behind their assigned chest. This was followed by the folding of blankets, each placed carefully within their respective trunks.

Everything at the monastery was filled with ritual, ceremony, and meaning. Willowing through the rituals was at first challenging for Aeden. He was accustomed to mimicking the movements of another, for that was integral to his martial studies. Here, there was less guidance. As a novice monk, he was expected to complete chores and tasks that no other did.

At first, he was resentful of the added chores. But as the days passed, so too did his anger. The hazing instead became a pattern to fill his mind. Anything was better than excess idleness. It was during those hollow moments of empty respite that his mind echoed with resounding thunder.

Vivid images of the final moments of his village's collapse replayed themselves in an endless loop in his mind. The scenes carved a molded path until finally there was a template of self-indulgent thought that consumed him.

He therefore grew to dread the meditations and hungered for companionship. Anything to fill the awful void of pictured death was better than solitude. For Aeden his days didn't start until after the first meditation and the end of breakfast.

Breakfast often consisted of a single egg, bread, and some old cheese. As was normal with each meal, a strict silence was observed. Aeden noticed the monks communicated through furtive hand gestures during mealtime. Gestures he was slowly learning.

Following the meal were more chores. This was when the monks were finally able to break their silence. Words, laughter, arguments, and camaraderie filled the air. It was music to Aeden's ears.

Depending on the day, half the group cleaned the kitchen and dining area as the other half went to the gardens in the courtyard. Aeden preferred garden duty. Something about digging in the dirt grounded him and settled his soul.

By midafternoon all the monks were required

to attend and participate in Noon Prayer. This took place in the main nave of the monastery and was conducted for the attending public. Aeden's first visit to the nave, after confinement, was strange. In his mind, he pictured the Imperial Guard lining the walls and the hulking Inquisitor staring menacingly at the monks upon the floor.

Those images faded to be replaced by a grueling two-hour event filled with chants, meditations, and judgments. The first few times were fascinating. The new ceremonies were fresh to his young eyes. The attending populace was a slice of Bodigan life. The freshness soon wore off, and the monotony of monastery life soon set in.

Late afternoon was Aeden's favorite time. It was the time immediately after a small meal and before dinner in which the monks were free to pursue leisure activities. There were board games, a library filled with volumes of books, and painting. Most monks took the time to get in a nap. Aeden spent his time with Odilo learning Heortian.

He was learning more and more of the language each day. From sunrise to sunset he was beside Odilo. He would ask the word for everything he could point at and anything he could think of. The result was that within two weeks he knew enough words to make a fool of himself. More importantly, he had earned a spot at the nightly table of a card game called *kayles*.

The games grew rowdiest after dinner. The senior monks retired to the second-floor rooms as the junior monks played. Gambling, strictly forbidden by Sancire scripture, was evident in hidden corners as card games flourished like flowers under the sun.

Kayles was normally a six-person game played in three teams of two. Although it was a source of entertainment and a method to pass the time, it was above all else the lynchpin to understanding the social dynamic of the monastery. It was through this game that brother monks would rotate teams amidst a few tables and share gossip, complaints, and poke fun of each other.

Aeden had been allowed to watch as the monks became more comfortable with his presence. It was Adel that had invited him to watch and finally to join them at the table. Adel was one of Odilo's recruits. Aeden had grown quite fond of him while in confinement.

Odilo had encouraged Aeden to participate in *kayles*, saying "this is best way to learn about brother monks and monastery talk."

Interestingly Odilo was nowhere to be found during the games.

It, however, was Adel who had truly convinced him to play. Armed with a youthful grin, charming personality, and flattering dialogue, he had convinced Aeden his Heortian was now good enough to earn a spot at the table.

Aeden presently sat next to Adel, his team member. Thomas, a pale, cheese-loving monk sat opposite him and was teamed with Neri.

Neri was interesting. He rarely spoke and when he did Aeden noticed a distinct accent. He had a darker complexion than any of the other monks. Neri rarely made eye contact and despite occasionally being quite physically close to the other monks, he was rather distant in all other respects, save for one.

Aeden remembered seeing him one day hunched over his trunk whispering sweet words. He was dropping in small pieces of bread at the time. It had seemed strange until Aeden had seen what Neri was doing. He had been feeding a squirrel. It had jumped into his hand. Neri's secret pet. It was one of those secrets that everyone knew but didn't much bother to spread.

The other team consisted of the monks Bosco and Jerome. They were a strange pair. Where Jerome was short and stout, Bosco was tall and lanky. They were always found together. It was rumored they bathed, ate, and shat together. They were lackeys of Monahan, the fat, mole-like monk that seemed to have it in for Aeden. Consequently, both Jerome and Bosco could be rather annoying. They would purposely make his life more difficult.

It was Jerome who would 'accidently' tip a bed pan when it was Aeden's turn to toss them. Bosco was trickier. After Aeden was released from confinement he had pretended to be helpful and pretended to have been impressed by Aeden's *interaction* with the Inquisitor. He flattered Aeden with compliments and would pretend to be helpful by giving him useful advice. Half of what Bosco had said was wrong, causing Aeden to fumble in Noon Prayer, and to make an ass of himself at the refectory. The problem was, half of what Bosco said was completely true, and when it wasn't true Aeden wasn't always caught doing something wrong. Following Bosco's advice led Aeden into trouble on more than one occasion. After a couple of weeks Aeden learned that he couldn't trust either one.

It was Aeden's turn to shuffle the cards and deal, for he and Adel had won the last hand. He quickly dealt out five cards to each player and finished by flipping over two cards. One card marked the trump card; the other card revealed the *triolet*, a card indicating which three of a kind would win the play pile.

Thomas quickly snatched up his cards and fidgeted with them as he put them in order and then went over them once more as if five cards were too many to keep track of. He reminded Aeden of a mouse working meticulously on a piece of leftover food.

Neri glanced once at his cards and collapsed them into a single pile held closely in his dark hands. He looked about with suspicious eyes as if constantly on the verge of taking offense. Aeden then watched as Jerome and Bosco spent a minute or so looking at each other's cards and whispering indiscernible strategies to each other.

Once everyone had settled, the lowest card began the game. Each person in turn produced their lowest card and then took a card from the face down deck to replenish their five-card hand. The five of arrows, the three of swords, a six of hearts, and a three of shields was played.

Aeden eyed the pile a moment, trying to remember the rules. He had played the three of arrows. He knew in terms of suits that arrows were the lowest when compared to the other suits. He quickly checked that he had the lowest number. He did, arrows beat swords for the first hand. He took the pile and played out a card. Adel graced him with a smile and a pat on the back. They were off to a good start.

"The barbarian can think," Bosco grumbled to himself.

Jerome chuckled, causing his rolls of fat to jiggle as he struggled to retain his cards in his bloated hand. Thomas seemed off put by the remark but said nothing. Neri merely glanced at the card played, scrutinized his hand for a quick moment before playing a high card, the queen of swords. Thomas followed with a low sword card.

Jerome's brow furrowed and he played a seven of swords. Bosco laid the king of swords with a smirk. Adel's thin face lit up as he struggled to hide his delight. He glanced at each in turn before slowly laying down the emperor of swords.

"Barbarians are winning," Adel said, taking the pile.

Thomas glanced up, fidgeted and smiled. It appeared he didn't much care for Bosco or Jerome either. Aeden watched Thomas a moment. Thomas didn't seem to notice as he reached into a fold of his robe and took out a small piece of cheese and began nibbling.

Adel led with a weak card, the two of hearts. Aeden glanced briefly at his own hand. He only had one heart and played it, the eight. The others followed, with Neri taking the pile. There were no clever rebukes as he organized his winning pile between him and Thomas.

And so, they played into the late hours of night. This was the nightly habit for most of the monks. It had become as much a part of Aeden's routine as prayer. Slowly Aeden's repertoire of insults grew and his knowledge of the monastery, its social structure, and political system began to unfurl itself, like a rose unfolding to the first kiss of Lenton.

Chapter 21

"Ignorance feeds irrational confidence." Saying of
Sawol

Odilo had tasked Adel with the tutelage of
Aeden. It was no easy task. Despite Aeden's
curiosity and inherent intelligence, there was a
stubborn streak that resided deep within. It was
like a vein of anger buried under a mountain of
ore.

"Let's start at the beginning," Adel said.

Aeden sat quietly, observing his newfound
friend. They'd spent a lot of time about the *kayles*
table, but this was different. The dynamic felt
more akin to teacher and student. It was strange
because they were so similar in age. And for
some reason Aeden already felt slightly resentful
that someone as young as Adel had been tasked
with teaching him. Why couldn't Odilo do it?

It was one thing for Adel to teach him
Heortian and another thing entirely for him to be
the expert in Salvare. It was a distinction that
Aeden couldn't ignore.

Back in the S'Velt things were different. Only
children were taught by the inexperienced.
Aeden had already taken a new name, passed his
coming of age rituals, and left behind the
threshold of childhood to become a man. It was
insulting.

Adel's voice droned on, interrupting Aeden's cyclical thoughts.

"Before there was anything there was the breath of God. It filled the void and sounded out in resonating tones, I am Salvare..."

This was stupid Aeden thought. Although his Heortian was still juvenile at best, he understood enough of the story to know it didn't make any sense. Adel continued to read, oblivious to Aeden's internal rants.

"...with each new breath, Salvare created the plants, the animals, and finally man. He..."

"How could one god do all this work," Aeden interrupted.

Adel paused from his reading and looked quizzically at Aeden. It was the look one had when they heard a statement of unbelievable stupidity. It was the look Devon often gave him when they were in the middle of one of their arguments. Adel, however, quickly masked his surprise and took in a breath before responding. Clearly, he took Odilo's orders seriously.

"People once believed there were other gods, long ago, and they were punished for it. Salvare, the one true god, spoke through the voices of his prophets and declared it so."

He looked at Aeden for a moment longer before delving back into his lesson.

"And He gave man female companions to help him bear children. He created animals to serve him, fruits to satiate him, and music to entertain him..."

Aeden nodded his head to indicate he was listening. In reality he was thinking about the game of *kayles* they had played the night before. It had turned into an interesting night. Although there was often some form of interesting gossip, last night one of the monks drew them out of their shells into the realm of momentary shock.

Thomas had been paired with a monk named Pate. Pate looked older than he really was. His balding head and portly features spoke of a life of idleness and a lack of discipline. He and Aeden were a bit like oil and water. Even though they were not on poor terms, like he was with Monahan, Bosco, and Jerome, they weren't on friendly terms either.

Thomas and Pate were leading for the majority of the night. Bosco complained throughout most of the game to the point where even his constant companion Jerome was getting irritated. Adel did his best to ignore Bosco's underhanded insults. It was Neri, the dark-skinned southerner, from the table over who had finally had enough.

Neri had thrown down his cards, turned to Bosco and stated in a whisper loud enough that the whole room fell quiet.

"You'd be shackled and sold as a dog to the lowliest woman in Sha'ril, who'd cut your tongue just to taste the sweet sound of silence."

After those words, he had stalked off in a cloud of disgust.

"Are you even listening?" Adel cut into Aeden's thoughts.

"Yes," he said sheepishly, caught in a daydream.

"What was I saying?" Adel asked.

Aeden glanced about the room searching for the answer.

"Something about a prophet?" he said.

"Not just any prophet, *the* prophet, the man who led the Church out of shadow and into the light."

Aeden nodded his head. He didn't want to be rude, not to his new friend. He didn't want to make life more difficult than it already was, yet a part of him couldn't help but rebel. Part of him didn't want to hear how there was only one god. It invalidated his beliefs. If Adel was right, then his real family, his village, would never ascend to the afterlife and eat amidst the gods.

"Can you name me the prophet?" Adel asked, momentarily sounding like Thomas.

"John?" Aeden shrugged.

Adel simply glared at him.

"Wait, no, it's Fendrel, or Geoffrey or something."

Adel's face went pale as his eyebrows knit

together in anger.

"You mock the Order," he said flatly, grinding his teeth and twiddling his fingers.

Aeden had noticed when playing cards that Adel twiddled his fingers when he had a bad hand or when they were losing. He also seemed to do it whenever he was corrected. So, despite not understanding the word "mock," he understood Adel's meaning. It was written in the set of his shoulders and across his face. Still, Aeden felt compelled to plead his case, to defend his people.

"You ignore the old gods, the true creators, and lecture me on a history you made up!" Aeden retorted.

"I didn't make anything up, it's written right here," Adel emphasized by jabbing a finger at the book open before him, "Bosco was right, you're a barbarian who cannot read, and cannot concede the truth when it slaps him in the face."

"This barbarian has earned his name!" Aeden practically shouted.

Just as Adel was about to respond Odilo entered the room. He didn't say a word. Instead he folded his arms across his chest in clear disappointment. He studied them a moment before speaking. He addressed Adel first.

"Brother, I chose you to cultivate your patience and deepen your understanding of the Book of Khein, but now I worry I chose poorly,"

Odilo paused and favored Adel with a stern look, "Perhaps you're too young."

Odilo's words were gentle but stung like the tip of a whip. Adel winced and dropped his eyes in shame.

"As for you," he continued, turning his gaze to Aeden, "I brought you in, sheltered you," he switched to Sagaru, "help you join new family."

It was Aeden's turn to feel shame. His face reddened and he glanced briefly at Odilo then to Brother Adel.

"I'm sorry," he managed to whisper before stalking out of the room and seeking his rooftop alcove.

Chapter 22

"Bribery is the sin of the unimaginative." 14:9
Book of Khein

Aeden sat upon the rooftop for a long time. He worked through the events of the previous day over and over again. The more he thought on it, the more he realized he'd been out of line. Adel was merely doing his job. He was simply teaching what he believed, right or wrong, it didn't matter. And now Aeden had stepped upon that burgeoning friendship with a heavy boot.

He wasn't invited to *kayles* that night. Not that he would have gone, for he knew it was far too soon to ask for forgiveness. Adel loved games and was the one largely responsible for organizing the *kayles* tables and teams. And Aeden had just managed to squash one of the most important socializing events at the monastery.

In fact, the two monks hardly spent more than a minute together since the argument. Odilo took over his tutelage of the Holy Order of Sancire. The stories Blaise often told at night became his escape from reality.

As the days stretched into weeks, Aeden fully began to realize how deeply he'd hurt Adel. There were few exchanges between them. So Aeden set out to rectify that.

Aeden spent the next few days finding out everything he could about the brother monk he'd offended. He found out that Adel loved pastries. One called king's delight was his favorite. So, in an effort to win Adel back into his favor he sought out Bosco, knowing that he had connections to the monastery's black market.

It was a testament to his desire to appease Adel that he spoke with the strangely disgusting monk. Bosco had the strange habit of constantly wiping his nose on his robe when he thought no one was looking, and he had been doing it when Aeden approached.

"Shouldn't you be cleaning bed pans?" Bosco said.

Already Aeden was irritated. He really didn't like the tall, skinny monk. Aeden took in a calming breath remembering why he had approached Bosco in the first place.

"I need a favor," Aeden began before being cut off.

"A favor? Why would I help a stupid barbarian?" Bosco stuttered in shock, turning to walk away.

Aeden placed a hand on his shoulder. Bosco jerked away as if he had been touched by the devil himself.

"Touch me again and I'll make sure you're kicked out of the monastery."

Aeden took a step back. He hadn't considered being kicked out and although he doubted Bosco had the ability or authority to make it happen it still gave him pause.

Bosco saw this moment of weakness and relished it.

"Odilo had to fight pretty hard to keep you here after your stupidity with the…" Bosco glanced about before whispering, "Inquisitor. Your stupidity has marked this monastery on the Emperor's map!"

Aeden didn't realize how hard this would be. He needed a new tactic. The words of his gevecht master came to mind: *timing and rhythm are everything in a confrontation of any nature.*

"You're right," Aeden said.

Bosco was disarmed.

"I shouldn't have been so stupid," Aeden paused for a moment, gauging Bosco's reaction, "I want to make it up to the brother monks, but I need a favor to do so."

Bosco turned back to face Aeden. His mind was clearly working.

"What do you want?"

It was now Aeden's turn to think. He was hesitant to open up to Bosco at all. He felt if Bosco knew the true reason for Aeden's motivation he would somehow ruin it.

"I want money to buy something…" he

finally said in a whisper.

Bosco regarded him oddly before responding.

"I could just turn you in for the suggestion," Bosco replied.

"And I would tell them you approached me, they'd investigate both of us."

Bosco fell silent a moment. He looked down the corridor and used the top of his robe to wipe at his nose. He turned back to Aeden.

"Then you will need to do something for me."

Chapter 23

"Stupidity is often the mark of ignorance, but at times defines the desperate." Book of Humors, Library of Galdor

Had Aeden known what Bosco's greater plan was, he would never have come to him. Aeden was stubborn, however, and once he had made up his mind to do something it was hard to become sidetracked. Dannon used to tease him about being as stubborn as Vintas in the Barre Mountains.

It was two days later that Bosco approached him and told him what he had wanted. Bosco had asked the impossible, and from the gleam in his eye, he knew it.

Aeden presently stood in the crypt, hidden in shadow. His heart was beating loudly, drumming its rhythm against his ears. His mind was strangely blank. The aroma of fear and doubt lingering along the outer recesses of his juvenile mental state had dissipated like an afternoon storm.

The crypt was quiet. It was a refuge of sort. A stuffy refuge filled with the smells of spices, grain, damp, and dust. A cluttered space used as storage for the kitchens, for the wine the monastery sold, and candles for the services to name a few.

Few people came down here. The cooks would frequent the crypt for meal preparation. They were easy to avoid. They would get what they needed and leave. It was the cellarer he had been worried about.

The cellarer's responsibilities included accounting for what the monastery had and what it needed to order. It was an important job and a slow and boring job. Aeden's fear of a vigilant cellarer watchful of his domain was exaggerated.

The soft sounds of snoring assured Aeden that watchful was far from the correct word to describe the man. Lazy perhaps, or complacent and old may have been better, but certainly not watchful.

Aeden slipped past and immersed himself in shadow. He paused beyond the line of sight of the cellarer and waited. He strained to hear movement. Nothing. Silence responded with the thrush of blood pounding within his ears.

He crept forward toward the empty space before a red door cast in darkness. His skin prickled with some unseen energy. His mind flashed to Odilo's admonishment from the last time he had visited the crypt. He then thought of Adel. How he had hurt his friend. How he needed to rectify his mistake. Bosco's smirking face was the final image Aeden allowed to pass through his mind before bringing himself into the present.

It was Aeden and the mysterious red door. Bosco's task now seemed all too simple, yet strangely difficult. What were his exact words?

"Bring me the book from beyond the Red Door."

Were there many books? How would Aeden know which one to bring? How did Bosco know what lay beyond the door? Did all the monks know once they passed the stage of being a novice?

What if there was another red door? Aeden had walked the monastery twice, looking for any other red doors. He hadn't seen any, but what if he had missed it and Bosco hadn't meant the crypt at all?

He took in a steady breath knowing the thoughts were useless. What had the master often told him, *"this excessive clutter will get you killed one day,"* he had said it jabbing a finger into his skull.

Aeden closed his eyes for a moment. His mind fell silent again. He opened them and took a step toward the door. His hand was shaking ever so slightly.

He took in a breath and placed his hand on the wooden door. Oddly there was no handle. How could he have forgotten there was no handle?

His arm pulsed strangely. Aeden pressed against the door. It didn't move.

He chided himself silently. If it had been that easy Bosco wouldn't have asked him to get the book.

He spent a moment studying the door, looking for a keyhole of some sort. There was none. His fingers traced the stone framework. Flowing script of some foreign language graced the stone, unblemished by time. His skin tingled slightly. It was similar to how he felt when he first picked up the Templas blade. The sensation soon faded and his dilemma only became more pronounced.

If Aeden tried to kick or break down the door the cellarer would certainly startle from his sleep. He wondered how long the old man napped for. Were the cooks coming down soon again for food preparation? It was difficult to judge the passage of time without a window to witness the cycle of the sun.

Maybe he could push it open if he found the right spot.

Aeden began to push on various parts of the door. It refused to move.

In frustration, he leaned against it and placed a hand on the frame molding. Again, a tingle crept slowly up his arm. Was the molding the secret to opening the door?

Aeden traced the edges of the frame looking for a hidden switch, a crack, a handle, anything.

He found nothing.

His head was becoming foggy. Was he hungry? How long had he been down there?

Aeden struggled to shake the growing weariness and persisted. His fingers paused on a particular set of script. His fingers felt like they were being pricked by needles, yet the surface appeared smooth. The muscles in his arm began to contract of their own accord. He must be getting close, he thought.

Undeterred, Aeden began to push harder on that particular spot on the frame. His arm pulsed with some unseen energy. His mind grew fuzzy and his eyes became heavy. He pushed harder. He must almost be there.

A flash of pain seared through him. He yelped as energy shot through his body and repelled him across the crypt onto a heap of sacks of grain. The world grew dark as Aeden drifted into unconsciousness.

Chapter 24

"The most adept among us lie more than most, despite an aversion to it." Book of Humors, Library of Galdor

Aeden awoke with a startling headache. It felt like a steely finger had reached into his brain and was poking at it with startling tenacity.

He rubbed at his eyes in an attempt to banish the pain. After a few steady breaths, the throbbing subsided and he opened his eyes. Standing before his sleeping mat was Odilo. It was odd to see him so early. There were routines to be followed.

Odilo beckoned to him and Aeden followed him out of the room. They made their way about the courtyard and to the second floor. Aeden's mind was now alight with curiosity. His headache temporarily forgotten.

It seemed Odilo was walking him to the abbot's quarters. He knew it had to be in response to him attempting to open the red door. He should never have listened to Bosco. Bosco was a manipulative idiot.

They now stood at the threshold to the abbot's room. The door was open. Odilo stepped through, but Aeden hesitated. He saw Monahan standing within, smiling. Maybe it was true, Monahan was trying to remove him from the monastery. Was this his last day? Where would he go? What would he do? He had no other friends. He had no family.

"Step inside young man," Blaise said.

Aeden did as he was told. He glanced at Blaise. A look of compassionate understanding graced his caring features. The abbot seemed distracted and tired. Monahan looked eager. Odilo stood slightly off to the side and was serious, but calm.

"You've been called in here for your recklessness and to account for your behavior," Monahan said.

"Brother Monahan, I understand your eagerness," Blaise cut in, "but please, this is a matter for the sacrist first and foremost."

Monahan's face flushed red at the chastisement.

"Novice Aeden, we are here to settle the matter in the crypt from yesterday. Brother Monahan believes that you had gone down into the crypt with the intent of purposefully trying to open the red door," Blaise paused only long enough to take in a breath, "I on the other hand have explained your condition."

Condition? Aeden was confused but did his best to hide it from his face.

"I understand you didn't want to tell the others about your white hair," Blaise took in a deep breath and looked down temporarily.

Aeden's eyes went wide. Did Blaise know about his mother? How could he? Aeden looked to the other monks. Odilo's face remained a passive mask of relegated concern. Monahan's beady eyes narrowed and the smile had disappeared from his mouth. The abbot appeared slightly distracted.

"It's ok, these men will not spread any rumors," Blaise said calmly, "some would say being struck by lightning at a young age is the mark of Salvare. If the price is the occasional headaches and blackout, well," Blaise shrugged, "you wouldn't be the only monk here to have passed out while working."

Monahan looked incredulously from Blaise then to Aeden. It hadn't gone as he had expected at all.

"But, he had purposefully touched the red door!" the mole-like monk stammered.

"Being that there were no witnesses we only have novice Aeden's word," Odilo said without emotion.

Blaise looked back to Aeden, "did you purposefully try to touch the red door."

Aeden shook his head.

"There, you see brother Monahan, not everyone is as sinister as you'd like to believe."

The abbot yawned in the background.

Monahan was clearly angry. He stood there fuming and thinking. Just as Blaise was about to dismiss Aeden, he spoke.

"There is the matter of why he was in the crypt in the first place and why he was asleep on the job!"

Finally, Aeden's mind calmed and clarity prevailed.

"Another monk suggested I see if the cellarer needed any help, but I think the smells and dust triggered a headache and I don't remember what happened after that."

Aeden was looking down and glanced up to see if anyone had bought his lie. Monahan clearly had not. Blaise simply smiled. Odilo looked away and began to exit the room.

"Brother Aeden..." the abbot began.

"Novice Aeden," Monahan whispered in correction, but the abbot took no notice.

"...will repent and say ten prayers," the abbot finished lazily.

Blaise placed a hand on Aeden's shoulder and ushered him out of the abbot's quarters. Monahan was clearly angry and seemed ready to debate the issue further. The fat monk looked about the room and found himself alone with the abbot and Aeden looking back at him with a smile.

As Aeden walked away he heard Monahan pleading with the abbot.

"I know he did it..." Monahan said in an

angry whisper.

"...there were no marks..."

The last words faded into obscurity.

Chapter 25

"One lie opens up an endless stream of lies in an attempt to save face, banishing honesty to the fearful depths of insecurity." Verse from the Bocian

Aeden sought out Bosco. He had nearly been kicked out of the monastery, forced to do more prayers, all for what? Bosco would come to understand what it meant to cross the last member of the Thane Sagan.

Aeden tore through the corridors with angry purpose. His heart beat heavily in his ears. Each audible thump was a call to war. His eyes were furious coals, eagerly searching for the tall, gangly monk.

Aeden spotted him farther down the corridor with Jerome. Why did Jerome have to be there? The slow-witted, overweight monk would only be another set of eyes. A witness. Aeden didn't want any witnesses. Bosco's word versus his would instill doubt. Two monks speaking out against him would certainly get him into trouble.

With great discipline Aeden stifled his anger. It was just enough to stuff it back down his throat, until he could come up with a better plan.

He needed Bosco alone.

Noon Prayer was wrapping up as Aeden

glanced over toward Bosco again.

"You seem distracted," Thomas said.

Aeden looked at the cheese-loving monk and shook his head.

"I keep imagining the Inquisitor in here," he lied to distract from his true purpose.

Aeden didn't like to lie, in fact, he hated it when others lied to him, however, when he wanted to accomplish a task nothing would stand in his way.

"Me too," Thomas whispered back.

The two of them had spent more time together since Adel still wasn't speaking to him. It was awkward because Aeden had become the noticeable absence at the *kayles* tables. In other words, he had become persona non-grata within certain circles of the monastery.

It made it easier for Aeden to spend time learning Heortian. Today, it made it easier to follow Bosco and consequently Jerome without much issue.

It turned out that finding Bosco alone was far more difficult than Aeden had originally thought. At every moment of the day Bosco and Jerome were together. They ate together, they slept on sleeping maps purposefully moved closer together, they always had the same work assignments together, and they shit together.

The more Aeden watched the two from a hidden distance, the more disgusted he became.

Bosco would constantly wipe his nose on his robes. Jerome had frequent bouts of flatulence that contended with the monastery bells for supremacy of sound and vibrato.

The final bell, ending Noon Prayer, rang out. Aeden watched for a moment as Bosco and Jerome left the grand nave.

"I'll see you later," Aeden said to Thomas.

Thomas merely nodded before heading to the kitchens in hopes of finding the cheeses unattended.

"Wait," Aeden called out to him as a simple idea unfolded in his head.

Thomas stopped.

"Could you do me a favor?" Aeden asked as he approached.

Thomas regarded him quietly for a moment, only glancing once more toward the refectory.

"What is it?"

"I was supposed to tell," Aeden paused, constructing a lie was no small feat, "I was supposed to tell Jerome that he is supposed to report to the sacrist at once."

Aeden's mind was still working out the details when Thomas replied.

"Why don't you tell him?"

"I can't stand those two. They keep trying to get me in trouble," he said.

At least the last part was the truth. What had

his gevecht teacher once told him, "*If you're going to lie to someone, the more truth you use, the more believable the lie. Stop lying!*"

Thomas nodded his head briefly. It was a good sign.

"And let Bosco know that he's supposed to get more candles from the crypt."

Thomas regarded Aeden oddly for a moment. Aeden attempted a smile.

"I'll give you my portion of cheese for the next week," Aeden followed up.

That seemed to clinch the deal. Thomas nodded and smiled.

"For a week," he said before walking off toward the awkward pair.

Chapter 26

"Fear through intimidation is as old as Verold itself, yet never lasting." Canton of Sawol

Aeden spent the next twenty minutes hiding in the crypt. At first Aeden thought he would wait for Bosco outside the kitchen door, but realized if Bosco took the nave entrance, Aeden could miss him altogether. Therefore, he waited in the dank bowels of the monastery.

It felt strange being back in the crypt so shortly after having gotten in trouble for his prior visit. Anxiety and anger rolled around his insides, battling for control. Aeden glanced about for a distraction. He had been expecting greater security measures.

Nothing had changed.

The cellarer was asleep. The supplies were stacked more or less where they had been before. The subtle aromas of spices, dust, and mildew permeated the air. And the red door remained stubbornly closed.

He had begun to question his last-minute tactics. His thoughts preyed on him the way a shroud cat stalks the wild elk of the Gwhelt. He shouldn't have involved Thomas. Guilt bubbled to the surface. What if they questioned Thomas as to who ordered them? Would Thomas in turn lie, or say that Aeden asked?

No, Thomas was quite straight-forward, he'd most likely tell them verbatim, nothing more, nothing less.

Maybe Bosco would wait for Jerome to visit the Sacrist and they'd come down together. What then? Would Aeden threaten them both? Would he have to actually hurt one of them?

Violence wasn't normally his first reaction to anything, but at this point he was so angry he didn't care. Sometimes it seemed violence was the only thing people paid attention to.

The light tap of approaching footsteps alerted Aeden to Bosco's approach. The tall, lanky shadow of Bosco stretched across the floor before the monk's visceral appearance.

Aeden stepped out of the shadows and placed a thick hand over the other monk's mouth. He simultaneously had scooped up an arm and twisted it behind Bosco's back.

Bosco attempted to scream. A muffled puff of air and a deep-throated mumble were barely audible.

"Shut up or I will break your arm," Aeden whispered into Bosco's ear.

Bosco fell silent. The power over him felt good.

"It's now your turn to uphold your end of the promise," Aeden continued.

Aeden slowly peeled his fingers from Bosco's mouth. They were now wet with saliva and whatever perpetual run-off Bosco had dripping from his nose. He wiped his hand on Bosco's robe and placed his hand on Bosco's shoulder just by the neck.

"Pay me what you owe," Aeden whispered threateningly, "and then we'll have little need to talk again."

Bosco fidgeted slightly. It was a futile gesture against Aeden's iron-like grip.

"I don't have the money," Bosco said.

All the prior emotions Aeden was wrestling with boiled over. The inner conflict between fear and anger was decided. Anger had won.

Aeden twisted Bosco's arm further, bringing the tall monk to his toes. Aeden then swiftly shoved him forward toward the red door.

"Please..." Bosco began.

Aeden wasn't listening. He no longer cared.

Bosco was attempting to struggle. It was a weak and useless gesture.

Aeden pressed the struggling monk to the red door. Bosco yelped. The smell of burnt skin startled Aeden out of his anger. That was strange. The thought was soon whisked away by hidden hands.

Aeden let go of Bosco and walked away, slipping through the shadows to the nearest stairway and out of the crypt.

Chapter 27

"The repayment of debts is rarely so gratifying as incurring them." Canton of Sawol

The following day Bosco paid Aeden. It was more than they had agreed upon. A bandage was upon one side of his face. Aeden briefly wondered what lie Bosco concocted to cover up the true reason for the burn marks on his face. Aeden decided he didn't much care. He had other things to do.

Aeden wasted no time as he sought out Pate. He was one of the few monks allowed to go beyond the monastery walls. Pate was tasked with community outreach. His main function was to entice wealthy patrons to visit the church and have their sins prayed for. This was all done for a small sum of money of course.

Pate smuggled in king's delight for Aeden. In turn Aeden would gift them to Adel. Adel would accept them. In fact, it was hard for him to refuse them. This allowed for a friendlier exchange of nods and such as they passed each other, but it didn't overcome Adel's discomfiture.

All that work and he had only succeeded in mildly improving the situation. He knew he had hurt his friend; he just hadn't realized by how much.

Faith was a funny thing.

Aeden needed a better plan. He decided then, to shadow Adel, to find out more about him. He stalked him through the corridors like a cat stalks its prey. He remained hidden in shadow and concealed his step as he'd been taught for years by the masters in the S'Velt. It paid off.

It took nearly two weeks, but Aeden had uncovered Adel's hidden passion. A secret he'd somehow managed to keep buried from the prying eyes of ever nosy monks. He learned that Adel was a skilled artist and loved to draw. He didn't just draw anything. He drew his fellow monks.

One day, Aeden waited until Adel was done drawing. He watched as Adel placed sheets of parchment back into a small box and slid the box behind a loose brick. Once Adel had checked the corridor and left, Aeden slipped into the room and uncovered Adel's secret drawings.

Aeden flipped through the pages of sketches. He saw a drawing of Neri huddled over his pet squirrel. There was another of Thomas nibbling on a piece of cheese. Adel had drawn Bosco and Jerome whispering to each other. It was the last drawing that had caught his attention. It was a sketch of himself.

Adel had depicted him with long hair, body armor, muscular, and warrior-like. It was odd seeing himself in his old garb and brought on a twinge of emotion. Aeden dropped the sheets back into their hiding place. A hint of sadness stabbed at his insides. Sadness for having hurt Adel, and a deeper, hidden sadness for all that he'd lost.

He left Adel's secret drawing spot and resolved to win him back.

In a last-ditch effort to earn coin, Aeden worked every unwanted chore of the monastery. He prayed longer than the other monks. Aeden already knew a certain number of prayers had to be accomplished per day, to ward off the sins and avarice of the wealthy.

He emptied the slop buckets, something that not even the well-paid monastery servants wanted to do. He worked the grinding stone, to mill wheat for bread and spent hours mending torn robes, pricking his thumbs more times than he could count.

After nearly three weeks, Aeden had earned enough money to bribe Pate once more. This time it took more convincing. He had to persuade Pate to purchase supplies from High Street, a nicer part of Bodig that resided next to Rat's Alley. Pate said he disliked Rat's Alley and was afraid of getting robbed and detested the number of whores that would offer themselves to him. In Pate's words, *"whores are Salvare's test of servitude, a pleasurable abomination if there ever was one."*

Rat's Alley was a neighborhood of servants for the rich and a large number of bastard children. It was a place of pickpockets, thieves, and prostitutes. He told Aeden the only way he'd go was if he had a full bit. A bit was a quarter of a silver dinar. It seemed excessive and it was more than Aeden had. It also seemed strange that a man who feared being robed wanted more money.

Only through excessive bargaining, did he convince Pate to sell his leather armor from S'Vothe and use that money for whatever activities he desired. Strangely, at mention of this, Pate's eyes lit up and a strange grin fought for control.

It had taken three days for Pate to sell Aeden's armor and use the money to purchase the supplies Aeden had asked for. Three days of Aeden waiting impatiently, wondering if he'd wasted his time and effort. Three days feeling ashamed at selling the armor his father had given him for his last trial. But in the end, it had been worth it.

Pate finally came back with the art supplies Aeden had requested. It then became a different waiting game. A game, in which, Aeden waited for the perfect time to present the supplies to Adel. Yet, the longer he waited, the more he realized there was no perfect time. So instead of making it awkward, he sought help in crafting a note in his own hand, and left the gift along with the note in Adel's secret drawing place.

Chapter 28

"Beauty can be misinterpreted as love with such frequency that the object of desire becomes a fixation that only love can cure." Canton of Sawol

Two long months passed before the beginning of Hearvest. There were celebrations in the streets of Bodig. They were celebrations that Aeden was only able to view while sitting on a roof under a small overhang near the main courtyard. The ceremonies were a welcome distraction from the idle thoughts that seemed to always circle back to his lost home and family.

It was a strange cycle of self-torture. He'd want to remember, for he felt his thoughts and memories served as a way to honor his people. If he kept them alive in his heart, they would be safer and happier until the day he could avenge them. The memories would always lead to him arriving upon the charred remains of S'Vothe. Twisted, blackened bodies with outstretched hands that reached for the sky as if seeking to fend off terrible deaths.

They were images forever fused into his young mind. His throat would constrict with emotion as he choked back tears in a valiant effort to hide his emotion from others. Distraction was the only way for him to remain sane.

Learning to speak Heortian had become his

greatest distraction, with *kayles* a close second.
Adel had finally accepted his apology. He had
discovered the pencils and paper he'd bought,
with Pate's help. They never spoke of it. Instead,
one day, Adel invited him back to the *kayles*
tables. It was as though nothing had ever
happened.

He had improved drastically in spoken
Heortian and understood more than he could
speak, but reading was another story. The
characters used to represent words were
confusing, too similar to each other. The whole
affair was rather tedious. He was struggling to
learn in an effort to read through the volumes of
books available in the monastery library. Aeden
figured the books would be a welcome escape
from the drudgery that had become his life. His
efforts were slow going and frustrating.

Far easier were the hand gestures used
almost exclusively during mealtime. Aeden
learned the signs for all the different foods, a
dozen simple phrases, and a few dozen objects.
Therefore, despite the silence observed in the
refectory, lively conversations would take place
in a symphony of hand movements.

Aeden's newfound language skills were
allowing him to make friends. With every word
learned a new piece of gossip unfolded its ugly
head. Aeden had learned that the monk who had
burned himself in the plaza was from Sawol. He
learned there was a growing rift between the

Church and the Emperor as a struggle for power ensued. The most obstreperous of which was to the north.

Yet, despite his newfound skills, he learned little about the Emperor's Inquisitors. It seemed another taboo topic he could add to his growing list. It was frustrating. The Red Door, Draccus Fiends, and Inquisitors. The more forbidden the subject it seemed, the more curious he became.

Understanding more Heortian brought on another frustration. Monahan. He had only become more obnoxious in his efforts to embarrass Aeden. It seemed Monahan's goal to be ever-present whenever Aeden fumbled in his attempts to communicate more complex subjects and his missteps in Sancire protocol.

Aeden's worst guffaw was at Noon Prayer a few weeks before. He had been guided through the process of judgements. It had seemed simple enough. The attending patron would sit through prayers and approach a monk of their choosing afterward. The attending monk would then listen to their woes and inform them of the number of prayers that would relieve their suffering. The patron would make an offering; the monk would refuse. The man would insist, and the Church would become a few coins richer.

Aeden had mistaken *sigloi* for dinar, not realizing the difference between the currency of D'seart and Heorte. Furthermore, he misjudged the wealth of the customer and had offered prayers far too cheaply. Monahan had witnessed the transgression and reported it to the sacrist. That night Aeden had spent hours prostrated before the other monks.

Apparently, money was a primary concern for the Church and deserving of greater punishment than other transgressions. It hadn't been his first offense. The only benefit from recited prayer was that he found himself learning the language more quickly.

Jerome and Bosco seemed to do their best to irritate him during the day, and whenever they were rotated to the same *kayles* table at night, they did their best to belittle him as they played. Although Bosco rarely made eye contact when he mumbled his insults.

Aeden's only consolation, during those subtle insults, was seeing the small scar that now marked part of Bosco's face.

"Don't mess with the Thane," it was something Devon used to like to say.

Aeden spent plenty of time with Odilo and came to respect him and like him. He learned that Odilo hadn't always been a monk. Aeden got the feeling there was more to his past than he let on, but whenever he would ask too many questions, Odilo would simply smile. Despite this mystery, Aeden could tell he was a simple man that was straightforward and honest. Qualities that he realized were of great importance to him.

Life was improving as he learned the role he was to play. Ceremonies began to make more sense. The daily routine became a blanket of security in a world full of unknowns. Therefore, it was strange and memorable when the routine was broken.

It was an uncommonly cool day when the Holy Order of Sancire of Bodig hosted a unique event. It seemed rarer these days that the Holy Order was able to do much of anything. The monks were still restricted to within the walls of the monastery. The magistrate of Bodig wasn't pleased by the last demonstration. Immolation caused too many to talk, to question, and to disobey. Worse still was Aeden's physical assault on an Inquisitor. Today of all days was not a day for disorder.

Aeden had finished Morning Prayer and completed his chores. Presently he could be found sitting in the small alcove on the roof that had become his refuge. The wind was gentle and spoke of greater things. It whispered as it swept past the white-stoned corner. It whistled as it traveled through the rain gutters and it caressed as it graced his cheeks.

He was watching the foot traffic beyond the monastery walls. His curiosity of what lay beyond grew with each passing day. Although he had seen much on his first day, it now felt long ago. The images were faded and watery. The wide street out front, the red-bricked buildings, and the alley around the corner had become his outside world. It was too small for his liking.

Today, however, he was content. There was enough activity to keep his mind occupied. Below, on the cobble-stoned street, guards were at their posts. They formed a staggered line on either side of the road, spaced evenly apart. Their tall spears were capped by polished steel heads. Red shirts with the images of a single oak and a single sword were worn over chainmail armor. Their helmets were tall and mildly reminiscent of a particular part of male anatomy.

"Pssst, Aeden!" came the hushed whisper of Adel.

Adel and Odilo were the only ones Aeden trusted enough to disclose the location of his secret alcove. The only other time Adel had come was when Abbott Filbert had requested to speak with him. That was in regard to him placing a lock on his storage chest. Apparently, possessions were communal and he wasn't supposed to have anything of value that required a lock. Luckily the abbot was so disengaged with the daily running of the monastery that Aeden simply told him he must have been mistaken. The abbot had shrugged and walked off as if the whole effort had been a waste of time.

Aeden had spent a great deal of time with Adel over the last couple of months. Their friendship grew steady and strong.

Despite much of time his time being spent with Adel, Aeden still sat with Odilo during meals. He found Odilo's peaceful nature to be calming. He also realized Odilo was a great source of wisdom and information. Sometimes Aeden wondered how he knew so much.

A monk's life seemed so sheltered that he knew Odilo must have led a more secret life before joining the monastery. It was a hidden desire to uncover that secret that also drove Aeden insane with curiosity.

"Come on," Adel whispered up to him.

What could it be this time? Had Monahan said something in an effort to get him into trouble? Aeden was curious and frustrated. He slid down a smooth section of roof, slipped down a column and landed near Adel, in a corner of the courtyard, hidden by fruit trees.

"We need to get ready!" Adel whispered, impatience painting his features with a look of concern.

"Ready for what?" Aeden asked as they peered around the trees before stepping briskly across the courtyard.

"The High Priest of Bodig and the Archduchess of the Second House of Bodig are coming," Adel said with a goofy grin.

Someone important was coming to the monastery. That meant chores and their best robes with the ceremonial red sash.

They hurried down the stone corridor. Beige arches flashed past in a blur as they rounded a corner. Adel and Aeden nearly ran into Jerome and Bosco. They came to a sudden halt. Bosco's hand slipped from his robe. The folds of cloth slipped away from his nose. There was a startled moment of exchanged expressions. Bosco was the quickest to recover and don a look of utter disgust.

"There you are, these hallways need to be swept before the high priest and archduchess arrive," he said authoritatively.

Jerome stood staring at Adel and Aeden with all the intellectual acumen of a bovine. Bosco shoved a bony elbow into his friend's fat arm. It was all the prodding Jerome needed.

"Well, get to it," Jerome said slowly, emphasizing Bosco's initial orders.

The strange pair handed them brooms and bitter expressions. Aeden grabbed a broom with a mild shrug. Adel looked at Bosco with narrowed eyes before he followed suit.

The awkward pair soon shoved past and disappeared around the corner. Aeden waited a moment longer before asking his question.

"Who's the archduchess?" Aeden asked, hoping he pronounced the word correctly.

Adel paused as if surprised Aeden had never heard of her.

"Alina Cynesige, the Holder of Keys. She's the third in line to succeed the Bodig throne and one of a dozen who could potentially lay claim to the Heorte Empire. Obviously after King Illian Benbow."

"She's the one who spoke to the king on my behalf?" Aeden muttered.

Adel looked up, confusion written upon his face.

"What?"

"Nothing," Aeden said.

He realized that only a handful of people probably knew the full ramifications of his actions with the Inquisitor. Distraction now was key. Plus, he enjoyed annoying Adel, it sometimes reminded him of his conversations with Devon.

"Heorte Empire?" Aeden asked.

"You don't know of the Heorte Empire? It's part of the reason we met," he stated matter-of-factly as he swept a particularly difficult corner.

"I've heard of the Heorte Empire," Aeden retorted, baiting Adel.

"I remember first seeing you. It's funny the memories that stick to one's mind. You stood out like a red-haired Calenite in Sawol. Odilo already knew, before the burning, that he wanted to recruit you, which seemed a little crazy, no offense..."

"None taken," Aeden said, listening intently, waiting for Adel to get to the point.

"But you looked like a wild, barbaric warrior out of some storybook."

"Thanks," Aeden said, attempting his most barbaric looking face.

"You're not scary now! I already know you're harmless."

Aeden smile inwardly.

"You were saying about the Heorte Empire."

"I was obviously getting to it," Adel continued, "Heorte as you know is made up of three kingdoms. To the north is Gemynd, to the south Sawol" he said, pointing as if one could tell their location from where they stood. "We're in Bodig, which is in the middle."

Adel leaned against his broom.

"Each has their own king, along with major and minor houses of nobility. Take the archduchess for example, she's part of a major house," Adel paused, scratching his nose, "Whichever king holds enough power and is in line for succession becomes the next emperor. It gets confusing because the seat of power may change, although I believe the last two emperors have held court in Sawol."

Adel's tone changed and his face became

serious, "It's rumored that Emperor Jarin the Bold wishes to abolish the practices of Sancire. If he were free to destroy each monastery, he would."

"He's the emperor. Can't he do whatever he wants?" Aeden asked, suddenly curious.

"Blaise says it's because he knows the people still hold Sancire deep within their hearts."

Aeden nodded; however, his mind was already on his next question.

"Why's he called Jarin the Bold?" Aeden asked.

"Here we start again, questions, questions, questions!" Adel said teasingly.

"That's not fair, I smuggled you a king's delight a few days ago, and I know you already ate it!"

"True. I'm not even going to ask how you accomplished that," Adel said, doing his best imitation of Thomas. His face taking on the stern expression of one disappointed in a moral edict being broken.

"I don't even remember what we were talking about," he continued.

"The Bald Emperor," Aeden replied.

"Right, and it's Jarin the Bold, not Bald Jarin" Adel stifled a chuckle, using that moment to recollect his thoughts. He continued to sweep for a moment before looking back up at Aeden, "You know I don't know why he's called Jarin the Bold. I just know that whatever names he had been called before he didn't like and people died for it. Their bodies were left on spikes along the King's Road."

"That's awful," Aeden said, visualizing the scene.

"Odilo saw it," Adel replied, "Thankfully I've never been farther south than the River Lif."

Adel paused, looking suddenly at Aeden. A gentle breeze swept through the corridor. His face became pinched with concern.

"We best prepare, I think Jerome and Bosco tricked us," Adel stated as though the idea of misconduct had just entered his mind.

The two moved with purpose down the empty corridor and entered an unoccupied barracks. They leaned the brooms against the wall in a corner and quickly donned their red ceremonial sashes. With haste, they made their way to the central nave.

"Finally," Thomas whispered in concern, the faintest smudge of cheese still graced the side of his mouth, as he looked at them the way a teacher would a failing student.

Aeden and Adel arrived, kneeling beside Odilo and Thomas. Bosco glanced back and seemed annoyed. He tapped Monahan on the shoulder who also turned to glance at the arriving pair. A flash of amusement and disgust rolled over his stout features as he studied them briefly with his mole-like eyes.

The sound of a massive bell shook them loose of their rivalry. The monks then began to chant in low humming tones as unarmed guards stepped into the expansive nave. Candles flickered with their passage, as beams of light fell through the circular windows, casting the men in their holy embrace. Polished armor reflected the light giving them the appearance of divinity.

Following the procession was a young woman flanked by an older man. The man wore a stern expression and a scar that ran down one half of his face. His clothes were fine, but odd. They appeared to be a cross between ceremonial armor and clothing befitting one of the Holy Order of Sancire.

Aeden hardly noticed the man for it was the young woman who had caught his attention. She couldn't have been more than sixteen years of age. Her skin was white and unblemished. It was her hair that first caught his attention. He had grown accustomed to everyone having heads of dirty yellow while living in S'Vothe. Only he and his mother had been the exception, with snowy white hair. In the monastery, short cropped hair of brown was most common.

The archduchess on the other hand had the blackest hair Aeden had ever seen. As she passed under the shaft of circular light, her locks were cast in a bluish sheen. It fell gracefully upon her ceremonial dress, made from a silk of the deepest red in a simple Bodig cut. Its lines were elegant, tracing the curves of her youthful body.

Aeden struggled to ignore the lines of red clinging to her contours. Each step allowed the thin fabric to shift and conform to her enticing shape. Her slender frame held an air of regal authority and childlike beauty. He was forced to think on other things as he felt a stirring in his loins.

As she passed, she glanced toward him as if she could feel his piercing gaze. Her eyes were large and expressive. There was no malice, simply curiosity and amusement. The sounds of chanting and the ringing bells faded into the background as he studied her features, as if trying to memorize every detail. Within a heartbeat, he broke eye contact, knowing to stare was to risk impropriety. With a deep breath, her Bodigan dress pulled taut, she too looked away and swept past. The scent of wild flowers followed her like a belated shadow.

For Aeden, the details of the ceremony fell into a foggy haze. Captivating glimpses of beauty were punctuated by drawn out speeches in a formal dialect of Bodig that Aeden long stopped trying to understand. By the end of it all his legs had grown numb. His friend Blaise struggled to stay awake, and the air within the massive room became stuffy and filled with the smells of too many men. It left Aeden longing for the archduchess to walk past just to fill his lungs with her perfumed scent.

He struggled to catch another glimpse of her but only succeeded in finally catching the interest of the angry looking man next to her. With a whispered warning from Adel, he relinquished his efforts and surrendered to the chants and prayers. His mind, however, wandered, dreaming of her face and dark shining hair.

Chapter 29

"Fear of the known can mask logic with the same swiftness as the hand of ignorance." Canton of Sawol

For the next few days, Aeden couldn't get the image of the archduchess out of his mind. She robbed him of sleep and stole his focus. Her form spilled into his mind like a hot mist that refused to leave. Every imagined interaction turned into ceremony as he raised her from icon to deity. His heart throbbed with anticipation, excitement, and longing, intermingled with feelings of guilt. He was ravished by hunger, ignorance, and a thirst for knowledge.

He found himself thinking less and less on Dannon and the loss of his home and more on the archduchess. It was a welcome reprieve, but it tore him in two directions. Temptation and imagination swelled with the rising tide of adolescence, as honor and memory fought to retain control.

His mind was so confounded that he found himself not paying attention to the simplest tasks. Aeden couldn't remember ever feeling this conflicted. It was as if his emotions had wrestled for control and kicked rational thought to the wayside. It was a strange feeling that he had trouble shaking loose. Aeden needed to tell someone, lest his mind wrest control from all normal interaction.

His first instinct was to tell Odilo, yet his pride wouldn't allow it. He was finally making progress in Heortian. He was beginning to fit into the monastery and hadn't been punished in weeks. Telling Odilo would only admit weakness and frailty of purpose to a man who never seemed to waver. In S'Vothe there was an expression that summed up his sentiment, "*one shouldn't steal water from the hand that measures it.*"

Adel, although a friend, was too young and too close to Odilo. Aeden and Adel talked about plenty, but often they simply joked around. A lot of their fun revolved around mimicking Jerome and Bosco. Although, as the restrictions on the Monastery continued, more and more of their time was consumed with getting their hands on some sort of pastry. Adel's fondness for pastries was only outdone by Bosco's irritation for life.

There was Thomas. They were not so close, even though Thomas would often trail Adel and him like a lost puppy. He was like their pet, or a quiet shadow that enjoyed pointing out others' lack of piety. He was loyal, quiet, and shy. Aeden knew all he'd need to do was sneak some cheese out of the refectory to get him to listen. There had to be a better option.

Of the junior monks that left Neri. He was strange and not necessarily the most trustworthy. Neri also had the habit of twisting one's words and interpreting a different meaning. He was quick to judge, sharp witted, and a bit of an outcast. At times, he reminded Aeden of a vulture waiting to pluck the eyes of the unwitting.

No, it was better to leave Neri to his pets.

This left Aeden in a bit of a conundrum. There were many other monks, but he didn't much interact with them. The only person that bubbled to mind was Blaise. The old-man storyteller who seemed filled with a passion for history, a smile for most jokes, and little tolerance for the gossip that often circled the monastery.

Blaise, it was. Aeden had decided.

It was early afternoon. The sun's light had settled upon the city of Bodig like a coppery blanket. The air was hot and stiff, inducing greater feats of laziness than he had ever seen in his homeland.

As others contended in an unseen competition of comatose indifference, Aeden sought Blaise. He cut through the still air like a fish through water. His eyes held the predatory gleam of the vulturine. The courtyard was empty and still like a painting.

There was no Blaise to be found amidst the sun-soaked plants. Aeden whisked through the sultry air toward the refectory. It, however, rested in silence. He then carved a path to the prayer hall. The nave sat in quiet solitude, basking in two pools of circular light, empty and serene.

Aeden decided to try the cloisters, where he knew most would be hard at work sleeping. His mind churned over his decision to seek out Blaise. The more he searched, the more confident he became that he had made the right decision. Blaise was not only wiser than most, but he was knowledgeable on a wide range of subjects. Perhaps he would have a story or two of the archduchess. That would allow him to further populate his daydreams with details of her life and their possible interactions.

Aeden rounded a corridor and almost stumbled into Jerome and Bosco. They blocked the corridor, each wearing devious expressions. Bosco puffed out his chest in an effort to appear larger as he looked down at Aeden. His normally bent frame was momentarily straight. Jerome was husky enough that he didn't need to inflate himself with bravado, despite his shorter stature. His expression was as vacuous as ever.

"Where do you think you are going *novice*?" Bosco asked, stressing the last word.

It was interesting what time could allow for. Given enough time, one could forget anything, even the most grievous of acts. For Bosco, enough time had passed to have forgotten the momentary pain of the red door. His brazen attempts at bullying had increased. It was gradual at first, like a child testing the temperature of the water before jumping in.

"That isn't your business," Aeden replied.

Bosco took a step forward and laid a spidery hand on Aeden's shoulder. It was a curious approach to bullying. Strangely over the last few days they had made more overt attempts at blustering. Each time would end with Aeden walking away. The whole affair was beginning to get irritating.

"We think it *is* our business," Bosco huffed.

Aeden looked them over and glanced briefly at the hand on his shoulder. There were so many options that flared to mind.

His heart beat a touch quicker as he readied himself for action. It had been a while since he had trained in the gevecht.

Part of him thought it might be fun to physically engage them, which was ironic because it was one of his least favorite activities growing up. He didn't mind the stone fist training or the forms and weapons movements. Although it was monotonous striking a leather bag filled with gravel, or moving through the same basic movements over and over, it was an opportunity to let his mind wander.

Combat training required constant vigilance and a certain sense of pride to further stimulate a sense of aggression. Aggression wasn't normally part of his psyche. And when he did get angry someone almost always got hurt.

Aeden looked the two monks over. Their gray robes hung quite differently. Bosco had a tall, narrow frame. Aeden imagined he looked a bit like a skeleton underneath, as evidenced by the knobby protrusions that formed a poor excuse for shoulders. Jerome on the other hand, filled out his robe mostly in his rotund midsection. Although Aeden hadn't caught him personally, he knew he had to be sneaking in food. At the very least, he was part of the well-hidden black market that had been given a new breath of life once the monks were ordered to remain within the monastery walls.

These monks likely had never seen a day of combat. Their footing was all wrong, the set of their shoulders indicated a lack of balance, and their movements were mildly clumsy. Aeden knew anything but a verbal altercation wouldn't be fair.

"Have you seen Blaise?" Aeden asked.

Jerome and Bosco looked at each other briefly as if wondering why in the world he wanted to see Blaise. They obviously arrived at the conclusion that if it was important enough for Aeden to see him, then it was important enough for them to know why.

"Tell us why and you may pass."

"I want him to tell me some more about

Sancire history," Aeden replied without hesitation.

Bosco removed his hand from Aeden's shoulder but didn't move out of the way. Jerome looked up at him as if wondering what their next move was.

"We know plenty of Sancire history," Jerome retorted.

"So, you're offering to teach me?" Aeden asked, mildly amused.

"No," Bosco replied before Jerome could say anything.

"Ok, then I'll be on my way."

Aeden took a step forward. Bosco stepped to the side to block his passage. Aeden tried to skirt him on the opposite side.

Again, Bosco moved to stop him. Aeden looked back, knowing that the only other way to the cloisters would be through the transept to the second floor. He didn't feel like backtracking that far.

"Why don't you take your pet to the field so he can graze," Aeden said to Bosco.

"I already ate," Jerome retorted.

"Yes, and you still have some hay on your lip."

Jerome's eyes narrowed and Bosco's face turned red. Aeden knew he was only stoking the fire, but he couldn't help himself. Stupidity for stupidity's sake was one of his greatest aversions.

"I don't want to hurt either one of you," Aeden said.

This elicited a chuckle from the two of them. Aeden had enough of their stupidity. All he wanted was to seek out Blaise. His mind was already swirling with a torrent of emotion and their nonsense only served to fan the flames of emotional incognizance.

If he were back home, he knew what Devon would do; tackle the problem head on, regardless of the consequences. Perhaps some of that logic was required now. It was apparent that Bosco was the leader. He didn't want to hurt them but he also wanted to send a clear message, don't mess with me.

"How about you clean out bedpans for a week, and then we'll let you pass," Bosco said with a sneer.

Aeden's anger boiled over. Without thought Aeden took a sliding step forward. His weight was balanced and low. He hooked his right foot behind Bosco's heel as he drove his shoulder into Bosco's sternum.

He was temporarily reminded of his interaction with the Inquisitor. All likeness peeled away under the frailty of Bosco's frame.

Bosco was upended like a child struck by a bull. One moment the bullying twosome were blocking the corridor, the next Jerome stood in stunned silence as he and Aeden watched Bosco tumble up into the air and land heavily onto his back, on the cool, hard stones. There was a muted thump as Bosco's head hit the ground.

Aeden glanced briefly at Jerome who remained unmoving, before looking down at Bosco. Bosco groaned and began to rub the back of his head. Once seeing Bosco would be fine, Aeden tore past, heading down the corridor. He hurt Bosco more than he intended, but it wasn't entirely his fault.

"Things will be different soon," Jerome shouted as Aeden stalked off.

Anger trailed him like a dark shadow. They clouded his mind to Jerome's idle threat. He focused instead on finding Blaise.

He glanced at each passing room.

Still no Blaise.

Aeden paused for a moment to calm his beating heart. It did little to improve his mood.

Why had Bosco pushed him? If only they had left him alone he'd never have hurt him. It was clearly their fault. Yet, part of him knew that Odilo would have handled it quite differently, and when he found out he would be most disappointed.

Aeden shook the thoughts loose and decided to continue searching for Blaise. He had started the afternoon looking for Blaise and he was damn well going to finish what he started.

Aeden realized he hadn't yet checked the second floor. He turned a corner and came upon a stairway. He took the stairs two at a time as the words of one of his gevecht teachers came to mind, *"temper your ability for violence with your ability to reason."*

Shame flushed his face as the onus of his mistake sank into the pit of his stomach.

He passed the library pausing to look inside. Blaise was known to sit and enjoy a good book on occasion. There were a few monks reading and a couple that were in the meticulous process of copying texts.

It was an endeavor that Adel recently had him undertake in an effort to drill Heortian characters into his head. He used scrapped bits of vellum and subpar ink of course, they were expensive items. Glancing about he did not see the jovial figure of Blaise.

Aeden continued down the corridor. He rounded a bend and walked parallel to the courtyard. To his right the stone archways looked down upon the garden. To his left the stone wall was occasionally punctuated by wooden doors. Voices carried beyond the closed door that led to the room of the abbot.

Aeden paused at the sound of Blaise's voice.

"...there is precedent; however, I must reiterate the fractured state of the Church may look upon such a pilgrimage with suspicion." It was the gentle baritone of Blaise, raised in slightly urgent tones.

"It's not the Church I'm concerned with, I'm sure our brothers to the north and south will welcome us. It's the Emperor that may have issue."

This time it was the nasally words of the abbot that barely permeated the wooden barrier and drifted to Aeden's waiting ear.

"The emperor is the reason for the fractured state of affairs." Blaise paused as Aeden took a step closer to make sure he didn't miss anything. "Monks on empire taxed roads may not ..." the next part was muffled by a bird taking flight from one of their nesting spots in a stone archway.

"You don't understand, the boy's interaction with the inquisitor necessitates this, there just isn't much choice in the matter," came the whining response of the elderly abbot.

"I assume you have already given word to the deacon to the north?" Blaise asked.

"You know very well that wouldn't be wise, I might as well inform the High Priest of Gemynd what we intend. There is no choice in this matter," the abbot's voice trailed off.

"Choice is a matter of perspective dear Abbot, one I think you failed to consider," Blaise said with anger. "Sacrificing the safety of one is unacceptable in the eyes of Salvare."

"At this point it's a decision of safety of the group over the individual," the abbot's voice took on its own tone of anger, chasing Blaise's response into the shadows.

A moment of silence had followed.

Aeden almost didn't realize the conversation was over. It was the turning of the door's latch that spurred him to action. Without waiting to awkwardly explain his presence, he turned and ran. A few final words trailed him as he left. They were the abbot's response.

"Once cornered an animal does what it thinks is right."

Chapter 30

"Excessive curiosity is the devil's own brew."
Superstition of Treton

Aeden had trouble sleeping that night. His mind hovered over the words he overheard, like a predatory bird circling over fallen prey.

What pilgrimage was the abbot referring to? Were they talking about him? Why had Blaise gotten so angry?

He tossed and turned for a few hours before he resolved to get some answers.

His curiosity and anxiety was enough to temporarily forget what had happened with Bosco and Jerome. That, or the alternative was more than Aeden wished to face. Banishment from the monastery and the brother monks hung about him in a heavy cloud.

He slipped off his blanket and crept through the dark chambers to Adel's sleeping mat.

"Wake up," Aeden whispered as he shook Adel.

Adel groaned as he turned over and pulled his blanket more tightly about him. Aeden shook him gently again.

"What is it?" Adel moaned.

"I want to talk."

Adel slowly sat up and rubbed at his blurry

eyes. He looked at Aeden for a moment as the world resolved into focus.

"This is a time of silence and reverence for Salvare," Adel said sleepily.

"I'll throw in a few kind words his way," Aeden said, tugging lightly on Adel's arm.

Adel glanced about the room. The other monks were sound asleep. The brother nearest him shifted on his sleeping mat. Adel's eyes finally settled back on Aeden. He nodded his head slightly.

"Fine, let me use the chamber pot first," Adel whispered.

"I'll meet you in the courtyard," Aeden replied.

Aeden sat idle in the dark courtyard. The night air was cool and peaceful. Stars cast the sky in a gentle blanket of muted light. He didn't notice any of this as fear sidled up to him, peppering him with questions.

What if he was chosen to leave on the pilgrimage? What if the Inquisitor came back, tearing through the monastery like a thresher through a wheat field? Could he fight off an Inquisitor and win?

The shadowy shape of Adel approaching, tore him from his thoughts.

"What's going on?" Adel said as he settled

himself onto a stone bench beside Aeden.

"What are you doing here?" Aeden teased, not sure how to start.

"What!" Adel said, starting to get up, "You asked me here."

"I know, it was a joke," Aeden replied more quietly.

He wasn't sure how to start. What had Dannon once told him, *"Sometimes it's better to simply jump in than to dance about the fire."*

"I overheard the abbot talking to someone earlier today," Aeden said.

Adel regarded him with tired eyes as he sat back onto the bench.

"Do you know whom?"

Aeden paused. He wasn't sure if he should mention Blaise.

"No, I couldn't tell."

Aeden watched Adel roll his eyes.

"So, what was it they said?" Adel asked.

"Something about a pilgrimage."

Adel leaned forward, "did he say what the pilgrimage was about?"

"No, but the other monk, err, person sounded upset, and wanted to know if the abbot had sent word to a deacon."

Adel looked about the courtyard. The trees were cast in the faint sheen of moonlight. The blood oranges hanging from the trees looked like dark orbs.

"Did he say which deacon?" Adel asked.

"I don't think so, but it sounded like the abbot didn't want to send a message to that deacon," Aeden continued.

Adel sighed heavily into the night.

"You woke me up, you are defying monastery edict," he took in a breath, "all so you could ask me if I know about a pilgrimage that the abbot may have been referring to, and some unknown deacon that you don't know the name of, as he talked to some unknown person?"

Aeden blushed in the moonlight. It did seem a little vague now that he thought about it. He had been hoping that Adel would somehow know more about what he had overheard. Maybe waking Adel hadn't been the brightest idea.

For some reason, he was reticent to mention his hidden fears. More secretly he wanted to know if the abbot would send him away from the monastery, alone on a pilgrimage. He wanted to know if the abbot had sent word to the Inquisitors. Were they already coming for him?

"I'll make sure we win the next hand of *kayles*," Aeden pleaded.

"And how will you accomplish that?" Adel asked.

"Prayer?"

"I'm leaving," Adel said, rubbing his eyes and standing up.

"Wait, I know how to get hold of a king's delight, I know how you rarely get to eat them anymore."

Adel paused and looked at Aeden's silvery outline before sitting back down on the cold stone bench.

"Fine, carry on."

Aeden struggled with his next words. He was already dreading the extra chores he'd have to do to maintain his promise to his friend. He hated emptying bed pans. There were a dozen other things he would rather do.

"Well, I was rather hoping you'd be able to figure out which deacon the abbot may have been referring to," Aeden said carefully.

"You're incredulous, I like you, but you really are incredulous."

"Yeah, I know," Aeden said shrugging his shoulders, but he pressed on, "So? Would you know which deacon?"

Adel kneaded his temples as if he had developed a sudden headache.

"Everyone knows there's little love between Sawol and Bodig, maybe he's referring to Deacon Saron," Adel stifled a yawn with his hand, "or the deacon from," Adel paused again in thought, "there's another in the Monastery of the Cave, but I can't remember her name."

"He didn't say a name, but I think he was referring to the north."

Adel scratched his head in thought.

"The deacons to the north wield a lot of influence, some even command small armies. They're responsible for enforcing Sancire Law. I've only met one before, and he seemed more interested in money and power than in prayers."

"What would a man of god need an army for?" Aeden asked.

"God doesn't always step in to fight the battles of ambitious men."

It seemed strange to think of monks fighting. He'd seen the monks of this monastery and none of them seemed the fighting type. Yet, he had seen so little of Verold.

"Which deacon did you meet?" Aeden asked curiously.

"The Deacon of Somerset. I was only a boy, yet I still remember him riding in on a tall black stallion. His robes were dark and fine, like a lord's. I was all the way in the back, so I didn't get much chance to see his face, but I do remember he interrupted prayer and told us of our important new task. No more judgements for thirty days, as we were to spend our time praying for the armies of Fendrel the Great."

Aeden's curiosity was sparked anew.

"Who's Fendrel the Great?"

"You mean who was Fendrel the Great," Adel corrected.

"Sure, I meant who *was* he."

Adel smiled amusedly. Good, keep him amused and he'll keep talking, Aeden thought.

"He was the king of Sawol," Adel stated slowly, a smile still on his face.

"I may be a barbarian, but I'm not stupid," Aeden replied, he thought Adel was going to go into greater depth than a mere title.

A week ago, they had been discussing some topic or other and stumbled upon the story of Chronum the Destroyer. Adel was deep into the story of an early man of incredible power who challenged the church and killed thousands of the early Church Inquisitors, when Aeden finally realized Adel had been talking about one of the Thirteen. He had been talking about the god Kegal, husband of Gauri.

Aeden was smart enough to keep that nugget of information to himself.

"I know, I just forget what you know and don't know," Adel said soothingly. "He died in battle years ago."

"Did you see the deacon again?" Aeden asked, switching subjects, trying to get back to the original reason he'd dragged Adel out of bed.

"Yes," Adel said thoughtfully, "with the archduchess, wearing the Holy Armor of Sancire."

Thoughts of the archduchess robbed him of coherent thought.

"Alina Cynesige..." Aeden whispered almost reverently.

"That's the one," Adel replied. "So, the abbot's planning a pilgrimage?" Adel said trying to get back on topic.

Thoughts of dark hair splayed across a pillow were yanked from Aeden's mind. They were replaced with the image of an impossibly tall figure clad in black.

Aeden decided he wouldn't dance about his fears any longer. He woke Adel for a purpose.

"I heard the abbot say he was worried about the Inquisitors," Aeden said quietly, almost too quietly to be heard.

Adel nodded slowly.

"That's why you woke me," Adel finally said as realization dawned on him.

"Do you think the abbot would send me away to draw the Inquisitors away from the monastery?"

"They'd kill you," Adel said, "no, he couldn't. He wouldn't."

Adel's voice became firmer as he seemed to convince himself.

"Do you think the Inquisitor has forgotten about me?"

Adel remained silent for a moment and

looked off toward the blood-orange trees. The faint light of night played with their leaves, casting them in hues of grey and black.

"No."

Aeden had feared as much.

"Should I run?"

Adel now looked to his friend. He saw the emotions playing across Aeden's face. There was a hint of fear, but more prominently displayed was determination. Aeden's bravery was inspiring.

"I think you're safer here," Adel said firmly, "they wouldn't dare come back to the monastery after what had happened."

Aeden nodded his head slowly. Questions still played at his mind.

"What do you know about *them*?" he asked.

"That we're not supposed to talk about them," Adel responded, "but if you really want to know more I think Thomas knows more than I."

It was a rare admission on Adel's part, to admit Thomas knew more than him. There seemed to be a small competition of who was more knowledgeable.

"Great, let's go wake him," Aeden said enthusiastically.

"What?"

Adel's face took on a stern visage. He looked

ready to leap into an argument about right and wrong and the rules of the monastery. Aeden spoke in an effort to avoid another disagreement.

"I'm joking," he said with a smile and small shrug, "I know you just want to go back to sleep."

"Well you did wake me from a particularly good dream," Adel replied.

A gentle breeze played with the trees in the courtyard, lightly rustling their leaves. Aeden's mind churned over all the questions he had. For some reason, he was hesitant to let Adel leave. Aeden knew that once he was back under his blanket, he'd simply stare at the ceiling, his mind working itself into exhaustion.

Adel stood.

Aeden looked at his friend in the faint light. His shortly cropped hair had grown a touch long. His paunch was barely noticeable on his otherwise slender frame. And for some reason Aeden felt a great affection for him. He was suddenly thankful to Odilo for introducing him to Adel.

"Let's go," Adel said.

Aeden remained seated; one more question was nagging at him.

"Do you know what's behind the forbidden door in the crypt?" Aeden asked seriously.

Adel turned to look at him. His face was a mask of temporary confusion, followed by feigned annoyance.

"You certainly have a penchant for asking about the forbidden," he said, "No I don't."

Aeden smiled.

"Just checking. Last question," Aeden said, "Do you think the archduchess would invite a young monk to dinner?"

Adel only shook his head. He smiled and started walking back toward the cloisters.

Aeden got up and followed him. The smile fell from his face as he walked.

"You know Salvare's watching and protecting us, don't you," Adel said in an effort to comfort him.

Aeden only nodded. He appreciated Adel's words, he simply didn't believe them. Somehow, he felt that not even the Thirteen could keep the Inquisitors away.

"Let's get back to the symphony of farting monks," Aeden said.

Adel laughed as they walked down the corridor back to the room of sleeping monks. The sound of Adel's temporary laughter danced in Aeden's heart.

Chapter 31

"Anticipation often fuels the imagination to staggering heights of stupidity." Anonymous

The next day, Aeden finished his chores following Noon Prayer and was situated comfortably on the roof alcove, he enjoyed frequenting. Traffic was slow. A few days before, there had been the frenzied activity of a small group struggling to upright a tipped cart. Today, Aeden was left with nothing but his thoughts to entertain him.

Aeden thought on his talk with Adel. He thought about Inquisitors and the archduchess, and about being sent away from the monastery.

He took in a slow breath and attempted to clear his mind. It only partially worked.

A couple nights ago, Blaise had told the story of Ansuz the Imprisoned. Aeden closed his eyes and felt the steamy breath of the city wash over him and stir memory. The story replayed itself before his inner eye.

After the death of Huta, the son of Magis then known as Ansuz, the lands fell into a period of darkness. Verold felt old and brittle, as night settled heavily into the hearts of men. Pleasure was but a thought and a memory, and joy had been forsaken. Even the beautiful Bellas, wife of Ansuz, stopped her painting and sat despondently in a wreath of dying flowers. Verold had dissolved into the muted shades of grey and brown.

Salvare watched over this dark period knowingly. His weary eye observed the last of the Scapan in the hope that humanity would be worth saving. He saw Verold weep at the passing of Huta. Shrines of the darkest stone were built and imbued with the ashes of the false god. People traveled far and wide to cast their prayers upon his ashes, to touch the shrines, and beg for the light to return.

Ansuz witnessed the people's pain. He ignored the whispers of Salvare and unleashed his magic upon the darkened lands. He created an island of unequaled beauty. He cast it in perpetual light, so that twilight's deep purpling was the only shadow cast upon the ground. He shaped the forests, the water, and the soil into shapes and colors never before seen. He then shaped a city from the rocks, the trees, and the sands and called it Bryn Yawr.

When Ansuz had finished, he sat back and saw what he had created was good and beautiful. He called upon Bellas to cast her weary gaze upon perfection. Her heart leapt with joy and she resumed her painting. She painted until her fingers hurt and her eyes fell blurry. Soon people flocked to Bryn Yawr and sang the praises of

Ansuz above that of Huta, Ghut, and Zhov.

Salvare grew angry as he was ignored. Men stole his glory. Men worshiped men, when he was the true and only god, deserving of their praise. Salvare reached down and tore the very fabric of Verold. He wrapped the lands of Bryn Yawr unto itself, casting it in shadow. He then breathed into Ansuz' nostril the breath of ever-lasting life, cursing him to immortality. Salvare then banished him to the distant lands of Templas and chained him to the Hidden Cliffs of Desolare.

Blaise had turned the story into a moral tale of Salvare's mercy, power, and greatness. Aeden ignored most of the latter, for he felt the Thirteen were the true gods. Three of whom had been mentioned by Blaise as men playing at gods, members of the Scapan.

The story had stirred the deeply buried emotions Aeden had worked so hard to stuff under layers of platitude. At first anger bubbled to the surface. But with anger came the bitter taste of sadness.

The story of Ansuz reminded Aeden of his lost home. It was too easy to imagine an eternity away from all that one loves, one knows, to reside within the infinite realms of immortality, writhing in despair. Just as emotion began to tug once more at the brittle strings of his heart, he heard Odilo's voice, soft and hesitant.

"Aeden?" came the hushed whisper.

Aeden sighed as he gathered his thoughts and stuffed his feelings back down his throat. Within a moment, he was back in the courtyard behind some fruit trees. The familiar sweet scent of blood orange, hung heavily about him as he glanced about for Odilo.

"Let's go, there's going to be an announcement at dinner," Odilo stated from behind, startling Aeden.

Announcement? Was this to be his last night in the monastery?

"After you," Aeden said with a gesture, as a pit opened in his stomach.

Odilo nodded and limped off.

Dinner was normally a quiet affair. Gray-robed monks would sit and eat. Most began meal with a silent prayer and most would finish by taking their bowl to the kitchen. Today, however, was something different. There was tension in the air. It wasn't the desperate feel of worry that befell a group upon news of someone's loss. Instead it was the gossamer feel of hidden anticipation. Monks sat fidgeting in their chairs, breathing in the nervous energy that had settled over the table like a pall.

Aeden's eyes glanced briefly at those he knew and finally paused on Blaise. The older monk sat near the head of the table and wore a placid expression. This in itself was telling for his normal countenance was that of a man mildly amused at some unseen joke.

Aeden took a seat between Odilo and Adel.

His heart was pounding heavily. He thought on his options. Where would he go? His home of S'Vothe was not an option, nor was the greater S'Velt Valley. He had no interest to travel to the desert kingdoms. That left north, to Gemynd or south, to Sawol.

"You look pale," Adel said quietly, looking at Aeden.

Aeden's mind was swimming with thought and he had a difficult time reigning it in.

"Where would you go if you could travel anywhere?" Aeden whispered.

Odilo glanced at them and made a gesture for silence.

Adel nodded his head and accepted the chastisement. Aeden looked about to distract himself.

There were two baskets filled with barley bread adorning the center of the table, as of yet, still untouched. Creamy butter sat enticingly in pewter bowls. Fresh candles flickered and burned along the walls. Their oscillating flames danced like restless snakes.

Clearly something important was about to transpire. The only gossip Odilo had heard was there was to be an announcement. He wasn't a good source for monastery chatter, for he rarely partook in such guilty pleasures.

Aeden did recall a few monks whispering of drastic changes lurking in the shadows as they played and gossiped at the *kayles* tables. Of course, as with most gossip, there was nothing substantial to be gleaned.

Aeden glanced once more at Blaise. A shadow of fiery discontent had settled about the older man in an uneasy aura. He wondered if the announcement had something to do with the visit of the archduchess a few days before. An image of the archduchess frolicked in his vision. Her dark hair was splayed across silken sheets as her eyes danced and played in the light.

The footsteps of a heavyset monk scraped their way into his mind, tearing him from his imagination. A few eyes turned toward one of the entryways to the dining hall. It was the abbot. His thick body was momentarily cast in equal parts light and shadow. The faint wisps of gray on his balding head swayed as if bowing their own subtle greeting. The purple tinged bags under his eyes spoke of a night without sleep.

"Senior," the voices of the surrounding monks broke the silence.

"May the Holy Order rise again," the abbot said in response.

Abbot Filbert's voice was tired and weak, like

burnt parchment. His thin and nasally voice spoke up again. Every monk turned to listen, with eager thirst, as if they had been waiting for months.

Monahan glanced briefly at Jerome then to Aeden. His bloated face was redder than usual like the angry mask of a blood moon. Monahan squinted his narrow eyes and shook his head as a crooked smile fought its way onto his mole-like face. Was this about Aeden attacking a brother monk?

Suddenly a small sense of panic welled up inside of him. Aeden quickly glanced about, but no one else seemed to notice the exchange.

Of course, he thought, they needed an excuse to get rid of him. They couldn't just throw him out without reason. He had almost completely forgotten of his interaction with Bosco and Jerome. He now regretted pushing the weaker monk, yet the memory of the skinny monk sailing through the air still made him smile.

"Times have changed. It seems there no longer is the peace that was promised to us," Abbot Filbert paused and looked at each monk in turn. His eyes lingered for a moment on Aeden.

Aeden squirmed in his seat thinking of how he should defend himself. Really it hadn't even been his fault, but he knew that both Jerome and Bosco would have their own version of events. How could he have been so stupid as to let his temper get the better of him? The abbot continued.

"The brotherhood of the Holy Order of Sancire once stood strong, united, and resolute. It is now fractured and broken like too much glass. Petty bickering and infighting has cast the Order in shadow," again he paused.

Aeden took in a breath to speak. Monahan caught his eye and raised an eyebrow. Jerome fought to hide a smirk on his face, and Bosco did his best to wear an expression of pained regret. Just as Aeden was about to stand and plead his case, Adel cast a hand on his shoulder.

"Wait," the younger monk whispered.

Aeden was rarely one to heed another's advice. His failure to listen had often gotten him into trouble in S'Vothe. He glanced at Adel and saw his earnest expression. Aeden swallowed a lump in his throat and remained seated. The abbot continued, oblivious to the exchange.

"It seems that now we must strive to remove ourselves from this shadow and renew our faith by looking to the past. The past holds the key to the future. The strict rules of the First Age, that bound us, shall remold us into the light."

There was a quiet murmur that swept through the room like an ocean tide. The swelling current of thought overpowered the traditional silence of the dining hall.

"Silence!" The booming voice belonged to

Blaise. His face was masked in the red glow of angry displeasure. "Listen to the words of our dear abbot and reserve judgment for once understanding has dawned on your thick heads," Blaise said with emotion bleeding through his voice.

Filbert glanced toward him. Surprise rolled over his features like a cloud passing through an otherwise clear sky. Aeden was growing more anxious with each passing moment. The Thane valued honesty, integrity, and honor. In their culture, it was important to be the first to admit wrongdoing. It was considered cowardice to remain silent as others spoke of their misdeeds.

Guilt sat heavily upon his shoulders as he once again decided to speak up. The abbot beat him to it and all he could do was sit and listen as he was accused.

"That's why we must go forth and solicit those to the north and south, before the strange and twisted customs of Sawol claim our ways as their own. We must remind the people of the power of faith, the strength and unity of the Church, and that the Emperor doesn't rule all things on heaven and earth. We will shine a light on our strengths and cast the corruption of the Empire and their heathen ways to the seventh level of hell."

This was not what Aeden had expected. As a weight was lifted off his shoulders. confusion muddied his mind and cast a pall over the other monks at the dining table. Only Blaise seemed to fully understand the meaning of the abbot's words.

"I don't understand," Aeden whispered to Adel.

He was rewarded with a stern look from his friend and the abbot's pinched voice.

"Of course, let me simplify," the abbot, said a mild look of annoyance crossing over his face, "The Holy Order of Bodig will set forth on a quest to spread the word of Dominer the Pure." He paused and took in a shaky breath before announcing, "The Book of Divinus has been found."

Aeden raised his eyebrows and mouthed the word "pilgrimage" to Adel. Adel shook his head.

The hush of a moment ago, was broken as monks clamored to be heard. Voices rose and fell as a dozen debates sparked to life across the room. The abbot slunk quietly out of the room as confusion, fear, and anger grappled for supremacy.

Aeden observed the confusion. A strong hand grabbed his arm, ushering him away. It was Odilo. Aeden quickly grabbed a loaf of bread and followed his friend out, into the cool stone hallway, away from the agitation of the dining hall. The candles' flames bobbed and twisted at his passing.

"I can't believe they found the Book of Divinus!" Adel exclaimed.

He had followed Odilo and Aeden as soon as they had stood.

"There is much going on here, and we are glimpsing but the surface of a larger pond. It appears the ceremonial gift from the archduchess was of greater value to the Church than anyone could have guessed," Odilo said contemplatively.

"Not everyone," Aeden whispered.

Adel and Odilo turned to look at Aeden. They both held a look of curious doubt.

"Blaise, didn't you notice him a little more agitated than normal? He must have known." Aeden said.

"That means he probably knows more than half of the bickering lot in there," Adel replied.

Odilo cast a hand on Adel's shoulder, "they are our brothers, each and every one of them."

Adel cast his head down as if in apology, "you're right, I forget myself."

"Ok, so we're all forgetting ourselves right now," Aeden said with exasperation in his voice, "maybe we can find Blaise and see if he can remove some gray from the matter."

Odilo smiled and Adel looked at him quizzically.

"Remove some gray?"

Aeden paused, knowing his Heortian was

still juvenile at best.

"You mean clarify? You could always say 'shed some light on the matter'," Adel offered.

"Shed some light on the matter?" Aeden said as if testing out the words on his tongue, "that sounds stupid."

Adel shrugged as Aeden caught sight of Blaise. An angry shroud hung about him like a curtain. Odilo placed a hand on Aeden.

"Perhaps now is not the time for questions."

Despite curiosity's tugging inquisitions, Aeden agreed and let Blaise slip past, disappearing around the curve of the stone corridor.

Chapter 32

"Competition at times is bred from the fear of not belonging." Saying of the Gemynd

Aeden had difficulty sleeping that night. His mind was alight with curiosity. It whittled the hours away under the weight of cognition. He lay unmoving as the morning bell rang out, making a sound similar to a thousand monks chanting.

Aeden was exhausted and felt little motivation for the early morning routines. It was a light kick from Adel that caused the excessive thoughts in his mind to scatter like a flock of startled birds. He placed his feet onto the cold stone floor and began the monotonous routine of rolling his sleeping mat. He then folded and stowed his blanket.

As he stuffed his blanket into the trunk, he allowed his hand to grace the soft fur of the shroud cat skin within. Memories accosted him, entering through his fingertips and swept through his mind like an afternoon storm. He closed his eyes and saw Devon mocking a younger student fumbling with the gevecht. He remembered the hours of dark solitude he spent locked away in a stone room. Images of sitting on an outcrop overseeing S'Vothe and the S'Velt Valley lingered like Dannon's kiss. The memories soured in his mind. The twisted and burned remains of his village, the Master, Borin, Dannon, and the kovor, singed their way into his thoughts.

He closed and locked the trunk, casting his memories into shadow.

With a heavy heart, he followed the other monks to Morning Prayer. The courtyard adjacent to the cloisters was a watery gray. A cool mist clung to the morning with a hidden tenacity mirroring the clouded aspect of his heart.

The silent line of monks weaved their way past the courtyard, down a long corridor and to the central nave. There was the usual scattering of the unusually devout in attendance. They sat quietly, watching the procession of gray-robed monks enter the lofty space and settle onto their simple floor cushions. Small clouds of dust lingered heavily in the empty spaces within.

Aeden recognized most of the older faces. Each was cast in the pale light of early morning. Without fanfare, as was routine, they began their chanting prayers. Aeden had learned much of the routine and language quickly, the chants being one of the first things he learned.

"Ready light burns anew with each branching day
Whispering the lord's crystal song, spreading
flame
Scattering ash, and revealing his sacred verity

"Remember us, the children of flame,
Who cast out those of obvious blame,
Reining fresh the breath of light
For all of us to gaze upon his awesome might,

"And deliver us from those angry lips
So that glory sharpens and purifies us
From the ever-lurking hidden depths."

The prayers were repeated three times in low voices. Aeden was still reminded of the rumbling growl of the shroud cat. The reverberating voices echoed hollowly within the chambers of his chest and off the cool walls of the monastery.

The monks then stood, formed a line and quietly exited the nave. None glanced back as they moved down the corridor through an open wooden door and toward the dining hall. The weight of silence remained with the group as they brought out foods from the kitchen for the morning meal. Steamed oats, bread, and milk were placed upon the dark wood of the table.

Halfway through their meal Abbot Filbert showed up bringing another small plate of bread and butter for himself. A few eyes looked at the tired old monk, while others simply focused on their meal. Aeden glanced up, out of the corner of his eye, finding it strange to see the abbot again. The abbot often took food in his room. The rumor was he received fresh goat's milk, berries, and sweet rolls from the Red Market. Purchasing food, however, was strictly forbidden.

Filbert waited until the monks finished their meal, but before they began their chores to address the gray-robed group.

"There will be a pilgrimage," Filbert began, his voice taking on a new pitch of nasally discomfort, "The honor of accompanying the Book of Divinus beyond the Red City is an important task. I will only choose a handful of you."

The abbot closed his eyes for a moment and rubbed his forehead. He glanced about, seeing dozens of eyes trained firmly upon him. He began to speak again, but his voice faltered. On his second attempt, he squeezed out a few words, "By the next moon I will have decided. Devotion, discipline, and dedicated piety are the route to salvation."

The old monk then quickly stood and walked out. It was a rather undramatic close to his half-hearted attempt at a speech. His half-eaten bread lay unceremoniously upon his plate, hinting at his frame of mind.

All eyes watched him leave.

None spoke, a sharp contrast to the night before. Adel looked to Odilo who remained seated, slowly finishing his meal. Blaise gazed about the table as if daring anyone to talk. He then grabbed his plate and that of the abbot and took them to the kitchen. Monahan, Jerome and Bosco stood in unison, removing their plates and moved toward the kitchen. Their faces wore the placid expression of forced piety. The sudden change in demeanor was almost humorous to watch.

Aeden had the feeling that more than he could understand was transpiring. Despite being confined to the white walls of the Sancire Monastery; he was beginning to glimpse the greater world. It was as if Verold itself was forcing itself through the untended cracks and fissures so as to freely walk the corridors and whisper its changing tide into Aeden's young, deaf ears.

Afternoon couldn't come soon enough. Aeden had been waiting since the day before to ask Blaise questions. He had hoped to work near him in the gardens, but Blaise, as the sacrist, had other chores to attend to.

The day seemed even longer because most monks were doing their best to show their discipline and devotion. Most did this by working in silence. Many doubled their efforts, especially when others were watching. A few took it upon themselves to chant prayers as they worked. The change was startling. There were always a handful of monks, like Odilo, who were strict with their practices, prudent in their decisions, generous in their actions, and warm hearted in their dealings with others. This, however, wasn't the norm.

The most obvious reason for the sea change was likely the result of the recent restrictions still emplaced on the monastery. The monks wanted their freedom. Within the walls, life was sheltered from the political machinations and daily activities of the outside, but not completely. It was getting harder to ignore the whispering of the wind. Change was no longer relegated to back alley shadows. It had reared its ugly, diffident head, and people were reacting the only way they knew how, with fear and rumor.

People spread the seeds of gossip across the Red City and beyond the maroon hued walls to the greater kingdom of Bodig. The monks knew change was coming and many wanted the opportunity to explore or leave before things grew worse.

Word had made its circuitous way southward that the peasants and nobility were unhappy with the tithes charged in the north. Monks were growing fat off the people in exchange for prayers and the promise of salvation.

To the south whispers of reform swept across the land, striking fear into those who opposed change. Imperial soldiers marched and camped along the wide border to the southern kingdom in a diplomatic show of force.

From his secret alcove, Aeden watched and listened to his slice of the city. More often Aeden would see imperial soldiers walking the streets in addition to an increase in Bodig Guards. People seemed more anxious. Judgments lasted longer after Afternoon Prayer and ate into the free time of the monks. It was enough to make most anyone believe a pilgrimage had to be better than life within the monastery walls.

"I found Blaise," Adel whispered loudly, sounding out of breath.

Aeden glanced about to make sure no one else heard. No one had. In fact, the area was strangely devoid of people. He worked his way down from the roof and joined Adel by the fruit tree.

"Let's find out more about this pilgrimage and book," Aeden said, extending his hand as if gesturing for Adel to lead the way.

Adel gave a quick mocking bow before leading the way with an excited Aeden in tow. Aeden wore an aura of enthusiasm about him like a newfound cloak. He barely noticed as they passed other monks and walked up the wide stairway to the second floor. They made their way to the library where Blaise sat flipping through a book with the focus of a hawk. Warm light filtered in through glass pane windows in a rainbow of color.

Aeden and Adel stood before him, their patience as thin as a Dimutian razor-leaf. Apparently, their excitement radiated beyond them as though their souls had carved their way out of their bodies to tap the older man on the shoulder. Blaise looked up startled, the book in his lap slipping closed and nearly falling from his lap. A smile made its way onto his lips.

"What is it I can do for you fine, eager young men?" Blaise asked with a hint of amusement in his voice.

Aeden's stomach suddenly fluttered as he remembered his prior altercation with Bosco. Originally, he was going to confess to the sacrist before asking about the archduchess. He had changed his mind about asking Blaise of the archduchess and all thoughts of confession had flittered away. Now they had come rushing back like a flock of riled birds.

Adel looked to Aeden, who in turn looked to Blaise. He decided it wasn't the right time. The Book of Divinus was more pressing. At least that's what he was able to convince himself. Aeden didn't feel like prostrating himself before the other monks yet again.

"We'd like to know more about this pilgrimage and the Book of Divinus," Aeden said with hope bleeding through his tone.

"Well now, you certainly know how to ask a lot without seeming to ask much! Those are two weighty topics," Blaise said, rubbing his chin thoughtfully. "Which is more important to you and I shall begin there."

"Pilgrimage," Adel blurted simultaneously as Aeden said, "Divinus."

"I see, well that complicates matters. How about this? I will tell you about both, but the abbreviated version because of the hour of the sun," Blaise said, gesturing toward the prism of light pouring through the windows and spilling onto the floor.

The younger monks nodded their approval and scouted for comfortable positions to better listen without distraction. Blaise gathered his thoughts as he watched the two take their seats. With a serious look, he began.

"The book of Divinus is said to be as old as time itself. It predates the first age. Its pages were inspiring young minds to greater feats of virtue at a time when idle minds had yet to think of the idea of subjugation. Kingdoms, empires, and useless wars were nonexistent then."

Aeden sat and listened, his ever-curious mind already filling with questions and tearing into the logic of the story. It was one of his personality quirks that rankled his gevecht teachers. *Stories must be heard for their layers, their depth, and their meaning, not picked apart by idle minds attempting to squander intelligence to the wind,* a favorite quote from one of his teachers drifted through his mind, stifling his questions into oblivion.

Blaise continued, incognizant of Aeden's mental wanderings. "...it is the foundation of the Holy Order of Sancire. Before the Book of Divinus people were lost, worshiping the wind, the water, fire and earth in equal measure, assigning properties of life, intelligence, and divinity to each. These were the dark times when great powers were allowed to men, given to them to shape the world. A time when the written word was only beginning to take root in a way now lost and incomprehensible, a time when stories were accepted as fact. It was out of this darkness that Salvare breathed life into a young man, Galvin Dominer.

"He is now known as Dominer the Pure, for he was a vessel of the Holy Spirit. His hand was guided by the light to correct that which was wrong. He cast away temptation, weakness, and sought the strength that the purity of mind and body delivered to open oneself to the divine.

"Once he finished translating the word of Salvare to text, he began his holy pilgrimage. He began with a small group and gathered followers at every town he visited. Word of his wisdom, his compassion and the message from the book, spread to the towns ahead of him. Many people waited to hear his message. Others were fearful that the old gods wouldn't allow such strange new ideas to be tolerated. They readied themselves with the simple tools of the time, using them as weapons to ward off the gathering group that followed Dominer.

"It was one town in particular, Treton, which resisted his message the most. They weren't open to the light, to understanding. Their small minds prayed to their old gods as folk prepared for battle."

Blaise paused for a moment, looking at the two in turn, his face taking on the drama of his story. Adel searched his pocket for sweets as Aeden sat quietly.

"Dominer was ready, for he had been forewarned by Salvare. His group waited for ten days and ten nights, watching the patterns of the town. By the tenth day it had become obvious that Treton was beyond saving. The people were hopelessly lost in the old ways, lost to the light, and needed to be cleansed so that their eternal souls could be saved.

"And so Dominer and his followers set fire to the town of Treton and they prayed as they watched the walls burn, looking like ten thousand candles in the night. But the old ways were stubborn and backed by the Scapan, a small group of shapers skilled in the ancient arts of the arkein. It was the greatest of the group, Magis, who called upon the power of the old arts to cast down fire from the sky, wreathing Dominer in flame."

Aeden's curiosity was now like a fully fed

fire. Blaise sensed this and took a brief moment to pause, allowing the tension of the story to build before continuing.

"Dominer was still true to Salvare and called on him for protection, but he had fear in his heart and gave the text of Salvare to his closest follower, Sha'a, who swore to protect it and keep it safe. Salvare saw this lack of faith and chose to let Dominer face Magis unaided. The wreath of fire grew as Magis called upon the elements ruled by the old gods. Dominer sat in the center of the circle, silently, accepting his fate. He burned slowly from the unnatural flame, but didn't cry out once as he showed his final act of faith, thereby proving himself to Salvare and earning the name Dominer the Pure."

Blaise took in a long and slow breath. He glanced briefly at his hands as if they held some interesting piece of information unseen to the casual observer. Aeden sat listening, hoping for more. Adel scratched his head idly, waiting for the story to continue.

"Times have changed," Blaise finally said in a voice that sounded older, brittle, tired. "The Book of Divinus offered hope, but," Blaise's voice cracked and he took in a slow steady breath. "People no longer believe as they used to. There is an air of decadence and entitlement that didn't exist before. As much as the Archduchess of the Second House may press for conformation to the old ways, those days may no longer be here."

Aeden's ears perked up at mention of the archduchess. He was hungry for more information, to hear about what she liked, where she came from, any scrap of information to fill his dreams. Blaise, however, continued on his own tangent, ignoring Aeden's starving imagination for more mundane matters.

"The Emperor does not wish to see the Holy Order rise to the prominence it held only a hundred years earlier. Those with power and influence know this. Those without, simply wish to be left alone, ignoring the tedium of ritual that they believe is the Church. Without the right person, without the hand of Salvare guiding the way, another pilgrimage is likely to end in death."

His final words were nearly a whisper. The light that once flickered and danced in his eyes now faded to a dull gleam. His eyebrows were knitted together in a semblance of a frown as he studied the floor.

"So, you think we shouldn't try to spread the word?" Adel asked in mild surprise at the older monk's attitude.

"No, that isn't what I'm saying," Blaise rubbed his forehead absentmindedly. "I don't wish to take anything from you or to give you the wrong idea. In fact, it is likely that my old age has addled my mind and crossed my vision. I don't see things with the brightness and simplicity of youth. Now shades of gray layer the world in a wide net that at times seems to threaten my own beliefs, but don't let it swallow you up too," he said this last part wagging a thick finger in Adel's direction.

Bells clanged somewhere in the distance singing their dinner song. Monks shuffled into motion as if conditioned by the sound to stir into action. Aeden and Adel were no exception. Only Blaise remained seated, studying the cracks and fissures that spider webbed the cool stone floor.

Chapter 33

"A false face can only be held for so long." Saying
of the Gemynd

For Aeden the days passed more quickly
than he initially imagined. There were several
reasons for this. One, he was enjoying seeing
many of the monks' false attempts at greater
piety crumble with time. There was so little
discipline and such a lack of enforcement that
only those with a fervent belief remained faithful
to their pious devotion. Two, he had resumed his
practice of the gevecht. It felt good to move his
body, sweat, stretch, and exercise. The forms at
first came as a challenge, but as the days passed
they again began to reveal themselves and
allowed him greater clarity of thought and better
sleep. Last, and in Aeden's case the most
important, was his final understanding of the
Heortian writing system. Adel had been
spending months with him and still Aeden had
continued to struggle. Perhaps the silence of the
monastery spurned him to greater heights. Or
perhaps it was because of his resumption of the
gevecht, but either way the result was the same.
Aeden was finally able to begin reading the
books in the library.

He spent hours each afternoon and hours at
night combing through the books in the

monastery library. It was as if he had just discovered food and realized he hadn't eaten in months. His hunger for the dusty leather tombs was insatiable. The more he read the more he learned. Aeden soaked in early Church history, a book on saints and saintly deeds, church medicine and miraculous cures, as well as a history of Bodig. Every book he read kindled the hope to discover more about the archduchess.

A hidden more desperate part of him wished to uncover information on draccus fiends and his homeland. This of course was fanciful thinking. Draccus fiends were nothing but a myth to most people, something the Church frowned upon, when the myth wasn't furthering their own cause.

As for Jerome and Bosco, they unsurprisingly gave him a wide berth, no longer attempting their intimidations. Even Monahan seemed to be giving Aeden more space and when they did cross paths, he refrained more often than before from casting scowling looks of hatred and disgust. Of course, at meals and prayers they both ensured that they sat as far from each other as possible, this was only natural for false piety can only go so far.

Time passed as it normally does, in graduating fits and starts. Periods of entertainment glided by unimpeded, whereas chores and other mundane duties crawled past an ever-watchful eye. Each passing day marked itself upon the mental calendars of everyone waiting for the abbot's announcement.

So, it was on a clear and unusually cool night that the full moon had finally shown its wide, glowing face. That following morning, monks were ever more eager to show their solemn devotion to what they believed the Book of Divinus revealed. It was the day that Abbot Filbert was to announce who would join the pilgrimage and who would remain behind. Even Odilo seemed to be affected by the weight of the moon and the impending decision.

The folding of blankets and rolling of sleeping mats became a practice in diligent patience. Each movement was made with uncommon awareness reminding Aeden of home. The gevecht provided a medium for one to practice atori, the art of paying attention to everything while still keeping the mind clear and alert. Today was the first day that Aeden realized atori could be applied to more mundane tasks.

His teachers preached, "*Attention belongs to the moment, every moment, not just those of particular choosing.*" Despite their words, he had lacked the maturity or desire to fully understand their meaning.

With an air of excitement about him, Aeden followed the other monks to Morning Prayer. It was still dark when they entered the nave.

Candles flickered at their passing, struggling to light the interior. The procession of gray-robed monks solemnly found their cushions and took their seats.

Aeden glanced about, surprised to see how many were in attendance. It was as if the pious energy of the monks, hollow as it was, drew in a greater crowd. After a belated pause, the stillness transformed into a quiet storm. The monks had begun chanting. Their low tones reverberated off the walls, playing with the shapes and shadows of the corridors lining the nave.

The last sounds of the chant echoed into silence. The monks stood as though the crowd had broken into applause, but of course they had not. With great formality, they formed a line and walked out of the central nave and toward the dining hall.

To Aeden it felt as though they were walking a little faster than normal. It was as if the excitement the monks felt gave speed to their movement. Aeden fell in line behind Adel.

"Good service this morning," he whispered.

Adel made no motion to indicate he heard.

"You see the fat guy picking his nose in the back?" Aeden prodded.

Still Adel remained quiet.

"Today's the day," he continued.

Adel merely nodded, not wanting to break the vow of silence before daybreak.

Aeden smiled.

They entered the refectory, making a procession into the kitchens, each bringing out their breakfast. Every action was routine, yet there was the underlying feeling that everything was somehow different.

In S'Vothe, once a year, there was a holiday of sorts in which the instructors would switch roles with the students. Everyone looked forward to the change, the camaraderie. Rarely did any student make an instructor do anything too extreme for everyone knew the following day everything would revert back to normal. Today had a similar giddy quality.

The breakfast was nothing unusual; a single egg, bread, and some old cheese, except this time the quiet brought on a new texture. Somehow the hush of the hall seemed more pronounced, tangible, like one could reach out and grasp a piece of it.

As usual, Aeden sat between Odilo and Adel, as far as possible from Monahan and his crew.

The breakfast passed incredibly slowly. The anxiety in the room reached a crescendo that sought to overcome the sticky silence. Aden wasn't the only monk who glanced at the doorway in hopes of an appearance by Abbot Filbert. As thick as the hope was, the breakfast passed without event. To make matters worse, Aeden was assigned kitchen duties by a senior monk, along with Jerome and Bosco. Odilo and Adel were fortunate enough to get garden duty.

Most of the monks filtered out of the dining hall without a word as the kitchen crew attended to the plates, leftover food, and general tidying up that came with kitchen duty. The sun had finally made its belated appearance and the monks were allowed to talk. Few chose to, fearing their voices would break the palpable silence and negatively affect their chances of being picked for the pilgrimage. Aeden remained quiet because there was no one he wished to talk to.

The morning soon transitioned to afternoon. Chores were accomplished and Afternoon Prayer quickly followed. Once again, attendance seemed higher than normal. This prolonged Judgments, the time after prayer when townsfolk approached the monks for advice and penance.

People lined up to speak with the monks. Many simply complaining of small ailments and hoping for an easy cure or prayer to help with their malady. Others came with minor family squabbles or neighborhood feuds hoping for sagely advice.

By the time judgments were done, there was only an hour of leisure before dinner. Aeden decided to sit at his favorite alcove on the rooftop overlooking his small slice of the city. He figured if he was somewhere out of the way, he could clear his mind, relax, and daydream.

A cool breeze swept across the Red City, beckoning Hearvest to relinquish its grasp so that Vintas could enter the stage. Aeden closed his eyes and allowed the wind to whisper away his thoughts. The sounds of the greater city filtered to his ears, jumbled voices, echoing animal calls from a distant market, and the rumbling of carts upon the stone roadway.

An image of the archduchess crept subtly into his mind. She smiled and his heart felt warm. He closed his eyes again in an attempt to pursue the fleeting image. Try as he might Aeden had a difficult time daydreaming. After a few moments, he gave up and glanced down the street toward the distant rooftops sloping gently toward the River Lif.

According to *Knowledge of Bodig*, a book he recently read, the River Lif was an important trading route that at one time connected with a channel that traveled north to the Dath River. This route traveled past two of the major cities in Gemynd all the way up to Staggered Falls. If one remained on the river traveling west, they would make it to the Imperium Gulf, a slice of open water between Imperium and Dimutia. Closing his eyes, he could see the map as clearly as if it were before him. The images sparked memory, and Aeden was reminded of a recent dream.

The night prior he had dreamt he was on a

great ship traveling the dangerous waters to Templas, to seek out those who had made his sword. It felt so real that when he awoke his feet felt unsteady below him as if he had been standing on a swaying deck for months. He smiled at the memory and opened his eyes.

Without further preamble, Aeden slipped down the column and to the courtyard below. The blood-orange trees, that populated what he liked to consider 'his' corner of the courtyard, only held a few fruits as the season was drawing to an end. He passed the trees and the vegetable garden as he made his way to the stone path that carved a square about the courtyard. Aeden cast a quick glance toward the sky, attempting to judge the time. As if in response a bell rang out, speaking the dinner hour.

His stomach turned uneasily as excitement and a hint of fear tugged at his emotions. Aeden had grown comfortable at the monastery and was worried that some of the people he liked would be chosen for the pilgrimage and he'd be left alone. He felt like Odilo would certainly be picked, perhaps Blaise. Most of the truly pious were kinder; their departure would leave a hole in the monastery that would be hard to fill.

A more hidden and repressed fear bubbled to the surface. What if the abbot announced Aeden was the sole monk chosen to leave? What if the abbot had made a secret deal with the Inquisitors, sacrificing Aeden to save the monastery?

"Aeden!" Adel shouted before realizing himself.

Adel was still much like a child in many ways, more so than Aeden, despite being a few years older. Aeden liked this quality about him, it was refreshing. It made it easier for him to forget his guilt, forget the death of his people, but never for long.

A hidden shadow haunted his thoughts and tugged at his emotions, reminding him of his duty, his failure, his fear, and his neglected honor.

Aeden's fingers slipped from the lock of hair he always kept with him, a habit that he had formed without realizing it. Memories washed away as if overtaken by a rogue wave.

"Do you think he'll make the announcement tonight?" Aeden asked, clasping a hand onto the monk's shoulder, swallowing away the rising lump of emotion in his throat.

"He'd better, the day's been dragging by like cold dripping honey."

"You think your day's been slow. I spent half the morning watching Jerome pretend to understand piety and watching Bosco attempt to smile. It was awkward. He looked like a scared dog."

Adel looked thoughtful for a moment.

"I don't think I've ever seen Bosco smile, what a truly terrifying experience."

Aeden laughed. His merriment was quickly followed by a stab of worry. What if Adel was chosen, then who'd he have left to make jokes with? He attempted to stifle the emotion.

"You and Odilo will likely be chosen," Aeden said, trying to sound nonchalant.

Adel cast an eye to Aeden, studying his expression for a moment.

"Only Salvare knows."

"And the abbot," Aeden said.

"Right, and the abbot," Adel replied.

"Do you think that he might send me to *them*?" Aeden asked softly.

"No," Adel answered, turning to face his friend, "and if he did, then they'd have to face me as well."

Somehow this made Aeden feel better.

"Plus," Adel continued, "I think Salvare is saving you for a more spectacular death."

Aeden stopped and stared. It wasn't often that Adel used dark humor. The smaller, slightly older monk had a huge grin on his face. Aeden couldn't help but smile in return.

"A death where I'm ripped apart by naked, desirous nymphs."

Adel stopped at the threshold to the refectory and gave Aeden a dirty look, before stepping into the room and finding a seat.

Aeden stood at the doorway for a moment,

his stomach churning away at a hidden knot of anticipation.

"Fear is but an old friend who's worn his welcome," Aeden whispered to himself as he followed Adel in, remembering the words the widow Ayleth had told him more than once growing up.

The dining hall was already full. Normally the dinner bell rustled many from sleep and they'd wander in, rubbing their blurry eyes, taking their time to stumble in. Today everyone looked bright-eyed and anxious. Even the candles seemed to flicker differently.

A hand clasped Aeden's shoulder. Turning, Aeden saw Odilo. Odilo smiled, his eyes twinkling as if he had just heard a good joke. Aeden scooted over making room for his friend, pushing Adel none too gently, earning him a mock stern look.

Blaise stepped into the doorway looking for a seat. Many of the monks looked up, forcing Aeden to look back toward the entrance. He silently cursed himself for choosing a seat with his back to the entrance. He'd now be forced to look over his shoulder every time a monk's eyes tracked a newcomer in the hopes it would be the abbot.

Blaise nodded to a few of the monks in greeting and took a seat. Aeden watched him for a moment before glancing over the contents of the table in a feeble effort to quench his fluttering stomach. Barley bread, butter, salt, and a rounded dish with a red spice he hadn't tried before, adorned the dark wooden surface. A bowl of simple fruit lay on either end of the table. He studied the fruit for a moment as he noticed a few monks glance toward the doorway again.

Aeden shifted in his seat, as did Adel, to glance at the doorway. Odilo remained seated facing forward, ever quiet and content. Monahan stood at the doorway surveying the room in a knowing manner. His round face seemed to hold a secret as he smirked upon the seated crowd. Jerome and Bosco were quick to follow. The three of them circled the long table, eyeing a few available spots toward the end.

As Monahan was taking his seat, yet again monks looked to the doorway. It was becoming tedious, but Aeden couldn't help himself and he looked back once more. It was Abbot Filbert. Some of the earlier fidgeting had stopped and a deeper quiet settled over them like a widely-cast net.

"Senior," the monks said in unison, their voices forming a counterpoint to the silence.

"May the Holy Order Rise again," the abbot replied with greater strength in his nasally voice than normal.

The abbot surveyed the scene in a way that Aeden imagined a king would. A haughty air of self-righteous betterment surrounded him, giving him the appearance of greater importance. It would seem that there would be an announcement today after all.

The abbot cleared his throat and the monks stirred in anticipation.

"Please, don't wait on my account, grab your dinners, eat!" He said.

One could almost feel the disappointment in some of the younger monks' faces, Aeden's included. With a shuffling of feet and general noises of movement, the monks made their way into the kitchen to retrieve their food.

Aeden grabbed a wooden bowl that lay stacked on a shelf. He waited his turn as each monk stepped forward. Each monk held their wooden bowl in front of them as one of the kitchener's staff slopped two large spoons of pottage into their bowls. The pottage was a mix of grains, vegetables, and meat.

Aeden's bowl was filled with the mushy soup-like content. He nodded briefly to the serious cook then stepped forward following the monk in front of him. He recognized the dark haired, pale features of Thomas. Aeden watched as Thomas grabbed a large hunk of cheese and couldn't help smiling to himself.

The image of Thomas sniffing at it and hiding it in his trunk passed through Aeden's mind. Aeden grabbed a piece for himself and an extra one to give Thomas later. He then followed the gray-robed figure back into the dining hall.

Once seated, none stood on ceremony as they dove into their meals. Monks plucked at the bread on the table, some smothering it in butter before soaking it in their pottage. Others grabbed at the salt and spice to flavor their meal. Aeden tried a pinch of the red spice in his pottage. It added a tingling flavor similar to spicy pepper and garlic, a definite treat.

It wasn't until most of the monks were nearly finished with their meal that the abbot broke the relative silence.

"Monahan, would you please," Filbert said, gesturing toward the portly monk.

Monahan nodded to the abbot and struggled a moment to extricate himself from the bench. He then stepped past a vaulted archway and out of the refectory into a smaller room usually used for storage. It was one of the entryways to the undercroft.

An image of a thick, red door, untouched, resting heavily in the middle of an otherwise over-filled basement leapt into mind. He hadn't thought on that door for weeks, which was strange since he was normally attracted to the unknown. Perhaps now that he was more comfortable at the monastery he could find out what was behind the door.

Within a moment, Monahan returned with a

small leather-bound book. His sausage-like fingers began the tedious task of finding the correct page he had marked to read from. His mouth opened and he licked his lips before he began.

"A passage from the Book of Divinus."

A few startled expressions were chased about the room, jumping from face to face as if fleeing from the far end of the hall. Aeden figured they must have copied the holy text to ensure its preservation, while the abbot deliberated on who would join the pilgrimage.

"And so, the blood of bulls and sheep, the ashes of Treton's fall, venerate those who have passed, so that soldiers of Salvare may populate the lands, enduring hardship and disease, knowing the judgment of the lord within their hearts, so that the fruit of heaven may bestoweth powers of purity and sanctity upon those whose souls are clean of virtue and beholden of the light."

Monahan carefully closed the book and walked to the abbot. Filbert held out his hands, accepting the text with a gracious bow of his head. Aeden watched in fascination.

"What in the hells did that mean?" Aeden whispered to Adel.

Adel elbowed him sharply in the ribs. Neri looked up from across the table and smirked. Monahan returned to his seat and Abbot Filbert addressed the waiting monks.

"It's our turn to spread the holy word of Salvare, the pilgrimage begun by Dominer the Pure will resume at the Fallen City of Treton and continue northward through Gemynd before going seaward to the great southern kingdom of D'seart.

"Those who will accompany the book will have to be brave of heart, strong in character, and accepting of Salvare's way. It has been a difficult task for me to choose who will go and who will stay." The abbot paused, affecting a look of deep concern, before continuing, "Remember those who remain, will reflect the virtue and strength of the monastery, and as per order of the magistrate will be allowed beyond the white walls of our temple and onto the streets of the Red City once more."

There was a pause as the abbot allowed the words to settle in. The monks looked at each other, many smiling in excitement. Quite a few had lost some weight under the strict rules, while a few grew rich from their brother monks' desires.

Aeden felt a weight lift off his shoulders. If he wasn't allowed to join the pilgrimage at least he'd have the opportunity to further explore Bodig. Maybe there was a chance he would run into the archduchess. His elation was cut off by the nasally voice of the abbot.

"As for who will accompany the great book," the abbot paused, pulling out a piece of parchment. His old fingers fumbled for a moment as he struggled to unroll the text. "Brother Bosco of The Plains, Brother Neri of Sha'ril, Brother Adel of Bodig, Brother Odilo of Bodig, Brother Thomas of Gemynd, and Brother Aeden of…" Abbot Filbert seemed to search for words, then seemed to think better of it and continued.

"For those who I have not called, please understand the decision was difficult and required hours of prayer and the guiding hand of Salvare. For those who have been chosen, please meet me in my room."

With that, the abbot stood, holding the copied text of Dominer the Pure under his arm. With one last glance about the room, the abbot strode out, leaving the monks to chew over his decision.

Chapter 34

"And so their feet tread upon the ground with the sanctity of the lord deep in their hearts." Book of Divinus

Aeden looked at Adel who wore a similar expression of shock. How was it they were chosen for the pilgrimage?

"It appears we're to be on an adventure," Odilo said, ushering them out of the room.

Outside the refectory in the cool stone corridor was Thomas. Standing nearby leaning against the wall was Neri. They were like salt and pepper. Where Thomas was pale and blue-eyed, Neri was dark skinned with ebony eyes, studying the group with a detached expression. The last to exit the dining hall was Bosco's tall, skinny frame. He ducked into the hallway, his face a carefully concealed mask of disdain.

"Let's get to it," Thomas chirped as he fidgeted with his hands, earning a few looks.

Aeden glanced about at the group. Were they picked for their youth and potential stamina? Aeden wondered if someone didn't want them around the monastery. His mind instantly went to Monahan, but if that were the case why was Bosco part of the group? Before his thoughts could travel too far into the shadowy corners of church politics, Neri spoke.

"Interesting group he chose, isn't it?" he said to no one in particular, his words echoing Aeden's thoughts. "I wonder how a novice was chosen for the pilgrimage," his eyes briefly settling on Aeden, emotionless as a wide body of water.

Neri's look of detached indifference clung to him like a second skin, marking his words as more of a statement. One that Aeden was wondering himself, but didn't dare ask. He realized he had been harboring the secret desire to leave the monastery and see the greater world. If he had been forced to stay while Odilo and Adel left, he would have been miserable.

There was a secondary and underlying emotion that refused to go away. It remained wedged deep within his throat like a thorn. It was the hidden fear of the Inquisitor. The dark, hulking mass that barely moved when Aeden had shoved him. What if he had been chosen as bait to lure the eyes of the empire away from the Holy Order of Sancire, Bodig?

He stuffed the thought away as he watched the group make their way down the corridor toward the stairway to the second floor. He followed. From there it was a quick jaunt to the second level. They followed an open-aired corridor around a corner toward the abbot's quarters. From this side, they could see the final light of day. The sun was setting, casting long fingers of golden light upon one edge of the courtyard below.

The group paused at the threshold.

Aeden looked across the courtyard toward his hidden alcove, realizing for the first time he would no longer need that spot to see the world. Part of him felt saddened at the thought. Thomas stood next to Adel and Neri, all eagerly waiting at the threshold of the abbot's room. The door stood open, waiting.

"You may enter," came the muted nasally voice of the abbot.

Thomas, Neri, Adel, and Bosco entered, leaving Odilo and Aeden standing in the vaulted corridor. Aeden was still leaning on the stone railing. Odilo stood next to him for a moment looking across the courtyard toward the corner with the blood-orange trees.

"No more dreaming, it's time to see Verold for what it is," Odilo said with a light grip on his arm.

Odilo's hand slipped away as he turned and entered the abbot's room, his slight limp and bald head now infused Aeden with feelings of warmth and security. Aeden nodded briefly to himself and followed him in.

The room was quite lavish. There was a tall wooden cabinet filled with books. Silver candelabras stood like luminescent sentinels in each corner, casting back the darkness. A bed rested languidly in the corner. Last, a simple table and two chairs hid behind the open door.

Most importantly were the items on the table. They drew Aeden's attention like a bear to honey. It was the Book of Divinus, a map, and six leather purses.

At the center of the room stood the squat figure of Abbot Filbert. He looked at each of them appraisingly, a glint of intelligence twinkled in his eyes. Aeden had always assumed he was rather daft, but now he began to reassess the older monk.

"My brothers, welcome and congratulations!" Filbert said with a dramatic flourish. "Your devotion and discipline to the old ways have garnered you a place on this sacred task." The abbot glanced significantly toward the book resting heavily upon the table. "There are some things you must know before you depart, for the roads may not be as safe as they once were."

Bosco glanced about as if looking for an exit. Neri raised an eyebrow but otherwise remained nonplussed. Thomas appeared to be the ever-perfunctory student, nodding his head in apparent understanding. Aeden just stood quietly, listening.

"I have dispatched pigeons to our sister monasteries in Gemynd," the abbot continued.

"We have pigeons?" Aeden asked innocently in surprise.

Odilo placed a hand on his shoulder as if to

calm him, as the abbot gave him a stern look.

"As I was saying, I have dispatched pigeons, and yes we have pigeons." His overly narrow-set eyes locked onto Aeden's waiting to see if further interruption would follow. It didn't, so he continued. "Two have returned. One with a message of welcome, the other with a word of warning. It appears the son of Geobold has died, leaving Gemynd without a legitimate heir. This has begun a quiet power struggle for the throne as the Emperor's soldiers have set up camps to deter unwanted behavior and ensure the peace.

"As monks of the Holy Order of Sancire you should have no trouble. You'll still be welcomed into peoples' homes, allowing for warmth and food, to rest your travel weary legs. However, I'm a realist and expect there will be times you need to pay out of pocket. Upon the table are six, coin purses to be used only in dire need, and most importantly to secure passage aboard a ship for your eventual journey south."

Bosco now looked white in the face as Adel gave Aeden a broad grin. Aeden took a step closer to the table and leaned forward to look at the map that lay next to the worn Book of Divinus.

"I see Brother Aeden has taken an interest in the map," Abbot Filbert resumed. "Please, stand around, for it shows the path I wish you to take."

The monks squeezed behind the door and

stood shoulder to shoulder in the tight space looking down upon the map. It was a crude piece of leather painted in faded lines demarking political territories and the rough location of key cities. A fresher red line showed a simple path traversing a few key cities.

"Since Aeden seems to be the most eager, I only think it appropriate that he be responsible for your navigation." The abbot then took a moment to appear pensive. It was a passable act that lasted the length of a slow breath. "Odilo is the most senior of you and shall be in charge. Thomas, you are familiar with Gemynd and will provide whatever insight you feel is necessary to your brother monks to prevent any," the abbot looked up thoughtfully as if trying to find the word he was looking for painted on the ceiling, "cultural misunderstandings. Neri will do the same for the southern leg of your journey, providing language and translation as needed. Last, Bosco."

The abbot glanced at Bosco then to the old copy of the Book of Divinus. "It will be your duty to keep the holy book safe, only to be shown to the monasteries marked on the map, so that they can make copies of it, before you resume your journey.

"May Salvare watch over you, guide your steps, and the light be bright upon your backs."

The abbot then watched as each monk took a

purse. Aeden rolled the map and held it firmly in his hand, his other hand clutching the coin purse. Everyone watched as Bosco reached for the Book of Divinus. The energy in the room was palpable as though they feared the book would burst into flame upon contact. Bosco picked it up and nothing happened, the feeling passed like a wisp of smoke.

"Take this to help keep it safe," the abbot said, handing an oiled cloth with elaborate markings to Bosco.

With those final words, Filbert shooed them out, with outstretched hands, as if herding chickens out of a coop.

PART THREE
Pilgrimage

Chapter 35

*"The virtue of the spoken word can paint a picture
that will fill a thousand pages." An Arkeinist's
Written Manual, Second Edition*

Gemynd was an interesting place. In the
first age, there was a history of draccus fiend
attacks that forced the residents to live in the hills
and underground. Toward the end of the first age
the draccus fiends became fewer in number and
retreated to The Isle of Fire far to the north. This
allowed the nomadic peoples of Gemynd to settle
and build cities.

The sudden freedom to build, created an
artistic renaissance of architecture and expression
heretofore unseen in Verold. Great cities were
born and dedicated to various ideals of
aesthetics.

By the end of the second age, Gemynd had

become one of the greatest kingdoms of the land.
Soon thereafter, news of this wealth spread and
drew in the wild tribes from the Gwhelt. There
were numerous raids, in which institutions of
learning were burned to the ground, wealth was
stolen, and women were taken as slaves.

The nobles of Gemynd reacted by seeking out
the secret members of the *Syrinx* to enlist their
services to defend the land. They were only
partially successful, for they found a member of
the Arkein, but not a true defender. The wizard
they found was twisted and although he did play
a large part in ending the raids it was at a terrible
and bloody price. Since that time, any form of
magic was looked upon with great distrust and
zealous anger. It was because of this the annalist
despised any interactions with those to the north,
the rhabdophobes of Gemynd.

It was on a cool Lenton day that the annalist
made it covertly into Petra's Landing. He had
already traced Aeden's steps from Bodig through
the countryside, towns, villages, and cities of
Gemynd. He had asked his questions, uncovered
hidden records, digging ever deeper into the
master arkeinist's past, trudging through
memory in an effort to seek the truth, the sharp
edge of fact that shaped reality.

Each relived memory cast upon paper was
like a weight upon his chest. Revelations of truth
threatened to unburden his heavy heart of the
load he carried, the onus of a long-buried hatred

for the man he sought.

Each difficulty the young Aeden endured was like a sliver of starlight piercing the otherwise dark night sky. There was less joy in uncovering these hardships than the annalist had originally thought. And now he was in a dangerous city, yet again risking his life, for duty to his king, responsibility to the realm, and the survival of his people. It was his last stop in the three kingdoms before heading to the deep southern deserts.

He needed to be careful. Having studied magic, his blood now coursed with the arkein, an intransmutable energy that marked every person of the second order or higher. Petra's Landing was infamous for "blood sniffers" as they called them, ambits of singular design, to detect the presence of magic.

The annalist knew he would have to be quick about his work, attentive to his surroundings, and furtive in his dealings with the populace. Nothing less would do. Hunting the history of Verold's most powerful man required all the skills a master annalist could bring to bear.

Chapter 36

"Beginnings have a way of burning themselves into memory." Saying of the Gemynd

The monastery bells clanged their morning song, rustling monks from restless dreams. Aeden was already awake, his mind had whittled away the hours of night, imagining the path before him. Attempting to imagine the unknown was as difficult as trying to drink from a waterfall, something Devon had dared him to do once. A wry smile made its way to his lips for the span of a breath before he sat up in bed.

As had become his routine, Aeden rolled his sleeping mat and stowed it behind his trunk. His movements were clumsy and distracted. He then folded his blanket and set it inside his strongbox. It took him a moment to fiddle with the lock, one he had purchased from the monastery black market in exchange for doing some unwanted chores.

He glanced about the long room, noticing the other tired-eye monks going about their business. No one was paying him any attention, it was too early, and the only source of light was a fat candle burning in a far corner.

He pulled back the thick skin of the shroud cat to reveal the dark Templas blade sheathed in its midnight scabbard. With a quick and deft

movement, he removed the sword from the trunk
and slipped it under his robes. Aeden hadn't
touched the cool handle since he had arrived at
the monastery, it felt good. His hand tingled at
first contact and a renewed sense of purpose
settled over him with confidence.

Aeden took a moment to retie the rope sash at
his waist, securing the sword to his hip. He
looked down at the folds of his loose-fitting gray
robes, made an adjustment before grabbing the
small leather purse and the rolled leather map.
He tied the purse to his belt, which now felt
heavy and tight against his hip. The map he
slipped into a makeshift pocket he had sewn into
a fold a month before. With one last look upon
the shroud skin fur, Aeden closed and locked the
trunk. It was time to begin a journey.

The refectory was uncommonly quiet and
dark that morning. While the other monks went
to Morning Prayer the six chosen for the
pilgrimage, sat about an overly long wooden
table and consumed a simple breakfast of rolled
oats and buttered milk. There was no talking as
was customary. Instead they eyed each other in
short glimpses as they ate, anxious to start the
trip and fearful of what the road would bring.

Slowly and one by one, the monks finished
their meals and brought their wooden bowls to
the kitchen. They rinsed them in a standing basin

of water and set them aside to air dry. Without ritual or further ado, the group slipped out into the dark, stone corridor and toward the nave.

Aeden fell in behind Adel, following the overly excited Thomas.

His stomach twisted into a knot of anticipation and struggled to digest his meal as if he had inadvertently swallowed a stone.

"Where's everyone?" Aeden asked in a faint whisper.

Adel glanced about as if noticing for the first time that it was strange to not see any of the other monks.

"I thought we'd get more of a sendoff than this…" Aeden continued.

"Strange," was all Adel said before Thomas stopped and looked at them.

The two of them fell silent.

They rounded a corner and came upon the large open space of the nave.

The nave itself was cast in shades of gray as the morning light had yet to cast its luminescence on the white-walled monastery. The monks passed their cushions without a second glance and came up short. Aeden noticed them first, his eyes having adjusted to the dim yellow pools of light, cast from fresh sputtering candles along the wall.

Standing within a fold of shadow were all the

monks of the Holy Order of Sancire, Bodig. At their approach, the abbot opened the doors to the nave, letting in the first slivers of pre-dawn light. A waft of cool air swept in, speaking the gentle note of Hearvest.

"Found them," Aeden whispered.

Adel rolled his eyes and smiled.

The grey-robed monks lined the walls of the nave much like the imperial soldiers had shortly after Aeden had first arrived. So much had changed. It was odd to think he was leaving the safety of the monastery walls.

He would no longer need to get up and fold his mat. He wouldn't have to attend morning prayers or administer afternoon judgements. He would no longer play *kayles* with the other monks. He would no longer sit upon his hidden alcove and dream of Verold.

He was going out into Verold.

Aeden went down the line of monks. Many he knew only in passing. He recognized some from the *kayles* tables. He nodded a greeting to Pate. Aeden smiled at a monk named Jonathan. He passed Jerome without so much as a hello.

He nodded to Monahan who wore a heavy expression of immeasurable indifference, yet his beady eyes spoke of a hidden plan. He shook the hands of many of the monks, not having been in the monastery long enough to develop the true sense of brotherhood that those who came as children had.

It was before Blaise that he paused. The bear-like monk wrapped him up in a hug and whispered in his ear.

"Keep them safe brother Aeden. I know that of the chosen, you are the one who can. The roads aren't safe, don't trust everything you see or hear, listen to your heart and avoid the Imperial Guard when possible."

Aeden withdrew from the bear hug and took a step closer to the massive monastery doors. Adel was ahead of him, standing before Abbot Filbert. The abbot stood there appraisingly. His face was half cast in silvery strands of light.

Adel shook the abbot's hand and stepped outside following Thomas, Odilo and Neri. Aeden glanced to his right and saw Bosco with his head close to Monahan, his face a mask of keen interest.

Aeden shook the smaller hand of the abbot and stepped out into the pre-dawn morning. He glanced at Adel and saw him wipe a small tear from his eye. Odilo stood by him wearing a look of compassion. Neri seemed nonplussed to leave. Thomas stood, studying the sky with a faint look of nostalgia, his hands clutching a small bit of cheese.

Finally, Bosco emerged and the group of six was ready to truly begin their pilgrimage.

They quickly moved down the wide stone

steps and onto the red-cobbled street of Bodig. There was little traffic at this hour. Storefronts were shuttered and streets lamps had run out of their nightly oil, leaving everything to shine a dull gray-red. The sky shone a brilliant violet as the sun worked its way out of its nightly cradle. The monks breathed in the city air and followed Odilo down the labyrinth of streets toward the northern gate.

The sights were a welcome distraction from the fear of leaving the safety of the monastery. It had become home for the monks, and even Aeden was feeling the queasy effect of apprehension play upon his innards.

He suspected they were all processing it in their own way. They were no longer within the monastery walls. They could speak if they had so chosen, but instead they chose silence. It blanketed them as they walked. It defined them as they swept through the awakening city.

With the determination of pious action, they crisscrossed alleys, passed wider streets and finally found themselves upon a boulevard, waking with the rising sun. Already merchants were opening stalls as the early risers, mostly the elderly, graced the city streets.

Aeden didn't recognize this section. He glanced about as they passed through a tall gate embedded within a wall of red. The whole city, he had read, was divided into sections to purposefully increase the number of fallback positions if the main walls had been breached.

The streets were offset, staggered, winding, and sometimes dead-ended at walls or buildings, all in an effort to befuddle an enemy combatant. The consequence was few people truly knew the entire city of Bodig, it was simply too confusing.

The boulevard sloped gradually downward, toward a tall wall now highlighted by the first rays of light. The semi-translucent bricks glowed a gentle maroon. It was an image Aeden would never have imagined in a hundred story tellings.

There were larger, wider buildings lining the broad street as they approached the looming city wall. The buildings had no windows, just oversized doors. There was a greater flurry of activity in this quarter of the Red City, mostly younger, well-muscled men moving about with great purpose.

"Amazing isn't it," Adel said, having caught Aeden's wandering eye for a moment.

The unspoken silence had been broken.

"I had no idea a city could be so busy," Aeden replied.

"You should see the ports on the southern side," Adel said with a flourish. "They also have some of the best pastries in the city," a grin formed on his boyish features.

"Alright, we're going the wrong way, let's turn around," Aeden announced rather loudly, "pastries are to the south."

Adel shook his head. Thomas looked confused. Odilo paused, looking back, noted the interaction between Adel and Aeden before smiling and continuing. Neri simply ignored them.

"You sure we're going the right way?" Aeden asked more quietly, "I thought we were supposed to make a left, a right, then two lefts, go straight over the hill, pass the market and then take a right."

Adel smiled, "Or was it four lefts, then two rights and under the hill?"

Thomas chimed in, not understanding their humor, "we're nearly upon the city gate, of course this is the right way."

Adel and Aeden looked at each other for a moment.

"Maybe I'm reading the map wrong," Aeden said, pulling it out and pretending to examine it, "I'm pretty sure the blue part demarcates land."

He said the last scratching his head.

Adel coughed to mask a laugh. Bosco wiped at his nose and ignored them. Odilo and Neri continued walking ahead.

"Blue marks water," was all Thomas said.

"Makes sense," Aeden responded seriously.

He turned to watch men carrying impossible loads upon their heads and shoulders.

Soon the monks were upon one of the massive gates of the main wall. Tall wooden doors reinforced by black metal, stood open, allowing a waft of air to tunnel into the city. It brought the smells of spices, sweat, and death.

The group of six monks passed through the gates, garnering a few looks from the workers, a few paused to nod their respect, and some grunted a simple prayer greeting, *"may the light be upon your back."*

A wide road already lined with carts trailing into the distance, traveled northward away from the capital. A small town of sorts had grown up outside the city walls. There were wooden structures that had the hobbled appearance of a quick assembly. Wagons and carts were scattered about in a semi-orderly fashion. City guards were posted near the city gates overseeing the chaos as Bodig inspectors, merchants, and traveling salesmen discussed prices. It was a chaotic and organized mess.

Odilo had turned and paused, facing the city wall behind them. Aeden turned to see what caused the senior monk to stop. Swinging gently and suspended from the red-brick wall were a series of cages. Each cage contained a person in various states of decay. Aeden couldn't have been more shocked if Odilo had turned to punch him in the gut.

He was transfixed by the sight.

Part of him wanted to turn and look away. Another part of him was morbidly curious. As much as he wanted to look away, he could not. Aeden held his hand reflexively to his nose as the smell of rotting flesh, blistered by the sun, created a stench unlike any other.

The cages on the left held the barely living; their heads were shaved and tarred. Their skin was burned by the sun as intense thirst robbed them of coherent thought. The cage in the middle held a naked man of indeterminate age whose body was held together by rope. His limbs had been severed from his torso only to be crudely attached by hooks and ropes, all suspended from the iron ring at the head of the metal coffin. Those on the right held the decaying remains of men with crude signs strapped to the bars, "thief," "rapist," murderer."

He had seen death's hand before, but in S'Vothe the dead were treated with respect and burned in pyres. They were never allowed to decay. It was revolting. Even the metal bars of the cage were in a state of atrophy. The wind, the rain, and the corrosive effects of too many wasting human bodies, had painted the joints and edges in various stains of red, white, and yellow.

Aeden swatted at an angry cloud of flies that buzzed about the scene. Groaning and desperate pleading cut through the din of merchants like the hiss of a startled newborn draccus weasel.

The sounds turned his stomach.

"They're called gibbets. They're here to punish particularly severe criminals and function as a statement of warning to potential criminals," Adel whispered to a shocked Aeden.

Aeden glanced at Adel. His young aquiline features seemed unaffected by the cruelty of the punishment. It was in juxtaposition to moments before when tears stained Adel's eyes at the prospect of leaving home, his family, his friends. Was this normal? Was the unreality of death too far removed from juvenile mental wanderings?

Odilo had already begun murmuring a quiet chant that was soon taken up by the small group of monks.

> *"Passing life, fading light*
> *Release this soul to flight*
> *So that peace sought*
> *Hard one and fought*
> *Becomes eternal light."*

The monks did this at every gibbet, hands raised in prayer. Merchants and city inspectors paused to watch them pray, some whispering the same words under their breath. A quiet settled briefly over the area as if Salvare himself had stepped onto the scene, ushering those present into silence. Even the groaning stopped as tortured ears strained to hear the sacred words of passing, so that they too could leave their mutilated existence and find peace in the afterlife.

The prayers stopped and the trance was broken. Debate over taxes and the value of wares resumed, as the monks left the final gibbet that contained nothing more than the tattered rags, bones, and bits of decaying flesh of what once was a man.

Chapter 37

"The road oft frequented can bring greater disquiet than the one less traveled." Book of Khein 8:4

The stone road was long and heavily traveled. The kingdom of Bodig was far larger than Aeden could have imagined. They had walked for hours, and as far as he could tell, they had only made it a quarter of the way to the first monastery marked on the map.

It was a warm day that only served to lengthen the passage of time. They had left behind the hubbub of the Red City and fell into a quiet rhythm. The road fell away before their feet as the sun burnt away the few stray clouds that were unfortunate enough to remain. It wasn't until the early afternoon that they stumbled upon their first respite from the sun.

Ahead was a caravan along the side of the road. Three loaded carts sat heavily upon the cobbled stones. A tall, young man stood watch and eyed their approach. Another older man, with a balding head, clasped a hand onto the younger man and yelled out to the monks.

"Welcome brothers! Please come and join us for some rest, food, and shade," he said in an accent that Aeden couldn't place.

"Thank you friend," Odilo shouted in return, startling Thomas.

The monks hastened their step and entered
the small circle of shade, cast by the towering
goods, stacked on the carts. Two women stepped
out from a cart, one older and one younger. The
younger one caught Aeden's eye. She wore a
simple dress of sorts, but its thin fabric clung to
parts and hid others in a manner that beckoned
to him in a non-clerical manner.

"Have a seat, you must be tired and thirsty,"
the older man said as he stepped forward
offering a smile.

Thomas placed his hands together in thanks,
as did everyone else, except Bosco and Aeden.
Bosco seemed too discomforted to make the
effort. Aeden on the other hand, was still mildly
distracted, for at that moment the girl caught his
eye and smiled a smile of knowing innocence.

"Have something to drink, it isn't much," the
older woman said, handing a water skin to Neri.

Neri took a quick sip and handed it to
Thomas. Thomas didn't drink and instead
handed it to Adel, who handed it to Odilo. Odilo
took some water and handed it to Bosco. Bosco
took a long pause to quench his thirst before it
finally arrived to Aeden.

The water was stale and tasted of minerals,
but he was thankful for something to quench his
thirst. Traveling as a monk seemed to have its
benefits.

Aeden glanced once more toward the man's

daughter. Her young form seemed so pure, so innocent.

"It's less common to see monks traveling the roads these days, with recent events being what they are," the man said offhandedly.

This tore Aeden's attention away from the distractions of adolescence.

"What news do you speak of?" Odilo asked calmly.

The woman looked to the man, who in turn rubbed at his forehead. The greater weight of the Imperium settling temporarily upon his shoulders.

"The Inquisitors' Army has moved to surround the town of Willow Hill," he said quietly, as if afraid of being overheard.

"Why?" Neri asked bluntly.

None of the monks objected, they were all thinking the same.

"We assumed," the man paused, "meaning no offense, we're people of the Church," he said turning to look back at his family, "that *they* marched as a response to the immolation."

Odilo nodded his head, "The seat of Subdeacon Lief is within the Willow Hill Monastery, along with Abbot Favian, both have vocally opposed the emperor," he said so softly that Aeden could barely hear him.

Odilo's eyes looked heavy.

Aeden watched Odilo for a moment, uncertain of how to comfort his mentor, before another thought wrestled its way to the surface.

Aeden pulled the map out from his pocket, as remembered images of the monk in the Red City plaza burned within his mind. He then recalled the Inquisitor within the monastery walls, along with a contingent of Imperial Soldiers. The last image to resolve itself before his mind's eye was the impossibly large figure of the Inquisitor. His menacing shadow swallowed the light.

The images dissolved into watery pictures of broken emotion.

Why Willow Hill?

Moving on a smaller town would be easier, he imagined. No town magistrate. No seat of some king or great noble house to impede their efforts. The townsfolk would have little recourse but to capitulate to the Inquisition's demands.

Aeden glanced at the map. Willow Hill was to the east, and thankfully not on the great North South road.

"Have you heard or seen any more of *them* along the roads?" Thomas asked.

Odilo stepped closer and placed a placating hand on Thomas' shoulder. Adel looked equally curious. Bosco slunk back, as if fearful of the entire conversation.

The man simply shook his head. He wiped again at his forehead.

"Where are you headed," Odilo asked, changing the tone of the conversation.

"The Red City," the man said, gesturing to his carts, "we've got the finest pottery this side of the Dath River," he said proudly, feeling more comfortable with the new topic.

"You hail from Somerset," Odilo stated.

The man seemed mildly surprised, but the expression passed from his face quickly. "Yes, you've heard of our craftwork then I see." He said the last touching his nose.

"You make very fine wares, but as simple monks we have no need for such beauty and extravagance."

"It's a shame, had you asked, I'd have offered anything of your choosing," the man replied.

With those words Aeden glanced once more at what he assumed was the man's daughter. The older man saw the glance but mistook it for curiosity, or a chance to move past the sensitive topic of immolation, imperial movements, and inquisitors.

"Illiana why don't you grace our guests with a song," her father stated with the authority of age.

The mother brought out some dried meat and stale bread as Illiana began to sing. Her voice was as sweet and pure as a mountain spring. They ate and listened. A gentle breeze rustled the wagon's tarp. The shade was cool and comfortable.

Tattered thoughts of fearful men were washed away by food, song, and the warmth of the day.

Soon enough her song ended and the food was finished.

"What can we offer for your kindness," Odilo asked.

The man looked to his wife before looking at Odilo. "A prayer for our second son, he's been injured and his arm can't lift what it used to."

"Can I see him?" Aeden interjected, before realizing he may have spoken out of turn.

If Odilo was irritated, he didn't show it. The man nodded his head, "of course, he's in the back of our wagon."

The man led Aeden to the cart. The other monks followed with curiosity. The third cart was laden with personal effects. Inside a boy of approximately twelve lay on top of a blanket that was laid amidst pots, pans, bundles of clothing, and other effects.

"Hello," Aeden said as he climbed into the wagon.

The other monks and the father stood outside, watching in earnest. Aeden knelt as best as he could next to the boy as Odilo led a healing chant.

"Oh Salvare, father of life, mother of health
we call upon you for your strength,

your power over us,

send goodness to this body..."

Aeden listened to the low chanting tones of the monks as he whispered to the boy.

"Where does it hurt?"

The boy pointed to his right elbow. Aeden nodded to him and smiled.

"May I place hands upon you?" Aeden asked.

The boy nodded.

"...as your children we ask of you

send down a sliver of your power

power from the divine love..."

The prayer continued as Aeden felt along the boy's arm for muscular tension and bone placement. As part of the gevecht every member of the Thane Sagan was trained in simple healing arts. They learned to brew their own herbs to reduce the pain and swelling that came from stone fist training. They learned how to manipulate stagnant blood to allow it to flow properly. They learned how to reset simple bone misalignments so as to help create a greater bond with each other and to allow training to resume as rapidly as possible.

Aeden finished massaging the line from the boy's neck to his wrist, softening the muscular tension to better slip his elbow into alignment. With a firm grasp at the base of the elbow and another hand near his wrist, Aeden quickly straightened and pulled the boy's arm. There was a muted crack, drowned out by the chanting monks.

The boy flinched but didn't make a noise.

"Try moving your elbow now," Aeden said.

The boy did as he was told and surprise rolled over his features, followed by a warm smile and a quick hug.

The chanting stopped and the boy jumped off the wagon followed by Aeden.

"They fixed me pa," the boy said gleefully.

The father placed one arm around the boy as a smile crept onto his aged features. His tired eyes gleamed with pride as he glanced down at his son before returning his attention to the monks.

"Please let me offer you something for your journey."

Odilo looked at the others before responding, "If you could spare a skin of water we'd be grateful and hold you in our prayers."

The man gestured to his wife as he thanked the monks again. The wife returned with a skin of water and handed it to Odilo. With smiles and hand waving, the groups said their goodbyes.

The monks resumed their journey down the road. They had only walked a dozen paces when Aeden was stopped by the young girl he had been enraptured with. She had caught up to them and held a leather strap in her hand. It was of decent quality and a buckle was fastened to one end.

"For your trouble," she said as she handed it to him, her hand lingering for a moment on his.

Aeden stood there dumbfounded and unwilling to move as though a bird had landed on his hand. She smiled, casting warmth into his heart and turned back toward the laden carts. He watched her dress shift as she walked away. He then looked down to the leather belt in his hands. He already knew what he'd use it for when the opportunity of privacy presented itself.

He turned and joined the monks, stuffing the belt as best as he could into the makeshift pocket in his robes.

The following hours were less comfortable. The Templas blade swung uncomfortably at Aeden's side as the hilt bit ever deeper into his hip. Sweat gathered on his forehead in annoying beads and thoughts plagued his restless mind.

"Do you think we're safe on these roads?" Adel asked out of the blue.

Aeden glanced over. It seemed to be a rhetorical question, one he had been pondering.

Bosco dropped his robes from his nose and glanced over, curious. Thomas fidgeted, as he often did when anxious or deep in thought.

"The Inquisition is not very large," Odilo

responded carefully, "and the farther from Sawol we travel, the safer we become."

Neri grunted.

"Do you think they'll come for us?" Aeden asked, curious to know more and worried about his small band of brothers.

Odilo didn't respond at first. Instead he seemed to contemplate the question and the best way to answer.

A gentle breeze picked up and swept through the North South road in unseen eddies. The sun ducked behind a cloud and hid its gaze from them, before Odilo decided to answer.

"I don't know."

Chapter 38

"Manipulation is the hidden truth social graces ignore." Book of Humors, Library of Galdor

The following day was even warmer than the day before. The sun had come out early and burnt away the remaining clouds. Their water skin had run dry, and they were still some distance to the next town.

Most spoke very little, save for one.

Bosco attempted to ward off discomfort through his sheer number of complaints.

"I thought it was Hearvest, why has Salvare cast the sun of Sumor upon us?" he complained.

Neri mumbled under his breath. Aeden couldn't understand it and wondered if it was one of the languages of D'seart.

It didn't matter.

They marched along, dutiful to the ever-watchful eye of Salvare.

As the other monks thought on prayer and their mission, Aeden thought on the Thirteen. He thought about his fallen villagers. He remembered the draccus fiend. Finally, his thoughts settled upon the idea of responsibility.

He still had a duty to avenge his greater Thane family. Yet, as before, he couldn't see a way to make that happen. Ignorance still blanketed him the way it blanketed the fervent believers peppering Verold.

By midafternoon they were able to hitch a ride on the back of a partially loaded wagon traveling north. Aeden found it challenging to sit comfortably with his sword hidden under his robes and offered his seat to an overly thankful Thomas.

As he stood, he watched the gently rolling hills of the countryside slide past. There were fields of various sorts on either side of the road. In the distance, there was the occasional stone wall, demarking one farmer's land.

Simple houses were evidenced by lazy wisps of smoke, creeping away from dark chimneys. There were trees and there were flowering bushes. Butterflies flitted about in half-drunk patterns of flight.

"I've got a question," Adel said, breaking the lull of passing scenery and rumbling wagon wheels.

Aeden glanced over and smiled. Adel loved games, whether it be mental puzzles, interesting questions, or card games.

"If you could talk to a famous person from history, who would it be and why?"

Adel looked at each monk in turn as if daring them to answer.

Thomas chipped in first. He enjoyed sharing his knowledge and intellect with others.

"Simple," he said, "Dominer the Pure. He's the founding father of the Church of Salvare, the vessel in which Salvare spoke through to transcribe the book of Divinus, and led mankind out of the Dark Period."

Adel nodded.

He then looked around, waiting for the next monk to speak.

Aeden was thinking. Who would he want to see? The archduchess? The first kovor? Or did he have a greater longing to see those he lost? His friends? Dannon? The stone carving of his mother came to mind, and he knew.

"I'd want to see Rajah," Neri said, "the original Lion of the Desert."

It was unusual to hear him speak. The others remained silent, waiting for the reason why. There was none. Typical Neri.

"I for one," Adel said, continuing the game, "would like to have met Prince Adam Wolf."

Thomas raised an eyebrow. Bosco wiped at his nose and looked away. Neri and Aeden clearly didn't know who he was talking about. Odilo remained unreadable, with just a hint of a smile gracing his eyes.

It wasn't the reaction Adel had been hoping for.

"As one of the most famous clairvoyants to have ever lived, he predicted that the Templas Empire would go quiet. He knew that Kresimer's sisters would die long before their time, and that Lord Bristol would have only one daughter."

"Who cares," Neri said.

"It's how insanely accurate he was that makes me care," Adel said.

"If he were so great, monuments would be built in his name, songs sung and we'd all know of him," Neri countered.

"Neri has a point," Aeden said.

"That fame is the marker for success?" Adel responded, "I disagree, I think that knowledge is what made him interesting and powerful."

"Why's the daughter thing important? I could guess with an even chance what sex a baby would be," Aeden said, playing devil's advocate.

"It showed that the prince could predict something as mundane as a single birth over a hundred years before it ever happened!"

Aeden nodded his head. That was impressive. If he could predict the future...he let the thought languish.

"I have one," Odilo said.

His voice was calm and cut through the argument like a knife through wool.

"Rulf of the Plains," Odilo said with a strange smile.

"The Silent King?" Thomas whispered.

Odilo nodded his head.

"Wasn't he also known as the Torturous

King, responsible for more gruesome public executions than any other king in history?" Adel said intrigued.

"That's the one," Odilo said.

"But why?" Adel asked.

Bosco looked up, curious.

"It's rumored that he was known as the Silent King because of a debilitating disease that deformed his skin. He wouldn't even allow his physicker in the same room. The physicker would have to shout his questions across a closed door to assess his health," Odilo paused and looked at his brother monks, "and it's my belief that he was scared, angry and lonely. If he knew that he was cared for, despite his appearance, that Salvare loved him, then perhaps he would not have killed so many innocent men."

No one spoke for a moment. The sounds of the cart over the cobbled road filled their ears.

"Odilo wins," Aeden said, conceding.

Adel merely nodded as the wagon finally came to a stop at a fork in the road.

A weathered wooden sign stood at the crossroads like an old sentinel who had long forgotten his purpose. The farmer smiled and said his farewell, his face creasing into a maze of age spots and lines.

The monks offered their sincere thanks and watched the old man use his switch to spur the two half-starved oxen forward. The cart rumbled down the rutted road to the west, leaving the group of six monks standing on the main north-south stone road.

According to the farmer, they were only a few miles from a town called Berkshire. It was a relatively small town that was ruled by a duke known for his proclivities with younger men.

The town itself rose in prominence when the emperor decided to garrison some of his imperial soldiers there. Their purpose was to enforce the road tax and to act as a base of operations for any small issues or uprisings. Mostly the soldiers dealt with bandits and highway robbers. Apparently to good effect, for thus far they had encountered no such trouble.

"Let's make it to Berkshire, perhaps there we shall find some food and rest," Odilo stated with a warm smile, the short scar on his cheek folding awkwardly.

Bosco grumbled a complaint. Thomas did his best to ignore it as Aeden and Adel stood further back quietly mocking the lanky monk.

Their jests concealed a more hidden worry. The imperial presence was a reminder of the state of contention within the Imperium. It was a reminder of the Inquisition.

The walk to Berkshire didn't take long. There was a simple forest that carpeted the gently rolling hills. Cutting a plain swath through the hills, cleared of trees, was the stone road north. As the monks crested a hill the town revealed itself to them.

The buildings of Berkshire appeared to hug the main road like a child would its mother. Businesses stood, lining either side of the thoroughfare, each competing for attention. There were a few east-west cross streets that led to smaller buildings and fenced plots of land with animals in pens and crops in neat rows.

A large stone garrison stood apart, standing squat near a wooden fortification. In the distance, at the far end of town, was a road leading to the east and a small hilltop clearing. A castle graced the hill, overseeing the town the way a midwife watches over a pregnant woman.

The group of six descended the hill. The town came into sharper focus as they neared. There were the familiar smells of humanity that replaced the scents of earth, still water, and broken leaves.

Bosco held his robe to his nose.

"Nothing like the stench of human waste to remind one of their humanity," Aeden said taking in a breath.

Neri grunted in amusement.

"Or to remind you that your nose works," Adel replied.

Thomas looked at them before offering his own nugget of wisdom.

"Herlewin says that humanity is nothing more than the excuse the ruling class uses to *save* people from themselves."

Thomas was looking out at the stone barracks as he spoke.

Aeden followed his gaze and suppressed a shiver.

Directly ahead of them was a simple and small fortification. It looked more like a shelter used during inclement weather. Surrounding the edifice were a group of imperial soldiers. Their demeanor spoke of quiet boredom.

Two were seated and playing cards as the other lounged lazily, leaning against a fence as if he needed support to maintain his posture. All the while a pennant with a golden draccus fiend hung suspended from a pole, flickering gently in the mild wind and marking their allegiance to the emperor.

The soldier leaning against a fence, stood up. He lazily tracked the incoming group with the half-assed confidence only a young, bored soldier could muster.

"Brothers, you will find no shelter here," the soldier stated flatly as the group approached. He looked directly at Aeden and continued, "You can take your group elsewhere brother."

Aeden eyed the soldiers standing there, observing their stance, weapons, and armor. Did the man think he was in charge of his fellow brothers?

"Thank you kindly, we are just passing through town," Odilo said with a calm and gentleness in his voice that disarmed the soldier.

The young soldier glanced back toward his comrades as if for support.

"Ask them about the monks," one of the soldiers playing guards said, reminding the young man.

The soldier nodded and looked back to the band of monks.

"You from the Holy Order of Bodig or Willow Hill Monastery?" the soldier asked perfunctorily.

"We're a band of brothers from the Plains, and as far south as D'seart, traveling north," Odilo offered before any of the other brother monks could speak.

The soldier looked over the group again eying their simple gray robes and lack of possessions.

"Passing through then. Be on your way," he said gruffly.

Without further delay the road weary monks walked through the town of Berkshire. It was a quiet town with few people walking the streets. There were a large number of taverns and brothels.

Scantily clad women leaned idly upon the

railings of some of the buildings lining the main thoroughfare. Their lips were overly red and their cleavage was forced upward by corsets in a lavish display of promiscuity.

"We shan't cast our eyes upon such temptations," Thomas spoke to no one in particular, his pale face paler than usual.

Aeden was starting to get a better feel for Thomas. It felt as though the abbot had chosen him as a verbal moral compass for the others. Odilo on the other hand was more of a silent moral compass, using his actions rather than his words.

The sun began to set, casting the sky in a startling array of color. Bosco began to grumble quiet complaints. Adel drew quiet. Odilo looked about seeking a suitable place for the night.

They were still a few days away from the first town on the map. Despite the distance there were a few townships before then, at least one of them had to be more open to the monks from the Holy Order of Sancire.

"Pssst," the sound was akin to a hissing snake.

Aden glanced about, but it was Neri who caught sight of the woman beckoning them. She was older, with gray hair pulled tightly into a bun. Her face was wrinkled and stern, but more from a life hard lived than from old age.

Neri walked closer to investigate, the other

monks following the way a flock of birds follows the leader.

"I have a place to rest your weary feet," she eyed them carefully for a moment, her eyes heavy. "I only ask for a good word as payment," the last came out quietly as if she were afraid of the very words.

"She wants an indulgence," Thomas said with mild exacerbation under his breath.

Aeden turned to Adel who responded by shrugging. It was ironic that the man who would occasionally sneak some extra cheese from the kitchens was concerned about praying for someone who offered a place for the night. Such was the role of morality, a personal affair of skewed perception.

It was Neri who answered.

"Not every monastery operates under the riches of a powerful patron, some make due with earning what money they can from the local populace," his words sounded slightly angry, offended even. "You from the Gemynd should know this more than most."

The woman watched the monks with trepidation, "I will include a hot meal of course," she said at last.

This seemed to be the words they were looking for. Bosco's tall, hunched frame was already following her, followed by Neri and Adel. Odilo turned to Thomas.

"The brothers need this," he whispered.

Thomas nodded but still seemed upset by the idea and was further offended by Neri's words. Aeden passed them, knowing that his stomach would be happy for a hot meal and his feet would feel better once he was off of them.

The woman led them down an alley that smelled like a combination of rotten cheese and rank meat. Whatever hunger Aeden felt was quick to pass. They weaved past a few side doors to a door that was worn with age and neglect.

The six gray-robed monks stepped inside and were accosted with the strong odor of perfume. They stopped in a small lounge of sorts. Faded red chairs sat on either side of a fireplace. At the moment, the fireplace was empty, blackened from prior use. Frayed curtains covered the sole window. A crude painting of two women playing with each other adorned the far wall.

As the monks did their best to avert their eyes from the painting, a woman stepped into the room. She wore nothing more than undergarments. Her cheeks were rosy, her lips overly red, and her face powdered white in an effort to hide her age. Gray lined her hair, which was pulled up and piled atop her head. As soon as she entered the old woman shooed her away the way one would a stray dog.

"I must apologize for her appearance," the woman who led them in said with true concern in her voice.

Odilo spoke first before any of the other monks could put in a word.

"It is understandable. We are simply humbled to have been invited in for a place to sleep and a hot meal."

"Of course, of course. Let me show you to your room, and then bring something warm to eat."

The lady smiled an awkward smile, it was apparent she wasn't used to the sensation and she looked more like a growling animal than a person. She turned and led them down the corridor to a set of rickety stairs. The stairs creaked and groaned like a despondent Hearvest wind.

Bosco muttered something about the impropriety of it all as they ascended. Thomas was ashen faced, yet curious. Adel was smiling and Aeden knew he probably had a joke simmering in his head.

"It's the best I can offer, which in this town is already a risk. Please don't let anyone know I've let you stay here, it could cost me more than you know," the older woman said, a frown settling comfortably onto her face.

"Of course, we understand," Odilo replied with a smile of reassurance.

The woman eyed them for a moment with her mouth half open as if weighing her words, "there are pleasures other than food if you have the coin and the inclination."

"Not tonight," Odilo said as he stepped into the room.

The woman nodded as she slipped away with an air of disappointment following her down the stairs.

Aeden glanced about and saw there was a single large bed and plenty of floor space for all of them. He set about securing a cleaner looking corner of the floor. Aeden pulled his hood over his head as he lay down. He fell asleep before the food was brought up.

Chapter 39

"A warm welcome isn't equivocal to the warmth of hospitality." Saying of the Gemynd

The days to Nailsea passed uneventfully. The weather had become cooler, near perfect traveling weather. Past the Berkshire Hills it had become flat again. The stone road northward was now surrounded by a mix of evergreens and deciduous trees.

Aeden drew in a breath, inhaling the sweet scents of the morning, a mix of pine needles, moisture, and earth. The monks had slowly grown accustomed to the idea of long days with little food. For Aeden the walk was far more comfortable once he readjusted his sword. He had used the leather strap given to him by Illiana to secure the Templas weapon to his back, underneath his robes. He no longer had a heavy weight tugging on his belt. He no longer worried about kneeling or sitting. He realized a moderately comfortable life was a happier life.

The forest slowly yielded to small farms. Plots of land reclaimed from the trees carved out niches for rows of food and for sheep and goats to roam, picking the earth clean of vegetation. The sun had settled into its midday nook, casting a wary eye upon the band of traveling monks.

They shared the road with a few carts, some

wandering Calenites, a cleric from the imperial seat, and a bearded man from Gemynd. It was the first time Aeden had ever seen or heard of the Calenites. The small group of Calenites was heading north, to answer their "calling." What initially stole his attention was their red hair and green eyes. It was unlike anything he had ever seen.

In his homeland, they had always described devils with flaming hair and eyes made of emeralds. Strangely he wasn't frightened, but instead was curious. They spoke Heortian well enough to be understood and spoke more often than many of the monks wished. Yet for all their words, they said very little.

The Calenites had been driven from their home over a century before and had been wandering in search of a new place ever since. According to their beliefs, they were promised a perfect strip of land, described as "*a place of green that touches upon azure waters, fertile and rich, peaceful and bountiful.*"

They had yet to find a place fitting that description and continued to search. For many in the Three Kingdoms they had become known as the Drifters, the people without a home. Some took pity upon them and gave them temporary shelter or food. Most steered clear of them. Aeden found them interesting. He was eager to gobble up all the information on the Imperium he could.

He attempted to engage the man from Gemynd, but was rebuffed for his efforts. The imperial cleric seemed nervous. He uttered something about inconstant bowels and scurried off into the woods, to not be seen again by his wandering group.

The farther they walked, the more people they encountered, and the greater Aeden's curiosity grew. It was as if his mind had been lying dormant, hidden in a veil of ignorance that was only now slipping from his eyes. He would pester Adel with questions only to reach the limits of his knowledge. Thomas was proving to be quite knowledgeable and the most willing to confer his wisdom to the youngest member of the group.

And so Aeden began to learn more about the history of Bodig and the customs of Gemynd. Consequently, they too began to form a friendship. Tenuous at first, like the foundation of a building on sand, it grew.

So, it was no surprise that Thomas was deep in an explanation of Gemynd traditional weddings when they fell upon the city of Nailsea.

There before them, stood the towering statues, dating back to an era long since passed. The statues were worn, weathered by the ages, but stood as a monument to a time before Salvare saved his people from a pantheon of petty gods. They dwarfed the trees about them, towering sentinels of Nailsea.

The Holy Order of Sancire had tried to remove them only to have the population turn angry and hostile. In response, the Church renamed them, Dominer and Sha'a. The people accepted the change and only a few remembered their true names as the centuries rolled past. It was interesting how time had the habit of erasing old memories while more deeply instilling old habits.

"Beautiful aren't they," Adel said in awe as they passed below, like insects staring upon giants.

"I didn't know men could build such things," Aeden replied, his eyes transfixed, recognition rolling over his features.

He knew the faces carved upon the weathered stone, the way a mother would know a child despite having parted years before. They were Anat and Baal, the twin gods of war, siblings, and lovers. They were part of the Thane's pantheon of thirteen.

"I didn't know you'd recognize Dominer's face and that of his lover, Sha'a." Adel said.

Aeden was temporarily at a loss for words. He couldn't tell him their true names. How could he explain the atrocities attributed to Baal, or the lengths Anat underwent to placate her sibling lover? He was only left with lies, something he was growing to despise, yet felt ever more compelled to do.

"Everyone knows their faces brother," he said.

Neri grunted. Thomas ignored him and stared at the statues, reaching out a hand to touch the side of one of the toes. The stone was as smooth as a Sumor cherry, as if a thousand thousand hands had graced that very spot.

Adel looked at Thomas. The burden of the quick lie was lifted from Aeden's chest as attention was now diverted elsewhere.

"To bring us luck and peace," Thomas said matter-of-factly as if it were common knowledge.

"If I lick it, will it bring me greater luck?" Neri asked sarcastically.

Thomas fidgeted.

"He's only playing brother." Adel said.

"Is it only that particular spot?" Aeden asked to distract brother Thomas from his irritation.

Thomas couldn't help himself. He was well read and only enjoyed a well-aged cheese more than sharing his knowledge.

"In Gemynd there's a saying for these statues: 'only a dunce shall rub once, although twice shall suffice, thrice will grant god's everlasting advice.'"

"There are more than these?" Adel asked.

"Of course, but most have been destroyed. According to Herlewin's *Anthology of Gemynd*, it was the Heretic King that ordered them to be broken to pave the way for Salvare."

Curiosity and worry fought for control of Aeden's young mind. It was worry that settled upon his shoulders and wrinkled his brow. He knew the power of the old gods. He glanced at his brother monks for a moment before jogging back to the well-worn toe of Baal. His fingers traced an invisible sign along the smooth stone as he whispered quietly to the old god.

"Please take no offense, spill no blood, for he's but an ignorant child before your grandeur," Aeden then touched his finger to his chest after uttering a prayer of forgiveness in his native tongue of Sagaru.

Images of his broken village bled into his mind and tore at his heart. He hardly noticed they'd arrived upon the city of Nailsea.

The city rested in the shadow of the great gods of Anat and Baal. It was a city that had long ago spilled past its initial city wall. A larger city wall had been built to encapsulate the growth and it too failed. Now a town rested beyond the walls of the city. Many of the buildings had the permanence of stone and the weathered appearance of age.

"Watch your pockets and your purses, this part of town has more than its share of pickpockets and thieves," Odilo said with certainty.

The other monks looked at him with mild surprise. Bosco clutched at his purse as Thomas looked around as if he could be robbed any moment. Aeden let his thoughts slip. He grew more vigilant, watching over his adopted brothers the way a mother bear does over her cubs. He had grown fond of these men and was beginning to regard them as family. Weak family, that needed the protection of a keen eye and sharp sword if need be.

Despite his ever-watchful eye, the gentle tug of curiosity begged to be heard.

"How does Odilo know of this place?" Aeden asked Adel in a hushed whisper, his eyes glancing about.

"Like you, he has a past and is covetous of his secrets."

"Covetous?"

"It means he protects them like a mother would her child," Adel explained.

Aeden nodded and looked toward Odilo. He walked in front of the group, confident and serene. So much so that it was easy to overlook his mild limp. It reminded him of when he had first met Odilo in the Red City. Odilo had been in the square, praying for a brother monk in fiery protest of Imperial rule. It was Odilo that had led him to safety, introduced him to the Order and vouched for him.

Another thought chased his initial one.

"I'm *covetous* of my secrets?" Aeden asked, affecting a hint of surprise in his voice.

"Please, you're one of the vaguest people I've ever met!"

"It's true," Thomas said in concurrence with Adel, his hands fidgeting ever so slightly as he slowed to join their conversation.

Aeden didn't know how to respond and felt himself grow quiet. He reflected on their words and tried to think of times he'd been purposefully vague. Was it when he was asked about family? His home?

The six monks passed through the spillage of Nailsea without issue and travelled into the heart of the city. Taller stone buildings lined the streets. Each wore the same faded skin as the last, facades worn with age and use. Merchants had carved out niches on the lower floors of many of the buildings.

The city proved to be a welcome distraction from mental wanderings.

In certain respects, Nailsea reminded Aeden of Bodig, with one major exception, the color of the stones. There was very little red to be found here. Most buildings were a boring, dull gray. The more exquisite buildings were whitewashed and smooth. Storefronts abutted the street in a vain attempt to ensnare the passerby. Clothiers catering to both Bodigan and Gemynd fashion fought for space on the busy street.

Aeden was temporarily distracted by the setting. He watched people go about their business. He imagined their daily lives. He then imagined Odilo within the city at a younger age and his curiosity blossomed like a flower to the sun.

"How long have you known Odilo?" He asked.

"He came to the monastery about eight years ago," Adel said as if recalling something someone else had told him.

"Do you know where from? The abbot said Bodig."

Adel cast a glance toward Odilo. Odilo walked farther ahead unaware of the exchange. Neri was near him followed by the lanky figure of Bosco.

"Bodig is used to describe the central kingdom as well as the seat of the king in the Red City. It can get confusing at times, but normally most people refer to Bodig as the kingdom that stretches between the two rivers, and the capital city as the Red City."

Aeden felt rather ignorant. He had read of the Red Castle, knowing it was the seat of the king. He knew it was within the walls of the Red City and that the Red City was within the kingdom of Bodig between the River Lif and the Dath River. Despite this he couldn't help but feel he was only scratching the surface.

Thomas cut in, not wasting an opportunity to educate. "Actually, not all the claimed land belongs to the kingdom. The Empire lays claim to a part, Sawol another, and Gemynd yet another still. It gets pretty confusing, especially once you make your way westward toward the delta and northern islands."

Aeden nodded his head. Thomas looked ready to say more, but Adel beat him to it.

"You wanted to know about Odilo right?"

At times, it seemed like there was a mild competition between the two.

"I don't know what city he came from. Do you?" Adel asked Thomas.

Thomas merely shook his head.

"There was gossip that upon his arrival he was rather," Adel paused looking for the right word to describe the scene without offending, "wild."

"Like me," Aeden said, feeling a hint of pride at sharing traits in common with Odilo.

"You were more like a stray cat, disheveled and unruly," Thomas cut in.

Both Aeden and Adel looked at each other before laughing. Thomas had a way of accidently implying humor. His matter-of-fact way of speaking was awkward and at times entertaining.

Thomas looked at them quizzically before catching sight of a creamery.

"Oh no, we're going to lose our brother," Adel said mockingly.

Thomas didn't hear him. Aeden merely chuckled.

Aeden pulled out his map and studied it for a moment.

"Just as I thought..." he said thoughtfully.

"What?" Thomas asked.

Adel looked over, waiting for Aeden's joke.

"If I'm reading this right, there should be a giant block of cheese on the next corner," he said seriously.

Adel coughed in an attempt to stifle his laughter.

Thomas gave Aeden a strange look.

Bosco glanced back and narrowed his eyes, as if their whole interaction was distracting him from the important task of being annoyed.

They walked in silence for a spell, each dwelling on their own thoughts. Aeden's thoughts wandered to those in his group. He was still curious about Odilo. In a way Odilo reminded him of his old master, a quiet, wise man, filled with experience that was wrapped in a blanket of mystery.

If he couldn't find out more about Odilo, perhaps he could satiate his thirst by bothering Adel with more questions.

"Have you ever made it this far north?"

Aeden asked as he looked about.

"Once as a child, before I joined the Church," Adel turned away so that his expression was lost to Aeden's reaching eyes.

"I never asked why you joined," Aeden suddenly asked, as if he could sense the weight of memory upon Adel's chest.

Adel didn't reply at first, instead he watched as the people ambled past. They wore simpler clothes than those from the Red City, and it appeared beards were the fashion. It made sense as they were closer to Gemynd. Men of Gemynd wore their beards proudly once they were of age. They were the mark of wisdom and manhood.

"My family fell on hard times after the emperor raised taxes a third time, to fend off the weakened income from a multi-year drought. I was the youngest child of four and they could no longer afford me. I was a burden instead of a help, unlike my older brothers and sister. So they sold me to the Church for a silver dinar."

If Adel was bitter, it wasn't apparent in his voice. His expression was neutral as if he had been relating someone else's story. Finally, after a long moment he looked to Aeden.

"What's your story?"

Aeden swallowed a lump that had formed in his throat. He had a feeling Adel would ask and had been debating how to respond. This was likely one of the moments that defined him as vague, yet how could he tell him a draccus fiend had attacked and destroyed his homeland? Adel wouldn't believe it. More than likely he'd think Aeden was making light of the situation. If he left the part out about a draccus fiend, he'd still have to include the minor detail of where he was from.

When Aeden first arrived at the monastery, he got the strong impression that it was wiser to hide his origins. Only Odilo seemed to know, yet he never alluded to it or said a word. Aeden followed Odilo's example and whenever asked, he would redirect the question as best as he could. It made for some hurt feelings and awkward conversations. This seemed to be another one of those times.

"You don't need to tell me now, when you're ready is fine," Adel said, reading Aeden's expression.

Relief washed across Aeden's face. Adel was a better friend than he deserved. He allowed Aeden to walk the rest of the way through the city in silent contemplation.

The monastery of Nailsea was situated on the top of a small hill. Unlike the Red City Monastery, it was surrounded by plots of cleared land. A well-worn dirt road made a circuitous route up the hillside from the main body of the city. Sheep dotted the northern slope, looking like puffs of white clouds had landed upon the countryside.

As the group approached the monastery, a young monk ran down the rutted roadway to greet them. Clinging to his robes were bits of bramble and wool. Sweat was upon his brow and his young cheeks were flushed.

"Welcome," he said as he stood stooped before them, struggling to regain his breath.

"Thank you, I assume you know who we are," Odilo said, eyeing him in amusement.

"We've been expecting you," the young man resumed, his breath returning to normal. "Please, follow me."

The building was similar to the monastery in Bodig. Its walls were white and the central nave was tall and wide. A tower stood off to one side with a copper circle capping its high peak.

Within the nave, two circles carved into the roof, let in the afternoon light. The nostalgic feeling of home swept over Aeden. It was a strange sensation because he'd only been away from the monastery of the Red City for a few days. Furthermore, it wasn't his real home, the home he'd grown up in. That home had been ripped from him so savagely that at times he wondered if it had ever existed.

"The abbot is most excited to see you and the book you bring," the young monk said, leading the group farther into the heart of the monastery.

They passed a few open rooms, each filled

with sleeping mats still upon the floor. These were obviously the cloisters.

"Many of the monks are also eager to know about life in the Red City, it must be fascinating living in the heart of the kingdom, near the seat of the king."

"I'd know more if we were allowed out," Aeden said under his breath.

"You live so close to Family Benbow, you may know more than us," Odilo said, trying to divert attention from Aeden's words.

"The Benbow's are a secretive lot senior," the young monk responded deferentially before looking to Aeden, curiosity sparkling in his wide eyes.

"You're the one, aren't you?" He said with awe in his voice.

Aeden looked to Adel. They exchanged a look of curiosity.

"The one who what?" Aeden asked.

The young monk looked about conspiratorially before responding, "the one who knocked down an Inquisitor."

Neri grunted.

"More like gently nudged," Aden replied.

Before Aeden had a chance to stick his foot further into his mouth, Odilo interjected.

"Our brother is looking forward to learning about the differences and similarities between our monasteries."

The young man nodded his head. He rounded a corner and stopped so abruptly that Bosco bumped into him, grumbling under his breath as he did so.

"The abbot would like to see you now," he said looking at them, curiosity carved deeply into the shallow lines etched onto his otherwise youthful face. He gestured toward an open door.

"We're excited you're here," he whispered to the younger Bodigan monks before scurrying off to some unknown task.

Chapter 40

"Change is fundamental to life, whereas resistance often leads to failure." Saying of the Bodig

The abbot was unusual in appearance. He was the juxtaposition of Abbot Filbert. Instead of soft, rounded features, he had a sharp vulturine visage. His shoulders were broad, speaking of the hours of physical labor he undertook alongside his brother monks. He was tall and it was likely that women would have found him attractive, if he were wearing robes other than that of the Order of Sancire.

"Welcome," the abbot said in a strong, masculine voice. "I'm Abbot Gilbert."

The monks drew their hands together and nodded their greeting.

"We've been looking forward to your visit, both the archduchess and the abbot of the Red City have sent word of your arrival," he stated.

At mention of the archduchess, Aeden's face lit up. Part of him wondered if he had been mentioned, if she remembered the stolen glance they had shared. It was fanciful thinking of course.

Gilbert looked them over, his eyes finally settling on Aeden. He studied his tall, broad frame, then his youthful face, burdened by life, before continuing.

"You must be hungry and tired from your journey. I would like nothing more than for you to eat and get some rest, but what kind of example would that set for your brothers toiling outside?"

A smile crept onto Aeden's face as he watched Bosco physically blanch at the idea of hard physical labor. Thoughts of the archduchess faded quickly and were replaced by curiosity.

"Of course, before we enjoy the work of Salvare, let's stop by the library. There are scribes eagerly waiting to copy the Book of Divinus."

"Of course, Abbot, we'll follow you," Odilo said in gentler tones.

The abbot nodded solemnly and walked out of his simple chambers. He led them down a corridor toward the library.

"Everything looks so clean," Aeden commented to Adel.

Gilbert responded, despite being several steps ahead of the group. "We take our mission to Salvare seriously; piety is only seen through action. We therefore strive to prove our worth in all our actions," he looked back toward Aeden, "which includes silence when there is nothing of value to be said."

Aeden wasn't stupid and understood when he was being told to be quiet. His ears burned in embarrassment as if he had been corrected for urinating in the hallway. Adel glanced at him then to the others. A few surprised expressions were momentarily evident.

The abbot led them through a tall archway and into a room with soaring, graceful windows. The late afternoon light fell upon the scene in curtains of luminescence. The light touched upon each desk, which stood tall and narrow upon the carpeted stone floor. Scribes sat on simple stools immediately behind these desks, hunched over open books. They had the look of predatory animals, half-starved, with curved backs protecting their prey.

Wooden shelves lined the walls filled with texts and scrolls. In the corner was a chest filled with bound books, empty, waiting for words to grace their pages. The air smelled vaguely of leather, dust, and a metallic scent that Aeden couldn't place.

Gilbert stopped before one of the desks. An elderly man took a moment to finish whatever he had been copying, before carefully placing his quill into a pewter well. He looked up with watery eyes.

"Our brothers from the Red City Monastery are here," Gilbert said, gesturing to the small band of monks. The old man looked over, his eyes struggling to focus, as if anything beyond a few feet was a blur. "All other work can be put on hold for now," Abbot Gilbert stated matter-of-factly.

"Of course, senior," the old man's voice was like stretched parchment, brittle and ready to crack.

Without further hesitation, Bosco stepped forward, holding the Book of Divinus in his overly long fingers.

"I'm tasked with watching the book senior, I will therefore remain here," he said, casting a darting glance to Odilo.

Odilo raised an eyebrow, but otherwise didn't respond.

"So be it. The rest, please join me in god's work," Gilbert said as he strode past the old scribe and back into the hallway. They weaved their way through the corridors to a side exit. The fresh air brushed past like a trailing silk scarf. It brought the sounds of monks toiling in the soil, splitting wood, and the shearing of sheep.

The hours passed in arduous intervals of backbreaking work. Clouds drifted overhead, lazily indifferent to the drudgery below. And a Hearvest wind swept in from the east, bringing the smells of turning leaves and the subtle hint of moisture.

The work was grueling, but enjoyable. Something about pushing his limits made Aeden feel alive. His muscles ached, he was covered in sweat and a smile graced his lips.

Aeden had been tasked with splitting wood.

The heft of the axe felt familiar in his hands, even comfortable. It was a subtle reminder of home; the way the scent of freshly baked bread reminds one of home. The memories tugged at his heart and threatened to rob him of the moment, but something about smashing iron through wood staved his sadness.

The evening bell rang loudly, beckoning the monks to dinner. As Aeden put down the axe, his stomach rumbled heavily, like the growl of a young shroud cat. Aden caught sight of Adel and Thomas jogging up the hill toward him. He waited for his friends.

"How was splitting wood?" Adel asked.

"Great," Aeden replied, rubbing his hands together. "What were you two doing?"

"Odilo, Thomas, and I were helping sheer sheep," Adel replied.

"More like running around trying to catch them and hold them down," Thomas said.

"It was more exciting than I would have hoped for," Adel continued, pulling some brush out of his robes.

"You should have seen some these sheep, it was like try to hold down an angry cow," Thomas piped in, his breathing still heavy from exertion.

"That does sound more exciting than chopping wood, perhaps I'll try that tomorrow," Aeden said with a sparkle in his eye.

"I hope to be on the road again by tomorrow," Adel said, as he turned to walk back toward the monastery, following the others.

"You think they'll be done copying the book that quickly?" Aeden asked, walking alongside him.

"Probably not, but the abbot is a little intimidating," Adel stated in muted tones, casting a quick look about.

Thomas nodded his head as if in agreement, but his face was passive. He was always the interesting mix of youth, piety, and forced discipline. Adel on the other hand was far more youthful when around Aeden and far more pious when around Odilo.

"I don't think he's so bad," Aeden said.

Adel shook his head in disagreement. Thomas looked up, interested.

"I'll explain," he continued.

"Please, we're all ears," Adel replied.

Aeden smiled at them.

"I haven't seen any fat monks here, it seems like the rules are strict for everyone, not just whomever he doesn't like, and he looks like he could fight an Inquisitor if he had too."

Thomas fidgeted in thought, "the first time I saw you, I thought you looked pretty mean, like the captain of some soldiering element."

"You mean a platoon," Adel corrected.

Aeden smiled again, "or a company."

"How would you know?" Thomas asked, genuinely curious.

Aeden remained silent at first. He could feel their eyes upon him the way one feels the stalking look of a predator.

"That was from another life," he said quietly.

Aeden's smile turned sour in his mouth as thoughts of his home permeated his mind, sending images of blistered bodies and scorched earth through his brain.

"Are you feeling alright?" Adel asked concerned.

"Just hungry, I think I'm not used to swinging an ...," Aeden paused not sure of the word in the common tongue, and seeking an excuse to distract them from his thoughts.

"Axe," Thomas offered lightly.

"Yes, axe," as if he had known the word all along and merely forgotten.

The monks began to file into a semblance of a line, as they entered the white-walled building. They made their way to a room bordering a courtyard of sorts, where large basins of water rested heavily along the wall. The monks splashed water onto their faces and rubbed it over their hands in a quick cleansing ritual. The liquid spilled out of the troughs and spattered upon the stones, soaking an already wet floor.

After washing the grime from his hands and the sweat from his face, Aeden followed Adel, Thomas, and the other monks to the refectory. It was twice the size of the dining hall in Bodig and for good reason. There were far more monks here. It seemed odd to Aeden that so far from the capital city there would be such a large population of monks.

Dinner was far more elaborate than anything they ate back in the Red City. They had barley bread, butter, fava beans, vegetables, salted pork, and sweet cakes.

Aeden caught Adel's eye and saw the smile that spread across his face was as wide as the River Lif. Adel's addiction to sweets was almost as notorious as Thomas' affinity for cheese.

Adel wasn't the only monk glancing in their direction. On several occasions, he could feel the stare of the other monks. When Aeden would look up, they would look away.

The monks from the Holy Order of Sancire, Bodig ate their fill as the other monks ate in greater moderation. During the meal one monk sat in a corner, abstaining from food as he read from The Book of Khein. His voice was drab and monotone, like the sound of dirt being tilled.

After dinner, it was much the same as back in the Red City. They washed their dishes in a semi-orderly fashion. The monks were allowed to speak again and the sounds of conversation rolled off the walls in waves of gossip and excitement.

The abbot retired to his room, bidding the monks a night filled with pious dreams. A few stood, watching him leave, a temporary hush falling over the group. Abbot Gilbert rounded a corner and disappeared from view. Aeden watched in curiosity.

Those watching him leave then turned and spoke in excited tones. A wave of questioning elation swept through the group in a quick encompassing gallop. Almost immediately the small band of traveling monks was accosted with questions, as the monks from Nailsea were eager for gossip and news from the capital.

"He's the one who knocked down an Inquisitor..."

"I heard the Red Monastery has been marked by the Emperor, is it true?"

Had they mentioned the Inquisitor? How did they know? Questions continued to pummel the group in an excited flurry. Aeden felt somewhat like a cornered animal as they were surrounded and interrogated. It was difficult to follow who was asking what. The questions built to a crescendo until finally Odilo had enough. He clapped his hands together loudly, startling those near him.

"My brothers, we are very excited to be here, and we wish nothing more than to share and learn, but perhaps a more organized forum would be more conducive."

Aeden always listened when Odilo spoke, for he had a way with words that would cut to the heart of the matter without offending. Aeden imagined the diplomats he had read about in *Bodig a History*, spoke in such a manner. He tucked away each mannerism and each speech Odilo gave in case he ever needed to resort to such diplomacy.

"How are the roads," one of the Nailsean monks blurted out.

"Safe and easy so far," Odilo responded.

"How about the number of imperial soldiers? There has been talk of massive troop movements to the north," another monk questioned.

The Bodig monks looked at each other.

"We have seen no such movements."

"We have some questions too," Aeden jumped in, his mind spurned to action by the last question, "What have you heard of the roads to the north, toward Old Treton and northward to the city of Gemynd?"

A few different monks spoke simultaneously, making it harder to discern each thread.

"Geobold's son died of consumption." "Imperial troops move to surround the city." "A new group seeks to lay claim to the throne."

The words were further garbled by the

murmuring voices of the monks, discussing what important gossip should be passed along, while some debated the merits of gossip altogether.

"We're aware of Geobold's son's death, what is it you have heard about a *new* group?" Aeden asked, garnering a look from some of his brother monks. Aeden glanced at them and shrugged his shoulders. He wanted to know if it was safe to travel north. His eyes returned to the surrounding group.

One of the older monks stepped forward; he was clearly senior to the others.

"We don't wish to spread gossip that we cannot confirm," he gave a significant look to the other monks. His expression suddenly reminded Aeden of Blaise. "But there has been talk of a group of mystics claiming to be led by the reincarnate of Dominer. They claim Elias didn't die of the consumption, but that the hand of their true god struck him down for claiming fealty to the emperor before the king."

"That's ridiculous, how can one claim to be the reincarnate of Dominer without Church authority?" Thomas exclaimed.

Odilo took a step toward Thomas and lay a hand lightly on his shoulder before speaking, "What my brother is wondering is how you came by this information."

It was the older monk that spoke for the group, "We encounter travelers from the south heading north, and those from the north heading south. Nailsea is a city at a crossroads, infamous for the twin statues guarding it. People who come to the monastery for judgements, talk. Of course, I cannot divulge what judgments were passed or what was said specifically, Church doctrine is very clear on such matters."

"Nor would we ever imply that you should tread on such doctrine," Odilo interjected calmly.

"However, it has become apparent, even in our sheltered bit of the world, that change is coming to the North. Gemynd is at its own crossroads, so to speak, and as our fellow brothers we simply wish to see you make your pilgrimage safely." He took in a deep breath and glanced at them with an expression of forced kindness. "The rumors of troop movements are nothing more than that, rumors, based on speculation and idle banter. The mystics, however, have already declared themselves and have been actively gathering followers, this much is known for even Abbot Gilbert has stated such."

This garnered its own small discussion. Adel glanced significantly at Aeden. Neri took a step away from the group and Odilo raised an eyebrow.

"We trust you in this and appreciate your candor and earnest well wishes," Odilo said after a small pause.

"Would you recommend a certain route

north? Any precautions for safe travel?" Aeden asked, the burden of Blaise's words "*Keep them safe brother Aeden,*" echoed in his mind and resonated in his heart.

Before any of the monks could respond, Odilo jumped in, "Our young brother is eager, but perhaps tomorrow is better suited to such a discussion." He glanced about and nodded to a few and smiled his most placating smile.

Aeden's face flushed in anger. Neri was the one who placed a hand on him, whispering as he pulled him away.

"Not now brother, let's see who comes forward and how reliable they are," his words were laced with emotion and stymied Aeden's own feelings.

There was a scattering of talk as monks splintered off from the group to get ready for bed. Aeden moved to a basin to rinse his face and was approached by Adel.

"Don't worry about Odilo, he is only looking out for us," he said softly.

Aeden wiped his face on his sleeve and glanced to Adel.

"I know," was all he said before finding a vacant sleeping mat and retiring for the night.

His mind churned over the words that had been spoken. It sounded like revolution was trying to slink past undetected and settle its heavy burden upon the kingdom of Gemynd.

Chapter 41

"Mental stimulation accents the tedium of life."
Anthology of Gemynd

Aeden was saddled with thoughts that night and felt sluggish the following morning. His muscles ached as he sat up. His back was sore, for he must have slept on his Templas sword for a good portion of the night. He rubbed wearily at his gummy eyes as the morning bells clanged incessantly in the background.

There was already a flurry of activity as the monks of Nailsea were up and about, accomplishing chores with a fervor. Adel caught up with Aeden as they grabbed brushes and helped to scrub the stone floors of the cloisters. They struggled to keep up with the other monks, who scrubbed as if banishing dirt were an edict from Salvare.

Aeden caught a glimpse of Bosco as he hurried out of the sleeping rooms to make his way to the library. He had the ever "important" job of watching over the Book of Divinus, which meant he was unable to assist in the chores, prayers, and other daily rituals of the monastery. Aeden was certain he was avoiding chores, but he also had the lingering feeling that there was something more he was up to.

"What do you think he's up to?" Aeden

whispered to Adel, nodding toward the retreating figure of Bosco.

Adel simply shrugged his shoulders as he glanced about, making sure no one else heard.

Aeden carried on, as if oblivious that the sun had yet to rise.

"I think him and Monahan are planning something," Aeden hypothesized.

Thomas now moved closer and held a finger to his lips.

Aeden smiled.

"What do you think Thomas?" he said, goading the young monk.

Thomas turned red in the face.

Adel stifled a laugh.

The trio fell silent as the older monk from the night prior glanced over.

After scrubbing they went to Morning Prayer, which was followed by a small and simple breakfast. There were fresh eggs and bread.

Odilo was chosen to read from The Book of Khein as the other monks ate. Thomas, Adel, and Aeden stuck close to each other. Neri, who always seemed slightly uncomfortable with the company of others, stuck to himself. In many ways it almost felt as if they had never left the Red City Monastery.

When breakfast was finished, the monks resumed chores, but unlike the Red City, much of the chores were outdoors, beyond the monastery walls. Luckily the clouds lingered that morning, forming a gray quilt that shielded the monks from the intensity of the morning sun. The air was crisp and fresh, singing the Hearvest song.

Thomas, Adel, and Aeden were chosen to help clean some wooden stalls.

They were milling about by one of the stalls, enjoying the fresh air and looking out toward the city of Nailsea, when the abbot approached. His voice cut through the air like a knife.

"You three," he said sternly, "I've heard a disturbing rumor about talk before sunrise."

"That's an awful rumor, senior," Aeden replied, "We'll be on the lookout."

Thomas grew pale.

"You are guests here, and as such fall under my rules. I suggest you follow them, I do not tolerate insubordination." The abbot leaned forward toward Aeden, "one pigeon from me and your friends from the empire will be entertaining you instead."

Aeden swallowed a lump in his throat and straightened up. The abbot continued.

"I want these floors cleaned, filled with fresh hay, and the dirt scrubbed free from the wooden walls. Tomorrow is an important day," Abbot Gilbert ordered.

His hair was neatly cropped and his face freshly shaven. His robes looked clean, despite a full day's worth of labor only the day before. Aeden wondered if he kept an extra set of robes, or meticulously cleaned and groomed every night. Either way, he realized the small details of appearance and presentation added to his aura of authority.

"You two," the abbot shouted to a pair of monks, "watch over our brothers from Bodig."

Without waiting for a reply, the abbot stalked off to give orders to other groups along a flat expanse near the winding road, leading to the monastery.

Two young monks were jogging toward Aeden, Adel and Thomas. Aeden recognized them from the night prior, Simon and Gamel, although he couldn't remember who was Simon and who was Gamel.

"I think I've changed my mind about the abbot," Aeden said, earning a laugh from Adel and surprisingly a smile from Thomas.

"You don't want the abbot to catch you poking fun or he'll punish you," one of the approaching Nailsean monks whispered, Aeden believed he was the one called Simon.

This caught Thomas' attention as well as Aeden's. He had read about some of the older punishments meted out by the Order in one of the monastery's library books, although he couldn't remember which one.

"What do you mean by punishment?"

Thomas asked with genuine concern and curiosity.

Thomas was often curious and when he wasn't trying to live up to the sacred vows all monks were sworn to take: poverty, piety, discipline, and celibacy, he was expanding his knowledge in all things related to the church. Aeden imagined Blaise was much like Thomas when he was younger.

"It depends, but normally it's time spent in solitude without food or water." The monks swallowed as he scratched absentmindedly at his back, "and if the crime is deemed harsh enough, a public lashing takes place."

Aeden's curiosity easily won out over any propriety he may have been feeling as he asked, "When was the last time someone had been lashed."

If Odilo had been around, he might have interceded or apologized for him, but both Adel and Thomas seemed equally curious. It was a testament to their youth that they chose to let events play out.

"Just two days before your arrival," the young monks said, his tanned face wrinkling in concern.

"What happened?" Thomas asked, dropping his usual pious reserve.

"One of the monks challenged the abbot's orders. He broke the vow of discipline, and was punished for it," Simon said softly so that only those in the stall could hear. "Isn't it the same in your monastery?"

Aeden was about to speak but then thought of Odilo. Odilo would likely think before responding, knowing that his words would have implications beyond the moment. As Aeden thought of the possible ramifications of his rebuttal, Adel spoke.

"We have different methods …" Adel paused, grasping for words.

Thomas cut in, "It has been a while since anyone has challenged our abbot."

This seemed to pacify the young monk, but he still wore an expression of concern.

"Why are we cleaning these stalls?" Aeden asked in an attempt to change the subject.

"You don't know? Tomorrow is Market Day!" Gamel said as Simon nodded his head enthusiastically.

"I've heard of the Nailsean Market," Thomas said, interest bleeding through his tone like ink spilled onto blank parchment, "I had always thought it was a city sponsored event."

"Actually, it was the Church that created the market as a method to pay for repairs to the nave, after it had been struck by lightning," Simon said.

Aeden glanced up the hill toward the great white building. Sunlight fought to blind him as golden rays of light reached around the tallest tower and through the dissipating clouds.

"You won't see anything from here, besides it happened decades ago," Simon said, a smile starting to form on his lips.

Aeden quickly looked away, feeling rather stupid. Thomas smiled and Adel laughed.

"I didn't know," Aeden said, breaking into a smile and shoving Adel.

"Neither did I, but you just looked so surprised."

The laughter died down to smiles and amusement.

The hours passed quickly as they finished cleaning the slop from the stall floors and replaced it with fresh straw. Aeden and his brother monks, along with Gamel, were scrubbing away when the afternoon bell struck its musical chord.

"There's no formal afternoon prayer today and lunch is in our minds," Simon said as he approached with a bucket of water and soap.

Aeden got up and helped Simon with the bucket, pouring some of its contents into their own dwindling pail. He broke off a piece of soap and placed it next to the bucket. He dipped the bristles of his horse-hair brush into the water then rubbed it onto the soap before resuming the tedious work of scrubbing the wood.

Simon looked to Gamel who in turned looked to Aeden.

"What?" Aeden asked, feeling uncomfortable under the scrutiny of their glare.

"Nothing," Gamel said.

Simon looked ready to speak but then looked down at his brush as if ascertaining if it were soapy enough for the chore at hand.

"Is it true you knocked down an Inquisitor?" Simon finally asked, his voice trailing off into a whisper.

Aeden's face grew serious. He wasn't sure how to respond. He knew that it was a sensitive topic.

Thomas cut in, "we don't speak of them," he stated matter-of-factly.

Silence fell over the group for an awkward moment.

Aeden looked at Gamel then Simon, before looking down at his own brush. He wanted to say something. He wanted to know more about the Inquisitors. He wanted to break the awkward silence but couldn't think of what to say. Gamel did it for him.

"Is it true the walls of Bodig are painted with the blood of the dead?" Gamel asked with a most serious expression.

Adel and Thomas looked at each other. Smiles spread across their lips. Aeden knew the walls were simply stone. He had touched the red bricks himself. What was it the old master used to say, *"The greatest obstacle to wisdom isn't ignorance, it's the illusion of knowledge."*

It seemed no matter how far he traveled, ignorance was always there to greet him.

"No, they're a type of sunstone," Thomas said.

"Then why the children's song?" Simon piped in, equally curious.

Now Aeden was interested. He stopped scrubbing and looked up.

"What children's song?" Adel asked.

The Bodigan monks all fixed Gamel and Simon with their most studious expressions. Gamel looked to his friend. Finally, Simon nodded and Gamel began to sing. His voice was soft and sweet.

> *"There she blossoms, red and bloom*
> *Flaunting a face full o' death n' gloom,*
> *Turn from her n' try to hide,*
> *As she cuts into your side*
> *Until bloody walls are dyed."*

Gamel stopped almost as abruptly as he had started. The Bodigan monks looked at each other. Thomas was the only one that seemed unsurprised. He fiddled with his fingers as if anxious to say what he knew.

"Out with it," Adel said.

"It's about the Blood Queen, Kresimer."

Adel cut in excitedly, "the one famous for killing half the city?"

"…and hanging their dead bodies off the city walls." Thomas finished.

"Why'd she do that?" Aeden asked.

Adel shrugged his shoulders. Thomas shook his head.

"Maybe she was crazy," Gamel offered.

"She must've been before House Benbow came into power," Simon said expertly.

Thomas fidgeted with his hands again and decided to resume scrubbing. Aeden watched him as something he had recently read, bubbled to mind. It was from one of the long genealogies in the Red City monastery's library.

"Wasn't Queen Kresimer's birth name Benbow, before she married a Leigh?" he said

Adel's mouth dropped open for a heartbeat. Aeden didn't say anymore. He didn't wish to risk offending Adel again.

"He's right," Thomas said, "before she was a queen, she was simply one of a half dozen daughters."

"How'd you know," Adel said, attempting to hide his irritation.

Aeden appreciated Adel as a friend and loved

him as a brother, but thought it strange that he was so bothered when someone knew more than him.

"It's in Herlewin's *Anthology of Gemynd*," Thomas stated.

Aeden wanted to know more, but knew it was probably best to stay quiet. It was Gamel who jumped in to stave his curiosity.

"How'd she become the Blood Queen?"

Thomas didn't hesitate to share his knowledge. His eyes sparkled as he relished the opportunity to share what he knew.

"She poisoned her sisters. According to Herlewin, she took just enough as well, to make her sick and cast blame elsewhere. When she came of age, she was the only daughter House Benbow had to offer House Leigh. The king of Bodig, a Leigh, married her. She killed the king and became the Queen."

"Sounds simple enough," Aeden offered.

"Simple for a bloody killer," Adel offered, a smile cracking his otherwise serious face.

Aeden flung some water at him with his horse-hair brush. Soon all the monks joined in and all thoughts of cleaning had gone by the wayside.

By the time the evening dinner bell had struck, Aeden's arms felt leaden. It was the familiar comfort and soreness that he had felt a hundred times before.

The flat expanse by the road had been transformed in a day. Stalls had been cleaned as others were erected. Signs were pounded into the ground next to each stall. The air smelled faintly of soap and fresh straw. The animals had been moved to pens on the other side of the monastery to keep the smells and sounds farther from the next day's market.

There were already carts nestled into their coveted spots. Merchants were hovering over the scene like anxious carrion birds. Many had their own small fires going and the smells of stew and simple spices stirred their stomachs. They were the smells of home. Smells of warmth splashed upon the rolling hills of a faraway land.

Aeden smiled as he stood. He briefly stretched as he helped gather their supplies. The small group had grown closer over the course of the day, sharing stories of their homes. He found out Simon and Gamel were brothers whose parents were lost to consumption. He learned of Thomas' home and more about Adel. Luckily the dinner bell had saved him from divulging much of his own past.

The small group walked up the hill toward the monastery with supplies in hand. The supplies were handed over to monks waiting near the monastery doors. They stamped their feet before entering and made their way to the open-aired room filled with water troughs. As they had done yesterday, the monks cleansed their hands and faces as they whispered a simple prayer of thanks.

Dinner was a simpler affair than the day before. Neri was chosen to read as Adel, Thomas, and Aeden sought out Odilo. They found him already seated with bits of wool stuck to his gray robes. They joined him just as Bosco arrived with a few of the old, weathered scribes. The scribes and Bosco sat far from Aeden and his group, beyond view.

Food was passed and quickly eaten with the hunger of men who'd worked all day. The air was stuffy with the smell of sweat and salt. Candles burned along the walls and Neri's voice floated in the ripe atmosphere. His accent was more pronounced as he read, both lyrical and guttural.

The food was gone before Neri had a chance to read a second chapter, which was a blessing for he didn't seem overly excited to have been chosen to read while the others ate. The familiar scraping of moving benches, plates being gathered, and the table being cleared, drowned out Aeden's thoughts. Before he knew it, they were done with chores and done for the night. The abbot excused himself as the monks retired to the cloisters.

That night there was less of a formal gathering and more one on one chatting, as the monks had slowly grown to know each other over the course of a day and a half. Already there was a sense of familiarity and camaraderie. It was the warm feeling of fellowship that only shared experience can bring.

It was with a smile and a tired body that Aeden pulled a blanket over him. He closed his eyes and the world faded away. Aeden slept well that night.

Chapter 42

"Fire is the cleansing agent of Salvare's wrath."
Book of Khein 6:9

The following day was Market Day. Every
month the monastery hosted an open-air market
for the monks, local merchants, and farmers to
sell their wares. It was widely known as the best
market within a two-day's walk.

There was a definite cloud of excited energy
about the monastery that morning. It hung
diffusely in the air like spider silk. Aeden was no
exception. He too was caught in the web of
curious excitation. He quickly set to chores,
which were thankfully cut short. The monks
responded to a second set of clanging bells and
made for the nave for Morning Prayer.

The nave was cast in the glow of a thousand
candles. Already a sizeable group was in
attendance. There were far more people sitting
and waiting than any Morning Prayer in the Red
City Monastery. The group was diverse in age.
The young fidgeted in their seat. Muffled
coughing echoed grandly off the stone walls and
vaulted ceiling. The old sat quietly, solemnly
awaiting the arriving monks.

The gray-robed line entered and stood in a
formation not unlike that of the imperial army.
Their voices soon filled the chamber with prayer,

drowning out the shuffling of those in attendance. Many present, had their eyes closed. Others whispered the holy words to themselves in a quiet mumbling rhythm.

Prayers wrapped to a close and the monks left as earnestly as they had arrived. Each rank filed off, as they made their way from the grand nave to the humble refectory for a quick morning meal. Aeden was hungry and was looking forward to some food. He hoped as they walked, that he wouldn't be chosen for the morning reading.

The sun was still not up as the days had grown shorter. There was a chill in the air as the monks entered the dining area. They formed a line and worked their way through the kitchen, in silence, grabbing their plates. Adel was behind him, and the tall, lanky figure of Bosco was only a few people ahead of him.

A monk approached Bosco, tapping him lightly on the shoulder. By this point, Bosco was nearly to the entrance of the kitchens. A look of mild annoyance passed over his face. The other monk gestured for him to follow. A small wave of relief washed over Aeden as he knew he hadn't been picked for reading duty.

Once seated, the monks ate as Bosco's meek voice fought to be heard. His face was a mask of distaste as he read the story of Terric the Healer from the vaunted Book of Khein.

As breakfast wrapped up, Bosco was seen quickly exiting the refectory, likely making his way back to the library, to watch over the scribes and the Book of Divinus. As he stepped out, he covertly wiped at his nose with his robes. Aeden shivered in disgust. Did no one else notice his filthy habit?

Aeden briefly had an image of the watery eyed scribe looking up, catching Bosco in the middle of one of his nose explorations. He smiled to himself, grateful he wasn't cooped up in the library all day.

Odilo limped ahead of Aeden, joining Adel and Thomas. The morning silence was getting longer as the days grew shorter. It was irritating. There were times in which Aeden loved nothing more than to be left alone to his own thoughts, and there were times when he wanted to talk. This morning he wanted to talk. More specifically he wanted to know what the rest of the day was to bring and what he was going to be doing.

He remembered the whispered warning of the abbot and bit his tongue. Aeden had no wish to test the monk, and even less desire to see any of the Inquisitors again.

The sun was barely cresting the horizon as the monks stepped out, into the crisp morning air. Wisps of steam were uncoiling slowly from their dewy grasp. Down the twisting road, wagons were parked by different stalls, and merchants were already busy unloading and setting about displaying their wares.

The abbot strolled through this with a keen eye. He caught sight of the taller figure of Aeden and those milling about him. Gilbert made a beeline toward them as Aeden turned to face him.

"Here comes the abbot," Aeden whispered to the others.

"I need you, you, and you to assist with moving the fleeces from storage," he said, pointing to Aeden, Adel, and Odilo. "And you can help with the cheese from the basement," Gilbert said gesturing to Thomas.

Thomas' pale face lit up with obvious excitement. Adel glanced at Aeden with a bit of a smirk, half concealed on his face. They were thinking the same thing, Thomas wasn't going to be working so much as sampling and stuffing his cheeks with whatever he could find.

"Yes senior," the monks replied.

"Get to it then," the abbot said as he strode off to oversee the unfolding market.

Aeden waved to Thomas, "enjoy the cheeses!"

"Don't get lost under the mountain of fleeces," he responded as he walked back toward the monastery, a marked skip in his step.

"You think there's a stand selling pastries I could work at?" Adel asked with a bit of hope in his voice.

"Let's get to it," Odilo said, in a tone that could possibly be mistaken for a crude impersonation of the abbot. Adel's smile faded to assume a more monk-like visage as he followed Aeden and Odilo.

The storage shed containing the fleeces smelled of dust and earth. Aeden had watched the grandfathers of S'Vothe tend to the sheep. He had watched the older women's strong hands washing the wool in cold water before they began the laborious process of spinning it and winding it onto skeins.

As he grabbed a bundle and hefted it onto his shoulder, Adel asked what he'd been thinking.

"Why are these so clean?" Adel asked.

Odilo chuckled and Aeden smiled. He had seen enough sheep to know that their overcoat was often full of bramble, sweat, and toward the rear, a good smattering of feces. The fleeces before him were for the most part relatively clean.

"They rinse them in buckets of rainwater," Odilo explained, already walking out of the shed with his load.

This pacified Adel and he followed Odilo down the hill with Aeden on his heels.

By the time the sun was fully awake, the market was bustling with activity. A puppet show was already entertaining a group of children. The words of the puppeteer drew laughs and shouts of derision. His words carried above the din of the crowds.

"A monk there was upon his steed,

Gentle as a wooden reed,

His voice was wrought with words of hell,

So that all done deeds simply fell,

Fat were his lords of mirth,

But all they ate increased their girth,

Robbing from paupers and pikes,

Until one day all would be right,

And heads would roll upon the crowds

As all laughed, dancing to the clouds."

There was a smattering of applause. The children giggled at the movements of the puppets, as those who understood the puppeteer's words distanced themselves from his stand, wearing grim faces and tired eyes.

Aeden watched in fascination as hawkers walked amidst the growing crowds, shouting to those who would listen, as they attempted to sell their wares. The farming poor mustered at the outskirts of the market, selling what extra produce they had out of simple baskets.

"Not quite like the markets in the Red City," Adel said, looking upon the scene as he wiped sweat off his brow.

"It smells better," Aeden said.

"I'll give you that."

"There's still more fleece to bring down," Odilo said, clasping them on the shoulders, "then we can enjoy the day."

They hiked back up the hill for their final load. The sun was near its midday zenith and the few clouds that had dotted the sky, dissipated under its unrelenting glare. The warmth made Aeden feel lazy and he was looking forward to taking a few moments to relax and enjoy the scenery.

There were four bundles left in the now mostly empty shed. Not wishing to make another trip, Aeden carried two bundles as he followed Adel and Odilo back to the seller's stall. As he looked down at the market sprawled out before him, he saw the lazy entrails of smoke wafting up from the far side.

At first, he thought it was nothing more than the smoke of one of the food merchants. But soon the distant shouts of frantic people jostled that thought free.

"Fire!" He yelled as he pointed to the other end of the market, dropping his bundles.

Odilo glanced up and saw it before Adel had a chance to drop his load. Adel placed a hand to his brow and cast a long glance toward the market, tracing the origins of the smoky fingers now rising rapidly into the air.

"Let's get to the pumps," Odilo shouted as he

bolted down the hill, abandoning the fleece bundle on the grassy hillside.

Adel and Aeden didn't hesitate as they followed Odilo down the hill. Abbot Gilbert could be seen shouting orders as the monks abandoned their stalls and made their way to the pump by the well, carrying empty buckets.

Another set of flames leapt up into the air on the other side of the market. Children stood crying in the street as adults panicked, some began packing their wares, and others joined the effort of putting out the fires.

Despite the madness, Aeden's mind was alight with another possibility. His stomach was unsettled as the hard-earned knowledge of his childhood training beckoned to come forth through the layers of repression he'd built over the last year.

"Let's make a line," Aeden shouted as he approached the pumps.

A few of the monks looked up at him before slowly falling into a semblance of a line. One of the stronger monks was manning the pump as another held a bucket under its spout. The bucket once filled was then passed down the forming line, making its way to the fire. The flames now licked at the sky with a maddening fury. Black clouds of smoke spread across the market, fanned by a late afternoon wind.

The fire had jumped to a neighboring stall,

growing like some living entity. People were shouting and screams pierced the bedlam. They were the cries of pain.

Deep memories of the recent past welled up inside of Aeden. He glanced to the sky, half in fear that a draccus fiend was breathing fire from the heavens. Billowing charcoal clouds blotted out the otherwise blue firmament, but there was no sight or sign of a draccus fiend. His keen eyes then scanned the market.

He caught sight of a guard lying on the ground, unmoving. Aeden continued to look across the chaos of the marketplace and saw another Nailsean guard unmoving, face down on the ground. His heart dropped into his stomach as his initial suspicions were confirmed.

"We're under attack!" Aeden shouted.

Chapter 43

"The smell of fear is nothing like the smell of death." Saying of the Thane Sagan

The monks looked at Aeden with the startled expression of uncomprehending animals. None behaved the way they should have. As a boy in S'Vothe they would periodically hold drills to prepare for an eventual attack. Alarm bells would be rung as people ran to defensive positions where stashes of weapons lay ready.

Here, however, no one reacted. People continued to fight the fire. Monks continued with the buckets of water. Children continued to cry. And in the distance, the sound of drums beating irregularly upon the ground rumbled ever closer.

Aeden looked out to the tree line. It was there that he saw the first reflective glint of steel. A heartbeat later he saw horses burst forth. The sound hadn't been drums. They were the beat of hooves upon the battered ground.

They were majestic creatures, tall and strong. Their nostrils flared as they galloped toward the market. Men sat hunched on their powerful backs like predatory cats. The wind whipped at their determined faces, partially concealed by their helmets. A pennant snapped and unfurled in their haste, revealing the crest of the emperor, a draccus fiend with a single breath of flame.

Yet, the wind did not bring the sound of shouts or war cries. Rather it spoke of steely conviction, revealed by the set of their shoulders, the tenacious grip upon their spears and long swords. It spoke of the cold-hearted look of men resolved to kill.

Fear reared its ugly head. Aeden momentarily remained rooted to the spot. Had the Inquisitors found him? Had the abbot turned him in? It didn't make any sense. It was all happening too fast.

There was no more time for thought. Action and reaction were the only recourse. Aeden knew there was no point saving the market. Their only hope for survival was a good defensive position.

"Back to the monastery! Run for shelter!" He bellowed. His voice more resonant than even he imagined it could be.

The monks froze.

The impressive sight of war horses, rapidly descending upon the marketplace, transfixed them as if they had started upon a basilisk. It was infuriating.

Why was it when mortal danger was upon someone, they chose inaction? Was life so fragile and fleeting? Were people so complacent as to hand over responsibility for their well-being to unknown strangers?

Aeden was stupefied by their lack of response. It angered him. He felt his face flush hot as if a burning furnace was feeding his body. An enraged sweat broke out as a strange calm pacified his mental wanderings.

He glanced about, taking note of his surroundings. In the distance, he saw Abbot Gilbert. His tall strong frame was evidenced in his gait as he ran toward the incoming army. His robe billowed about him like a sail. His hands were held up, palms out. The war horses stammered ever closer. The abbot shouted, his words carried by the wind.

"In the name of Salvare, I demand you leave this place!"

The war horses didn't slow as they met him on the field. He looked insignificant and small next to the incoming mass of horses and men. A heavy war hammer was lifted overhead. It came down with startling force, smashing through the abbot's outstretched hands and into his skull. A muted thunk permeated the air for the span of a heartbeat and the abbot crumpled like a fallen rag doll. His head cleaved like a pig at market.

The dull crack of iron on bone seemed to wake the frozen populace. Startled screams hacked at the momentary hush as people began to run for their lives. Warriors on horseback cut through the market like a Vintas gale. The mocking pennant glared down upon the people of Nailsea.

Arms were thrown up in protective postures,

as swords sliced through flesh. Blood sprayed and speckled the beautiful manes of the horses. And the monks finally started their mad scramble up the hill, toward the protective walls of the monastery. They ran as if the lord Salvare beckoned to them. Gray-robed figures were seen slipping, sprinting, and scurrying in their desperate dash for safety.

Adel stood unmoving as he watched the massacre unfold. A sharp slap across the face woke his sleeping mind.

"Go to the monastery, protect the Book of Divinus," Aeden shouted.

Adel nodded, purpose filling him with strength. He glanced about as if suddenly awakened and joined the monks in their frantic retreat. Aeden watched him go then looked about for Odilo. His bald head and gray robes were heading down the hill toward the chaos.

"Odilo!" Aeden shouted, as he struggled to watch over his group, as if watching over a flock of dispersing sheep.

"Brother Thomas," Odilo shouted back as he headed down the hill.

Aeden glanced toward the retreating monks, ensuring Adel was part of the mad rush. He was. Unwilling to lose the man who had sheltered him, Aeden ran after Odilo.

His feet pounded the ground in a steady beat. The shrieks of women grasped at his resolve. The smell of charred skin sought to overwhelm him with guilty inaction. A gust of smoke caused him to cough in a sputtering gasp for air. It passed and he realized he'd caught up to Odilo.

The two now ran down the hill toward the stall Thomas was working. The unfolding scene fought to cut through his anger and immobilize him with fear.

The sounds of steel upon flesh cut through his awareness like a sickle through wheat. Children cried as war horses stammered about. The savagery of the imperial soldiers was more startling than anything Aeden had witnessed in his short life. It was almost too easy to forget that they too were men.

He was sickened, saddened, and more than anything he was angry.

"Odilo!" Thomas shouted, still clutching a wheel of cheese in his hands as if it would somehow save him from the madness.

Blood covered parts of his robe and hands. Aeden noticed his hands, they were visibly shaking. His eyes were wide with fear as he mumbled a prayer.

"We must get to shelter," Odilo shouted, reaching out a protective hand toward him, despite the distance.

Thomas left the relative shelter of a battered stall and ran toward them.

"No!" Aeden shouted with all his heart.

A tall man on a towering war horse caught sight of the fleeing monk. He reined his horse. Its magnificent head reared back in protest as it turned on a new path. The beast bore down on the frail monk. Thomas ran, oblivious. The horse crushed the broken body of a little girl as it galloped nearer.

It was the thundering beat of death. Odilo ran harder in an effort to save his brother monk. His feet were too slow. His body was too weak. With one swift movement Thomas was cut down. The wheel of cheese flew from his hands as his body fell lifeless to the bloodied ground. His final expression was one of surprise.

The fierce man on horseback did not hesitate as he reared toward Odilo.

Aeden reacted with every fiber in his body. Rage swirled about him like a gossamer storm. His thick hands grasped hold of his friend as the war horse settled upon them. Aeden caught sight of the startling green eyes of his attacker and the tufts of red hair under his helmet. A strange thought passed through his mind as he spun with Odilo in his arms. The soldier slashed with his sword, striking Aeden squarely upon the back.

Both Aeden and Odilo fell to the ground, struck down by the force of the blow. The soldier pulled on his reins and circled about. His war horse stomped by the unmoving figures as the man atop glanced about the burning market for more people to kill. A maniacal grin of religious fervor fixed upon his pale features.

Chapter 44

"Shock is the reflexive mind coping with a shattered reality." Text of Human Principles - Library of Galdor

It took a full day and half a night to control the fires that had swept across the marketplace. Citizens from Nailsea picked through the remains. Some were looking for friends, family members, as others sought anything of value. Nailsean guards were posted in a massive ring about the charred earth. Finally, gray robed monks were seen praying, chanting, and crying soft tears of sadness for those they had lost.

Aeden stumbled about, stuck somewhere between grief and outrage. His back was sore from where the attacker's sword had struck his Templas blade. His hands were numb and his eyes stung from the ash carried by the breeze.

After the attack, Aeden and Odilo had lay upon the beaten earth, lost, horrified, and scared. They watched through half open eyes as the war horses retreated away from the city. They stumbled to shaky feet, as the dust of reality settled firmly upon their shoulders. They watched as the Nailsean Guard rushed to defend the market and their fallen brothers.

They were too late. The market lay in smoldering ruins. Bodies were strewn about as if cast aside by some uncaring giant. Smoke clung to the air like some rabid animal, stinging the eyes and burning the noses of any who dared venture too close.

They wiped away tears of sadness and stifled feelings of anger as they picked through the bodies. They looked for their brother monks. Aeden forced himself to feel nothing. He refused to freeze as he had when his village had been destroyed. A village he should have sacrificed his life defending. Guilt lurked in the messy darkness of tangled emotion.

The two of them began with Thomas. They carefully carried his body away from the carnage to a spot unblemished by horses' hoof prints, blood, and smoldering ash. They whispered their prayers. They closed his eyes and they laid him to rest until such time that he could be properly buried.

As the day wore on, the line of bodies grew. They covered the green grass in neat rows. Their pale faces watching the movement of the sun. Their blood speckled clothing and horrendous injuries bespeaking a fate no one should have to endure.

Families claimed bodies. People wept and shouted. And through it all Odilo and Aeden continued to trudge along as if guided by some unseen hand, gifted with some unseen strength.

The truth, however, was far more mundane.

Both men had suffered tragedy in their lives. Both men had formed an irreconcilable bond that day. Their actions drew upon a deep well of tormented emotion. Their strength fed off each other as if some hidden link fueled them past their limits.

The monks from the monastery had finally made their way down. Even Bosco was amidst them. His face was a ghastly white as if it were trying to blend in with the white ash carried by the wind. Neri and Adel stood near each other, searching for their fellow band of pilgrimaging monks.

When Adel finally found Aeden and Odilo, his eyes burst forth with tears. His chest shook with heaving sobs of gratitude and racking helpings of fear.

As Aeden embraced his brother he whispered, "Thomas has been given to Salvare."

Adel nodded in shock and grief. His hands tracing a line over Aeden's Templas sword, slung under his robes, secured to his back. Aeden pulled away and looked at Adel. Adel had been too saddened to notice.

"We must organize an effort to care for our brother monks," Aeden's voice sounded firmer and stronger than he felt.

It was then that he noticed the Nailsean monks were looking upon him. They were looking for guidance, leadership. Their abbot lay upon the rows of dead and along with him laid their resolve. They needed strength, understanding, and above all, direction.

Aeden glanced about, the weight of the day attempting to rob him of his voice, of his dignity. He dug down into the pit of his heart and cleared his mind as countless hours of training had taught him to do and he spoke.

"We must be strong brothers. We must be strong for our fellow brothers who have fallen today. We must be strong for those who have lost family here today. We are the face of Salvare. We are the strength of the city. Let us pray for those who have fallen, and let us begin the task of caring for the bodies of those who have passed into the arms of our lord."

They were the words and the actions he should have taken with his own people. They were the guilty translation of conscience to the physical world. He knew they were watching.

By nightfall Aeden was exhausted. His body was starved and deprived of rest. One hundred and eighty-nine graves were dug that day. They were simple graves on the hillside near the market. Monks had begun the digging and the townsfolk of Nailsea had joined their efforts.

As the sun was setting, a long line of monks stood upon the hill and chanted. Their voices sang out a long and low prayer that echoed upon the shattered remains of the stalls. The sound penetrated the hearts of those present and carried with it the strength of hope and the power of renewal. It was then that Aeden understood the true power of the Church. It was the power of unity, faith, and community. It was the power of the masses.

Chapter 45

*"Pride is the sin of those who cannot see beyond
their own shadow." Book of Khein 2:12*

The next few days were filled with prayers,
grief, and the unceremonious chores of daily life.
A trudging routine was established as most
looked to their senior monk, James, to fill the
void. It had been deemed that on the third day
elections would be held to officially select the
new abbot. The elections meant the monks from
the Red City were free for longer parts of the day.

Strangely, many of the monks looked to
Aeden for leadership. Their fear dictated a need
for a show of strength. His reputation had
preceded him. He was already known as a monk
who took action. A monk who confronted an
Inquisitor to save his brothers. They craved
security and longed for someone who shared
their anger.

For Aeden, the days passed with this burning
anger seething within like glowing coals. The
injustice of it all seemed profoundly unfair. There
was a code of honor that warriors were to follow.
The Thane harped on this as part of their
intensive training. Hurting or killing the weak
and unarmed for the sole purpose of destruction
was not only frowned upon, it was taught as a sin
that would be rewarded with death in this life

and a special place of torment in the afterlife.

The emperor and his soldiers had extended far beyond their right and beyond the realm and sanctity of life. Aeden wanted nothing more than justice for his fallen friend Thomas and for the innocents slaughtered that day.

He was forced, however, to stifle his feelings for the other monks. He noticed most weren't dealing with their grief through anger, but instead were cast in the shadow of sadness and grief. For them he wore a face of strength and struggled to give hope.

He felt older than his years.

The business of praying and maintaining the monastery carried on as usual, despite the veiled anger Aeden felt or the pervasive gloom that stuck to the walls like a slick growth.

The scribes were still working day and night copying the Book of Divinus. It was a short book devoid of illustrations, but it was still a painstaking endeavor. The nibs of each quill used, had to constantly be recut. Quills were painstakingly made by the scribes during their non-copying hours. The ink paste they had created from boiling blackthorn, was dissolved in wine as needed to maintain a steady supply. And all the while Bosco watched and waited.

Aeden knew this, for he had stopped by the library on more than one occasion to check on the progress of the scribes. They weren't much happy for the visit. They were a solitary bunch that appeared to only tolerate the spoken word and the company of others. They were ideally suited to the task at hand.

Bosco, however, seemed overly interested one day at Aeden's visit. His usually drawn face formed a semblance of a smile. It gave him the awkward appearance of a man first learning to smile.

"How would you like to watch the fascinating work of the scribes for an hour?" Bosco asked hopefully.

Aeden had thought it strange and his curiosity welled up through the layers of anger and grief he had been harboring for the last few days.

"Why?" was all he asked.

Bosco regarded him thoughtfully for a moment as if he were trying to create the perfect lie. Instead he simply spoke, albeit softly, "to send a pigeon back to the Red City, to inform them," Bosco paused and the smile slipped from his face, "of our loss."

Aeden nodded and waved his hand, indicating for Bosco to go. The tall skinny frame of Bosco extricated himself quietly from the library. One of the scribes scowled, but didn't look up from his writing desk.

Aeden was glad for the reprieve. It was almost peaceful sitting in the room with the other monks. In many ways, he might as well have been left alone.

A soft light permeated the floor and graced the writing desks. Dust lingered in the air, hovering as small specks within the shafts of light, cutting delicately through the windows. The sounds of quills scratching upon the surface of parchments of vellum, hung delicately in the air. The voice of the sole reader was solemn and monotone. Every hour the scribes would change who read aloud as the others copied every word they heard.

The reader changed twice before Bosco returned. Aeden had hardly noticed. He had been lost in thought. His mind lurked on the events of a few days earlier. The dreadful images of the massacre at the marketplace unfolded in his mind like a sail unfurling to the wind.

He couldn't help but wonder if he had done something differently would he have been able to save Thomas. What if he had run down the hill sooner? What if he had drawn his sword and attacked the soldier on the massive war horse? A thousand what-ifs were fighting for control of his attention that Aeden was startled when Bosco rested a hand on his shoulder.

"Are you alright?" Bosco said, with what appeared to be genuine concern.

It was the first time Aeden had heard him speak with any sense of compassion. It was unsettling.

"Yes, thank you," he finally said as he stood, earning a sharp hushing "shhh," from one of the scribes.

He walked out of the room without looking back. The corridor suddenly felt warm and comforting despite its stone-cool chill. He simply stood there for a moment gathering himself and his bearings, before he made his way toward the central nave in the hopes of finding Adel.

He found Neri first.

"The other monks are speaking of your deeds," he said flatly.

This caught Aeden by surprise and he wasn't quite sure what Neri was referring to.

"I don't follow your words," he said in response.

Neri stared at him with the look of one talking to a child, "your actions at the marketplace, saving Odilo, organizing the effort of collecting the dead, and starting the task of burying them," he said with a minor hint of displeasure as if the whole affair hadn't played out properly.

Yet again Aeden found he was unable to connect with Neri. What was it that was so different about him that made it so hard to relate? Could the minor differences of culture create such a gap between two otherwise similar beings?

"Have you seen Adel?" Aeden asked.

"He's in the dining hall, as are the others," he said.

"What are you doing out here?" Curiosity was taking over.

"I don't like being in large groups, and Odilo felt Bosco should join them," Neri said.

"Thank you for the information," Aeden said awkwardly as he slowly moved away from the conversation.

Neri's words echoed in his head as he left him standing in the corridor. Neri was an odd man. He didn't speak often and when he did it was either to relate a misunderstanding of some sort or to correct someone based on a difference of perception. Neri seemed to view the world through a different lens. Aeden had always heard that D'seart was a unique place with very different customs and traditions. He therefore gave Neri's words little heed.

"I was looking for you," Adel said as he rounded a corner and practically ran into Aeden.

"I'm here," Aeden replied.

"They will announce the results of a secret election for the new abbot and Odilo thought it'd be good if we were there to show our support and cohesion."

"Should be fun," he replied, following Adel, although he wasn't looking forward to another clerical ceremony.

They walked without word down the stone corridors of the Monastery of Nailsea. Normally, there would have been other monks busy cleaning. Today the corridors were devoid of people. It was eerily quiet as if death still lingered in the air and demanded silence.

The monks were gathered in the dining hall. They were seated as if to have a meal, but it wasn't mealtime. No food rested upon the tables and the monks were quietly conversing with each other.

There was an air of excitement, nervousness, and grief that lingered over them. It was palpable but difficult to describe if one were to simply look at the gray-robed figures sitting there. It wasn't until more careful consideration was given to individual facial expressions, the fidgeting movements of their hands, and the low, somber tones of their voices that a picture could be painted to illustrate the mood. It was a picture that would have been painted in broad strokes of drab and gray.

Candles burned brightly, illuminating the scene in soft tones of yellow. Near one of the candelabras sat Odilo. Adel and Aeden took seats next to him. Aeden caught sight of James, the most likely candidate to become the new abbot, talking to another younger monk he recognized. It was the one who had greeted them on their first day. His curiosity about the whole process swelled.

"How do the elections work?" Aeden asked, hoping conversation would free his mind of its incessantly dark thoughts.

He hadn't really geared his question to anyone in particular. He had simply stated what he had been thinking out loud. Adel jumped in with an answer.

"There are a set of rules that must be followed, but every monastery is slightly different." He paused and looked at Odilo as if for guidance. Odilo simply nodded his head in encouragement.

Adel continued, "Generally a monk has to be over twenty-five years of age to be considered for the position, with at least eight years as a monk. Now some monasteries only promote from within, some purposefully think it best to elect someone from another monastery to keep things more civil and to introduce new ideas."

Adel paused in his explanation, as if thinking of what else there was to explain. Odilo looked over toward them and spoke, "If I may."

"Of course," Adel said quickly, his eyes tracking the incoming Neri and Bosco.

"There's normally a secret ballot that is cast by all the monks who have spent more than a month at the monastery. The votes are collected over the course of the day, tallied, and by the end of the day there is an announcement. In most cases the announcement is followed by a speech from the new abbot." Odilo rubbed his chin thoughtfully, a smile resting subtly upon his lips, "and if I'm not mistaken they're working out the finally tally now," he said pointing to James in the corner with the younger monk, Luke.

"What happens if there's a tie?" Aeden asked curiously.

"As far as I know that almost never happens," Odilo said looking toward Adel.

"I've never heard of it happening, but I'm sure it has. Normally there is a senior monk that seems most suited to the job and most people simply vote for him," Adel said expertly.

A hush fell upon the table and soon Aeden saw why. James stood facing them with his hands out in a placating gesture. His face carried the subtle expression of confused authority.

"Let us begin with a prayer for divine guidance from our lord Salvare," he began.

There were the sounds of shuffling feet, robes moving, and benches scraping across the ground as the monks stood. Then the prayer began.

"*Salvare, lord above all others, we ask for your strength,*

not to lend us power for unholy deeds, or to disobey,

but to better follow your will, to understand your desire

so that we can prostrate ourselves before your greatness."

The monks then took their seats once more. James remained standing, watching over them. His eyes paused on Aeden for a long moment before he began.

"A secret ballot was cast, and you, my brothers, have voted for whom you may have felt was best to lead, but…" James paused as he searched for the right words, pious, forgiving, and condescending, "recent events may have clouded your judgment and hidden Salvare's message from your hearts."

No one spoke, but there were quite a few displeased looks as monks turned to look briefly at each other.

"The lord always watches over us, protects us, and at times challenges us to atone for our weaknesses, our mistakes, our impure thoughts. Today he poses another challenge, one this monastery hasn't seen in over a hundred years," James looked about the table before finishing his thought, "A contested vote."

A faint murmuring swept across the room like ashes scattered by the wind. The murmuring died down, allowing James to continue.

"It appears Salvare has sought to test us in a trying time," he looked down at a small wooden icon he held in his hands. "The two votes are for myself," he took in a breath as if to control his emotions, "and the other for a very young brother from another monastery. Aeden of the

Red City."

Chapter 46

"Leadership is a quality best reserved for those who don't desire it." Saying of Sawol

The air grew still as if the breath of Vintas had exhaled a long, frosty breath. The stillness shattered and the monks broke into questioning conversation. A tied vote between an obvious choice and a novice from another monastery, was too much for most to stay silent.

Aeden briefly caught the angry glare of Bosco, the emotionless stare of Neri, and the broad smile of Adel.

"Abbot Aeden," Adel whispered, still smiling.

"Actually, he's still a novice and shouldn't have been considered for the vote at all," Odilo said without a trace of malice.

Part of Aeden felt proud, as if his father were watching him and finally approved of his leadership qualities. Another part of him was terrified. He didn't want to be stuck in one location for the rest of his life. The thought of being a monk and taking the vows were more than he wished to think of.

An image of the archduchess leapt to mind. Her dark hair splayed across a pillow as she smiled; it was an image he had dreamed of many times. The image was becoming mixed with reality. Aeden wasn't willing to give up on certain dreams just yet.

"I can't be abbot," Aeden said to Odilo.

"I know, I don't think you will be either, but a split vote normally has to be decided. It's possible that a monastic priest will have to decide."

"A what?" Aeden said, the words sounding familiar as if he had seen them before.

Adel jumped in pleased to offer what he knew, "they are part of the Church hierarchy. The rankings are novice to monk, to abbot, to monastic priest, to deacon, to archdeacon, then finally to high priest." He glanced at Odilo briefly.

"There are positions that are held with responsibility and authority that weren't mentioned, like the tithe counter, cellarer, kitchener, sacrist, and the almoner for example," Odilo piped in.

"And the carrier," Adel stated.

"Carrier?" Aeden was overwhelmed with how much he didn't yet know about the Church.

He was familiar with the positions within the monastery. He knew at the Red City Monastery that the abbot was Filbert, the sacrist was Blaise, Odilo was the almoner, and Monahan was the tithe counter. He'd talked of deacons and high priests, but he still felt remarkably ignorant at the lack of depth of his knowledge.

"The carrier is the man in charge of the pigeons, taking care of all the messages in and out of the monastery," Adel clarified.

"Actually, the carrier is a revolving duty and isn't a titled position with any authority like the others," Odilo corrected.

Adel nodded and twiddled his fingers, a habit Aeden had noticed him undertake whenever he was corrected.

There was a lull in the conversation. Aeden's mind spun as he struggled with his ever-changing reality. There was a reason he didn't want to be a leader when he was younger, it was too much responsibility. He always felt there had to be someone smarter, stronger, and better suited to leadership than himself. Why had he been chosen?

"Silence!" James shouted from the other side of the room.

The conversations died down as the monks turned to look at the older monk.

"Clearly we will have to resolve this as soon as possible. I suggest that for now I will take the position of abbot in everything but name and tomorrow we will send word to the monastic priest of Nailsea for an audience to settle the matter." James looked about the group.

Many of the monks were nodding their heads in agreement. Those who weren't nodding their heads turned to look at Aeden. It was then that he realized they expected some sort of response. He had been half voted in as the new abbot after all.

"I'm in agreement with Brother James. Until such time that we can get this matter resolved I suggest that we carry on with our holy work as was done under Abbot Gilbert, may Salvare watch over him."

Aeden's voice echoed more loudly than he intended and faded into silence. Odilo wore a strange expression half between pride and amusement. Adel was openly smiling.

"That's why you were chosen," Adel whispered.

Chapter 47

"The face is a mask meant to convey polite indifference." Caliph of Sha'ril

It was two days before they received a response from the monastic priest of Nailsea. It wasn't the response that either Aeden or James had been hoping for. Instead of making a decision and swiftly ending the matter, the priest referred them to the Deacon of Treton. In a way, it was almost perfect, for that was where the pilgrimage was supposed to visit next. But it did delay the uncertainty of the future.

It was Adel's theory that the priest of Nailsea knew this and simply decided to wash his hands of the matter and send it up the holy chain of authority. Whatever the reason, the monks were to travel the following morning, provided the scribes had finished their copying of the Book of Divinus.

In an effort to speed up their efforts, Aeden told them that they would leave with the book whether they were finished or not. This elicited some quiet grumblings and a few severe looks, but it also set a fire to their movements.

The next morning had come quickly. As they all had so few possessions, getting ready for travel was easy. A warm meal was provided after

Morning Prayer. The monks were given sacks of dried foods from the kitchener as they left the refectory.

The Book of Divinus had been hastily copied the night prior, only finishing before Morning Prayer. Bosco was once again in possession of the holy book, a look of self-righteousness transfixed to his thin features.

The Red City group was together again, standing at the steps of the monastery's western entrance. The notable absence was Thomas. His pale face, moral rectitude, cheese-loving person had been gifted to god and would no longer interject his words of knowledge, his awkward jokes, and his pious beliefs upon the group. He left a palpable gap that was only partially filled by the presence of James and a younger monk named Luke.

The sun was struggling to peer through an iron-gray sheet of clouds that blanketed the sky, creating a low ceiling. The air was cool to the point of being chilly. The grasses were damp with the morning dew, looking heavy and tired in the soft gray light. Standing in sheer contrast, were blackened parcels of land, lingering as burnt reminders of the imperial raid from days earlier.

The band of seven monks wound their way down the twisting path, toward the walled city of Nailsea. The stone road to the north passed through the heart of the city, predating the city by a few hundred years.

They passed through an arched entryway now more heavily defended by Nailsean Guards. Stone undercrofts topped by wooden living spaces, hugged the street. The monks walked passed the drab section of the city and cut right upon the wide and worn stone road.

The smells and sounds of humanity clung to the air like a leech upon fresh skin. Yet even the smells of pastries and baked goods were not enough to lift Adel from his look of mourning, or to permeate the determined gait of the traveling monks.

They passed through the city quickly and found themselves on a quiet stretch of road. Peasants were already working the fields in their final efforts to glean something from the land before the cold of Vintas forced them inside their homes. The sound of stakes being driven into the earth echoed mutedly across the fields as field masters used the end of Hearvest to delineate farming plots for the following year.

Had Thomas been with them, Aeden would have asked him questions about the whole process. Instead they walked without word.

James walked ahead with the not-so-subtle air of a man who wished to be seen as in charge. Luke kept up with his hellish pace. Bosco brought up the rear, already looking miserable as if the chill in the air and the rapid march were purposely there to annoy him.

Everything was almost normal.

It had taken them nearly five days to work their way to the Old City of Treton. They had stopped at a monastic cell in the woods for one of the nights, enjoying the warmth of a fire and the comfort of a good meal. The monks there were reserved, lean, and rigid. Nonetheless, it had been better than sleeping in the forest or a verder's hut for that matter.

The second day saw them crossing the Dath River, a wide and slow-moving body of water that separated Bodig from Gemynd. A small town near the river provided some food and shelter. It rested in the shadow of a large church-run windmill. Gemynd's grain was all ground by the millstones of Church owned mills, protected by the Gemynd noble house of Cox.

The ragged populace offered gifts and money in exchange for prayers and judgments, but Odilo declined, much to the protestations of the populace.

On the third night, they were able to find shelter with a farmer and his family. He let them warm themselves by the fire, for the days were turning cooler and the nights even colder. The leaves had fallen off most of the trees and lay dead and rotting upon the stone road.

The fourth day they happened upon another monastic cell. Unlike the cell in Bodig, this one was flush with precious metals, beautiful sculptures, and fat monks. It was a shock for them, but nice to have a warm meal and a straw mattress to lie upon for the night. They prayed twice as often, ate three times as much, and worked half as much as they did in Nailsea, all in the span of half a day and a night.

It was upon the fifth morning that they started once more upon the road north, then branching east on a well-worn path to the city of Treton. They left behind the comfort of the stone road and walked in solitude for several hours before the forest gave way to some open fields.

As they neared the old city, Aeden's stomach felt watery and weak. He caught sight of the ruins of the fallen city. They were nothing more than a few weathered pieces of stone that had been too large to be used in the construction of the rebuilt Treton, after the historic fall of the city. The sight provided little distraction as they branched off the main road and took a smaller road to the fortified complex of the Deacon of Treton.

He wasn't sure exactly why he felt nervous. Perhaps it was the fear that he'd be chosen as the new abbot, despite Odilo's reassurances to the contrary. Perhaps it was the stories he had heard of the power of the deacons of the Church. They had the authority to judge and sentence one to death if they deemed it Salvare's will. But more likely it was the pervasive fear that imperial soldiers would swoop on them out of the woods, mounted on their giant war horses, swinging their bloody blades, killing everyone he now knew and held dear.

Despite his fears, the final leg of their journey passed without incident.

Ahead of them stood the walled compound of the deacon. Instead of a white-walled monastery, open and inviting, there stood a squat gray structure that was reminiscent of a military garrison. Two slovenly guards defended the gates of the compound. Their demeanor was lazy yet alert.

A red pennant hung flaccid in the windless afternoon. The image of an oak tree and a sword could just barely be made out upon it.

"We have business with the deacon," James spoke out, ensuring he was cast in the light of leadership.

The guards took note of their gray robes and closely cropped hair and without word waved them through.

They passed wooden stables on the right. A few bored stable hands sat chewing straw upon bales of sodden hay. The neighing of large horses within the stables lent a gentle note to the air.

To their left was a round stone building with two chimneys spewing smoke. Those would be the kitchens. A few strong men in armor stood outside, as if waiting for something to occur. They had the vigilant look of eagles tracking their prey.

Directly ahead was the wide, low stone building of the deacon. A narrow stairway led to a single door framed by two narrow glassless windows. The building felt as old as the earth and as solid as a boulder.

Where were the poor, the huddled masses of the weak and sick? Wasn't the Church supposed to be a beacon of warmth, light, and openness? A place to help those in need? Aeden had been expecting mothers' holding their babies, hopeful of blessings or farmers with simple disputes seeking judgments, not the cold functionality of military-style buildings. Not the presence of strong men easily capable of violence.

Strangely, his group of shaven headed monks seemed out of place. Aeden felt he would have fit in better in his leather armor with his sword strapped obviously and proudly upon his back.

Letting go of his thoughts, he followed the other apprehensive monks up the narrow stairway, to the tight landing before a stout wooden door. Before any of them had a chance to knock, the door swung open on heavy hinges.

"Excuse me," a tall man in armor said as he stepped to the side allowing the monks passage.

The man was trailed by a younger man

carrying the items of the first. A squire of sorts Aeden thought. As soon as the monks entered the cool entryway, the tall man and his younger companion swept out of the room and closed the wooden door behind them, sealing them in the tomb-like entryway.

"Welcome brother monks, I've been expecting you," a dark-haired man in his thirties said.

He approached with open arms and a straight face.

"Deacon," James said nodding his head.

The man laughed a short, barking laugh before he spoke.

"I'm the subdeacon, Deacon Edwin is currently occupied. But I am in his full confidence and more than willing to confer any judgments in his stead," he said as he led them into another room that was lined with carpets. A roaring fire burned heartily along the far wall in a squat fireplace.

"I understand there is some dispute as to who will be abbot," the subdeacon said as he took a seat on a comfortable chair. "But before we delve into that business, please tell me of news from Nailsea." His dark, deep set eyes held the subtle hint of curiosity and expectation.

Aeden glanced about and noticed that there were no other chairs in the room, nor had the dark-haired man offered them food, drink, or somewhere to rest their travel burdened legs.

None spoke for a moment, leaving the subdeacon's words to fade into silence as his hooded expression turned into a frown. Aeden felt compelled to speak.

"There was an attack on the marketplace," Aeden said, his voice low, yet strong, "me and my brother monks were busy within the stalls or moving supplies from the monastery storehouses. A fire broke out on one side of the market followed by another on the other side, a distraction allowing the pre-invasion party to kill the Nailsean guards, before the main body swept through the town upon horseback, cutting down men, women, and children, including seven monks."

The subdeacon regarded Aeden thoughtfully for a moment, staring intently upon him. "Was there anything else?" he inquired.

Before anyone else had a chance to speak Aeden blurted out, "I caught sight of one of the raiding party. I saw his eyes; they were as green as grass and his hair through the gap in his helmet, red like flame."

The subdeacon then looked to the other monks present as if his gaze alone could decipher the truth, before settling upon Aeden once more. The subdeacon briefly raised an eyebrow as if in thought before allowing his face to become passive again.

"Interesting that you were able to get so close and survive," the subdeacon said rhetorically.

Aeden was beginning to realize that the subdeacon was a clever man. Despite the nature of his statement Odilo responded.

"It must have been Salvare's will, for brother Aeden speaks from the heart and his words are true."

"Yes, he does, doesn't he?" The subdeacon paused for a moment before changing tracts, "Let's move on to the real reason you are here, a tied vote at the monastery, and the continuation of a pilgrimage."

"Yes father," James spoke up in an effort to take charge.

Odilo's eyes showed surprise at mention of the pilgrimage. Neri remained tight faced, even more so than usual. As far as Aeden knew, the deacon wasn't made aware of their arrival. The faint words he overheard through Abbot Filbert's door echoed lightly in his head, a response to Blaise's simple question asking if he had informed the deacon, *You know very well that wouldn't be wise, I might as well inform the High Priest of Gemynd what we intend. There is no choice in this matter.*

The dark-haired subdeacon was clearly a shrewd man playing at a subtle game that remained veiled to the simple monks.

"You are both astute and wise," James said in

a blatant attempt to curry favor.

"You needn't flatter me," the subdeacon said with sharp eyes and a wave of his bejeweled hand, "I do assume you're seeking the position of abbot at Nailsea?"

"Yes father," he replied in a meeker voice that didn't suit him.

The subdeacon's eyes scanned over the others and finally stopped upon the youthful figure of Aeden. He pointed to him as he spoke.

"Step forward, I assume you are the youth that tied his vote?"

"I am," Aeden said with more strength in his voice than intended.

The subdeacon nodded his head as if in apparent thought. "You are obviously too young and the rules of the Church clearly stipulate the requirements necessary for one to become abbot."

At this point a wide smile crept onto James' face as he took a moment to gloat at the decision. Aeden felt a sudden burden lifted from his chest and resisted an urge to laugh.

"I'm not finished," the subdeacon said, his eyes glaring intensely as if he did not like to be interrupted by idle thoughts, "James will not become the abbot of Nailsea, Deacon Edwin has chosen another to fill Abbot Gilbert's place."

The smile slipped from James' face as quickly as if someone had reached forward and snatched it from him.

"Who then, if I may ask, is to fill that position?" James asked in a tightly controlled voice.

The subdeacon's eyes then looked over to the tall, lanky figure of Bosco.

"Bosco of the Red City Monastery shall be, and you shall be his sacrist, assisting him as is necessary in the daily running of the monastery."

Aeden looked over to Bosco. Bosco's eyes were averted, but the look of surprise Aeden had expected, failed to roll across Bosco's long face. Bosco's hand clutched at his chest as if he were suffering chest pain, but Aeden quickly realized he was holding the Book of Divinus within the folds of his robes.

"Ah yes, as for the book, please hand that to the young monk, it shall now be in his care," the subdeacon commanded, looking from Bosco to Aeden.

Bosco looked hesitant at first until he caught sight of the subdeacon's unwavering glare. With long fingers, he withdrew the carefully wrapped book and placed it in Aeden's strong hands.

Just then a side door swung open. An angry looking man with a scar upon one side of his face strode out. He wore light body armor with the circle of Salvare upon his chest, but strangely no weapons were on his person. He was followed by the most beautiful woman Aeden had ever seen, the Archduchess of the Second House of Bodig. He couldn't have been more surprised had the roof collapsed around them.

The scarred man hardly gave them the time of day until his eye caught the short, bald, and slightly scarred figure of Odilo. There was a pregnant pause in which the man studied him as if recalling some long dormant memory. He grunted, nodded briefly and stalked off.

Aeden, however, barely noticed. His attention was focused on the archduchess. Had he paid more attention he may have seen the subdeacon squirm in his chair. But of course, he only had eyes for the archduchess.

She wore a simple garment, layered to flatter her feminine features with a red sash elegantly tied about her narrow waist. Her dark hair seemed even darker and more beautiful in the flickering light of the crackling fire. She paused as she stepped through, her eyes finding his.

Aeden stood immobilized as if he had just sprouted roots. Time hung suspended for what felt like an eternity. In that moment, he studied every line, every shadow, every perfection that was her face. A simple smile passed over her lips so subtly that Aeden wondered if he had imagined it.

The moment was broken and she followed the angry-looking man through the room, passing the monks and moving beyond Aeden's field of vision. Aeden hardly noticed as an older man too stepped into the room. His robes were clean, finely woven, and of an expensive fabric, yet clearly demarcated him of the Church.

"I trust this matter has been resolved," the man said, his voice struggling to hide his disdain as his hands gestured loosely to the band of monks.

"Yes deacon," the subdeacon responded pushing himself from the chair.

The monks stood there a moment as if lost for words or action.

"You may go, spread the good word and walk in Salvare's light," the subdeacon said.

The monks didn't need further coaxing. They left the room and exited the heavy building.

Chapter 48

"The temerity of faith is one best left for men of god." Saying of Gemynd

The journey northward to Gemynd was not without incident. As Neri, Adel, Odilo, and Aeden made their way back toward the Old City of Treton they met with some trouble, yet ultimately, they felt a greater connection to their faith and their god. And in Aeden's case it was a subtle reminder of the power of the Thirteen.

The day was particularly cold as the first sign of Vintas was upon them. Snow fell in a light flurry as steely clouds obscured the weak sun. An occasional gust of wind would tear through the leafless trees and cut through their robes like a wolf tearing into a meal.

They had already parted ways with Bosco, James, and Luke, for they were heading back to Nailsea. The farewells were half-hearted and forced for the most part. Bosco took to his new role quickly, holding his head differently and looking down the length of his long nose as if peering at subordinates. James continued to sulk, despite his age, and wore an expression of despondent disregard. Luke was still young, younger even than Aeden, and smiled and waved his goodbye enthusiastically.

The pilgrimaging monks hadn't traveled far

when the unfortunate business all began. It was Neri who first warned them of something out of the ordinary, but not in any noble manner. It was his garish shout that pulled them from their thoughts and had them spin about to see what had surprised the trailing monk.

On the roadway stood a man wearing nothing but tattered rags for clothing. He was dirty and smelled of waste and decay. His feet were bare, blistered, and rough. Most notably he was missing his tongue, a clear sign of one who had lied or slandered someone higher on the social food chain.

He was clearly an outlaw.

The group was so caught up by the sight of the man that they failed to notice two other outlaws step onto the road behind them. Adel and Odilo had already worked their way toward Neri and the tongueless man in an effort to potentially offer aid.

This left Aeden toward the back of the group. It was Aeden who noticed the two men step onto the street with knives in their hands. They looked emaciated and mean. Their knives, though rusty and chipped, look menacing in their hands as their wild looking eyes searched the group hungrily.

Under different circumstances Aeden would have thought it almost comical that men without armor and nothing more than short knives were attacking a larger, healthier group. But he was with a band of monks, defended by the good-will of the people and their faith in god. In other words, it was up to him to assure their safety. Blaise's words rang in his head, *"keep them safe brother Aeden."*

With hands stretched out before him, palms out, he approached the larger one to the right. He took a few calming breaths and cleared his mind as he became alert to the subtle movements of the men before him. He watched their stance, the tension in their shoulders, and the darting look of their eyes.

He was briefly reminded of his training as a boy. Instead of a wild man before him it was Devon, his friend. Devon wore a smirk and held a wooden spathe. It was Aeden's task to disarm Devon rapidly and without any harm to himself. His father, the kovor, stood in the shadows watching.

The memory faded rapidly, replaced with the cold reality before him. These men were not his friends. They were here with a single purpose, to steal whatever they could, anyway they could.

The more he thought on it, the angrier he became. The monks were unarmed and these men wished to commit violence in the name of selfish desire, rather than work for what they needed. Images of imperial soldiers, sweeping through the Nailsean market on horseback cutting through the masses, fueled the simmering coals of injustice he had been harboring for the last few days.

Without hesitation, Aeden closed the remaining distance between him and the first man. In a rapid blur of motion, he broke the hand that held the knife and threw the man to the side of the road. The other man attacked as Aeden had expected, with the rusted blade thrust toward him.

He caught a glimpse of Odilo turning toward him and heard words echo in the background. They were lost to him as he engaged. His hand connected with the man's wrist as he turned his body and allowed the thrust to miss his body. He pivoted and applied pressure to the knife hand sending the man sailing feet over head toward the ground. The man fell in a heap and Aeden slammed a heavy palm onto the back of his neck. The connection of his stone-hardened palm to the soft backside of the man's neck was strangely satisfying.

The larger man with a broken arm glanced at his fallen friend then to Aeden. Aeden's eyes were pools of fury, dark and menacing. The man shrank back as if Aeden's stare had burnt his flesh. He scrambled backward to his feet and retreated rapidly into the forest.

At the other end of the small band of monks the tongueless man grunted something incomprehensible. Soon he too bolted into the forest, leaving the group momentarily stunned.

"What have you done?" Neri inquired as he pushed his way toward Aeden, half accusatory, half in awe.

"Nothing," he replied, looking down at the limp form of the man on the ground, his insides swirling as his heart pounded away at his chest.

"Why did they run and what happened to this man?" Neri asked in a rush.

Adel stepped forward and looked down at the man, whispering, "It's a miracle!"

Aeden glanced about looking at the others, noticing that all eyes were on him. Only Odilo seemed to have registered the last interaction, yet he stood quietly. Odilo took a small step forward and laid a gentle and calming hand on Aeden.

For a moment Aeden felt like he was going to react, but instead the storm of emotion slowly settled. Aeden had been ready to answer with the truth, but Adel's words caught him by surprise. For some reason Aeden felt compelled to lie. It was a simple transgression into an arena of ease and dishonor, one that would mark greater transgressions to come.

"I began to pray quietly as I saw the two men approach. As this man," Aeden pointed to the fallen form crumpled before him, "approached, I touched the Book of Divinus and he fell before my feet as if struck by the hand of god. The other man saw this and ran." Finally, his breathing was under control and his face fell into its usual passive countenance.

Neri narrowed his eyes as Odilo stood by his side. Odilo glanced at the fallen form briefly, uttering a quick prayer. It was Neri who spoke.

"Salvare's will has been done," he stated without sympathy as he stepped past the fallen form.

Aeden knelt by the fallen man and placed a hand on his neck. He was rewarded by a heavy pulse.

"He will live," he said looking up to Odilo and Adel.

"He'll live," Adel whispered as if the shock were only now slowly wearing away like ice at the beginning of Lenton.

"Salvare is merciful," Odilo said before looking up, catching Aeden's eye.

"Yes, and works in mysterious ways," Adel stated, looking at Odilo.

They nodded as they resumed their journey toward the stone road. The air somehow felt colder and thicker. The snow now began to fall in earnest, blanketing the ground in a thin film of white. The scene was beautiful and clean, a work of art that only Salvare could have produced.

Fear faded as heartbeats settled. Finally, a feeling of vigor settled upon the group as realization of their brush with death and god's work permeated their consciousness.

The clouds parted, allowing for a shaft of light to illuminate the roadway ahead. Snow danced in the light as it fell from the heavens. And even Neri had a faint, giddy smile upon his lips. They were alive and despite all evidence to the contrary, selected and protected by Salvare himself.

Sometimes belief in a thing is more important than understanding, Aeden thought. He cast one final glance back upon the now serene scene. The last remnants of his fight now rested as unseen prints under his restful gaze.

Chapter 49

*"Festivals disarm the masses, while leaving the
church armed with the tools of piety." Analogy of the
Order - Library of Galdor*

It was only a half day from the deacon's
residence to the Old City of Treton. The road was
covered in a light dusting of snow and the day
was cast in a misty gray. The bare branches of the
deciduous trees were plated in a layer of silvery
frost, while the evergreens cradled white powder
in the delicate embrace of their pine needles.

Aeden's feet were cold and his hands were
buried within the folds of his homespun robe in
an effort to keep them warm. Neri was paler than
usual and Adel had far less to say than normal.
Luckily, they knew they hadn't far to go before
the promise of warmth and food.

As they trudged along the roadway, they met
few others. Most were wise enough to stay
indoors, where a crackling fire kept them warm.
It was the smell of burning wood that let the
monks know they were getting close to Treton.

Aeden knew that the pilgrimage truly began
in the old city. It was there that history had left its
mark. It was the ancient city that had once defied
the church only to transform into sacred land,
thereby becoming one of the most devout and
pious cities in the Three Kingdoms. In a way, it

was one of the Holy Order of Sancire's greatest achievements.

The city revealed itself in fits, as a cold wind played with the low-hanging fog. Snow danced upon the mud-covered stones and dashed against stone buildings like handfuls of salt.

They had arrived during the Festival of Nettles, one of the numerous holidays sponsored by the Church. The holidays provided a respite from work and were often a time when lords would hold a feast for the peasants in the keep of their castles. Merchants, blacksmiths, and minor gentry would gather in their homes and eat until their bellies were full and their eyes were heavy.

Therefore, the streets were largely empty as people were preparing for their Vintas feast. The few people that were outside were huddled against the cold in thick cloaks or in the case of those with a little more money, warm furs.

The monks stood out as they walked down the street. For one, their gray robes marked them of Bodig, for the monks of Gemynd wore nicer robes dyed a deep blue. Two, their lack of Vintas cloaks made them look far humbler, disciplined, and pious. This drew more attention and attracted peasants, merchants, tradesmen, and women alike.

"May the light be upon your back," folks would utter as the monks trudged through the city.

The city itself was clearly as old as time. The roads were paved in worn stone, cracked and softened by centuries of use and weather. The streets curved about larger, windowless buildings, built during an era before the understanding of true and straight walls, relying upon girth for strength. Therefore, many of the homes were squat structures, with the heavy feel of permanence. Aeden imagined them as fat, stone giants resting on their backs, with their great big bellies forming the domed roofs.

As it was Vintas, the windows were covered in thick blankets in an effort to keep their stone homes warm. The golden light of flickering fires was hidden from view and only made known by the makeshift chimneys spewing smoke into the air.

"Excuse me, where can we find the Monastery of Treton?" Odilo asked a man wrapped in furs.

The man stopped and held up his hands in a sign of respect before answering. "Follow this road to the Mare's Inn, and then take the road to your left until you come upon it," he said with clouds of vapor escaping his lips with each breath.

"How will we know the monastery?" Neri inquired.

"By its newness and wealth," the man stated, rubbing his hands together.

"May Salvare bless your holiday," Odilo said in thanks.

The man bowed his head slightly and hurried off.

The monks found the inn quickly enough. It was a large building with glass windows and multiple chimneys. The windows glowed a faint red, beckoning the monks inside. Instead they followed Odilo, turning left down the stone road toward the monastery.

They didn't have to travel far before happening upon a tall building with impossibly long windows covered in fine stained glass. Golden spires capped two lofty towers, standing abreast two immense doors. Cleverly carved into one of the doors was a smaller door large enough for a man to pass through. Everything was locked up tighter than a widow's disconcerted frown.

Aeden withdrew his hands from the folds of warmth in his now damp robe. He clasped the metal knocker and banged the door twice loudly, his flesh threatening to stick to the frozen metal.

The monks stood there for a few minutes before knocking again. It was on their third attempt that they could hear rustling on the other side and a bolt being slid free. The small door within a door opened and a fat monk stood there looking at them, a candle burning gently in his hand.

"Come now, out of the cold you four," he

said quickly, ushering them inside with a swift movement of his blue-robed arm.

The Red City monks didn't hesitate as they walked inside hoping for warmth. The large monk closed the door behind them before speaking again.

"You're just in time for the feast, we've been expecting you," he said jovially.

The grand nave was dark and cold, lit only by the candle in the monk's hand. The faint yellow light reflected off the gold leaf and polished silver, hugging the graceful pillars. Aeden strained to see farther into the depths of the nave but was rewarded with shadow and darkness.

"This way brothers, to warmth and food," the monk said as he burnished his candle through the cavernous depths of the lavish monastery.

Aeden trailed behind the others, feelings of curiosity tugging at him. It was already evident that Gemynd was different than Bodig. It was colder, grayer, and the monasteries seemed richer, displaying their wealth in a wanton attempt to convince the masses of Salvare's greatness.

They arrived at a grand dining hall filled with oversized monks. A massive fire lent light, warmth, and a hint of smoke to the stone-vaulted room. Wooden tables lay side by side and were already covered in what appeared to be the first few courses of a grand feast. Servants were coming out with trays as they were greeted and ushered to seats.

Aeden was surprised. The others were in shock at the level of decadence displayed. An excessive number of candles were burning along the walls, providing more than ample light. None-too-quiet discussions echoed off the stone surfaces. It seemed to be more an atmosphere of celebration and gluttony than quiet contemplation.

"Eat brothers!" One of the seated monks said, gesturing to them with a half-eaten piece of meat dangling from his fingers.

Aeden glanced at Odilo and the others briefly before he reached forward and grabbed a chunk of pheasant. It was very mildly spiced, not nearly as much as some of the foods in Bodig, perhaps because of the weather he thought idly.

"Certainly different than Nailsea," Aeden said conspiratorially to Adel recalling the runner Luke taking them immediately to the strict Abbot Gilbert.

Adel glanced sideways at Aeden then quickly to Odilo as if speaking during mealtime was frowned upon.

"The rules are different here, just keep Salvare in your hearts," Odilo said, only partially looking at them as if he knew exactly what they were thinking.

This seemed to be what Adel had been

looking for. He dipped some horse bread into a bowl of beer before responding. "Nailsea makes me think of other things," he said quietly.

"Thomas," Aeden whispered, a sudden feeling of sadness welling up inside of him like a cold spring.

"Yes," Adel responded, pausing with a hunk of bread in his hand.

"I'm sure he's been guided into the light."

"Thanks to you, for properly burying him and leading the monks in prayer."

"I don't remember leading anyone in much of anything, besides Odilo was the one who started the prayers," Aeden said honestly.

Adel shrugged and dipped some more bread into his beer. The two of them remained silent for a time as a sea of conversation ebbed and flowed along the natural rhythms of dinner.

"Have some more," a monk next to Aeden said emphatically as he pushed a plate of dilled potatoes toward him.

"Thank you," Aeden replied, remembering to grab the plate with his left hand supported by his right at the elbow. It was a tradition of strength and deference among the Gemynd, according to Thomas.

"You're not from here," the man next to him suddenly said, with crumbs falling from his beard, and his blue eyes staring carefully at Aeden's gray irises and shortly cropped white hair.

"I was struck by lightning when I was young," Aeden said, remembering a story he once heard about a boy from a distant town.

"Graced by Salvare's own hand, marked for something special I see," he said slightly less seriously, "well, all the same, eat and enjoy. It is His holiday after all!"

Chapter 50

"And so, the Calenites fell upon the merciless blade of Sancire." Annals of Verold, Volume II - Anonymous

The days at the Treton Monastery passed uneventfully. It was a reprieve of sorts for what had happened in Nailsea and for what was to come. The time spent there was akin to sitting in the eye of a storm, firmly oblivious to the horizon.

The days were cold and snow fell about them in gentle sheets of silky white. The scribes worked with the attention and efficiency of neophytes, only half-hearted in their earnestness to complete the task. Chores were accomplished by a small army of servants as the glutinous monks ate, slept, and prayed, mostly in that order.

Aeden spent a lot of time in the library reading by candlelight. Adel was more withdrawn than usual. He was taking the loss of Brother Thomas harder than Odilo or Neri. In fact, Neri seemed to be unaffected, save for spending more time with the pigeons and the monastery carrier.

It was on the second week there, a particularly cold day, that Aeden stumbled across an interesting bit of information in a well-hidden book. In particular, a set of passages that related Dominer the Pure's attempts at gathering a following. The passage read was the following:

It is heretofore unknown and unheralded in account, but anonymity requires certain annals to preclude facts for their very nature may be deemed threatening to those vested in the current state of affairs. Therefore, it was upon the First Age of the Imperium, the Second Age of Man, and the hundred and fiftieth year of Calenite Law that Dominer, son of Galvin of Chur began an ambitious campaign in the view of self-pious belief. His actions could be seen as a response to the oppression of belief in all things ethereal. For history records a bloody time of persecution, fear, and mistrust. Agents of Calen were hidden by fold and cloth, devious to the point of absurdity. It was Dominer son of Galvin that spoke out against the atrocities of power, the trappings of wealth, and the deceit of the ruling class. His word echoed grandly upon the plains to profound effect; for followers swelled upon the earth in droves to hear his sermons, oblivious to the hidden demons of powerful men. Words of self-denial, restraint, and discipline, followed a call to greater action; so then a dichotomy of belief was founded, rooted in the efforts of a few to overcome the power of the pervasive. Dominer son of Galvin met Sha'a of A'sh and begot four sons, Sha'ril in honor of the mother, Gemynd to honor the mind, Bodig to honor the body, and Sawol in honor of the soul. As Dominer's children grew, so too did his affection for the people and the land, whilst his desire

*for change and liberty from Calenite Law swelled. It
was upon the eclipse of the sun during the hundred
and sixty first year of Calenite Law that the following
of sancire began their destructive emancipation from
those who wished to continue their iron rule; cities
were burned, lives were lost, and a religion was born.
With each victory Dominer grew in stature. Ballads of
greatness were cast to stone and sang upon the lips of
men. Even after his death upon the flames of Tretun
were the songs sung. Those who did not sing wept at
his loss but none more than his wife, who had drew
unto him unlike any other; Sha'a fled with her favored
son Sha'ril to the deserts of the far south, Gemynd in
his infinite wisdom deemed the north to be of greater
safety and took refuge amongst the windswept
mountains, Bodig chose to fight and stay in the land of
his birth, leaving Sawol to wander south of the mighty
river in search of creating a land of peace. And so it
was on the First Age of the Imperium, the Second Age
of Man, and the one hundred and sixty ninth year that
the Empire of Calen fell.*

Aeden's mind reeled with questions. If this
was an accurate account of history, it flew in the
face of all other accounts he had read thus far. It
contradicted Blaise's words and was likely
condemned by the Church. He was surprised to
have found it.

At first the book's old dusty cover beckoned
to him, the yellowed parchment and old flowing
script begged to be read. He was careful with the

pages for they felt ready to break at the slightest touch. He read as quickly as he could, eager to devour more, yet many of the pages were beyond repair, their words lost to the ages.

When he finally read what he could, he delicately closed the book with the gentleness of a first kiss. Aeden ached to know more, to uncover the hidden secrets of history, to better understand the present. He thought it equally strange and fascinating that such different accounts of the same history could be told. At times, he felt as if the very house of god whisked the wind from the lungs of the faithful, casting the light into shadow.

The more he thought on it, the more curious he became. Among the Thane there were numerous stories, parables his master called them. They served the purpose of delivering a moral principle, yet most people knew they weren't entirely true. This differed from the texts and words of the monks he met. Most monks seemed to place greater faith in the words of their books and the stories of the seniors, as though they were more than parables, they were living embodiments of what had truly occurred.

Many of their stories conflicted with what he knew to be true. This awakened a greater curiosity and set his mind aflame with questions. Were their stories true or were the stories he grew up with true? Part of him wanted to reject all that was not Thane, but he could almost see his friend Devon playing devil's advocate just to spurn him. The conversation played out in his mind as if the ghost of his deceased friend were there before him.

"You always questioned our stories, traditions, and methods, why would you stop now? You feel guilty for leaving me, leaving S'Vothe the way you'd found us? Burnt and exposed? Or is it you've come to your senses? The kovor's son finally acting as he should," Aeden imagined Devon smirking as if he had made an irrefutable point.

"I will forever deal with my guilt, but I'll make it right. I will do all in my power to set you free. As for my changes. I have grown. I have learned that patience begins with the self before being extended to others."

"So, the Temple of Boredom worked!"

"Maybe. But if I've grown why do I feel so angry," Aeden replied to the imaginary Devon.

"I don't think you're angry enough! You always were soft like a woman. But what did I expect from a boy raised by grandmothers. I'm sure you will soon forget all of us who perished while you watched from safety," Devon's eyes turned cold.

Aeden's heart beat strangely in his chest. Guilt surfaced like bile. The feeling tasted bitter in his mouth. He rubbed his forehead and struggled to bury his memories.

As he opened his eyes, he glanced down at the dusty book. He picked it up gingerly and replaced it in the hidden spot behind the other books. His guilt slowly subsiding as questions bubbled to the surface. As the Evening Prayer bell rung out its deep reverberating song, Aeden thought of the ancient Calenites and their once vast empire.

Chapter 51

"Inspiration can be taught to those with an open mind and willing heart." Canton of Sawol

Inspired by the texts he had read, Aeden spoke with Adel. He was curious about the different accounts of history, wanted a fresh perspective, and most of all he wanted to see if he could convince a friend to join him in speaking out against the atrocities that had occurred at the Nailsean market.

"What did you think?" Aeden asked inquisitively.

"It contrasts Blaise's story and would likely be considered a blasphemous account of Dominer the Pure," Adel replied carefully.

"I know, but the reasons for his struggle make sense. Why else would a man be driven to violence," Aeden saw Adel's face twist into a look of disapproval.

"It may seem to make sense, but that doesn't mean it's true. Dominer was inspired by Salvare himself, the one true god, to take proper action, to save the people," Adel said.

Aeden eyed him for a moment, feeling as though he was losing Adel's interest before he even had a chance to begin. What was it about certain beliefs that made people abandon all logic, Aeden wondered? It angered him.

"What are you afraid of? The truth? Why couldn't Dominer have both been inspired by Salvare and acted in response to the events of the time?" Aeden said pleadingly.

Adel's composure changed as he crossed his arms over his chest.

"I live with the faith of my god in my heart, I'm not afraid," Adel responded defensively.

Aeden pressed on, in the hopes of still convincing him.

"Perhaps god inspired him at the right time, it was all part of Salvare's plan to have Dominer rise up against the oppression of the Calenite Empire. How do we not know that Salvare isn't testing us, seeing when we will take action, to make positive change?" Aeden said, his mind searching for words to convince the doubting Adel. "Monks have already been demonstrating, as I saw when I first came to the Red City, but there has to be a more effective way," he continued.

"I don't know. What can we do but pray and set an example?" Adel intoned.

"Pray louder so that groups of people hear. Set the example through words and action to let the people know that it isn't right for those with power to simply squash those without. Why kill a marketplace full of monks and townspeople if not to send a message? We can be even louder and make ourselves heard."

"And what message would you send?" Odilo asked as he stepped into the room, a look of intense interest written upon his face.

Adel and Aeden turned to look at him. Aeden was startled and it showed, whereas Adel looked moderately guilty, as though he had been caught conspiring in some illicit scheme.

"That the emperor cannot be allowed to kill without cause, without repercussions," Aeden said, his voice trailing off.

Odilo merely nodded and looked thoughtful as he looked to Adel, "and your thoughts?"

"Brother, I don't know what to believe," he responded more quietly, "but I think that if Salvare wanted reprisal, He will do it in His own way in His own time."

"We can't be so swift to assume to know the will of god or be so quick to assume it is upon our shoulders to carry out His justice. Remember that in the shadow of ignorance further ignorance is born." Odilo said, looking to Aden.

"But we were there, you saw them cut the people down, you saw the banners and armor of the emperor, the bodies of the dead," Aeden said in frustration.

"You speak of inciting the people to act out, this is very different than drawing attention to an idea, and letting Salvare sort out the rest," Odilo said gently.

"What if it's Salvare's will that we speak out, we tell the people what we saw," Aeden said.

Odilo drew in a slow breath and looked at them both with compassion in his eyes, "because it is never Salvare's will to cause harm or be the spark that leads to death."

Aeden almost spoke again, for he knew in his heart that Dominer had led the people to resist Calenite Law. Instead he chose silence, knowing there was no use debating Odilo. He had no desire to step upon the friendship of either monk, despite the anger of the injustice that simmered within.

Swallowing his pride, Aeden stepped out into the hallway and sought a quiet space to contemplate recent events.

Chapter 52

"Words are often the spark that kindles a fire."
Canton of Sawol

The days grew shorter and became colder. Snow blanketed rooftops and rested lazily in rifts next to squat stone buildings. Time passed without much discussion of rebellion, death, or the empire. Instead, idle talk of the cold weather, prayer, and the slow progress of Treton scribes touched the lips of the small band of visiting monks. The laziness of the monastery became ever more evident as another holiday passed and yet another feast of glutinous proportions was forced upon already full stomachs.

At first Aeden had wrestled with the idea of talking about the massacre to others. As more time passed, he found it harder to stifle his anger and to resist the temptation of action. He found it increasingly difficult to sit quietly; to pretend nothing happened.

In the name of Thomas, he swore an oath to Salvare that those who perpetrated his death and the deaths of the other one hundred and eighty-eight present that day would suffer an equal fate. More quietly he swore an oath to the older gods of the Thane Sagan Parthenon that he would avenge his brother and help his soul find peace. He felt that by helping them, he would be one step closer to helping his own family, his fallen comrades of S'Vothe, attain their much-needed salvation.

Aeden finally had enough of idly waiting within the confines of the bejeweled monastery. Without asking for permission or letting the other monks know, he slipped out, into the cold grip of Vintas. He ventured into the city of Treton and listened to the people talk at taverns and inns. People would approach him, asking for blessings for themselves, their children, and their businesses.

Aeden happily obliged and enjoyed feeling useful. He needed a purpose in life. And part of him hoped that this distraction would allow him to let go of his anger. If not, it would show him the path he needed to take to fulfill his oaths.

As he deliberated and cast judgments he listened. Many of the citizens would offer money in return for blessings. Aeden would refuse, telling them they needed it more than him. The looks of appreciation, surprise, and as time passed, respect, became more frequent. He realized he liked the attention. He enjoyed the level of respect that he lacked as a novice in the Order and the respect he had lacked as a student of the gevecht back in S'Vothe.

Aeden made his visits more often and word spread of the honorable Bodigan monk who would freely give blessings and judgements for those who asked. Despite the cold weather, lines began to form, whenever he entered an establishment. People were reserved, yet eager. They didn't jostle or push, for he would not have tolerated that. Instead, they waited patiently for their chance to speak to the young gray-robed monk from the kingdom south of the Dath River.

Complaints of high taxes, the recent epidemic of consumption, and increasingly unsafe roads were common. Trade was being stifled by the need for more money to combat the rising threat of mystics that had grown ever more organized in their attacks of the capital city of Gemynd. Imperial soldiers were camped in the north, often residing where it pleased them in their attempt to root out the mystics and squash any potential rebellion. This often meant soldiers occupied residences, fine stone-built houses of the merchant class, as the families they displaced sought shelter in their businesses or among the peasants, or on the floor of the great keep of whatever lord they served.

As the cold months crept by, the mystics were able to conduct quick raids undetected and unhindered, despite the massive presence of imperial soldiers and Gemynd guards. Imperial collectors were rumored to be gearing up for another round of taxes to fund the effort, all in the name of greater safety and security. The people were being squeezed on all sides and it was beginning to show. To Aeden it was like looking at a bag stuffed so full of grain the seams were beginning to widen, threads were showing and individual granules fell to the floor in the form of heartfelt complaints.

To further add to the woes of the populace, it had been a dry Sumor, which in turn meant less wheat and less grain to fill the kingdom's granaries. Gemynd's economy, although based on the same gold standard as the rest of the Heorte Empire, was tied directly to their fields. The educated knew the economy was tied more heavily to their production of grain: wheat, rye, and barley, than it was their production of fine steel, which was traded and sold to the rest of the empire.

Aeden, however, was still not fully aware of the deeper machinations of government, the economy, and political plays of power. To him the problem was obvious and the solution was simple. Taxes were too high, forced upon the people by the greedy nobles who sat within the safe confines of their castles, as the common folk were forced to pay for ineffective protection, protection that they could have taken care of themselves.

Amongst the Thane Sagan, the idea of paying someone else to protect what they held dear was ludicrous. It was like handing over one's child to a stranger, hoping they would do a better job and be more invested in their upbringing than the parents themselves would.

Therefore, as people came for judgements and asked for blessings Aeden would also ask questions. He would learn more about the person, their position, their fears and then he'd tailor his judgements to include the ideas of personal security, freedom from excessive taxes, and the importance of individual liberty in following Salvare's path.

Slowly, greater crowds were drawn to his speeches and he found larger numbers of people nodding their head in approval. His prayers were tailored to his message and that message began to spread upon the lips of those who heard.

It was one speech in particular that sparked the anger and fears of the populace. It was Aeden's last night visiting the taverns.

He found himself at Mare's Inn. A large establishment, filled with hundreds of people. They had come to hear the young Bodigan monk speak.

The crowd parted as Aeden walked through. Hands reached out to touch his grey robes. Voices spoke out, asking for salvation, for the strength to feed their families, for a short Vintas.

Aeden nodded and looked each in the eye as he passed. He felt important. He knew he had an audience. If there truly was a Salvare, would he have allowed this opportunity to be squandered to fear? Aeden did not think so.

Action was the response to circumstance, he

knew this from his years of training. Hiding from fear only brings shame and guilt. He'd rather have died a hundred times than to feel the weight of those emotions lurk about his neck, dragging him ever deeper into an abyss of self-torture.

"Good evening," Aeden said loudly as he turned to face the crowd.

"May the light be bright upon your back," the crowd responded.

"Tonight, I will not be making judgements," he stated, looking about the massive room. The crowd voiced their displeasure. "Instead, I will speak to you all from what I've seen, from what Salvare has shown me."

The protestations died away as people murmured more softly to each other.

"Tonight, I will share what I know to be true, risking the anger of the Church and the wrath of the Empire, if you do not wish to listen, then please leave now," Aeden said with conviction.

He looked about the room, seeing the eyes of those gathered. There was heartache and fear, but underlying it all was anger. A few people shuffled out of the tavern, but most remained. Aeden nodded and smiled.

"I have prayed," he began, "I have prayed night and day for peace to come to the lands, food to fill our bellies, and for violence to be banished to the seventh level of hell…and do you know what I have seen?"

Aeden paused, taking in a breath and studying the lines of an old woman in the crowd.

"I've seen famine, fear, and death," Aeden nodded to himself, "I have looked death in the eye far too many times. I know its glassy stare. I know its fetid smell. It is lifeless, it is unmoving, uncaring, and final...

"I look around and do you know what I see?" Aeden paused for effect, "I see hardworking men and women. I see god-fearing people struggling to put food on the table, good people pushed to the edge of desperation, but why?"

Again, Aeden took a moment and looked about the inn. All eyes were on him. The usual din of the tavern had fallen away like the leaves after a Hearvest storm.

"Why?" he repeated, "The answer becomes obvious when one looks and sees. I have looked. I have seen. And I know who hoards the wealth, who controls the armies, who sends the tax collectors..."

People were now nodding their heads in agreement. Aeden pressed on.

"There once was a time when food was ample, families were strong, happy, when the voice of the people mattered, and morality was the rule of law, but that time has passed," he looked about, "we are now entering a new era. Brothers and sisters, mothers and fathers, friends...look around you, what do *you* see?

"I know what *I* see," Aeden continued, "I see strength. I see hope. I see the power of the masses. We are the many. We are the strong."

A few people mumbled agreement, while others listened intently.

"I have listened to Salvare's words, I have read upon the book of Divinus, I have seen Dominer's words laid bare. He would not have stood idly by while the lands were taken from him, while the rich grew richer upon the backs of the working class, while tax collectors stripped them of their savings, and imperial soldiers raided with impunity.

"No, I know what he did. He stood up. He stood tall. He swallowed his fear and shouldered the responsibility that all of humanity shares. He fought so that his children would be free. He rose up so that imperial rule would fall. He died so that we could be free…"

A few voiced their concerns, their fears.

"We don't want to die." "What can we do?" "We're not Dominer."

Aeden listened and continued.

"I was at the Nailsean Market when the imperial raiders came. I watched as they struck down Abbot Gilbert. I watched as men, women, and children were slaughtered. I watched fellow monks, men of god, struck down without mercy, without repercussion.

"Now where do they lay? What can they do?

Life is short. Time is not an ally we can befriend and depend upon. For what is life without action? What is life without freedom? What marks us apart from those who've truly lived? Is our legacy to feed the rich? To die under the sword after years of toil? To pay the tax collector so that others fight our battles?"

Aeden let his words fall over the crowd. The weight of his message and the layered implications settled over them like the first snow of Vintas.

"We cannot wait any longer. Death lurks in the shadows. It lurks as the shadowy tax collector, the noble lord hoarding our wealth, the imperial soldiers who rape and kill. We must act, for action is what defines life, and is the narrative that will define our legacy.

"We must act for our friends, for our families, for our children, and for our freedom."

The crowd, who stood mesmerized, took up the chant of Aeden's final words, "for freedom!" Shouting until it echoed beyond the walls of the Mare's Inn and spread beyond Treton, carried by travelers, merchants, and bards. Echoing into the annuls of history through song, which you'd know if you have ever heard the *Humble Monk of Bodig*.

For Aeden, the adventures into town, allowed the days to pass more quickly and alleviated the weight of the constant iron-gray clouds looming overhead. But for Verold, something greater was taking shape. It lingered in the hearts of the many, and ate at the souls of the few.

Chapter 53

*"Ale is the truthsayer alchemists have been
struggling to find since the birth of science."
Herlewin's Anthology of Gemynd*

It was a cold morning the day they decided
to travel north. Snow fell in angry sheets. The
wind howled as it swept past ice-covered
buildings. And thick white drifts concealed the
stone road.

The monks from the Treton Monastery had
given each Bodigan monk a long cloak and thick
furs. Aeden had been given new boots on one of
his nightly excursions, lined with rabbit's fur.
Yet, despite all the layers, it was still cold.

The monks trudged through the dark gray in
silence. There were very few people out. In fact, it
was odd for people to be traveling in this
weather, but Vintas was only beginning in the
north. If they were to wait, they could have been
stuck in Treton for months and none of the
monks wanted that. Talk of the great capital of
Gemynd was upon their lips and served to warm
their hearts.

Aeden was rubbing his hands together for
warmth when he heard the snorting of a pair of
yaks. He turned around, struggling to see
through the falling snow as it swirled about,
dancing to some unseen rhythm.

"Brothers, you shouldn't be out in the cold!" a man yelled to them above the din of Vintas.

The monks stopped and stepped aside to make way for the thick-furred animals, their Vintas coats covered in bits of white as their misty breaths steamed from dark nostrils.

"Brother Aeden?" the same man shouted again, this time in surprise. "Please, all of you come aboard; there is greater warmth in my humble cart."

The man pulled on the reins, causing one of the yaks to rear its head in protest.

"Stop it Maggie, let me drive for once, eh," the man said, attempting to sooth the agitated beast.

The monks squeezed onto the back of the partially covered wagon. A set of blankets had been stretched over a simple wooden frame and tied in place, providing a modicum of shelter from above and the sides, but let in a howling draft of air from the front and back.

They huddled together for warmth on the half-full cart. The man twisted in his wooden bench, his thick furs obscuring half his face. He turned his attention to them.

"It's not much, but I'll take you as far as you need to go," he said, his eyes fixed on Aeden.

Aeden recognized him after a moment's thought. Brom Dyer was his name, but he couldn't quite recall his story. If he remembered correctly, Dyer meant he worked with clothing.

Adel looked at him quizzically as Odilo answered.

"We're headed to the capital."

Brom paused in thought. He eyed the weather and then looked back toward Aeden.

"It's a long stretch of road," he began.

"Perhaps you've business in the capital?" Aeden offered.

Brom looked at each of the monks sitting upon the pile of his goods. His large beard covered most of his face, hiding his expression. His dark eyes were the only indicators of thought.

"I guess I can sell there just as well, and I've a brother who owes me money," he said half to himself before looking back toward the monks. "Fine, fine, of course. Then off we go to the capital." The man turned in his seat and coaxed the yaks forward, "let's go Maggie, you too Marie."

The cart lurched to a slow rocking rhythm over the slippery cobbled stones of the great north-south road.

"Salvare watches over us even now," Adel said.

"As does Brother Thomas," Aeden replied in a barely audible whisper.

The road was long, bumpy, and cold. The cart was buffeted by icy winds that cut through the blanketed shell like frozen blades of tempered steel. The winds howled, speaking of quiet desperation, fear, and impending change.

"We should bed down for the night, and my girls need some rest," Brom said as the wind whisked away the clouds of steam from his blue lips. "There's a place ahead, warmth and food, and more importantly good ale."

The driver turned to face forward, once again urging the yaks forward.

Aeden struggled to see through the falling snow, only to catch a face full of frozen tundra. He blinked his eyes and rubbed at his cheeks. They felt numb. He wanted to smile, but it hurt when his teeth were exposed to the bite of Vintas.

"Is it normally this cold?" Aeden asked to no one in particular.

There was a pause as if the other monks were debating to answer or simply sit shivering.

"This is an unusual year, could be a storm sent by Salvare to test us," Adel said.

"It'd be better if He were testing some other lot of monks. Man shouldn't live without the kiss of the sun upon his skin," Neri said with disdain, uttering more words than he had the day prior.

"How is it different where you're from?" Adel asked.

"Where I'm from is better than here," Neri

stated matter-of-factly.

Both Adel and Aeden looked at each other as Odilo stifled a smile within the hood of his cloak.

"Whoa Maggie, you can stop, we're here, we're here."

The cart slowed to a stop. Brom twisted in his seat.

"We're here," he said to the monks as though they hadn't gathered that from the stopped cart and his gentle admonishment to his more stubborn yak.

"Thank you kindly, do you need any help with tending to your cart?" Odilo asked.

"No, Maggie and Marie are cautious animals, don't much like the touch of strangers. I'll do rightly fine; I suggest you get warm inside."

"Thank you," Odilo said.

Aeden waited for the others to get off the cart. His back and legs were stiff with cold. He was looking forward to some warmth.

A two-story, wooden building stood as a barrier to the cold and wind. The small windows were half covered by snow, but a warm glow was still visible from the other side. The monks made their careful way up the half-frozen steps and to the heavy doors. They all piled into the warm room as a gust of wind followed them in.

A large fire crackled on the opposite side of the room. The orange flames spoke the quiet song of warmth. Chairs and tables were strewn about on either side of the room. A bard sang as his fingers carefully strung accompaniment on a simple lute.

There was a smattering of people. Aeden's eye took in the scene quickly. Only a few men seemed large enough and in a non-inebriated state to potentially pose a threat. There were a few engrossed by the music, tapping their feet or attempting to sing along. Most, however, seemed engrossed in conversation or were staring deeply into the bottom of their beer mugs.

"Brothers, welcome." A young woman said. "Will you be wanting a room or something to drink?"

"What've you to eat?" Adel asked eagerly.

"Stew and buttered bread."

"I'll have some of that," he replied.

Aeden followed suit, his stomach grumbling. Odilo and Neri ordered as Adel found an unoccupied table. A few eyes tracked them as they crossed the room. There was a polite nod from an older man. There was a glare bordering on curiosity from a younger mercenary, and a flirtatious smile from a young woman on the far side of the room sitting on another man's lap.

Aeden removed his fur cloak and touched his thawing hands to his cold cheeks, smiling back sheepishly. The sensation of warmth from the room, slowly spread like a thousand tingling needles.

"There is nothing like a little hardship to remind one of the simple pleasures," Odilo said as he rubbed his hands together.

"There's nothing like hardship to remember how few pleasures there are," Neri grumbled.

Adel looked to Aeden for a moment. They were both thinking the same thing; Neri seemed to have taken over Bosco's position of chief complainer, although with greater sarcastic wit.

"I brought a deck of cards from Treton," Adel said, looking hopefully at the other monks.

"Let's enjoy our meal first," Odilo replied, catching his eye, "then I'd love to play a hand."

"I'm in too," Aeden said quickly.

The three monks looked to Neri who at first attempted to look everywhere else but at them. He finally relented.

"Cards it is," he grunted.

"The bread and soup are two drams," the waitress said as she carefully placed bowls of soup before each monk, a fat slice of buttered bread rested atop the stew.

Another gust of cold Vintas air marked the room with its glacial reach. The fire flickered in silent protest and the woman upon the man's lap frowned.

Aeden looked up to see Brom lumber toward them. He had the wild look of a black bear wandering into town, searching for food.

"Stop pestering, I'll pay, I'll pay," Brom's husky voice cut in.

"Of course," she said, a look of annoyance passing briefly over her face, "two drams a piece."

"Bring me some as well will you," Brom said, placing a gloved hand on her arm.

She carefully slipped away. Brom watched her with a smile.

"Sometimes I forget what you've given up. It can't be easy not wanting after a woman like that."

"Salvare gives us strength and helps us on our path," Adel said.

"Of course brother, I meant no disrespect. It's just that it can't be easy is all. She's a fine-looking lass. I'd imagine she'd keep a man nice and warm at night."

Odilo smiled as Brom spoke, "we thank you for your kindness, but you've already taken us thus far, you needn't pay for our meals." He said in an effort to guide the conversation to safer ground.

"Nonsense, I'd best do right by Salvare's eyes if I want a piece of that salvation," he glanced about looking for the waitress, "how about some ale, what's music without ale?"

There was a lingering moment of silence,

filled with the warmth of the crackling fire, the lilting tune of a singing bard, and hot soup filling the belly. Fingers had thawed, hunger had been satiated and Adel had already pulled out his deck of playing cards.

"Cards, eh?" Brom said as if to himself, "I'd imagine you wouldn't care to make it interesting?"

Adel seemed slightly confused, "it's almost always interesting."

Brom smiled as Odilo leaned over to explain. Aeden leaned in too.

"He means wagering coin per hand."

Adel nodded as understanding dawned on him.

"Perhaps not so interesting tonight, however," he quickly said.

At this Brom exploded in a deep bellied laugh. Adel flushed in shame and Neri glanced about to see who had notice his outburst. Very few seemed interested.

"A round of ale," Brom said as the waitress collected plates. As she left he slapped her once on her thigh the way one would a good horse. "She's a looker."

Adel had already begun dealing cards to the other monks.

"What're we playing?" Brom asked.

Apparently, Adel hadn't thought to include

Brom in the dealing. Odilo quickly cut in.

"Kayles," he said, "Do you know how to play."

"Kayles? Do you mean King's High?"

"They're one and the same," Aeden replied, shocking the other monks.

Adel looked at him a moment, surprised. Aeden had learned about some of Gemynd, including their card games, by frequenting establishments in the evening as he conversed, dispensed judgments, and fought for the memory of Thomas. He, of course, didn't want to reveal that and simply shrugged.

Odilo had already gathered the cards so Adel could deal Brom in. They'd be playing individually as opposed to teams, as was normally done back in the Red City Monastery.

The waitress returned with five sloshing mugs of ale. She was careful to approach from the side, avoiding Brom's groping hands. Aeden thought he caught a mild smile part her lips as she caught Brom's eye.

By the fifth hand and the sixth round of ale, the small group of monks and the merchant from Treton had become progressively louder. Lips had loosened as the alcohol worked its hidden magic. Even Odilo seemed affected.

For Aeden it was his first time being drunk and he loved it. The world swam in his vision as his speech felt thicker and slurred. His body felt relaxed and the ever-important task of constant awareness seemed far less important, as if he had been transported to a place where fear was a distant memory struggling to take shape.

With a clouded mind, Aeden struggled to track the conversation that now spilled across the table like an upturned jug of ale.

"No drinks and no women!" Brom echoed again incredulously. "I'd rather be stabbed than live in the wretched lands to the south."

Neri's eyes grew narrow, "you'd likely be stabbed if you were in the south, for you have worse manners than the stinking barbarians of the Gwhelt!"

Odilo cast a look toward Aeden. Aeden only barely comprehended the words, clearly not enough to take offense. The argument continued oblivious of the insults inadvertently hurtled.

"You're drinking now," Adel stated innocently, seemingly confused by Neri's complex beliefs.

"Am I in the land of the A'sh? Do you see me surrounded by my brothers of D'seart? Only there does the true word of Salvare touch the hearts of men, showing the divine path of…" Neri suddenly seemed to catch himself and stopped abruptly.

Odilo now regarded him with a more careful look. Adel waited for Neri to finish as Aeden watched the whole interaction with detached curiosity and amusement.

"Who cares about all of that, why hide your women is what I don't understand," Brom cut in, stumbling over his words the way a child learning to speak would.

"Because they're to be protected. They are weak like children. Do you have children fight your wars? Do you wish for children to be touched and violated by dirty hands? Or seen with unclean eyes?"

The words burned through the hazy cloud that spun around Aeden's head. His eyes dilated and adjusted to the dim flickering light of the fire and candles as he focused on Brom. Brom's features changed as if he had just realized he'd hit a nerve.

"It's a crime is all, and doesn't seem right not having women folk out and about," Brom said in his defense.

Aeden started nodding his head in agreement. He loved women. He loved their delicate grace. He couldn't imagine a world where he wasn't allowed to gaze upon the beauty of the archduchess, to smell her as she passed, to think on her once she left the room.

"I think it's your turn to deal," Odilo said, handing the cards to Brom. "And perhaps pursue a different avenue of conversation."

Neri suddenly stood up and stormed off. A

negative cloud seemed to follow him, obscuring the light of the candles as he passed.

"Or per... perhaps it's time to call it a night," Adel said, stumbling with his words.

Chapter 54

"One man's rebellion is another man's bid for freedom." Isaac the Philosopher - Gemynd

The following morning Aeden awoke to a pounding headache. It felt like a woodpecker had become trapped on the inside of his skull and was attempting to peck its way out. Every sound was amplified. The very light, weak as it was, glared through the window angrily as if its very purpose was to drill a hole through his weary eyes.

It was a strange and altogether uncomfortable feeling, yet oddly comforting. In a way it reminded him of his humanity, his frailty, and subtly reaffirmed his inability to follow through with his burdensome obligation to duty.

"Now I remember why I don't drink," Adel said as he sat up and looked about, confusion settling upon his features.

"Good morning," Odilo said as he stepped into the small room. "Have some of this, it'll help," he said as he handed them each a small bowl of porridge, his voice cutting through Aeden like a Vintas wind through a Sumor tunic.

Aeden didn't much feel like eating, but he also didn't much care for the pounding headache. He took reluctant mouthfuls of porridge as he glanced about for Neri. The previous night suddenly washed over him like a bucket of cold water.

"Where's Neri?" Aeden asked.

"Downstairs, he said he needed some space," Odilo replied.

"And Brom?"

Odilo simply pointed to a heap in the corner, covered in furs. Aeden looked more carefully and noticed that there was a slight rise and fall. He had assumed those were discarded furs upon first glance. Now as the world came into focus, he realized differently.

He took another mouthful of the porridge. It wasn't particularly good. It tasted like the color gray.

"We should wake him and be on our way before another snow storm sets in," Odilo said, his words felt overly loud to Aeden. Why was he shouting?

"Can't we just go back to sleep?" Adel asked.

"No, and it'd be good to remember why the Book of Khein teaches moderation in action and discipline in forethought."

With those words, Odilo stepped over to Brom and kicked him gently in the ribs.

"Master Brom," Odilo said gently at first.

There was a startled snore that sounded like a choking animal, before the small mountain of furs shifted to reveal the Treton merchant.

"Have some porridge to recover your strength and then perhaps we can leave."

Brom peeled his eyes open accepting the soup into his large hands as he looked through the half-frosted window.

"I suspect this would be as good a time as any," he grumbled as he noisily slurped some porridge down his gullet.

Aeden watched him in fascination. He looked like a bear hovering over a tiny morsel, with his dark eyes, thick mane of hair and wild beard.

"If you need any help getting your oxen ready, these two have volunteered," Odilo said as he stepped out.

Aeden and Adel looked at each other.

"We did?" Aeden whispered in confusion, the wooden spoon threatening to fall out of his bowl.

Adel shrugged and blinked his eyes a few times.

"Well boys, I'd be glad for the help once I've found me a chamber pot!"

"Down the hall," Adel said.

"Really?" Aeden asked as Brom lumbered into the hallway.

"I don't know, but if he pulled out his snake right here, I don't think I'd keep my porridge down."

"Good point," Aeden took the last spoonful

of porridge and placed the bowl on the floor, "I guess it's time to get moving."

Aeden was briefly reminded of his early morning training in the S'Velt. The memory washed over him quickly before fading into the rhythmic thumping of his persistent headache. He had little desire to remember much of anything.

Within an hour, the band of monks were snuggled under layers of fur in the back of Brom's cart, as his oxen pulled them slowly toward the capital of Gemynd. They sat in silence, listening to the echoing rant of the wheels slipping and scraping over rock and ice.

The clouds were thick, but not so thick as to block the sun's buttery brilliance, melting through the steel gray in gobs of watery light. The hours faded under heaven's watchful eye as Aeden struggled with heavy eyes and shivering cold.

A gentle snowfall had begun carrying the soft note of life. It rustled through the trees, whispering and singing as it swept across the land. It cooed as it settled upon the thick furs, before finally resting peacefully in a thickening blanket of purity.

Aeden was so transfixed that he hardly noticed as they arrived at the outskirts of the great capital city of Gemynd. Had he been paying more attention he would have seen the road grow wider. He would have noticed the growing numbers of people plying the roadway. Finally, he would have caught sight of the scattering of snow covered buildings, that marked the countryside outside the frozen capital of the north. But he had noticed none of this. Instead, he sat quietly transfixed as if meditating upon the subtle nature of being, consumed by the weather and the slow rocking of the cart.

It was Brom that finally stirred him from his mental state.

"Gemynd, the capital that never forgot, the capital that never gave up."

These words had stirred more than just Aeden. His friend, Adel, glanced about as if waking from a dream. His mind was already filling with questions.

"What does he mean by that?" Adel asked, suddenly wishing for Thomas' presence.

"He's referring to their history. Gemynd actually predates the other capitals. There was a settlement of the Early People who lived here before its creation, or so I was once told. And there was a later history of draccus fiend attacks and barbarian attacks, yet it never forgot its roots and always rebuilt itself," Odilo said.

Aeden was suddenly awake and curious. Had Odilo said draccus fiend attacks?

"Aeden, look!" Adel said, his enthusiasm

clear as day.

Aeden turned in his seat, allowing the blankets to shift and a draft of cold air to slip under the pile of warmth. He hardly noticed as he gazed upon a thousand yellow lights, flickering amidst the white of snow.

"The lights, those are people," Adel said, his voice quivering from both excitement and the frigid temperatures.

He was right. They were the lights of a thousand torches. The golden light flickered off snow drifts and thickly blanketed buildings draped in powdery white. Ice formed broken clusters near the shore and by the bridges that spanned the many islands that formed Gemynd. The islands looked like small mounds topped by stone buildings, low and tall.

"Whoa Maggie," Brom's voice cut through the cold to calm the hairy ox.

"Is this normal?" Odilo asked as he leaned toward Brom.

Brom was silent for a moment as if considering his response.

"No, this smells like a blood moon in Sumor."

Aeden looked to Adel confused.

"A blood moon in Sumor speaks of bad things."

"Perhaps we should steer clear of the growing crowd," Odilo offered, still speaking to

Brom.

"There, there Maggie, you're startling Marie. C'mon, we'll go somewhere quieter."

Odilo nodded to himself as he readjusted the blankets to better cover his legs. Aeden adjusted to maintain an eye on the gathering band of lights. They were just close enough for him to make out body shapes and hear the rising voices of those arriving. It had the ominous feel of a distant fire, crackling and sucking at the wind, foreshadowing a devastating inferno to come.

A thump on the cart and a loud voice startled everyone to the core.

"Monks on the road, not safe monks, not safe at all."

Three men lumbered past, each welding a mean looking farm tool.

Aeden shifted in his seat so as to better get at his Templas sword if needed. It was only a mild comfort, for what could he do against such a large number of gathering men. He didn't like the feeling that was settling in his stomach. It was the flittering weight of nervous anticipation.

Slowly the wagon turned around. The view of the unfolding scene was ever more present from the back of the cart. Despite the cloud of impending violence, the monks were determined to continue their pilgrimage.

The sky still held the last embers of light, glowing a faint purple-orange above the strewn clouds. The faint light cast the islands and buildings of the capital in pale shadows. The biggest island was dominated by the largest castle Aeden had ever seen. Its towers were thick and tall. Buildings nestled close to its walls as if for protection, much like a cub to its mother. Only one bridge led to the island, flanked by its own towers. Fires burned in guard huts, highlighting the falling bits of snow in their feathery embrace.

Aeden was so caught up in the scene that he hardly noticed Odilo lean toward Brom.

"We thank you many times over, but Gemynd is where we must go," Odilo said to him.

Brom looked back and gave each of them a discerning look before pausing on Aeden. Aeden nodded ever so slightly. Despite his gut twisting uncomfortably within, he knew it was what Thomas would have wanted. Aeden needed to prove he wasn't afraid. He was through hiding. His hand slipped unconsciously into the pocket with Dannon's lock of hair. He fingered it for a moment as he looked at the others.

"Who am I to question Salvare's ways," Brom grumbled as he pulled on the reins, bringing the cart to a gradual halt.

Each of the monks thanked Brom in turn before hopping off the relative safety of the partially covered wagon. Brom cursed and yelled to get his stubborn oxen moving again in an effort to leave as quickly as possible. They snorted and complained before finally relenting and struggled to find purchase on the snow-covered road.

A light flurry whipped across the terrain as the monks stood by the roadside, huddled together under their thick furs. They were looking to Odilo.

"Let's find the monastery, we should find shelter and warmth there," he said.

The monks all nodded their approval. They trudged down the snow-covered road toward the swelling tide of torches and scattered shouting. As they drew closer the shouts became intelligible.

"Down with Geobold!"

"Burn the churches!"

"Stop the taxes!"

"They wouldn't touch the church. It's protected by Salvare, right?" Adel asked, a cloud of warm vapor escaping his pale lips, as a hint of fear shaped his question.

His question was followed by the continued vague shouting of the crowd, which grew more intense with each passing. An echoing response of neighing horses grabbed Aeden's attention. His mind spun as he was sucked into the past. Images from the market of Nailsea threatened to drown him.

He wasn't the only one. They all tracked the incoming horses. The strong riders, wrapped in armor and fur, clung to horseback with the same intensity of the Nailsean attackers. The crowds parted at their arrival.

Aeden's stomach clenched in fear, but he remained rooted to the spot. He watched, waiting for the bloodletting, the terrible screaming. It never came. Instead, the crowd grew more anxious, more excited.

The monks were no more than a hundred feet from the swelling masses. The crowds formed at the crossroads to the main island chains of the city of Gemynd. A wide road branching to the northwest climbed over a bridge, passed through the Isle of Repose, before continuing to the Isle of Castle Forge.

The last slivers of light faded, giving way to an emotional tide. The mob's mood was a fluctuating colostrum of angry torrents. Burning torches showed pinched expressions, flushed red from exposure to the cold. Bearded faces with dark eyes, tracked the movement of incoming horses.

The feeling of history unfolding at Aeden's feet, swept over him and settled upon him like a blanket. Curiosity tugged at each monk in turn, blinding them to danger. It robbed them of rational thought and whispered of Salvare's folly.

A thickly accented voice spoke up and the

shouting of the crowd died to an anticipatory murmur.

"One of Salvare's own has spoken of the atrocities of the rich, the despicable acts of the nobles, taxing, taking, and raping these lands. He has helped lead you to our own path, the path of the righteous!"

Aeden watched as the crowd seemed to grow tense with the energy of the words. A palpable anger was swelling. Who was the man referring to? The strings of destiny seemed to have formed a rich tapestry, with layers of fiber that remained hidden to the young Aeden. All he could do was watch and listen in an attempt to comprehend unfolding events.

The mounted horseman continued to shout to the masses.

"Tonight is our night. You have come to the right place, and made the right decision. Tonight, we take what is ours and send the thieves of Gemynd to be judged!"

A roar swept across the crowd like an untamed fire.

"Let Gemynd remember the true voice of the people, the voice of the Mystae. Follow and we shall lead. Listen and we shall respond." The rider pulled free a sword and pointed to a few of his fellow horsemen as he rode the length of the crowds. "Take them to the houses of greed, to feast on what is rightfully theirs!"

Another shout of approval leapt up from the torch carrying masses.

"For freedom!"

The mounted horsemen began to splinter from the group. They bore down different streets, leading groups of angry men. The shouts began to grow as fires were set to the wooden roofs of stone-built houses.

Aeden watched in disbelief. His sword hummed an icy song at his back, as he watched city descend into violence.

More people streamed toward the cacophony of sound. The monks were jostled as large men shoved their way roughly past. Aeden gave voice to the obvious.

"We aren't going to the monastery tonight," Aeden shouted over the din, startling the monks. "We have to make our way to the ports and leave before the city descends into chaos."

Odilo looked at him thoughtfully as Adel looked to the older monk for guidance. Neri watched the city burn for a moment longer before speaking up.

"Aeden's right. We set sail for Petra's Landing and then hire a sea going vessel to the safety and warmth of my people, leaving this frozen firestorm to the dastardly north."

"Adel?" Odilo asked.

Adel looked from Aeden to Neri back to the city of Gemynd.

"I agree."

Chapter 55

"Lies before the eyes of Salvare are transparent truths waiting to be judged." Archdeacon of Sawol

The small group of monks stood, shivering quietly behind a few wooden barrels, waiting on Aeden. It was fully night and the distant shouts of fighting, the glow of fires, and the smell of smoke permeated the air.

Aeden crouched in a dark corner that smelled of half-rotten fish. His fingers were bordering on numb and his nose was runny from the cold. He ignored the discomforts as he had in the S'Velt. Instead he focused on the words of a couple lone docks men.

"We should leave now," a deep baritone intoned.

"That wasn't the deal. Lord Bristol promised a hefty payment for passage north," a second voice countered.

"He also said he'd be here an hour ago, and there's no lord gracing these docks!"

"How'd you know, you've never met him!" the smaller voice rebuked.

"You never met him either! You ought change your name to Gavin the Idiot. Look around. There's no one on these bloody docks," the deeper-voiced man said.

"We wait until the candle burns half, then we cast off." There was a note of finality in Gavin's voice, followed by the grunting approval of the other man.

Aeden lingered a moment longer, casting a quick glance around the corner of a small building. He caught sight of a well-built man. His wide shoulders and thick frame were evident through his Vintas clothing. He was fiddling with the lines attached to a small barge floating in the frigid waters of Lake Stevol. Aeden figured this must have been the deeper-voiced man.

A smaller man paced the wooden deck looking toward the fires burning red at the heart of Gemynd. He had a pinched face, with a large head and a receding hairline. He was clearly upset. His shoulders were hunched and his brow was wrinkled in worry.

Aeden figured the smaller man was thinking what Aeden had been thinking; the city would never be the same. The smell of death was upon the air. It was carried by the wind and being deposited as ash. It fell as if mocking the snow.

Without further hesitation, Aeden slipped into the shadows and worked his way back to the other monks.

"It's me," he whispered as he approached.

Adel stuck his head out from behind the barrels, flashing a quick smile. Aeden joined the others behind their temporary concealment, his mind already working on two separate plans, neither of which seemed very church-like.

Taking the boat by force seemed out of the question. The others would never go for it, and he doubted any of them had much experience on the water. That left bribery or deception. Bribery would leave little money for the next leg of their journey. That left only one good option.

"Would Salvare object to a small lie?" Aeden whispered, his mind struggling to tie the pieces of a makeshift plan into place.

"Lies are what hold the church together," Neri uttered.

Odilo frowned briefly at Neri before addressing Aeden. "I would imagine if it served his greater purpose, bending the truth could be forgiven."

"Then I think I have a plan," he said, as he whispered a silent prayer.

Odilo strode confidently toward the docks. The younger monks followed his lead. With his head held high, he did his best to give the impression that the entire area was filthy. To Aeden and Adel it appeared that Odilo was doing his best Bosco impression. Odilo was able to imitate Bosco's best mask of barely contained disgust.

"Why the Lord Bristol chose these docks is beneath me!" Odilo said loudly, doing his best to adopt a mild Gemynd accent.

"I don't see why you're complaining, you're the one who failed to secure the luggage, leaving us with nothing but coin," Adel replied, his voice shaking slightly.

"You saw those brutes! They're burning the damned city to the ground. You think they'd stop for his house staff?"

"Where's this damned Gavin anyway," Adel stammered.

A larger man stepped onto the dock before them.

"Are you the Lord Bristol's men?" His deep voice cut through them like a knife through leather.

"We are," Odilo responded.

Another man jumped deftly from the smaller barge onto the wooden dock.

"Where's the Lord Bristol?" Gavin asked.

"He won't make it I'm afraid, we've barely made it ourselves," Odilo said, gesturing to the glowing fires of the city behind them.

"I told you we should have left," the large man said. The smaller man waved him off.

"You have our payment?"

"We have half your payment, the other half is at Petra's Landing," Odilo said.

Gavin eyed them for a moment, his shrewd eyes taking them in. Adel looked away as Neri

glared at him. Aeden adjusted his footing, ready
to fight.

"Let's go already, the city's burning," the
larger man said. "Get aboard, we'll discuss
payment underway."

"You forget who makes the decisions Bryce!"
Gavin said in offense.

Bryce stared at him with his hands in the air.
He held them up in mock uselessness. His face,
however, was painted in a far darker shade of
anger.

"We go," Gavin finally said.

"There we bloody have it, the Lord of the
Barge has spoken," Bryce grumbled.

The smaller man knitted his eyebrows but
gave in and set about untying the lines, throwing
them aboard.

"Well, get on board already, unless you're
waiting for the fires to spread to the docks,"
Gavin commanded.

The monks each hopped on board. The barge
rocked under their weight. Once all four were on
the barge Gavin gave a shove off the dock and
jumped aboard. Bryce began to work the large
oar in the rear. The barge rocked gently before
falling into a steady rhythm.

They moved slowly from the strangely empty
docks pushing through the small fragments of ice
that clung desperately to the water's surface. The
sound of water lapping on the bow was drowned

out by the distant sounds of Gemynd burning. The city cried out in pain to a despondent night that watched with indifferent eyes.

"Halt!" a voice shouted from horseback upon the dock.

The man, although clearly disheveled, had the look of nobility. He wore a fine wolf fur across his shoulders clasped together by a chain of gold. His horse was tall and spirited, clouds of steam escaping its wide nostrils. Its coat shimmered in the single light of the dock, casting the man and beast in hues of amber.

There was some blood on his clothes, but it didn't appear to be his. The look in his eye was half mad with fear, yet he still retained the countenance of nobility. Years of habit layered his mannerisms to such a degree that a night of terror could not fully wash them away.

The men on the boat looked back toward the docks. The monks froze in fear. It appeared the lord had arrived after all.

"Don't stop," Aeden said, "He was one of the attackers. He stole that horse and fur!"

Adel glanced up at Aeden then to Odilo. It was obviously too much for him to handle. Neri had a strange smile on his lips as Odilo appeared to wrestle with the morality of the situation. Aeden had no such qualms. He was determined to keep his group safe, all other concerns were secondary.

Bryce began moving the oar again as Gavin peered out toward the docks. The barge drifted farther away. The lord upon the docks dismounted and waved his arms frantically. Fear found his voice and it cracked with strain.

"Wait!"

"Why should we halt for you?" Gavin shouted back.

"We had an agreement!" the lord screamed.

Aeden quickly unfastened his coin purse from his belt and let it drop loudly in front of Bryce.

"Ten gold dinar to continue to Petra's Landing."

The larger man looked to the coin purse, his partner, and then to the man on the docks. He glanced once more at the closed leather purse before him. He made his decision and began to work the oar back and forth with greater effort. The wooden blade stirred and splashed briefly in the water, pushing them deeper into the icy waters of Lake Stevol.

The desperate shouts of the lord faded into silence and burned a guilty hole into each of them. Greed and self-preservation had trumped humanity. Salvare would have to forgive more than just lies that night.

Adel buried his head into his hands in the hopes of hiding from the truth. Odilo looked solemn. The usual hidden smile lurking beneath the surface did not grace his eyes. Instead they were cold and distant. Neri whispered prayers under his breath as Aeden struggled to think of what they'd do once the bargemen asked for payment.

Chapter 56

*"Desperation defines humanity to a greater degree
than a thousand well placed words." Herlewin's
Letters of Apology*

It took most of the night and well into the
following morning before they arrived in Petra's
Landing. The sky was a sapphire blue, free of
clouds and free of wind. The air was crisp and
fresh, holding the gentle note of salt from the
nearby sea.

Aeden was thankful for the kiss of the
morning sun. The night had been long and cold.
Normally the monks would have huddled
together for warmth, but last night had been
different. They each had been wrestling with the
final shouts of a desperate man, left alone on the
docks of a burning city. The agony of desolation
had befriended them each in turn, gifting them
with introspection and self-doubt. The once clear
lines of perception had shifted and now a man
was likely dead as they glided safely toward
harbor.

The closer they came to the stone outcropping
of Petra's Landing, the tighter the knot in
Aeden's stomach grew. His shivering body
robbed his mind of coherent thought. Not a
single solution of any merit had passed through
his head. The looming issue of payment mounted

with each stroke of the oar.

He wanted to ask the others but couldn't think of how to ask without raising the suspicions of the two bargemen. Instead, his mind was flooded with questions, boiling over from a cauldron of fear.

What if they had friends at the docks? How would they react when the monks showed they had only a fraction of the money they had promised? Were criminals treated similarly in Petra's Landing as they were in Bodig?

Aeden had an image of his body rotting slowly in a gibbet. The uncaring masses ignored his immortal soul as they passed underneath the rusting metal cage. His body wouldn't be properly burned or cared for and his consciousness would be forever trapped in the netherworld, waiting hopelessly for someone to avenge his shameful death.

"We're nearly there. We'll take the first half of our payment. Petra's Landing's dock fees have been going up year after year and this Vintas has been no exception," Gavin said, his face even more pinched than before. His cheeks were red, and his beady eyes glanced briefly at each of them in turn.

The words startled the monks. They looked at each other, before fiddling with their money belts. Worry was written across Adel's features. Neri looked irritated, borderline irate. His face was flushed red as he struggled with emotion. Odilo on the other hand seemed slightly resigned to his fate, as if it were all a form of penance.

Aeden felt he was the only one left to make intelligent decisions. Decisions that would either save them or get them all killed. He didn't like it.

"Use what you need from these two purses, your greater payment waits at a usurer in town," Aeden replied, purposefully ignoring the looks from the other monks.

"We'll take all your purses," Gavin said, "and you'll take us to the usurer."

"But, we'll have nothing," Adel stammered.

"Not my problem," Gavin replied, his hand resting lightly on the hilt of a long dagger.

"Let us keep at least one, the usurer will make up for the difference," Aeden stepped in.

"Fine," Gavin said.

Bryce grumbled just loud enough to be heard, "It better or you'll find yourself floating in Stevol."

The barge slid into port as Gavin jumped onto the waiting dock. There were men busily unloading a scow on the opposite side. They hardly glanced over as the arriving barge was tied fast to the pier.

For a moment Aeden was lost in the scene. His thoughts drifted away as his eyes drank in Petra's Landing. They had branched east and taken a channel into the city. To the north, a castle straddled a small hill that dominated the cityscape. Barren trees peppered the steep southern slope and snow desperately clung to crags and rocks. The eastern slope was far more gradual, with what appeared to be tightly pruned grape vines covered for Vintas.

Hugging a narrow stone pathway, along the channel, were brightly colored houses. White, yellow, and red facades faced the water. Their backs were tight upon Castle Hill. It was to the east of the hill that the city flattened and more houses stretched over a minor grade toward the bay.

"Get off, let's go," the larger man said gruffly.

The monks shuffled off. Aeden's attention settled firmly on his agitated stomach. It rumbled with a mixture of hunger and anticipation as he jumped from the barge and onto the solid wooden deck of the pier.

Bryce herded the monks forward as Gavin led the way.

"Where are you taking us," Adel asked.

Gavin looked back as if confused. His confusion quickly turned to anger as his hand settled on the hilt of the dagger on his hip.

"You're the one taking us to your usurer. No more games. You sold out your lord; you'll not do the same to us."

As if to drive the point home, Bryce gave

Adel a brisk shove, sending him sprawling onto the snowy pier. Aeden's protective nature flared to life and the fog clouding his mind dissipated as if a strong gust of wind had torn through, whisking it away.

Aeden turned to face Bryce.

"You the bloody hero," the deep baritone implored, his bearded face was more threatening than an angry bear.

Aeden shook his head and turned back around. Instead, he watched as Odilo helped Adel to his feet. The situation was falling apart and he began to fear for his brother monks. *Fear will rob your mind of clarity; remove the fear to overcome your adversary.* The words of his instructor drifted through his mind and sparked an idea.

"The usurer doesn't like a crowd. I'll take you to get your money," Aeden blurted out.

Odilo looked at Aeden with the blank expression of disbelief. Adel shook his head as if signaling him to abort his failed idea. Neri didn't seem to care much either way. Strange, since he was often the most volatile of the group. Aeden pressed on, to silence the other monks and to convince the two men.

"Would you rather deal with all four of us? Where we're going, a crowd would draw attention."

The two bargemen looked briefly at each

other, then at the other monks. The decision had a certain sense of logic. It certainly would be far easier for them to control one man instead of four.

"So be it, let's go," Gavin replied.

Aeden looked to the others, giving each a quick hug.

"Come on, my mother's less sensitive. You can touch each other after you've paid us," the big man spat.

Aeden ignored him and whispered quickly in Odilo's ear.

"Let's meet near the main pier at the northern harbor. And take this in case I don't make it."

Aeden discreetly shoved the Book of Divinus into Odilo's unsuspecting hands. Odilo caught his eye briefly, just as Bryce yanked Aeden away with a surprisingly strong grip. Aeden caught his balance and began to walk toward the stone pathway parallel to the waterway. He glanced back one last time, catching Odilo's worried intimation.

It was a look of concern, anger, and surprise. His eyes were gentle, the brow furrowed, and his mouth slightly agape. Aeden had been so consumed by it that he had ignored Adel and Neri.

A twinge of guilt crept in like a worm boring into rotten fruit. He needed to clear his mind of emotion if he was going to come out of this predicament alive.

He passed under a sign marked "*Use of the Arkein Is Forbidden by Writ of the King*." It sparked his curiosity, but not enough to engage his two companions in conversation. It, however, was just enough to let his mind travel down a new rabbit hole.

They reached the pathway and he turned left, putting distance between himself and the other monks. His mind was still working on a plan as he walked. A quieter part of town seemed best. The only problem was, he had no idea the layout of the city. He was walking blindly into the unknown and hoping for the best. He couldn't shake loose the image of a blind man stumbling into a pack of wolves with a butter knife as his weapon.

"How much farther," Bryce grunted as if sensing Aeden's uncertainty.

"It's been a while since I've been here, but I think we aren't far," he replied in an effort to bide for more time.

There were few people on the streets. Those that braved the cold were wrapped in furs for warmth. They walked quickly to their destinations, eyes down, and heads covered. None seemed to be interested in the trio, even less so Aeden's plight.

The stone and snow gave way to the waterway on his left. It seemed a touch precarious if the path hadn't been wide enough for a horse's carriage. Perhaps he could push them into the water and make his escape. He would have to be quick. If either one of them grabbed him he'd go in too. He wasn't sure how long any one of them would last in the icy waters.

"Whatever you're planning, it better involve us getting paid," Bryce huffed, walking uncomfortably close.

The three of them rounded the bend. The pathway narrowed. Here the houses were smaller and more cramped, as if they feared casting too wide a shadow. They were now in the penumbra of the castle atop the hill. The wind somehow felt cooler. It tickled the back of Aeden's neck and pricked uncomfortably at his exposed face.

Aeden was about to turn to address Gavin when a fist hit him in the back of the head. He staggered forward and only regained his balance when two ham-fists grabbed hold of him. It was Bryce.

"No more games little man," he said, his face inches from Aeden's.

Gavin had his dagger out and held it before Aeden threateningly.

"You've got no friends, it's time to pay, or it's time to swim."

Aeden glanced about desperately. His head

throbbed where he had been hit. His mind raced. He stumbled for words but could think of nothing. He thought of reaching for his sword, but it was buried under layers of fur. He thought of striking Bryce in the throat and releasing himself, but Gavin would merely need to lean in with the dagger to cut his throat.

Therefore, Aeden did the only thing that felt natural. He screamed for help.

"Shut up, you filthy shit," Gavin snarled, holding the dagger to his neck, the cold metal felt sticky and painful against his skin.

"What's this?" A man's voice shouted, approaching from Aeden's left.

Gavin backed off, slowly lowering the dagger. Bryce looked over but didn't let Aeden go. Aeden was still barely on his tiptoes and couldn't turn his head for Bryce's fist.

"We caught a thief," Gavin stated calmly to the approaching man.

"Legal matters are for those appointed by the High Sheriff, not peasants such as yourselves."

"We're merchants, not peasants. It's this foreigner who stole from us," Gavin retorted.

The man came close enough for Aeden to see. The man wasn't alone. Two of them stood there, both as tall and wide as Bryce. Swords hung menacingly at their hips. Leather armor was strapped over warm furs. The armor was emblazoned with the crest of The Fallen

Constable.

One was as bald as a newborn babe. The other had a notch carved out of his ear. Neither looked friendly. A life of fighting and hardship carved them into cold, mean, hands of the law.

"Hand him over and we will sort this matter out," the constable said.

"He owes us money," Bryce complained.

"What he owes can be considered a tax for keeping the streets safe," the other constable said pulling his sword free.

Gavin placed a steadying hand on Bryce's arm.

"Of course, we'll leave you to your work. We have three other friends to catch up with anyhow," Gavin said.

Aeden realized before Bryce, that Gavin was referring to the other monks. He needed to warn them, to help them.

"Let's go foreigner," the bald constable said, a vice-like grip nearly pulled his arm free of the socket as he yanked him forward, a cruel grin momentarily revealing itself.

"But it's them that tried to rob me," Aeden said in an effort to free himself.

"They don't have the gray eyes of the Gwhelt, I hardly imagine two merchants, lowly as they are, tried to rob a barbarian."

"Barbarian?" Aeden was able to utter before a

sharp pain cracked through the back of his skull, shuddered its way down his spine, and the world went dark.

Chapter 57

*"A prison of the body will stifle the mind until it
too lies in shackles." Herlewin's Letters of Apology*

Aeden drifted in and out of consciousness
like a wraith through a hazy night. His head
pounded in rhythm to his heart. And glimpses of
colorful buildings passed like running paints
upon an overburdened tapestry.

"He'd better wake by tomorrow," a voice
echoed faintly through the distant recesses of his
mind.

"They always wake up," another voice
replied in watery tones.

Silence cocooned Aeden for a moment as he
forced an eye open. The startling brilliance of an
overcast sky and snow-covered roads branded
his eyes with images of Petra's Landing.

"Last week you hit one so hard he never
woke," the first voice suddenly burst forth,
drumming upon Aeden's sensitive ears.

"Wasn't my fault, bastard been dipping into
the Tempest."

"Constable wouldn't be pleased is all."

The voices sounded distantly familiar as if
Aeden had dreamed them once before. He
struggled to open an eye again. He was rewarded
with the blurry image of an old, columned

building. It had the worn look of a threadbare cloak. An edifice lost to history only to find a new use and a new home.

"Toss him in already, we've got a few more hours to round up something better."

Aeden vaguely remembered feeling his body hefted on high, the faint feel of wind across cold cheeks, and the solid feel of a hard floor. He recalled the remote clunk of metal upon metal followed by darkness. Sleep wrapped its comforting arms around him in a gentle embrace.

Within the warm embrace of darkness Aeden dreamt. Aeden dreamt of the red door buried within the crypt of the monastery. The sounds of a distant voice permeated the dark shroud of delusion. The voice spoke in rhymes of a hidden god trapped by the arkein. It whispered of lines of ancient magic stretching across a tumultuous sea.

Aeden awoke with a start. His head throbbed painfully as he sat up. Stars ringed his vision as his eyes adjusted to the lack of light. A full minute passed as he sat there, waiting for the pain to subside. He waited for memory to wash back and fill him like a rising ocean tide.

He blinked away tears and forced himself to assess his situation.

"Dope's awake, he's not late, for there's no fate, but here," a voice rang out in the semblance of a song, yet completely out of key and partially incoherent.

Aeden slid back away from the sound. He wasn't alone.

"Slither away, like a snake, but he's a fake."

Aeden scrambled to his feet as his eyes adjusted to the dim conditions. There was enough light to slowly make out the stone walls. His eyes scanned the room. He saw a chair, a table, and what appeared to be a man.

Suddenly the stench of the room assaulted his nose and caused his eyes to water. The dark shape squatting by the door moved toward him. The hunched shape was like a mass of broken stones wrapped in clothing.

"A friend to take, or a man to hate, we shall rate or see," he uttered in a rasping and broken voice.

"Stay back," Aeden warned, his hand reflexively moving toward his Templas blade.

The handle was buried under a cloak and some furs, but he was comforted to find his sword still firmly strapped to his back. The man scampered closer like a wild animal inspecting another of its kind.

"Soon they peek, returning weak, for those they seek," the man hummed as he spoke.

The sound of cold steel being drawn, rang out audibly in the stone room. The hunched man came to a halt and titled his head and masked his eyes as if the very blade shone brighter than the sun.

"Fate's reward, is t'never be bored, bringing heaven's storm, and killing all those aboard."

Aeden took a threatening step forward and the man retreated to the corner opposite the door. The pulsing agony in Aeden's eyes intensified, causing him to grip his sword more tightly. The image of his father standing under an overhang, studying him judgmentally flashed through his mind's eye.

The pulsing faded and a determination to escape, to help his brother monks washed over him. He stepped toward the door and noticed there was no handle. He pushed on the door. It didn't move.

"Fevered man, holding fate's own hand, sinks like falling sand," the hunched man sang out more loudly than Aeden would've liked.

The tune continued as he watched Aeden through curious eyes. Eyes that were only half here and half masked by the glossy look of someone gone mad.

Aeden spun about as he heard a soft splashing thump. The man hadn't moved. A rat? He looked at the door again and glanced through the metal bars. All he could make out was a lone flickering candle in a wide hallway. He strained to hear for a moment. The sound of snoring traveled faintly down the corridor like a gentle note.

"Where am I?" Aeden asked the man.

The man played with the ground, drawing random patterns, no response.

Another sloshing thunk drew Aeden's attention to the far side of the room. He walked over, investigating the floor. A puddle was evident and a few small chunks of what appeared to be salt were scattered about the floor. *Why would there be salt on the floor,* he thought.

He traced his boot through the puddle and broke apart some of the soft salt. It had the consistency of powdered sugar. He leaned forward onto the wall only to retract his hand. A thin sheen of water was trickling down the cold surface. He followed the water source to the roof.

Was that a hole in the roof? He stood on his tip toes and used his sword to probe the roof. Chunks of snow fell through along with some old, rotting building materials. He jumped back and blinked his eyes and coughed up whatever had landed in his gaping mouth.

Maybe the Thirteen were watching over him after all, or was it Salvare? *Too much time with the monks,* he thought briefly.

After wiping his eyes free of tears, he glanced about for anything to allow him to better reach the roof. There was a table and a chair. It was almost too easy. He sheathed his sword and grabbed the table.

"Sword's gone quiet, hissing like a giant, waiting for self-reliant to echo free..." the man fell into a spasm of coughs.

Aeden eyed him for a moment before using the coughing noises to mask the sound of dragging a heavy wooden table across the room. It still felt painfully loud to his ears. He came to a stop on the other side of the room, breathing hard. The sound of his heart rushed through his ears and pounded away angrily within his head.

He strained to listen to anything beyond the closed wooden door. He feared guards rushing in. Aeden wondered for a moment if he'd be willing to cut them down in an effort to escape. The door remained closed and his mind wandered back to the hole in the ceiling. *How old was this building?* He thought curiously.

Once on top of the table, Aeden pulled out his sword and began to work at the hole. This time he shielded his eyes and kept his mouth closed as it rained debris.

"Escape to the roof, our soldier's on the loose," the man now began to shout.

Aeden sheathed his sword and risked a quick glance at the deformed man. The man's face was pulled by the temporal hands of a devil's fate. Aeden tore his gaze loose from the man's contorted features. The singing continued unabated.

"Masquerading ruse, brothers shall pass, they

shall see, entertaining muse…"

He hefted himself up through the narrow hole he had created. Bits of roof fell free and he lost his grip twice, nearly crashing down into the room, before finally hefting himself onto the cold, snowy canopy.

A thick gust of wind threatened to push Aeden back into the prison he'd escaped from. His heart beat heavily in his chest as he struggled to believe his good fortune.

"Up there!" A brutish voice shouted.

Aeden just realized the singing of the hunched man had stopped. It was replaced by the rough voice of the men who had brought him there. His heart sank. He looked about for his next move.

The sound of one man scrambling after him set fire to his movements. Glancing down he saw it was too high to jump. His only option was to make it to the next roof. He braced his feet as best he could before leaping to the nearest rooftop. The impact knocked snow free and for a moment he madly scrambled for purchase.

Aeden's feet found the lip of the roof line and his descent was abruptly halted. He didn't hesitate as he clambered around the roofline toward the next building. The sound of his pursuers never felt far behind.

He was able to leap and run across two more buildings before gravity caught up with him.

Aeden made one final leap to a smaller building. As soon as he landed, he felt the weight of his body and the burden of the snow, tear through the poorly crafted roof. He fell upon a bed of straw amidst a few startled animals.

There was a brief moment where a goat stared stupidly at him before they all fell through the second floor. He hit the ground floor with a jarring thud. His spine tingled as though a hammer had been taken to it.

A family of four sat in stunned silence. There upon their floor was a stranger clad in furs, surrounded by two goats, a dog, some straw, and a pile of snow. A cold wind howled through the hole in their ceiling and the goat bleated in response.

Aeden pushed himself to his feet, dusting himself off. He quickly checked for injuries and was relieved to find himself more or less in one piece. The child pointed to Aeden as though the others hadn't seen him. The mother gripped her child, and the man stared with the same blank intensity as the goat.

"I'm sorry for dropping in," Aeden said with a half-smirk as he stepped out the door, his adrenaline pumping and thoughts of Devon briefly passing through his head.

It had started snowing. A light flurry danced in his vision as his eyes readjusted to the night.

"I see him!" A voice shouted from a nearby

house.

Aeden wasted no time as he bolted down the street. The sound of cursing and labored breathing followed him for the first few minutes. His feet slipped and struggled for purchase on the ice-covered roads. The sun had slipped behind the black canvas of night. Stars, the faint sliver of moonlight, and a few street lamps provided the only light. Shades of silvery gray cast the scene in hues of despair, apathetic to Aeden's plight.

He ducked down alleys. He ran past homes, taverns, and shuttered businesses. By the time his breath was strained and his heart was pumping wildly, the sounds of cursing faded away. His pursuers had finally given up. Aeden was free and as he soon realized, thoroughly lost.

Chapter 58

"Providence is often more than mere coincidence."
Matters of Fate, Book of Galdor

$\mathbf{A}$eden had spent a long, cold night shivering upon the streets of Petra's Landing. He walked in shadow, hidden from the reaching light of a partial moon. Silver strands of light played with the city in a spidery dance of enchantment.

The hours stretched passed, before Aeden finally stumbled upon the northern harbor of Grace's Fortune. The sun had begun to force its gentle way into the sky. Clouds parted at its behest, and warmth finally began to make its way into Aeden's heart.

"Brother Aeden!"

The voice was all too familiar. Aeden's heart leapt with joy. Had it only been a day? He had been worried that the others would have left. Or that they would have been found by Gavin and Bryce. His mind had tormented him with wicked images and horrible scenes, each iteration causing him to spiral further into darkness.

Adel ran forward and embraced him. Aeden smiled and hugged him back.

"The others are safe? Odilo, Neri?"

"Of course, we're all fine. The light of Salvare

has watched over us, just as you've helped protect us."

A sudden tugging at Aeden's heart threatened to tear away the fragile barrier he had so carefully built up. It was a curtain of promulgated strength. One he had cast about himself to protect him from having to feel too much. Yet, now after so many days, feeling so drained, the damn broke.

The death of his father, his friends, of Dannon. The brutal murders of the monks at Nailsea, Thomas lying upon the earth by a wheel of cheese. They all tumbled forward and tears flowed freely upon his face.

"We're safe brother, because of you," Adel had continued, pausing once he saw Aeden's state. Adel spoke again, "Neri helped us secure a ship. It was the strangest thing. We've passage southward. Away from all this! South to where it's warm. Everything will be okay now."

Adel looked at Aeden with a mixture of concern and brotherly love.

"They're waiting. We leave at dawn's breaking."

Aeden hastily wiped the tears from his swollen eyes. His face felt cold and numb. With a ragged breath, he stifled his emotions and followed Adel toward the vast northern port.

His heart was twisted in knots and his stomach felt like leaden stone. Aeden barely noticed the stone towers, that stood as sentinels upon the end of the fingers of land, extending into the bay. Walls of stone protected Petra's Landing from the wrath of the sea and from those who wished to invade. Wooden piers jutted out onto calm waters, straddled by the largest sea-going vessels Aeden had ever seen.

Ships of unbelievable size floated in the docks. Hives of workers moved about in a frenzy of activity, loading and unloading goods. Crates, barrels, and sacks lined the piers and were carried upon the backs of overly-muscled men.

"This way," Adel said.

Aeden tore his gaze from the ships and the waters they floated upon. He focused his attention on the young brother monk's back. The thick furs of his cloak swung lightly as he walked. Bits of snow clung desperately to the course hair of the fur lining.

Just ahead, Odilo's scarred face turned to meet his gaze as though he felt him coming. A smile creased his features, although it barely touched his eyes. It was as though the passage of time had finally worn away at the innocence of his soul.

"We must board now, or risk losing passage aboard the *Seventh Sage*," Odilo said, ushering them toward the wooden planking running up toward the main deck of a three-mast ship.

The ship rose and fell to the rhythm of the sea

in a gentle undulating manner. Aeden walked quickly up the plank and jumped onto the deck of the wooden vessel. It was far larger than the barges, schooners, scows and smaller caravels he had seen.

"Head to the sterncastle, C'ptn'll see ya now," a man shouted from the busy deck.

Aeden, Neri, Odilo, and Adel stood like stunned animals on deck. None of them knew where the sterncastle was. Men shuffled around them as they made the ship ready for sea.

"That there is the c'ptn's quarters," a younger man pointed as he passed.

The galley was cramped. They climbed a set of stairs to the extended poop deck behind the mainmast. Toward the stern of the ship was another raised structure looking a little like a miniature castle. The name now made sense as the group approached the open door.

"We were told to see you once onboard," Odilo offered.

The captain was flanked by two other men. He didn't acknowledge them immediately. Instead, he continued to study a chart laid out across a wooden drawing board. He nodded to one of the men who shoved his way past them before turning to the monks.

"Ah yes, the four monks traveling south," he said in near perfect Heortian.

His face was deeply tanned, as were his

hands. Wrinkles about his eyes spoke of his age. He was shorter than Aeden would have thought, and his features reminded him mildly of Neri.

"My second master will show you to your living area, familiarize you with the ship, and most importantly the rules."

The second master was a taller man and despite the layers of clothing, appeared to be thickly built. His brow was furrowed and he squinted at them as he stepped out. His hands were balled into fists and he looked ready to fight.

"This way," he said in a tone that belied his size and appearance, it was almost gentle in nature.

"This is the mizzenmast," he pointed to the stern beam that currently contained a folded sail. "This area is the poop deck, you aren't allowed unless captain, first master, or myself say," he lumbered past not waiting for a response.

They made their way down the stairs to the main deck.

"This's the galley, here is often busy, better to stay out of the way," the second master continued.

Aeden glanced about trying to guess how many people were onboard. There were people up on the masts and the webbed shrouds that stayed the main mast, on the three different levels of the deck, and from what he could tell, there were more below.

Ahead was an arched wooden alcove, crammed full of sacks and a few barrels tied down. Thick ropes hung on hooks along the side walls. A single ladder led to the foredeck.

"Forecastle, don't go there," the man pointed to the front of the ship. "Food is eaten here," he pointed to the open area below the poop deck behind them. Several sacks, smaller barrels, a single wooden table and bench were all squeezed under heavy wooden beams.

The man then led them down the open hatch to below deck. Immediately a dozen smells assaulted Aeden's sensitive nose. The smell of stale salt water, fresh tar, and a sweet musky scent hung over the tapestry of odors like a lingering note.

"Don't touch supplies," the second master said as they walked past men adjusting cargo. It was dark, cramped, and cold. There was barely enough room for them to walk single file through the center of the ship. It reminded Aeden of the overfilled croft at the monastery. Just as there was a door off limits, here most everything was restricted. His excitement of being on the ship was already beginning to wane.

The air was damp and there appeared to be tiny leaks allowing water into the main hold. Small dark shapes scurried into hidden corners behind stacks of supplies.

"You live here and sleep here, top deck allowed twice a day." The second master looked about with a bit of a smirk before disappearing up the stairs to the main deck.

"This should be fun," Aeden said, trying to sound positive.

Neri grunted in disapproval as he lay upon a few sacks.

"Fun? I already feel sick to my stomach," Adel replied, his face looking ashen in the relative darkness.

"Think on the warmth of the south. May Salvare watch over us," Odilo said the last faintly.

It was barely overheard because of the shouting above and the creaking of the ship.

Chapter 59

"Nature's mood is nothing more than the expression of Salvare's wrath." Saying of the Gemynd

The next week passed slowly. The winds were strong and buffeted the ship. The *Seventh Sage* creaked and moaned in response, as if its very soul were complaining. Bilge water seeped into the hold and smelled of grimy salt and human waste.

The boatswain had tasked the monks with manning the pumps, which proved to be a constant job. They were relieved by members of the crew on occasion, yet there seemed to be no known schedule. Their arms ached, their backs hurt, and their stomachs were never quite satiated.

Sleep was an escape, and when it came, the rocking of the decks permeated their dreams. Food was a privilege. The rations were meager at best. They usually made due with sea biscuits, salted meat, and watery wine. The occasional warm food; bread, and beans, was reserved for the officers, then the crew.

Aeden had only been on the main deck a half dozen times and each day had been like the last. Steely clouds loomed low and large. The dark waters of the Black Sea churned and foamed like a mad beast.

"She'll eat you in a sea minute if you let 'er," one of the crew members said, slapping him heavily on the back, as he stared out to sea.

In an effort to distract themselves, the monks played cards. They only played on a handful of occasions, but it proved more difficult a distraction than silently manning the pumps did. Conversations were sporadic and half-hearted.

Adel was constantly sick and never strayed far from a bucket. His voyages topside were to throw the contents of his bucket overboard, often to the jeers and insults of the crew.

Neri was in a foul mood. Odilo seemed the worse for ware, and Aeden couldn't claim to feel much better.

The boredom led Aeden's mind to wander astray. He engaged Neri several times and convinced him to teach him Adhari, the language of the deserts. It was slow and he mostly learned how to name things, but it was better than sitting in the idle boredom of inaction.

He learned the naming conventions of the A'sh. Neri's full name before donning the robe of the Holy Order was Neri Qasim Sha'ril. Qasim was his family name and Sha'ril was the city he was born in. As with all brothers of the Holy Order, Neri had abandoned all but his given name to Salvare. Aeden found the more he learned Adhari the more the culture opened up to him, filling an overly curious mind with thousands of questions.

These questions served to frustrate Neri. Aeden continued to be bored. Adel remained sick and Odilo was quieter than usual. Therefore, when the weather slowly changed and the days became longer and warmer the mood of the crew finally began to improve.

The sun made its first true appearance somewhere south of the Disputed Islands. Warm light filtered down below decks and splashed everything with a hint of color. The men topside were heard singing to pass the time. A colorful mix of accents stained their song in D'seart hues.

Aeden was manning the pumps and Odilo sat nearby. Aeden fiddled with the pump handle, debating whether to engage Odilo in conversation. The last few tries hadn't gone over well. Odilo had mildly rebuffed him. Aeden didn't wish to bother him and truthfully didn't want to be ignored by the man he so respected.

"You ever thought you'd be on a ship headed to the desert kingdoms?" Aeden asked Odilo hesitantly.

Adel was sick by a bucket, trying to stay as close to the middle of the carrack as possible. Neri was curled up toward the bow upon sacks of grain. Neither of them likely heard his question. Aeden, however, ignored them and glanced at Odilo through the corner of his eye.

He was wondering what sort of response he would get today.

Odilo regarded Aeden for a moment. His scarred face looked thinner and paler, but had regained some of the merriment it had lost over the previous days.

"Not recently," Odilo said.

Aeden stopped working the pump and looked up expectantly at Odilo. There was a moment of silence as Aeden waited with anticipation flittering about his gut like a trapped butterfly.

"It has taken me a few days to come to terms with our recent actions," Odilo started again; "I understand there is great mystery in the works of Salvare. I understand there are agents that work against his will and at times deciphering his intent can be difficult."

Aeden didn't say anything. He simply nodded his head. He knew Odilo needed to talk. In fact, he hoped that he would continue to talk.

"You're a good man Aeden, misguided perhaps, but you bear no ill-intent. I believe you to be an agent for good, an agent of Salvare," again Odilo paused as if collecting his thoughts, "but I can see sadness in your heart."

Aeden looked away momentarily. How had Odilo seen this?

"You hide it well, don't worry, I doubt many others have seen it."

"How do you know?" Aeden asked, worried of the response.

Could Odilo read his thoughts? Aeden had heard rumors that Imperial Inquisitors could read minds. Did Odilo know how his home had been destroyed? His family had been violently ripped from him? That everything he knew had been burned to ash?

Odilo was silent for a moment. The distant shouts of the seamen above, filtered through the deck. "*Half sail, square the rigging, steer into the wind.*" Their words combined with the sounds of sloshing water and feet upon the deck.

"My family was taken from me at an early age by greedy men," Odilo broke the relative silence.

At first it seemed as if that was all he would say. Aeden remained still so as to not disturb the gentle note of solitude that hung in the air between them. Had he pushed too far? Odilo took in a breath and began.

"I too have been tested by Salvare. I too have felt his wrath, have felt great anger deep in my belly, and I too have made poor decisions."

Odilo's eyes remained downcast as if looking for words in the moist planks of the hold.

Aeden looked at him for a moment, wondering what to say. Eventually his curiosity won out.

"What happened?" he asked.

Odilo looked up and raised an eyebrow. He nodded his head as if to himself and smiled for a moment. Not his normal smile. There was no happiness or warmth upon his lips. Instead, it was the smile of a man who's conceded his fate to the gods.

"It was dark. There was no moon that night." Odilo's eyes took on the faraway look of recollection. "I awoke to the sound of a crackling fire and the smell of smoke. I stumbled outside to see the cause, only to find my village was afire. I struggled to shout, but my lungs filled with smoke. My eyes stung with the ashes of the fallen as armed men atop horses swept through the village, killing, burning, and raping."

Aeden's eyes dropped to the floor as images flooded his mind. Odilo continued.

"Those of us that were young enough were spared. My brothers were too old and were killed, but not me. I was taken prisoner. I was to become a slave to be sold in a market to the highest bidder. I was so full of anger those days. I believed in nothing but myself, trusted no one but myself."

Odilo's words faded to a whisper. Aeden had stopped pumping now. The only sound was the wind howling down the open hatch and the creaking of the wooden beams as they strained against the sea.

"I wasn't going to be sold, so at my first

opportunity I escaped. I ran as far as my little legs would take me, as fast as they could move. But it wasn't fast enough. I was caught and punished," Odilo unconsciously rubbed at his thigh as he spoke, "They broke my leg and threw me in a prison. It was there that I remained for years. I saw people come and go, except for one. One stayed as long as me. He was an older man with piercing gray eyes, a man from the Gwhelt. He taught me your language, taught me to channel my anger into something useful."

Odilo suddenly stopped. Aeden was leaning so far forward he almost slipped off the small stool he was sitting on.

"But how then did you become a monk?" Aeden asked, all sense of propriety lost to curiosity.

Odilo regarded him for a moment.

"You know this isn't something I normally talk about," he said.

"I'm sorry," Aeden suddenly blurted out, imagining how he'd feel if someone were to pry into his own life, although a part of him wished someone would. He needed a release for all his buried anger.

"No, there's no need to apologize young brother. You've sacrificed much for us, for this mission. You clearly have a big heart, although I wonder if this is the role you were meant to play. The Church isn't for everyone," Odilo said, glancing ever so briefly toward Neri.

"What do you mean?" Aeden asked, worry creeping into his voice.

Ever since he had left the S'Velt the Church had become his new home. His fellow monks had become his new family. Where would he go if it wasn't for them? What would he do?

"I'm not suggesting you leave brother Aeden, however, I can't help but feel you may have a different calling." Odilo glanced about as if searching for the right words, "Not everyone is suited to the daily routine of monastic life. You have a strong spark of leadership and are quick to act when needed, but…"

Odilo looked at the ground for a moment and closed his eyes, rubbing absentmindedly at his scar.

"You had asked how I became a monk," Odilo started again in an effort to ease Aeden's fears, distracting him with words.

Aeden nodded his head slowly. His mind was still on Odilo's words. What would he do if he were not to become a monk? He hadn't given it much thought. He found it easier to not think on the future, it was less painful.

"Then let me tell you," Odilo began, "While in prison, we were occasionally visited by monks from the Holy Order of Sancire. They would come in clean robes, unafraid of the filth of the prisons. They would give us bread and weak wine. They would pray for us, and they would place hands on the sick, even those that the guards didn't dare beat.

"One monk in particular took an interest in me, I remember, for he too had a scarred face. He taught me the prayers. He taught me how to read, and eventually he taught me how to find peace. He must have argued on my behalf, and likely paid a small sum, but one day I was free to leave. He told me I could go anywhere I wanted, but that if I chose, I could go with him and become a novice at the Church."

"What happened next?" Aeden asked eagerly.

"I chose to go with him."

"What became of the monk who saved you?"

Odilo paused a moment, catching Aeden's eye, evaluating him.

"He grew to a position of great power, becoming the Deacon of Somerset, although that was years ago. It seems he's risen to greater levels of power since then, and I'm not sure if he would recognize me now, even if we crossed paths." Odilo had a strange look upon his face.

"Can I ask another question?" Aeden said.

Odilo looked at the younger brother and suddenly smiled.

"What is it you wish to know?"

Aeden hesitated before blurting out, "What's

behind the red door in the crypt?"

Odilo laughed out loud. It was a robust laugh, filled with the pent-up energy of a dozen weary nights. Neri stirred in his sleep on the far side of the hold. Adel glanced over, holding the bucket desperately in between his legs.

"I don't know," he finally said.

Aeden had one more question. He wanted to know more about the Inquisitors. He looked at the smile on Odilo's face. He decided now was not the time. The question slipped from his mind like a coin through water. Aeden caught Odilo's eye and smiled too, enjoying the mirth of his brother monk.

Chapter 60

"From the breath of competition exhales anger, frustration, and triumph." Book of Khein 6:12

By the second week the *Seventh Sage* had cut a wide swath about the Disputed Islands and traveled south toward the Gulf of Galdor. It was off the coast of Sawara when the wind died and the sea became uncommonly still.

The monks had been allowed on deck as there was little to do. The air was thick with humidity and as warm as a Sumor day. The ocean was as still as glass. There wasn't a cloud in the light blue sky. But the attention of the crew wasn't on the scenery about the floating carrack, but instead rested intently upon the main galley.

Men hung off the railing of the poop deck and forecastle, angling for a better vantage point. Hooting, betting, and hollering dominated the stagnant air. Thick accents washed off the flaccid square-rigged sails. Shouts of encouragement echoed grandly from the sterncastle to the bowsprit. ·

It was an odd sight aboard the *Seventh Sage*. Normally the men worked in two separate shifts, rarely awake at the same time. Today, however, was different. They crowded the bow and stern with eager anticipation. And in the center of it all were two men eyeing each other wearily.

They were both stripped to the waist and barefoot. One was thickly muscled, with deeply tanned skin. He moved with the grace of experience and age. The other was tall, younger, and startling pale, with a spate of white hair, growing where he had once been shaved bald.

"Come on Aeden!" Adel shouted in a manner unbecoming a monk of the Holy Order.

Aeden glanced up and smiled. It was his fifth bout and he was having a blast. The warmth of the sun melted away his concerns. The movement and competition had drawn him in like a fly to honey. Before he knew it, he had been challenged and had gladly accepted.

Now he faced the ship's reigning champion, Hamal Badi Agir. He was not only the reigning champion, but was also the boatswain. The man was responsible for stowing supplies, operation of the bilge pump, and he was the man who metered out punishment when sailors failed to follow orders.

Aeden instantly recognized the man had skill. He had likely trained and fought elsewhere, before becoming a crewman aboard the *Seventh Sage*. It was times like these that Aeden's mind struggled to wander, much like a spirited horse with a fresh bit in its mouth.

Hamal darted in, feinting with a jab and then came in low for a takedown. Aeden had anticipated this, for he had watched him do it three times before with other members of the crew. He brought up his knee to strike him in the face. Hamal was too quick and swatted it to the side and shoved Aeden back.

Aeden struck the center mast, his breath temporarily stolen from him. He stood there a moment panting under the unrelenting sun. His own sweat stung at his eyes. He blinked repeatedly as he stepped to the side.

It had been too long since he had trained and competed. He had grown soft among the monks he realized. Realization of such things always befell him at the most inopportune times.

"You fight like a woman!" Hamal taunted him, his thick accent drooling over each syllable.

The spectators cheered out Hamal's name. It was taken up by both ends of the ship and turned into an echoing chant, "Hamal, Hamal, Hamal!"

Aeden glanced up briefly, looking for support. In that moment Hamal launched forward. A fist caught Aeden flat-footed on the side of the head. He staggered and reformed his defenses. His face quickly grew numb.

"Be gentle with her, you've spilt her moon's blood!" Another crewmember squawked.

The red-hot feel of anger began to seep into Aeden's veins. The dull throbbing of pain drummed away into silence. He had been waiting for Hamal to tire. That was the wrong strategy. He seemed to feed off the sunlight while

Aeden wilted under its scrutiny. The humid air sucked at his lungs and sapped his strength. He felt lazy when he should have felt lively.

"It's when you're tired, cold, and hungry, that you must dig the deepest, train the hardest, and overcome your adversary." The words of his teacher drifted through his mind, lending strength to his tired legs. Although he couldn't help but wish for it to be a little cooler.

Hamal thrust forward again. Aeden side stepped the attack and back handed Hamal in the face. He then stepped diagonally into him and placed one hand on Hamal's forearm while his other hand struck with the speed of a striking cobra.

A spurt of blood erupted from Hamal's crushed nose. He yelped as he staggered back. Aeden's eyes held the fierce look of death. He was already moving forward, the momentum of his attack only just beginning.

"Aeden!" a strong voice called out through the haze of anger, pain, and blood-crazed onlookers.

Aeden froze with his fist in midair. He had thrown another punch without realizing. A punch he had trained a thousand times before. One he had practiced on stone to harden his fists. One that would have killed Hamal had Odilo not called out to him.

The weight of the humidity settled upon his

sticky skin. Slowly the throbbing pain returned. His head pounded awkwardly as he gazed at the sprawled figure of Hamal. Hamal lay on the deck looking up at him half in fear, half in awe. Aeden then glanced at those leaning over the railing of the forecastle deck. A dozen sun-tanned faces looked down upon him. Some had the gleam of bloodlust still in their eyes. Others looked away as if shamed by his penetrating gaze.

None of their looks registered. Aeden was caught in a world of moral confusion. Was he really willing to bash this man's face in over a friendly competition? He had to believe he was better than that.

Aeden extended his hand. It hung there silently in the afternoon air for everyone to see. Hamal spat upon it and pushed himself up. He eyed Aeden darkly for a moment before he stalked off. The crowd grew quiet and Aeden continued standing there. The sun glared away brightly, glittering off the emerald green waters, off the Gulf of Galdor. It remained indifferent to the struggles of the mortals below.

Chapter 61

"Knowledge is the seed from which sprouts power." Caliph of Q'Bala

"**Y**ou showed much courage today," the captain said hours later, clasping a firm hand onto Aeden's shoulder.

Aeden remained quiet. Despite having done well or perhaps because of his success, most of the crew had increased their distance. Many eyed him warily. Others turned their backs to him as he walked the deck. He was therefore quite surprised when the captain had invited him to the sterncastle.

"Strange weather, I can't remember a time that we went for so long without wind, it isn't natural. Soon wood worms will begin boring into the hull and we'll have our hands full tarring the leaks and manning the bilge."

Aeden nodded in silence, waiting for the captain to reveal his wishes. There had to be a reason he was asked up to the sterncastle. Did he want him and the other monks to man the bilge pumps even more then they had been? It didn't seem fair with so many idle crew members. The shorter man carried on, unconcerned with Aeden's mental wanderings.

"Pray to your god for wind, for ours hasn't been listening. The longer we sit in these waters the greater our risk. We have goods to offload. These men have wives to see, children that need to be fed. As I assume you too have a family waiting for you."

Aeden cringed. He did his best to hide his expression, but he couldn't help imagine the last time he saw his father. His twisted, burnt body lay beside Sagas, the sword of the kovor and every kovor before him.

"Do you not see your family?" the captain asked in a low and serious tone, bordering on offense.

"I pray for my family, for they have passed into the afterlife," Aeden said stiffly.

"It is said that tragedy at such a young age is a gift from Ghut and marks one for greatness." The captain regarded him for a moment, scrutinizing him as if he could discern Ghut's mark with a careful visual inspection.

"I don't feel marked for greatness," Aeden said quietly, unsure of how to respond.

"The greatest of us rarely feel as entitled as those who've been handed everything."

Aeden contemplated his words for a moment. There was truth to them and they cut through his mind like a hot knife. He looked about for a distraction. He found it tucked into a corner by the captain's simple bed. It was a book with a single word, plated in golden flowing script upon its cover.

"What are you reading?" Aeden asked, pointing to the book.

The captain's gaze traveled to the corner and a mask of displeasure passed across his features. He quickly covered the book with a simple cloth.

"The eyes of the unordained shouldn't look upon the Bocian." He berated.

Aeden ignored his tone as his curiosity was peaked.

"Bocian?"

"It's the holy book of the prophet Sha'a, from our sacred home of Q'Bala."

"So, that's where you're all from," Aeden stated as if it had been a question praying on his mind for some time.

"No, most are from there, but not all of us. You have met one from the deep deserts of A'sh. In fact, it is your performance from earlier that has begged this meeting."

Aeden's face flushed momentarily in shame. He had almost killed Hamal in their most recent contest before the eyes of the crew and before his fellow brother monks.

"You have some skill," the dark man continued as he gestured to the lower galley. "Perhaps you could teach some of those skills to my crew, for these aren't the safest waters," he continued, pressing on through the silence. "Of course, you'd be repaid for your efforts."

Aeden looked about for a moment, unsure of how to respond. He looked about for the crew. Was this a trick? He saw a few had fallen asleep in the limited shade under the forecastle. Others sat below the poop deck practicing knots, drinking watery wine, their voices carried faintly through the wooden deck. And as always, there were lookouts on the masthead and bow. The masthead rested high above the waterline, just above the main skysail, affording a wide view of the waters about them.

"In exchange for better treatment of my fellow brothers, greater food rations, and…" Aeden paused looking about.

He caught sight of the great chart spread across the drawing board within the captain's quarters. There were markings upon it, a ledger next to it, and fascinating tools that stood oddly upon a shelf. Curiosity plucked at him as it often did.

"And I want to learn how to navigate the ship."

The captain glanced back to the chart, then to Aeden.

"You've a keen eye young warrior monk, but know navigation is a long and difficult study. Most do not comprehend such things. Perhaps learning to tie knots would be a better place to begin."

"If I learn to tie your knots, will you teach me

navigation?" He asked.

"You learn the knots and teach my crew how you fight and I'll teach you navigation," the captain said, extending his hand.

Aeden reached forward and shook his hand. The captain retracted his hand shaking his head.

"No, that's of the north. We shake hands like this," he grasped Aeden's forearm and indicated for him to do the same. "Good, now go. My second master will coordinate training with you."

True to the captain's word the second master sought out Aeden. Over the course of the next few days Aeden spent his time training members of the crew. He ran them through various forms. Most had a decent foundation to work with, likely a result of having been at sea for so many years. The rocking motion of the ship taught them to carry their weight low.

Just as their lessons slowly progressed, his lessons in knot tying progressed. They were puzzles for his fresh young mind. The first few he learned were incredibly easy. The later knots were given to him already tied. He would spend a minute or so examining the knot, then he'd untie it, only to retie the knot. This earned him startled expressions and rowdy praise.

As a child, he had learned a few knots back in S'Vothe. His father had been adamant that he have a basic understanding of every aspect of village life. He had learned to milk the goats; sheer the sheep, felt wool, weave clothing, straighten a sword, mend armor, repair a wall, and tie simple knots. He didn't let the crew know, however, for he rather enjoyed the praise.

It was therefore, on the third day when the winds finally resumed, that Aeden was once again invited to the sterncastle.

"*Suya qan cetmek*, blood cannot be made into rain, but you have proved me wrong. I had given you my word under the eyes of the ever watchful Ghut, and will now fulfill my obligation."

Captain Nawfel Murad Q'Bala led Aeden into his quarters upon the sterncastle. Resting before him was a chart carefully painted upon the finest vellum Aeden had ever seen. All of Verold was expertly depicted, with consideration for outlying islands, and excessive detail was heaped upon the coasts, bays, and inlets of the continents.

"This is the most precious item aboard this ship, don't let any other captain tell you otherwise," Nawfel said, his dark eyes drinking in the features of the map. "It's both a tool for navigation and a thing of beauty. Use it incorrectly and you will be hopelessly lost. Use it correctly and you will always sail true."

Aeden nodded his head as if he already understood the intricate inner workings of navigation at sea. The captain smiled. His missing teeth were ever more evident in close proximity.

"The chart is useless without understanding the basics of terrain recognition when near a coast and angles for when out to sea."

Aeden looked to the captain, "angles?"

"The math of triangles. Understanding the mystery of the triangle allows one to plot a point on the map," the captain replied and placed a firm finger upon the map as if for emphasis.

Aeden looked carefully at the map then at the instruments on a nearby shelf.

"Is that what this one's for?" Aeden asked, pointing to a long staff with three perpendicular cross sections.

"You've an astute eye. Yes, without the cross-staff a captain cannot determine the proper angles. You want to try?" He said, pulling the cross-staff off the shelf.

Aeden nodded his head as he peered at the device.

"Come, we must do this outside," Nawfel said.

Aeden stepped outside to the quarterdeck. He looked up at the blue sky, using his hand to shield his eyes from the intensity of the sun. The day was already warm and humid. His skin was sensitive to the sun from his bouts under its intense gaze.

"The key to using the cross-staff is positioning. You must place it correctly on your cheek in the exact same spot each time, and you must stand on the same spot of the ship facing two different directions, otherwise your angles will be inaccurate.

"Watch me first," Nawfel said as he held the device up to his cheek.

The length of it was approximately as long as his arm. The three transoms were able to slide up and down the length of the staff. Lines were carved up the length in regular intervals and filled with black ink. At the end of the center transom were two holes. One was filled with a bit of smoked glass held in a metal ring.

"You must brace yourself with the movement of the ship and line up the device with the sun and the horizon, sliding the appropriate transom based on the time of day to get your angle."

The captain held the cross-staff firmly to his cheek with the transepts forming a vertical cross in respect to the horizon. He lined up the center transept so as to catch the light of the sun through the smoked glass, and so that the bottom circle lined up with where the water met the sky in the distant horizon.

"You see," the captain said, "Now I slide the transept so that both the sun and horizon are within these circles."

He pointed with his other hand at the metal

rings on either end of the perpendicular transept.

"Art and science is what this is, bleeding the truth from Ghut's masterful creation."

Aeden stood, watching in fascination. The ideas of triangles, congruencies, angles, and distances slowly revealed themselves to his ever-curious mind.

Chapter 62

*"Nature's fury can only be imitated by the
greatest of the arkein." Lost Scroll of the Scapan*

The winds finally picked up. They swept
across the sea with angry purpose. They moved
as though they were making up for the stillness
of the days prior. Lightning tore across the
darkening sky in flashes of powerful brilliance.
The once emerald waters turned dark as
undulating waves crashed upon the bow of the
Seventh Sage.

"Reef the mainsails, gallants, and topsail!" the
Captain screamed above the brewing storm.
"Loose the storm sails, man the bilges, secure the
deck."

Men scrambled to their duties. Sails were
furled slowly as men struggled against the
winds. The approaching storm had come with
such speed that normal preparations were only
now underway. The second master was shouting
orders and helping tie down everything top deck.
The boatswain, Hamal, was in the hold, double
checking the barrels, sacks, and trade goods. If
they shifted during the storm, items could be
damaged or worse yet, the boat could capsize.

"Soon there will be more water than can be
pumped, Ghut will seed the oceans with his
tears, as Marduk battles from below," Hamal said

as he looked over the monks with a wild gleam in his eye.

Adel's face blanched. Odilo looked to Neri then Aeden, before watching Hamal climb back to the galley.

"Marduk?" Adel breathed.

"The god of the sea and master of the winds," Aeden replied.

Adel and Odilo both looked at him quizzically as the ship rocked underfoot.

"What? I ask questions," he said.

The ship suddenly lurched and the monks were suspended in the air for a moment before it came crashing down. Water splashed about the forecastle and washed down the galley, pouring into the hold.

"Time to begin our duty," Odilo said as he moved toward one of the bilge pumps.

"We'll work in pairs," Aeden replied, moving toward the other pump at the stern of the ship.

Adel glanced up as the midship hatch was closed. The hold fell into darkness. The smell of bilge water hung thickly in the air. It burned their noses and stung at their eyes.

"I guess we'll work in darkness," Aden said, feeling his way toward the pump under steerage.

"If Salvare swallows this ship, its crew, and foul stench, I'd pay my weight in dinars," Neri uttered, feeling his way toward Odilo.

Aeden's eyes adjusted to the faint light spilling in through the steerage hatch. Water drained in through the opening in smattering showers as the ship was rocked by the sea.

"The darkness shall be the end of us," Adel whispered.

Aeden stumbled as the ship moved, before finding purchase and positioning himself next to Adel. If he was going to die he wanted to die next to a friend.

"It's not the darkness that'll take us, but the unrelenting sea," Aeden replied.

"Thanks, I feel better," Adel whispered.

Aeden couldn't help but laugh. The sound of creaking wood, struggling against nature's fury, was momentarily drowned by his delirious amusement.

"What's so funny? Death?" Adel asked, his voice slightly higher pitch than normal.

"My father used to tell me that 'Cowards die a thousand small deaths every day. It's the brave who only have to face it but once.' And only now do I finally understand what he meant."

The sounds of the storm enveloped them in a symphony of violence. Heavy rains fell from the firmament as if unleashed by heavenly hands. Lightning allowed for brief flashes of light as thunder rumbled deep within the belly of the *Seventh Sage*.

"Lord of light and life,

Deliver us from the jaws of death,

And bring us the peace of understanding…"

Aeden listened to Adel's prayer as he glimpsed his still form in the dark hues of shadow. Stillness had claimed him and stolen his attention. The ship lurched awkwardly and Aeden slipped to the side, grasping hold of the bilge pump. He continued to listen to the prayer as he positioned himself to work the pump for all he was worth.

The hours droned on and Aeden's arms grew leaden with exhaustion. They worked in complete darkness as the steerage hatch had long since been closed. Only the sounds of the waves slapping the bow of the carrack and the rumblings of thunder could be heard.

Adel had fallen silent.

"You think we'll make it," Adel said at last.

Aeden was startled out of his thoughts. He stopped his work at the pump, his arms tingling from fatigue.

"Of course we'll make it. We have the Book of Divinus aboard. Salvare wouldn't allow such a precious item to be lost at sea," Aeden said with strength in his voice, despite his own fears playing desperately in the back of his mind.

"It's your strength in trying times," Adel said, "that's why you were chosen."

Aeden remained silent. He wasn't sure if Adel was talking just to hear himself speak.

"That's why you were voted in as abbot in Nailsea," he continued. "I wish I had your faith."

Aeden didn't reply at first. Adel's words were the heartfelt honesty of one waiting for the arms of death. Such honesty often made Aeden feel uncomfortable and at a loss for words.

"Faith is the mask one wears when the unknown beckons," Aeden said after a moment.

"But I know what comes," Adel responded, "a watery grave and Salvare's loving embrace."

"Knowledge is but one half of your religion, faith is the other," Aeden replied.

Adel became quiet. Aeden resumed working the bilge pump. The storm continued to rage.

"Why did you say '*your*' religion," Adel suddenly asked as if a realization dawned on him.

Aeden was at a loss for words. Back in S'Vothe he was renowned for talking even when he shouldn't. In the Bodig Monastery there were times he was chastised for commenting when silence was demanded. Now he had nothing to say. No words. No thoughts. Yet he felt the need to justify himself.

Just as he was about to speak, a loud crack fractured the droning storm. It was different than the roaring rumble of thunder. It was sharper, angrier. A moment later wood splintered apart and the howl of wind tore into the hold.

Chapter 63

"Death comes for us all." Proverb of the Thane
Sagan

"What was that?" Adel screamed.

Aeden's ears were ringing. He looked about for Adel. He saw him huddled by sacks of grain. He then thought of the others.

"Odilo, Neri, are you okay?" Aeden shouted.

There was a short pause before Odilo shouted back.

"We're okay, you?"

"Adel and I are fine. What happened?" Aeden asked.

"No idea," Odilo responded.

The steerage hatch swept open and one of the crewmen shouted through the opening.

"Pirates!"

Aeden didn't hesitate as he scrambled for his hidden sword. He had sandwiched it between a couple of barrels, hoping to keep it both hidden and reasonably dry. Once in hand, the grip felt cool and comforting. He slipped as he ran to the wooden ladder leading out of the hold.

Aeden climbed to steerage, finding himself just below the sterncastle. He stumbled as the ship lurched underfoot. The wind howled as it whipped through the vessel. Men screamed orders. Faint battle cries fought against the torrent to be heard.

Once his footing was moderately secure, he swept past the tiller, then past the table and bench and onto the galley deck. It was slick with rain and seawater. Gusts of wind hurled across its surface, threatening to sweep everything off the deck.

Sheets of water fell from the blackened heavens. Lightning struck a moment later. Its fiery light cast everything in shades of silvery white before slipping back to darkness. In that moment, a desperate scene was burned into his eyes.

Grappling hooks had bitten into the wood of the *Seventh Sage*. Two caravels flanked the ship as men were attempting to board. Hamal led a small group, cutting the ropes on the port side. The second master led another group starboard. The captain struggled with steering, attempting to battle a course into the waves to avoid being capsized.

"*Birakmak!*" the men from the flanking ships shouted. Their voices were carried and thrown about by the winds.

Two men had climbed aboard and were making their way toward Captain Nawfel. Aeden moved as quickly as he could on the slick decks. He bounded up the stairs and drew his sword.

"Stop!" Aeden screamed as he approached

warily.

The captain's first mate had already engaged a pirate with a long dagger in hand. Lightning flashed again. In an instant a dark-skinned man rushed Aeden. Strangely Aeden felt unafraid. He remarked upon the man's bare feet and black stained teeth. It was an odd sensation. His training took over as if it were a second skin.

He recoiled and brought up his sword. The clang of steel was lost to the weather. The shorter man cursed in a foreign tongue and parried. It all seemed to happen too slowly. Aeden watched as his attacker lunged forward. He remarked upon the strangely curved blade. He saw his own blade counter as he stepped to the side. It wasn't much of a fight. His opponent was passionate, quick, and intent. Yet he lacked finesse. He lacked the competence of the Thane.

Aeden whipped forward and sliced into the meat of his attacker's arm. The man howled in pain and dropped his sword. It clattered to the deck and was quickly swept to sea as the carrack was pounded by a rogue wave.

Fighting stopped for a moment as men slipped to the port side. Curses clung to the air like a tenacious mist. Fingers scrambled desperately for purchase. A few men tumbled over the railing and were lost to the dark waters. Sacrifices demanded by Marduk.

Aeden only barely caught hold of the railing.

The wind was knocked from his lungs. He nearly lost his grip on his sword. His scabbard, however, wasn't so fortunate and slid across the poop deck down to the galley.

The *Seventh Sage* creaked and moaned as if she were mortally wounded. Another loud explosion echoed across the expanse between one of the caravels and the carrack. Aeden caught sight of a brief flash of light followed by the sound of wood exploding in a shower of splinters. What sort of magic was this?

"Aeden, stop her cannon," Captain Nawfel shouted from the poop deck.

Realization settled upon him as a flash of lightning cast the captain's figure in light and shadow. He was pointing toward the source of the explosion.

"Father watch over me and give me strength," Aeden whispered as he climbed to the forecastle.

Once on the bow he braced himself on the foremast. A grappling hook and line were still firmly attached to the railing of the ship. Aeden took in a deep breath, clamped onto the Templas sword with his teeth and clambered across.

The wind buffeted him as he struggled to maintain his grip on the wet rope. His sword immediately felt far too heavy and he ached to let it go. The waves danced upon the prow and sprayed upward in giant plumes of salty mist.

The water stung at his eyes and threatened to tear him loose of his weakening grip.

Finally, Aeden reached the railing of the pirate caravel. He hauled himself onto their deck only to come face to face with a startled pirate. He kicked him squarely in the groin and threw the wheezing man overboard.

With his sword in his hand he looked upon the deck. He searched for the cannon. The ship was smaller than the *Seventh Sage*. It only had two masts, an extended poop deck and a short foredeck. Its lateen sails were reefed.

"Acele etmek!" a short man shouted.

Aeden caught sight of a small group huddled around a long metal tube. A young man was in the act of stuffing a metal rod down the hollow shaft. Another quickly placed river stone within, ramming it home with a ramrod. Off to the side the short man lit the end of a linstock, a long staff with a slow burning match.

That had to be it, Aeden thought.

He rushed across the deck. The storm raged about him masking his movement. The men now struggled as they ran the cannon back out. The ship heaved underfoot. Aeden braced himself as best as he could. The men stood back, placing a small block behind the wooden wheels. The breech of the cannon was primed with powder as the short man approached with the linstock.

Aeden swung his sword and sliced through

the wood of the linstock. The top half fell to the deck as the slow match sputtered. The man reacted immediately using the remaining portion of the staff as a weapon. The others turned to face Aeden. The realization that death was likely upon him settled firmly into his stomach. He should have killed the man.

The short pirate lunged forward and Aeden stumbled back. The other men moved toward him fanning out to either side. Rain splashed upon the deck in angry sheets as if taunting the crew.

Aeden's heart pounded away feverishly. Gusts of wind hurled over the railing, picking up the rain and sending it across the caravel in blinding curtains of despair. Nearly drowned by the wind was the sound of triumphant shouting. A lone voice stood out amidst the cacophony of the storm.

"Biz kazandik! Biz kazandik!"

"Do your dog ears hear this sound?" the short man grunted. "We take your ship, your cargo, and your crew."

Although he spoke with a thick grueling accent, Aeden understood every word. His heart sank as a pit formed in his stomach and his bowels turned to water. They had captured the *Seventh Sage*.

He was too late. He had been too slow and too merciful.

Again, he had failed those he cared about because of weakness. Fear had stayed his hand and robbed him of his freedom. He looked up, half expecting to see his father's disappointed features glaring down upon him. Instead, he was rewarded with a face full of rain.

"Dog, I speak to you. Lay down that sword. You are mine now," the man continued, his dark eyes staring upon him with a mad intensity. His words were like steel over a grinding stone.

Aeden glanced to either side and saw the others slowly approach him. Two more men climbed out of the hold with chains in hand. One of them caught sight of Aeden and drew a dagger with his free hand.

He knew when he had lost. Aeden let go of his Templas blade. It fell upon the wooden deck with a hollow sound, ringing out as if in pain.

Two men approached from either side, holding their sword tips to his neck as the shorter man approached and picked up Aeden's fallen sword. He held it up, examining it in the faint light of distant lightning.

"Where did a slave steal such a sword?" The man eyed him curiously.

Aeden looked back at him in defiance. One of the men hit him in the back of the head with the flat of his sword.

"You answer when spoken to dog," he said, holding Aeden's gaze. "Where did you steal this?" He asked again, this time painfully slow as though Aeden couldn't understand basic Heortian.

"It's mine, I didn't steal it," Aeden replied.

Aeden staggered to his knees as a blow struck him in the back of the neck. He hadn't seen it coming.

"Watch your tongue slave," the man spat upon the ground and walked off, holding Aeden's Templas sword in his hand like it was a favored prize.

Another man approached. He was thickly muscled and taller than the last. He held chains in his hands. He quickly bound Aeden's hands. He worked with the practiced efficiency of one who had done this a thousand times. He manipulated Aeden the way one would a sheep to be shorn. Manacles were then placed upon his feet. A small hammer drove the locking pin home.

The sound of the hammer upon the iron echoed loudly in his head. It was the sound of freedom being stripped away.

Chapter 64

"Freedom is a state of mind for some and a state of being for others." Proverb of the Sawol

The following two weeks were agony. Heat, hunger, and fever each played a hand by inflicting ever greater levels of discomfort. Shame was cast to the sea the day following the storm.

The winds had died to a slow breeze. The clouds gave way to the intensity of the sun and humidity clung to the air with desperation. The *Seventh Sage* had been captured. Half her crew had been slain or lost to sea. The other half had been split between the two caravels, slaver ships.

Aeden had been relieved to see that the other monks were, for the most part, unharmed. They too stood on the deck before the unforgiving sun. Its fingers of light probed every part of their naked bodies as they stood on the deck of the *Zafer*. Before them stood Reem Sati Agir, the short man Aeden had encountered the night before, the man who had stolen his Templas sword.

He eyed them carefully as other men checked their bodies. A dialect of the deep A'sh desert was uttered between the men. Calloused hands checked each of them for injury and disease. None were spoken to, for they were below their captors in every respect of the word.

Hamal was one of the crewmembers taken aboard the *Zafer*. He was the only man who chose to speak aloud. He was the only man from the *Seventh Sage* that understood their dialect. They shared a language and culture.

The similarities were but stagnant water at the captors' feet. Hamal was severely beaten for daring to question them. His echoing cries plagued Aeden's nightmares. His bloodied face was contorted in pain as one of the slavers pummeled him over and over. A look of boredom was etched on the captor's features, as if this were a job he'd undertaken a hundred times over.

"You see dogs," Reem said aloud, "this is what comes of defiance," his accent sounded like grated metal.

Reem looked down upon the crumpled form of Hamal. Reem shook his head in mild disappointment.

"He's damaged, throw him over," he commanded in Heortian so that the others could understand.

The translation wasn't necessary. Two muscular men picked up Hamal by his hands and feet. He attempted to struggle, but only weakly. His body had been broken. They swung him up and over the railing of the *Zafer*. The subtle splash of his body hitting the water was like a nail driven into each and every skull of the naked men who stood watching.

None dared speak thereafter. Not in the presence of their captors. It wasn't until they were shackled below deck that muted whispers were heard. Prayers, complaints, and pleas of quiet agony hung upon the stale atmosphere.

The air below deck was foul. It was thick with the scents of fear, excrement, and rot. Never had Aeden experienced such a stench. His nose burned. His eyes watered. His stomach turned and he lost all sense of taste, smell, and his desire for food.

When it came time to go above deck to eat, Aeden refused. Not out of disobedience, but out of fear. He was afraid he wouldn't be able to keep his food down. It was his first mistake under their captivity.

The sun was up. A few white clouds were painted upon the blue sky the day Aeden was first beaten as a slave. The other men of the *Seventh Sage* and his brother monks were all forced to watch. Punishment was a lesson for them all. Every bloody detail was meant to be remembered.

Aeden was tied down by his feet. His hands were bound and placed above his head upon a hook on the mainmast. His heart pounded strangely in his chest. He remembered being thankful for the smell of the sea. The fresh air gave him strength and gave him hope. A subtle hope that was nothing more than the whisper of a lover's secret.

An otherwise normal looking man stood to the side, watching. His eyes were intense and curious. Another approached from behind with a whip in hand. The smell of his sweat hung about him like a wet sheet.

Fear crept into Aeden's young mind as the anticipation of pain crept into view.

Snap!

The man lashed out, striking at the air as if to hear the crack of the whip. There was a playful grin that passed across his features. The smile disappeared and the whip cracked through the air again. This time the tail sliced through skin and muscle. Pain welled up through Aeden's back and down his legs.

He'd lost fights. He'd trained with stones, staffs, and all manner of weapons. He'd trained his body to be hard against strikes and soft against incoming attacks. He'd been beaten by fists, but never had he felt such a pain as that of the whip.

Each slash cut through the air and tore upon the naked skin of his back. Eventually he grew numb from the throbbing torment. He sagged against the mainmast. It was his only support, his only comfort. The rope about his hands bit into his wrists. Blood dripped down his arms as it did his back. He was too tired and too beaten to care.

"You'll eat dog," was all that was said.

Aeden was cut down. He fell to the deck in a heap. A man kicked him in his ribs. He reflected upon the surprise at the new sensation of pain.

"Up," the man said.

Aeden struggled. His arms shook and his back burned. His hands were slippery with his own blood. Despite the pain, he managed to stagger to the other monks. Odilo caught his eye. He nodded his head briefly in understanding and then glanced at the bowl of food they were all given.

Aeden ate. He forced the food into his mouth. Each mouthful of the tasteless porridge threatened to accumulate into a massive lump in his throat. With great will he choked down every bite.

He kept his head down and endured the only way he knew how. He shut off part of himself. He sectioned off a piece of his psyche. He ignored the pain, the physical torment, and withdrew into a quiet shell he had created deep within his mind.

Chapter 65

"Money drives the desires of men and eats at his wayward heart." Proverb of the A'sh

By the end of the second week Aeden's fever broke. The undulating movements of the ship, the confined quarters, chains, and stench had been unbearable. As the days grew warmer so too did the pestilent atmosphere of the hold. Perspiration, urine, seawater, and waste hung in the stagnant air in a suffocating aroma of distaste.

His back continued to bleed for the first few days. One of the crewmembers from the *Seventh Sage* had urinated on his back daily in an effort to keep the wound from festering. It must have worked for Aeden had begun a slow recovery.

Each day he allowed the sun to warm the wounds upon his back. Each day he ate his two meals in silence. And each day he swore to himself that he would soon be free.

Neri had fallen into a sullen stupor. Words, humor, and all attempts of communication had failed. He had withdrawn into himself and simply stared at the world with unseeing eyes. Odilo remained strong. He had lost that sparkling smile in his eye, but his spirit was firm. It was his words and his prayers that gave strength to many of the others. Adel needed them more than most.

Adel looked frightened. He hovered between shock and apathy. At times Aeden glimpsed bits of his former self. And as the days passed Adel slowly seemed to accept his fate. He took to the role better than Aeden could ever have. His posture changed to subservience.

Shouts from above distracted Aeden from idle thoughts. All whispers ceased as the sound of gulls rang in the hot air. The sounds of men working upon the deck were evident. Aeden imagined the sails being reefed as they glided into port.

He didn't know how much time passed before the hatch was peeled open. Sunlight peeked its wary head into the dark corners of the slaver's bowels. A gust of wind brought the smells of the sea.

Two men lowered themselves below deck, holding a piece of cloth to their nose. They moved quickly among the captured men, shackling legs and hands before freeing them from their group restraints.

"Move topside you filthy dogs," one of the men shouted in barely intelligible Heortian.

Aeden was closest to the hatch. He stumbled as he climbed up the short ladder. The chains at his feet clanked upon each wooden step. The sound was akin to the distant song of a forge.

Sunlight and heat attacked his tired body as he pushed himself onto the deck. His eyes struggled to adjust from the intensity of the glare as he took in his surroundings.

The *Zafer* had docked. On the other side of the pier was the *Seventh Sage*, her sails reefed, and the other caravel, *Ruzgar*. In the light of day, the splintered holes along the carrack's side appeared as small wounds upon her otherwise unblemished skin. Dotting the wide harbor were hundreds of smaller ships. Scows, cogs, caravels, and a few carracks provided a splash of color to the pale blue waters off the coast of a magnificent city.

Aeden shuffled to the starboard side as the others clambered to the main deck. His attention was now upon the city by the water. White buildings gleamed in the sunlight, climbing a gentle slope, which was capped by the largest structure Aeden had ever seen. A round dome dominated the cityscape, flanked by six slender towers. Gold capped the top of the dome, shining like a beacon to the gods. He didn't know there was so much gold in all of Verold.

They had arrived upon the fabled southern city of Sha'ril.

"Dogs, listen to your master," Reem spoke aloud.

Aeden couldn't help but notice that he now wore the Templas sword at his hip. He must have uncovered the scabbard from the *Seventh Sage*, for it hung sheathed before his eyes like a slap to the face.

"You will do well to obey. Speak when spoken to, not otherwise. List your talents when asked, and feel free to embellish, so my pockets may be lined with *sigloi*."

Over the course of the following hour they were washed down with salt water and scrubbed clean. Aeden had his wounds attended to and was given a simple shirt to wear to cover the scabs and deep scars lining his back. They were fed, threatened, clothed and talked to.

"Do not pretend injury or you will be beaten," Reem exclaimed, "stand proud on the block, but don't let your eyes linger."

Aeden only partially paid attention as Reem spouted rules for them to follow. He was grateful for the fresh air. It felt good to move, to stand, and to feel the touch of the sun upon his face.

Once the tirade of etiquette was done, they were led off the ship down a gangplank to the pier. A stream of goods and people entered the white city, sweeping them up in the tide of humanity entering Sha'ril.

Slave soldiers stood guard, unwaveringly. Their spears gleamed in the late morning light. Green pendants with a single sword burnished on their faces, snapped and furled in the light morning wind.

The former crew members of the *Seventh Sage* and the four monks, passed under the grand archway of Caliph Rajah. They walked in a two-man procession down the main street of Sha'ril. They were flanked and trailed by the slavers of the *Zafer* and *Ruzgar*. Reem Sati Agir led the shuffling group with his head held high. Aeden's Templas sword swung lightly by his side.

The day had grown hot under the intense gaze of the southerly sun. The white walls that gleamed so purely from the sanguine waters of port appeared worn with age. They were cracked, with crumbled corners. Despite their apparent age, they were blindingly bright.

Aeden's eyes watered under the scrutiny of their reflected light. His neck grew sore and raw from the metal clasp that bound him by chains to those behind him. Sand and dust filled cracks in the roadway and piled in corners along the sides of buildings. The occasional gust of wind hurled granules of the A'sh into his sunburnt face. The march through the tight streets of the bustling city had become an effort of endurance.

The scene only proved mildly more distracting than his discomfort. Sha'ril was the fabled city of the south. It was the seat of the famous Caliphate of A'sh, a ruthless empire that had once stretched from the White Sea to the Barre Mountains.

Aeden glanced about. The men ignored him. The children pointed and stared. They giggled as they watched the group marched through the street as if they were a parade for their amusement.

Skinny, hairless dogs scavenged the narrow alleys in search of scraps of food. Stone archways of varying height lined the main roads. They provided shade for vendors. They cast entryways into shadow and permeated the atmosphere with a hint of mystery. Hidden courtyards lay beyond.

Aeden hoped the small, scampering animal had caught Neri's attention. Hopefully it brought him a modicum of joy. It was funny that even chained, uncomfortable and captive, his mind continued to churn out thoughts unabated.

The sounds of bustling activity and shouting grew like the buzzing of a swarm of approaching bees. The roadway widened as the procession forced their way through the massive crowds. The lingering scent of perfumed oils and sweat hung thickly in the air.

Aeden coughed as they passed men covered in swaths of clothing to protect them from the glaring sun. Stalls were scattered about in no apparent order or fashion. Wooden trestles covered sections of the market, checkering the crowds in lines of light and shadow. They provided a smattering of protection from the desert sun.

An open plaza stretched before them as they worked their way past a stone archway. The tall minarets of the golden-domed temple stood as absurdly tall sentinels on either side of the market. The archways lining the perimeter of the square were covered in carpets, metal wares, and clothing. It was a colorful collage of merchandise designed to entice the buyer. Men sat upon simple wooden stools watching those who passed with the disinterested look of boredom.

The shouting grew more intense as they approached the center of the crowds and the center of the plaza. The smells of rotten fruit, the stench of sweat, and the stink of human waste clung to the air.

Reem turned, "stop here dogs," he commanded. "*Onlari izlamek*," he shouted to the other slaver-pirates who were watching over them.

Reem then left their group and slipped into the masses. Aeden watched him go with anger in his heart. Curiosity slowly replaced his anger with a sense of purpose. He looked about for a method of escape, somewhere to hide.

There were cages in the center of the market with more slaves. Men, women, and children were all for sale. Their lives worth nothing more than the coin of a wealthy man's purse. Soldiers guarded the cages as merchants perused the humanity within, as though they were nothing more than animals for sale.

Well-dressed men gripped slave faces in their hands and examined teeth. They gripped arms and legs in an attempt to assess muscle. They groped women's breasts and buttocks to assess their fertility. Aeden felt sick to his stomach. Realization slowly dawned on him. He was soon to be sold as a piece of property.

Reem returned and led them to the far side of the plaza. Aeden glimpsed an auction block and a rectangular area roped off and punctuated with soldiers. They passed wooden cages filled with slaves to be sold. His eye paused on suckling infants crying at their mother's teat.

An empty wooden cage rested heavily upon the white stones of the square. One by one the chains around their necks were undone and each was pushed roughly into the cage. Finally, the doors were closed shut. Aeden glimpsed Reem hand a shiny silver coin to a fat man in green and ivory robes, before he moved beyond sight.

The hours stretched by slowly under the sultry embrace of the day. The heat made his clothes stick to his body. His skin was red from the sun and his mouth was dry and thirsty. In that span of time he heard the shouting and haggling of slavers peddling their slaves. Men walked past his cage, looking inquiringly upon the fresh crew and the four monks. On occasion words were exchanged between one of the slavers and the perspective buyer.

It wasn't until the sun was a couple of hours

from setting that Reem returned. The green-robed fat man procured a key and the crew members of the *Seventh Sage* were called forward. The monks were told to remain behind.

Aeden moved to the far side of the cage and attempted to watch the sale of the crewmembers. They were led to the block one at a time.

"Salvare still watches over us," Aeden heard Odilo whisper.

He turned to see Odilo comforting Adel. Neri sat in a corner staring at a spot on the ground.

"He's forsaken us to this hell," Adel responded. "Salvare wouldn't allow men such actions."

"He's allowed far worse. Empires have been built on the backs of the less fortunate. It is the faith that He reserves judgment for that final breath that allows one to accept such atrocities," Odilo replied gently.

Aeden stared at Odilo for a moment. The fundamental idea of the Holy Order of Salvare flashed before his eyes, and its one glaring weakness now echoed loudly in his mind, *faith*. It was a word often used, but what strength did the word hold when imperial soldiers were allowed to slaughter innocents in Nailsea? What did faith do to stop the pirates from capturing the *Seventh Sage*? What would faith have done to stop the draccus fiend from destroying his home, his family, and his friends?

The answer was *nothing*. He required something more tangible, more powerful than faith.

"Seventh hell isn't punishment enough for them," Adel responded, anger evident in his eyes.

Good, Aeden thought, use your anger to remain strong, to retain a sense of self and purpose. He watched Odilo and Adel for only a moment longer before turning his attention to the auctioning block.

"*Hada sani kre gecelum!*" The green robed man shouted, gesturing for them to get out.

The four monks shuffled out of the cage at the direction of the fat guard. They were led past empty cages where slaves had been held and then sold. As they moved toward the auctioning block Aeden's stomach tightened. He was about to be sold as a piece of property. Would he be bought by someone fair? What type of work would they demand of him? Fear reared its ugly head and fanned the flames of anxiety.

He barely noticed the other monks, but they too were in the grip of despair. Instead, he was focused on the auctioning block as if it were a living thing. Its simple wooden design belied its somber purpose. Standing on the platform was a well-dressed man of indeterminate age. As they approached he began to speak to the crowds in a voice that carried across the plaza.

"*Dikket adiniz,*" the announcer shouted, gesturing a bejeweled hand to the four monks approaching.

Another guard stood at the base. Reem and his crew stood behind the platform. More guards ringed the plaza. Aeden realized escape would be short lived and complicated by the chains at his hands and feet.

The guard at the base of the steps evaluated them with a quick glance and chose Odilo to move up the steps first. With a shove, Odilo limped up the short steps and onto stage. The announcer seemed to cringe at his faltering step and began to speak as if to draw attention away from his deformity. Aeden couldn't help but wonder if the auctioneer took a cut from every human he helped sell.

"*Katual dezunin bir Salvare,*" he shouted, "*itaatker bir kapek.*"

"*Bir gumus sigloi,*" a man in the crowd said half-heartedly.

Aeden searched the crowd for the voice and recognized one of the men from the *Zafer*. They were trying to entice the crowd to buy. Instead of further offers, there was a moment of silence followed by another shouting voice.

"*Kases kupaki kapek!*" there was vile in those words.

Aeden glanced at Neri who had finally looked up.

The shout was now echoed by others in the crowd.

"*Kases kupaki kapek!*"

"What're they saying?" Aeden whispered to Neri.

Neri looked at Aeden with sadness in his eyes.

"They say, 'kill the dog monk.'"

Aeden glanced up at the announcer, who seemed uncertain of how to respond. The energy of the crowd was beginning to turn. How could words incite such hatred? How could words sway emotion to supersede reason and cause men to wish for violence?

It angered him.

Two guards stepped onto the platform with their hands on the hilts of their swords. They seemed hesitant as if feeding off the energy of the gathered masses. Aeden could only think of one reason they'd approach Odilo. The man who'd saved him from the guards of Bodig. The man who had spoken on his behalf and allowed him shelter, food, safety, and a brotherhood when he was at his most vulnerable.

They meant to kill a member of his adopted family.

Rage pulsed through his veins like scolding hot water. It bubbled over until his mind went quiet. The world narrowed in his vision. His ears pounded with the sound of his rushing heartbeat.

There was no more time. He needed to act.

Without thought, Aeden bounded up the stairs in short, precise steps. A shout echoed somewhere behind him. He ignored it. His eyes were fixed upon the guards. There was a predatory glare fixed to Aeden's face.

The guards looked weak. Without warning he struck.

One barely had enough time to partially draw his sword before Aeden swept his foot and broke his neck. The guard was dead before he hit the floor. The following guard only had time to look up before Aeden smashed him in the face with a stone-hardened fist. The chains slowed him down, but he still felt his knuckles bite into the guard's face as if he had punched through old parchment.

The guard stumbled. Blood spurted from his staved face. He fell off the platform gurgling incoherently.

Two more guards ran up the steps. He dispatched the first in two swift movements, disarming him with the chains between his wrists. His death was quick and painless.

The second was better armed, better dressed, and clearly better trained. The crowd grew strangely quiet as the two moved about on stage. Aeden's anger rolled quietly in the background. His skin hummed with emotion. He felt no weakness. He felt no discomfort. He had only one mission. Protect Odilo and his brother monks.

The man struck with remarkable speed. Aeden reacted before the man had fully committed to his technique. He side-stepped the thrust and grabbed the man's sword hand with both of his hands. Continuing his forward movement, he snapped the man's wrist into a lock as the man's elbow reflexively swept up into the air. Aeden stripped the sword from his hand and fluidly twisted his body, slicing through the side of the richly-clad guard.

The guard fell to his knees in utter shock. Aeden held the sword in his hands prepared to deliver the killing blow when a voice shouted out.

"Stop!" It was in Heortian and it had emanated from the crowd.

Odilo placed a hand on Aeden. Slowly the anger faded and the world resolved into focus. The well-dressed guard sat upon his knees. His hands were soaked in blood and held onto something. What was he holding? Whatever it was glistened slick and pale in the waning sun. Understanding finally dawned on Aeden. He had cut through the man's muscular wall and spilled his tubular organs.

Aeden suddenly felt sick. He turned away only to see the other guards he had felled. The world spun and he struggled to remain focused. He caught sight of a dozen sets of eyes fixed on him. Surrounding the wooden platform were soldiers, well-armed, with spears pointed toward him. It appeared they too stopped at the command.

Who had shouted the order?

"Sunin bicekleri kiluf!" The man from the plaza boomed.

Immediately the soldiers stood to attention with their spears held squarely by their sides, points skyward.

"Drop your weapon," the man then said to Aeden.

Aeden finally saw him, for the crowds had parted around him. He was an imposing sight. Not because of his size. Rather his mere presence commanded authority. He radiated power the way the sun radiated light. His fine robes graced his lean body in shades of emerald. A decorative helmet sat regally upon his head. Golden chainmail adorned the lower half covering his neck like a waterfall of rich armor. But it was his intense gaze that most marked him. Dark, brooding eyes under rich eyebrows, carefully trimmed. Those eyes were now locked onto Aeden's.

Aeden was enraptured by the man's gaze. He slowly put down the sword as if the man's eyes had willed him to it. The man whispered to another well-dressed guard at his side. The guard bore the same manner of dress as the one who now moaned with his intestines upon his hands. The guard moved forward quickly, cutting through the crowd with ease.

The guard walked up the steps and spoke to the announcer. The announcer looked at him dumbly as shock slowly receded to the hidden recesses of his mind. The announcer nodded his head briefly to indicate he understood. The guard then walked past Aeden and paused in front of Odilo. He lifted Odilo's chin as if he were inspecting him. With a casual and quick movement, the guard slashed Odilo's throat.

Blood squirted from his neck in ever decreasing bursts as his heart struggled to pump life to his brain.

What had happened? Why kill Odilo?

Aeden was too stupefied for anger. The casual manner of the killing shocked him into stillness. He was reminded of his inaction at the foot of his village. The horrible screams bubbled to memory. The terrible sounds of the draccus fiend and the more horrendous sounds of his home burning, cut across his guilty conscience like a hot knife.

But there was no mythical beast before him. There was only a well-dressed man, armed with a jeweled blade. There was his brother monk, his friend, and his confidant bleeding to death before him.

Aeden rushed to him and placed his hands

upon Odilo's bleeding neck. It was a futile attempt to save him. Aeden watched as the life faded from his eyes. Odilo managed to shake his head once. He didn't want further violence perpetrated on his behalf. Even in his final moments he was able to follow the teachings of Khein and walk in the path of Salvare. Aeden didn't understand.

Odilo's eyes slowly closed shut and he slumped forward. Aeden carefully lowered him to the blood-stained platform. A faint smile was upon his dead brother's lips. And Aeden wept.

PART FOUR
Sha'ril

Chapter 66

"And pack what goods are necessary for your journey, remembering the greatest good is that of pious action." Verse from the Bocian

The Annalist glided into port aboard a Bodigan caravel on a quiet Sumor morning. The first glimpse of molten bronze poured from the great jeweler in the sky, spreading its warmth upon the calm waters of the Port of Sha'ril. In the shimmering distance the Grand Temple of Anwar attempted to mirror the golden sun in a vain attempt at beauty.

He coughed as he stood upon the stern. The lapis waters lapped lightly upon the bow, calming his nerves. The annalist rubbed absentmindedly at his temples. He had been nursing a headache for days. The pain for a while was nearly unbearable, but manageable. It was the price he paid for his gift. Use of the arkein often exacted a price. Yet, for all his searching, he hadn't found what toll it took upon the Kan Savasci. He was beginning to wonder if the man he was investigating had uncovered the secrets of the *Syrinx*, the secrets that only the greatest of arkeinists, Magis, had been purported to discover.

"We've arrived my lord."

"I see that," the annalist retorted a bit too sharply.

He closed his eyes a moment and willed the throbbing pain in his head to subside. A wave of nausea invaded the shores of his mind before receding to a dull ache. He opened his eyes and took in the broad sweep of city before him.

The light blue waters formed a counterpoint to the white buildings that graced the shoreline. The magnificent city of Sha'ril seemed largely unaffected by the discord to the north. It was a welcome sight after all he'd seen.

"Ready the ship young master, I'd like to meet this new Caliph as soon as possible."

"Of course, my lord."

A man of no more than twenty years relayed orders and busied himself preparing the annalist's travel bag.

The annalist stood upon the stern deck a moment longer. The sun was already making its way into the sky and forcing its warmth upon the dry lands. He preferred to leave as soon as possible. By noon the heat would become unbearable. How Aeden survived the desert heat seemed almost as great an accomplishment as his defeat of the Bodig army at Vintas Pass.

The annalist was rubbing his temples gently when the young master returned with his travel bag.

"Everything's packed and your guards are awaiting you my lord," he said.

It felt strange having someone call him lord, but he understood why the king had given him the title. Titles command respect just as well-dressed guards paint the illusion of great importance. The annalist was more than apt to take care of himself, the guards might as well have been children dressed in costume.

"Welcome," a slightly overweight man in splendid robes said.

The annalist paused momentarily at the threshold of a cushioned chamber. He struggled to take in a level of opulence the king of Bodig would have begged to be privy to.

Pillars of gold were beset by jewels the size of his fist. They ringed the circular room. Tall, pointed archways connected each pillar. Suspended from these were curtains of the finest silk he'd ever seen. They looked as if they had been woven by a team of spiders, threading gossamer gold.

The man himself was flanked by two large and dangerous looking men. It wasn't the guards that caught the annalist's attention, it was the man himself. Dark, intelligent eyes watched him, calculating. They rested deeply within a once handsome face under carefully trimmed eyebrows. His slightly hooked nose gave him the predatory appearance of the much-feared siren eagle.

The annalist glanced at his two guards and dismissed them. If there was to be a play of power on a subtle level, he was going to win. The annalist watched as the new caliph raised an eyebrow.

"I bring the greetings of King Godwin of Bodig, High Priest of the Holy Order of Salvare, Holder of Keys, and Rightful Emperor of Heorte."

"And may I present..." one of the guards fell silent as the caliph held up a bejeweled hand.

"I am Jal Isa Sha'ril, Caliph of the mighty A'sh Empire, *Cesur Kimse*, Lion of the Desert, and once teacher and master of *Kan Savasci*, the great Blood Warrior."

Chapter 67

"True freedom stands on the backs of the enslaved." Caliph of Q'Bala

"**Y**ou now belong to me."

Aeden regarded his new master for a moment. Those intelligent eyes watched Aeden the way a predator tracks its prey. They were dark eyes, hiding their true purpose behind a benevolent mask. One Aeden refused to believe. He was now this man's property. It was a concept so foreign to him that he had yet to wrap his mind around its true ramifications.

"What would you have me do?" Aeden asked, fearing the answer.

"Isn't it obvious," the man replied in near perfect Heortian.

Aeden shook his head.

"That means yes here in the A'sh. But for the sake of entertainment, tell me what you think your purpose is."

Aeden felt like this was a test. He was reminded briefly of his father quizzing him after the Shrine of Patience. Although in a way it was more like the Witches of Agathon. He found it hard to read this man. Was it the cultural differences?

The longer he waited to answer, the more he

realized he'd better have a good answer. For some reason, he felt the man had high expectations of him.

"You wish me to fight for you," Aeden said at last.

The man shook his head in approval. It was a subtle gesture; one Aeden would have missed had he not been paying attention.

"It's more than that," Aeden continued.

"Yes," the master replied, his eyes slightly wider, interested.

"You want me to be part of your personal guard," Aeden felt like he was reaching, or perhaps being overly confident, but he also felt he had little to lose, how naive he was.

Silence followed for a span. The only sounds Aeden heard were the rustling of the wind through fine silk curtains that blocked the sun's light and the small movement of one of the guards behind him.

"You've a shrewd mind, but you're presumptuous."

Aeden remained silent. The words of the old S'Vothe master traveled through his head. *"Wisdom is learning to keep your mouth shut when you have nothing of value to say."*

"You are partially correct. Now I wonder what it is you think you need to better attain this position."

Aeden watched him for a moment, unsure if he should answer. Finally, the man raised an eyebrow. That was all Aeden needed.

"I want my brothers freed," Aeden said.

Despite the heat of the day the room grew cold. One of the guards moved toward him as the seated master's eyes were drawn into angry dark coals, glaring dangerously through him.

"That is your first mistake dog, falter again and I shall have another killed simply to amuse me." Some of the tension left the room and he continued, "I'll give you another chance, since you still wear ignorance like a veil upon your eyes."

Aeden was now uncertain what to say. Aeden believed him when he said he would kill his friends. There was an aura of power about the man that hung over him like a shroud.

"I would need my sword back."

"Where is it? Or should I say who has it?"

"Reem Sati Agir from the caravel *Zafer*," Aeden said, struggling to control his anger.

If it hadn't been for Reem and his crew, the brothers from the Holy Order of Salvare Bodig would be safe now, not slaves.

"You've a memory for foreign words, that's good. What else."

"I would need training in your language and customs," Aeden continued before hesitating to say his last request.

"And?"

"And I would need to know my brothers are safe," he said, hoping it wasn't too much.

Instead of anger there was laughter. It seemed forced, but it had to be better than anger, Aeden thought.

"Well spoken, so it shall be."

Chapter 68

*"The foundation of power stems from knowledge
in all things." Caliph of Sha'ril*

T he story of Aeden's tutelage is largely
uneventful. He was occupied from morning to
night under the careful eye of a team of
instructors. He had relatively free reign within
the Jal's compound. Every action, every test was
done with the pervasive threat of harm to his
brother monks. It was like a red cloud that clung
to the edges of his vision. It was a constant
reminder of the weight of his responsibility and
the standard he was to uphold.

Aeden's training was as diverse as Jal's
interests, however, if there was said to be an
overarching influence it would have been history.
The Jal once said, *"The key to understanding a
people is understanding their history."*

Aeden learned of the prior Caliphates of
A'sh. He learned of the Caliph Jal Rajah Sha'ril
whose empire stretched north to the Barre
Mountains, west to the Gulf of Galdor, east to the
Sea of Atland and even to the Isle of Mann off the
coast of Templas. He learned about the events
leading to the fall of the great empire. He learned
what led to a split in the empire. A minor
Caliphate was formed in the port city of Q'Bala
and the Desert War had begun.

Aeden was tutored in mathematics, one of his least favorite subjects. He didn't understand how knowing about numbers would assist in daily life. He studied Adhari, the language of the A'sh, reading and writing. There were instructors for small team tactics, teaching protection and attack. A different instructor taught him cultural idiosyncrasies. An old man with unusually steady hands and a shaky voice taught him chemistry.

The chemist had him practice titrations, distillations, the use of solvents and the creation of solutions. He learned how to take a simple plant boil it, apply the appropriate salt, and titrate the solution until he had the desired potency, to create a most deadly poison. He learned about the properties of dozens of plants, algae, fungi, and lichen.

Aeden practiced cultural dialogues, mannerisms, and the etiquette among the nobles. He furthered his training in their unique methods of hand-to-hand combat refined from years of warring with the Shadow Warriors of Q'Bala. Much of his training took place in narrow corridors, on the stairs, and in darkened rooms. He practiced assaulting from hidden alcoves, from the shadows. Training that was in stark contrast to many of the methods he had learned in S'Vothe.

He was allotted an hour a week to see his brother monks. Although the visits were infrequent, they were special. Neri and Adel were treated well. They worked as scribes for the most part, increasing Jal Isa Sha'ril's massive library. They were given a sole task, copy the Book of Divinus.

Once Jal Isa Shar'il had learned of the Book of Divinus he had a small army scour the city in search of the slavers. Once word got out that the Purser of Sha'ril sought out these men, it didn't take long for them to be found and the book to exchange hands.

Aeden knew that the Jal had spared the monks, not on his behalf, but for more personal reasons. Reasons beyond his immediate understanding. It felt as if every action, every thought was carefully mapped out to conform to a hidden plan. In a way, the Jal reminded Aeden of the subdeacon of Treton, although more ambitious, darker, and far more dangerous.

Chapter 69

"Friendship often rests on the back of the invested." Proverb of Q'Bala

"You let him die," Adel whispered under his breath, looking upon Aeden with empty eyes.

Aeden stood before Adel and Neri in silence. The small confines of the writing room were in stark contrast to the opulence of much of the Jal's small palace. The air was thick with fear and a sad desperation. It lingered on the writing supplies, clung to the wooden desks, and wrapped itself about the two monks from Bodig.

As Aeden glanced about, he fought against a rising tide of guilt. It wasn't as difficult a struggle as it had once been. His heart was no longer weak. It had been shored with stone and tears.

Although Aeden knew they blamed him for Odilo's death, he felt more at peace than he had before. He had overcome a lingering fear. He had taken the lives of the men who wished his brother harm. If he felt any guilt, it was that he wasn't fast enough or strong enough to take on so many.

"You killed four men, while in chains," Neri said quietly, "You cut through them like they were children."

Neri was clearly in shock. He didn't look up at Aeden as he spoke. Instead, his eyes held a faraway appearance, as though another soul entered his body to relate the story. Aeden couldn't blame him. Logically he should have been in shock too. Maybe it was because he hadn't realized he'd killed four men.

"Are you being treated well?" Aeden asked, in an effort to engage either one of them.

"We're prisoners," Adel finally said, looking down at the chains attached to his right foot then up into Aeden's eyes.

Aeden glanced about. They were alone. The guards were on the other side of the doorway. He was surprised how much freedom he had. The Jal must have known how important his brother monks were to him. He must have known Aeden wouldn't risk their lives needlessly.

"I will free you, that I promise," Aeden said with steely conviction.

"Empty promises fall on deaf ears," Neri said, "You don't know this place. You don't know the Jal. There is no escape."

Adel looked to Neri then back to Aeden, before casting his eyes helplessly to the ground. So much loss. Aeden was suddenly overcome with the image of Odilo gasping for his last breath as he bled out.

The events of the last two years threatened to overwhelm him.

He took in a long and slow breath. The lump that normally resided in the back of his throat was gone. It had been replaced with an angry conviction. He knew what he had to do. He just wasn't sure how to accomplish it.

His brothers needed to see strength, not weakness.

"You will be freed, I swear this on the Thirteen," Aeden said, strength seeping into his voice.

He looked at each one in turn before stepping out of the room.

Chapter 70

"The mind lingers when hope is lost." Canton of
Sawol

Aeden managed to visit his brothers again.

On one of his visits he brought a deck of
playing cards. He had convinced the Jal that the
more content his brothers were, the more
productive they'd be. It was a challenging
argument. The Jal enjoyed debate, mostly to test
Aeden's progress in Adhari, but also to assess his
state of mind, his weaknesses and his strengths.
This, however, meant that now, Aeden would
have to convince his brother monks to try a touch
harder.

They moved one of the tables toward the
center of the small writing room, allowing Aeden
to deal out the cards.

"Where've you been?" Adel asked with a
mixture of curiosity and jealousy in his voice.

"Busy," Aeden replied, not sure how to
respond.

"Must be nice wandering the palace
unrestrained," Adel said, lifting his chained leg.

At this Neri glanced up, nodding his head
briefly. Was he agreeing or disagreeing? The
customs of D'seart were so in contrast to Heorte
that Aeden was starting to get confused.

"He's had me training from morning until night," Aeden finally replied.

He paused for a moment as he picked up his cards. Neri was already sorting through his absentmindedly as Adel stared at his cards resting on the desk.

"I brought something for you, but you cannot tell anyone," Aeden said, looking at Adel.

There was a hint of curiosity on Adel's face.

Aeden reached into his pocket and pulled out a small honey-sweetened cake. Adel's eyes momentarily lit up as he instinctively reached for it.

Neri raised an eyebrow before a cloud of quiet distaste settled over his features.

"I've also brought something for you," Aeden said, turning to Neri.

Neri put down his cards.

"I don't like sweets," he began.

"It's not a sweet," Aeden said tentatively, attempting to undo the button on his other pocket.

Neri leaned forward looking at Aeden then to his pocket.

"I figured you could give him a better home than I could," Aeden said as he held out a cupped hand to Neri.

Neri placed his hands under Aeden's. Aeden allowed a small, white mouse to sniff around and make its way into Neri's hands.

Neri looked at the mouse, bringing it close to his chest. He murmured soft cooing words to it, before he looked back up at Aeden. He didn't smile. But he didn't need to. The change in his tone of voice was all Aeden needed.

"It's a she, not a he," was all he said.

"What kind of training?" Adel asked, crumbs gracing the corner of his lip.

Aeden played the two of arrows, starting off the game.

"He has me learning Adhari, simple chemistry, history, argument, D'seart culture," Aeden paused as he ran through a mental list in his tired mind, "etiquette and desert fighting techniques."

Neri stopped whispering to his newfound friend and looked up. Adel played a nine of swords. His brow was knotted in thought.

"That doesn't make any sense," Adel said.

"I know! I've been trying to figure it out myself."

Neri played a king of hearts and took the pile, playing a new card.

"There could be a reason for it all," Neri offered quietly.

His words halted Adel's hand and forced Aeden to look at him with intense curiosity. The room grew quiet.

"Well?" Adel finally said after a moment's pause.

"Jal Isa Sha'ril is an ambitious man. He didn't rise so rapidly through the ranks without killing a few birds."

"Birds?" Aeden asked, interrupting Neri.

Neri gave him an angry look. It almost felt like they were back in the monastery again, almost.

"It's an expression. Birds, people, they're one in the same."

Adel jumped in, "what's that have to do with Aeden's training?"

"Everything I'd imagine," Neri said slowly as if relating something difficult to a child, "the Jal wouldn't waste his time with Aeden if he didn't think Aeden couldn't help him attain greater power."

Adel nodded his head in understanding. Aeden, however, felt as lost as ever. How would he learning history or etiquette help the Jal gain greater power?

The game was interrupted by the door swinging open. In the door frame stood a dark-skinned man of average height. His robes were green and fine. A delicate armor of copper chain-mail hung over his chest. And his hand rested casually on the hilt of a curved sword.

"The Jal commands your presence," the guard said, staring intently at Aeden.

Aeden stood. He waved to his brothers and followed the guard out of the room.

Chapter 71

"Political power swells from the tip of the sword."
Caliph of Sha'ril

"**D**o you now understand why you're here?" Jal Isa Sha'ril asked, his neatly trimmed eyebrows arching slightly over his hooded eyes.

Had the Jal overheard his conversation with his brother monks? Is that why he had allowed the card game? Was it a test to see if he'd be honest?

Aeden stood uncomfortably within the magnificent library. Beautifully bound books lined the shelves, filling the walls. A large map of Verold had been carefully painted upon the domed ceiling, stretching the entire circumference of the room.

"You've trained me for a special purpose," Aeden responded carefully.

"Yes," Jal shook his head ever so slightly in approval.

Aeden glanced at the guards that stood to either side of him. He wondered briefly if he could kill them and the Jal, while still making it down to his brother monks before they were summarily executed.

The Jal studied Aeden for a moment before glancing at the table before him. Aeden followed his gaze. There upon the dark silk was his Templas sword, sheathed in midnight. He was surprised he'd missed it at first. For a moment it was the only thing he could see before falling back into shadow.

"Consider it a gift of sorts," the Jal said amusedly.

Aeden swallowed a lump in his throat. Something didn't feel right. Slaves weren't given gifts. He made no move to pick it up, despite a desperate longing to feel its hilt in his hand once more.

"It's interesting; the sword betrayed its last owner. Just as death reached for him, the sword failed him," the Jal continued.

"I don't understand," Aeden said slowly, wondering if it was his juvenile understanding of Adhari that was leading to confusion.

A guard walked forward and placed a basket next to the sword. A silken cloth covered the contents within.

The Jal now leaned forward ever so slightly. His carefully trimmed eyebrows accentuated his hooded eyes.

"Go on," he said, gesturing a jeweled hand to the basket, "have a look."

Aeden stepped forward and placed a hand on the silken cloth. For some reason, he was hesitant to remove it and uncover the contents within. Aeden looked to the Jal again as if for approval.

The Jal wore a strange expression, somewhere between bemused interest and self-satisfaction. Aeden pulled the scarf free.

A putrid smell accosted him before his eyes understood what it was he was seeing.

It was the head of Reem Sati Agir.

"You were telling me what you thought it is I want of you," the Jal said, sitting back upon the cushions of his chair.

Aeden remained quiet for a handful of heartbeats. He was still in shock. The Jal had just proven his power, his reach, his lack of moral consideration for anything that remotely stood in his way. He could more easily have purchased the sword, yet instead, he had brought the slaver's head to Aeden.

"You wish me to kill for you," Aeden began, his eyes moving to Jal Isa Sha'ril, "someone in particular."

Silence filled the room in response. It was a thick silence of echoing resonance; heavy with the burden of truth, the fear of failure, and the unspoken secrets that each desperately clung to.

"Continue," the Jal said, gesturing with a hand, although his face remained neutral.

"You already control the Purse of Sha'ril, which is a form of power in of itself, but there is another office of greater magnitude that would command ever greater levels of respect."

The Jal's eyes widened slightly, his dark

pupils glistening with interest.

"You've said quite enough," before Aeden continued the Jal had cut him off, "I see you learned how to divine truth from your lessons, yet I wonder how well you understand the politics of Sha'ril."

The Jal leaned forward in his cushioned chair. His dark eyes gathered in Aeden as if he were nothing more than an interesting collection of facts.

"You've found my sword," Aeden said without invitation.

"Ah, the sword, but of course. It was an easy task, yet its owner was not so pleased to part with it," the Jal replied.

Aeden watched Jal Isa Sha'ril now more intently. The man wore confidence the way a beautiful woman wears a form-fitting tunic.

"When you had spoken of 'your' sword, you failed to mention its name," the Jal said.

"It doesn't have a name," Aeden replied.

"Oh, but it does. This is no ordinary blade, not if I'm correct in my summation. It is one of a handful made long ago, by none other than the prophet Majorem," the Jal leaned forward and whispered as if fearing to wake the resting blade, "he called it Kan Savasci."

"What does it mean?" Aeden asked, silently repeating the name to himself, *Kan Savasci*.

"Fate Walker, Blood Warrior, it has many meanings, some I cannot understand or translate," the Jal paused, collecting his thoughts; "it is imbued with a unique characteristic."

Aeden wanted to ask what it was, but he knew he was playing into the Jal's hand. He didn't like being a puppet. He didn't like being played.

"Aren't you curious?" the Jal inquired.

Aeden stood silently, wondering if this is what his father had been waiting to tell him nearly two years ago. The thought of his loss still pained him, but the emotions were no longer fresh.

"Pick it up," the Jal said off-handedly, but something about his tone unnerved him.

Aeden looked at the Jal a moment longer before reaching for the Templas sword. It seemed to hum under his touch. His arm tingled as he clasped the hilt. It felt cool and comforting.

"Draw the blade," the Jal said.

Aeden drew the blade. The soft note of steel rang in the air.

The guards both looked to the Jal before pulling their own swords free.

The Jal held up a hand to reassure them.

"Interesting, so it is true," Jal Isa Sha'ril whispered.

Aeden saw the guards staring intently upon

him. He then thought of the other guards in the palace and of his shackled brothers. Now was not the time. He sheathed his sword and held it by his side.

"I give it back to you," the Jal said magnanimously, "having faith in the prophet Majorem, may his power never wane."

Aeden nodded heavily. Once again, the burden of responsibility threatened to crush him. The air felt thick with obligations waiting to be met. The bitter taste of revenge rose in his throat like bile and threatened to make him sick.

"We have much to discuss," the Jal's voice changed pitch and he leaned forward, finally gesturing for Aeden to take a seat.

Chapter 72

*"Struggle defines the shape of a man." Saying of
the Thane Sagan*

"**W**here are you going?" Adel asked.

Aeden stood at the doorway, not daring pass
the threshold. Guards stood not far from them,
ever watchful. Neri was hunched over in the
corner whispering to the mouse he cupped
lightly in his hand.

"I cannot say," Aeden replied. He looked
from Neri back to Adel, "I hope to buy your
freedom."

"At what cost," Adel asked.

Neri glanced up at Aeden for the first time
since he had come down. Aeden didn't dare meet
their gaze. The cost of a life for two would be
hard for them to understand. It was something he
didn't want to think about. He had spent a
sleepless night trying to justify what he was
about to do, yet couldn't come up with a rational
reason to move forward. He had hoped seeing
his brother monks would serve as the motivation
to follow through.

"I don't know," he said.

Again, silence stretched between them,
exacerbating the distance that stood from Aeden
to his fellow monks. Time had drawn an invisible

line between them, slowly pulling Aeden down another path, a bloodier path, a path leading to revenge.

"Then may the lord Salvare watch over you and guide your steps brother," Adel said.

His tired eyes met Aeden's for a moment and held the weight of the last months upon them in red lines running as tiny rivulets of blood cracking the periphery of his dark pupils.

"May the Holy Order rise again," Neri uttered, escaping back to the mouse nibbling upon some hidden morsel on his outstretched hand.

"May the Holy Order rise again," Aeden repeated almost automatically, the words sounding somehow different to his own ears. It reminded him of the words he was forced to remember as a boy for the trials of becoming a man.

He continued to watch them for a moment, almost reluctant to go. He leaned heavily upon the door frame as if for support. Their words echoing like rippling waves in a pond across the chasm of his mind.

With a tired breath, he nodded to them, even though neither were paying him any attention. Somewhere in the quiet recesses of his consciousness he knew that he was a monk no longer.

Aeden looked away and steeled himself for

the upcoming task. The cold hands of fate seemed to be guiding him blindly down some unseen path, a sadder and more violent path than the one he'd already experienced. He only hoped Odilo would understand.

Epilogue

"The trouble with the truth is that it needn't make sense." Herlewin's Letters of Apology

The annalist left the opulent rooms of the Caliph and exited the gilded compound of the Emperor of A'sh.

The sun was now fully in the sky casting its feverish light upon the lands in a vengeful act of malicious intent. The air was still as if the very city of Sha'ril had paused, taking in a breath, waiting desperately to exhale.

The heat slowed the annalist's mind. It preyed on his skin and sucked at what little moisture he had in his mouth. He licked at his parched lips as he replayed the exchange with Jal Isa Sha'ril.

There had been deceit in his eyes, in his words. There were so many layers of lies that the truth was hard to decipher. Even for one as skilled as he. The annalist, however, wasn't willing to kill the Caliph for answers. Not yet anyway. He had proven too powerful an ally against Sawol and the damned city of Q'Bala.

There were others in Sha'ril with information. Perhaps they would lead the annalist to the path of truth. The truth was all that mattered now. The hidden web that once divined would lead to the Kan Savasci's hidden fortress and to his weakness.

The annalist knew who he needed to seek out, for he still had questions that needed answering. Perhaps then he could find out who Aeden had been ordered to kill.

The pieces were coming together, just not nearly as fast as the annalist had promised. Not nearly fast enough in a time of war.

He just hoped the new Deacon of Sha'ril would have the answers he sought. Verold could only wait so long before being torn apart by those he had awakened.

THE END

Thank you for reading Part 0 of the Kan Savasci Cycle (a prequel to a grand saga). Please allow me a moment to entice you to leave a review. I know your time is valuable, and I will not ask for much of it. If you enjoyed this book let me know. I write on my own time, whilst holding two jobs. Your words let me know what you like and do not like. They inspire me to spend more time writing. Your review can be long and in depth or it can be a single sentence.

Ultimately readers getting the word out is the single greatest tool for an aspiring author. If you wish to know when upcoming books are coming out and to be notified of discounted sales dates, please email me at author.chaseblackwood@gmail.com (I never spam or sell emails, I hate it when it's done to me)

Last, for updates on the next book, blog, news; visit: www.chase-blackwood.com

Made in the USA
Middletown, DE
29 November 2018